Tales of Hardooth 4

COUNTLESS ENEMIES AND DISCOVERIES

Dara J. Carr

Tales of Hardooth 4

COUNTLESS ENEMIES
AND DISCOVERIES

Dara J. Carr

Harrison House Publishing

Tales of Hardooth 4: Countless Enemies and Discoveries
All Rights Reserved
Copyright © 2017 Dara J. Carr
Edited by Betty Powell and Linda S. Carr
Artwork by Eric A. Carr

Harrison House Publishing
www.theharrisonhousepublishing.com
info@theharrisonhousepublising.com
ISBN: 978-0-9974935-7-3
Library of Congress Control Number: 2017942839
Harrison House Publishing and the "HH" logo are trademarks belonging to Harrison House Publishing.

PRINTED IN THE UNITED STATES OF AMERICA

TXu 1-937-734

OTHER BOOKS BY

DARA J. CARR

The Semi-Dragon Tale

Revenge Cometh Forth

Here Are My Shorts (a collection of short stories)

Volunteer…Spy?

The Original Owlam

What New Things We Can Learn?

The Lies We Tell to Survive

COUNTLESS ENEMIES AND DISCOVERIES

1

Bonarain was sitting on the roof of the building. She was at a total loss as far as what she should do. She had seen several of the Cacktash personnel appear to be chopping up Owlamites in the fields near her hiding place. She was not sure whether or not she wanted to call out to any of the rest of her Team because she feared the worst. Had they been caught by the Cacktash and were being chopped up? The only time that she had ever felt this helpless before was when the firestorm weapon had first devastated the city of Owlam. She just sat there feeling sorry for herself. She hung her head and started crying again.

"We heard you," said Soolchakan calmly and flatly. "We heard you each time you sent out that message about Observation dimension."

Bonarain gasped in surprise and looked up startled. "You... aren't...*hurt*?" She sat there wiping her nose and eyes as she tried to get over the shock.

"No, I'm not."

"But...how?"

"As soon as I saw those kites come over, I tried to call out to the rest of the Team. I got Kiyalee and Chyning and we Jumped to the gorge. For some reason...you weren't listening. Once I heard you...calling out to all of us...about Observation, I knew that you were all right. So, I came to get you."

She stood up and looked out over the fields. "Who...was being...cut up...in our field?"

He shook his head sadly. "I don't know. Obviously... someone else ran into our fields...in a state of panic. Why they were panicking...I don't know. They were caught there and..." He looked off to the side. "Supreme Officer, Wilfadge is going to have his Team do a full roll call on all of the Owlamites. We have no idea...how many were killed...yet."

She looked at him in shock. "Supreme Officer...*Wilfadge*? What happened to...Holla?"

He shook his head sadly. "It seems that...she's one of the casualties. Right now, we don't know what all happened, but all Owlamites, that are still alive, have been called to the gorge... even the ones that were spying on Algothon...or any place else."

"What're we gonna to do?"

"A full investigation on these invaders. Who was involved, what are their plans, where do we strike back...the hardest?"

She took another look out over the fields. "I've got something to report as well."

"Don't waste the Supreme Officer's time...unless it's REALLY important."

She glared back at him. "Oh it is. I guarantee you...it *really* is."

He looked up, cocked his head to the side and raised his eyebrows. "Well then, let's go."

Together they Jumped to their unit in the gorge.

Kiyalee and Chyning were sitting in the dining area on the first floor. Neither one looked very happy. They nodded at Bonarain when she appeared but did very little other than that.

Kiyalee hung her head and sighed. "Wilfadge is going to start the full roll call soon. From what I understand...we've lost a lot of people...again."

Bonarain wiped more tears off her cheek. "How many... on the staff...I mean how is this going to affect the...chain of command?"

Chyning scoffed. "Who cares? We can always get the new chain of command after the roll call. Right now..." She looked away, placed her hand over her mouth and sniffled.

"Let's just sit," said Soolchakan. "We wait for our number to be called. We can still say...all of us are accounted for...which is a lot better than...many other Teams."

They sat in silence as the roll call was started. The only sounds that could be heard was someone sniffling or blowing their nose from time to time.

Outside the city of Owlam, Prok was strutting around like he was the king of the entire planet. He had several Cacktash personnel who were following close by. If anyone tried to question the authority of *Prominent King*, Prok, the Cacktash would attack them mentally and all arguments with him would end quickly with him as the victor.

Several of the Cacktash were rather disgusted with the thought of having to bow down to a non-telepath and non-Cacktash, however, it was convenient...for the moment to have this man in the current chain of command.

The gift that Prok had received from the Cacktash was a box full of electrified collars. He could place the collar around the neck of whomever he desired and with the little control box, he could give them a very nasty shock if they disobeyed his commands. Currently, he had three of the collars in use. Choya, Sarskatama and Shiganeea were the victims of the collars. He decided to make all three of the Investigator women, who were on the *Tuzine* team, his personal sex slaves. He had hold of leashes that were attached to their collars and he was parading around the area, leading the three, totally naked, women in an act of complete humiliation for the trio. If they tried to cover any part of themselves or pull against the leash, all three would get shocked. He was making full use of the plan: If one of you disobeys, all three get punished, therefore, you are all three dependent on each other for *absolute* obedience.

At night, Shiganeea was his primary target. Occasionally,

he would molest the other two women, however, he was more attracted to and had more fun with Shiganeea - even though she was totally repulsed and did very little to cooperate.

All of the people who had been there at Owlam for trading when the attack took place now ended up as work slaves. The Cacktash would attack them mentally and force them to do whatever was ordered.

The Cacktash were determined to find the manufacturing plant and the recipe for the *Tuzine*. They were now being frustrated by the fact that no one could find any manufacturing plant inside or outside the walls of Owlam. They found an abundance of crops and numerous places where there were all kinds of farming equipment. They were baffled by the fact that they could not find any homes. All buildings were storage for farming, water purification or power plants.

The only Owlamites that were inside the walls were all dead. The Cacktash had attacked, trying to strike fear in the hearts of all denizens of the city and instead were only confused by not being able to take a single one alive. Another conundrum was that fact that there were numerous Cacktash who were missing and no one could figure out how or why. They had just…vanished.

Susugam called some of the higher ranking individuals in. "I don't know what's going on here, Sirs. We went into that… useless little warehouse that the Owlams were using to bring out the *Tuzine*. The other traders are all being used inside this warehouse to dig up the entire floor. So far, all we're finding is undisturbed soil. No one dug up anything or made any form of a…tunnel…under that building."

Back Breaker, Chowsiyma looked rather bored. "Are you sure that this was the only place that the Owlams were bringing the drug from?"

"Yes, Sir," said Susugam adamantly. "All races and creeds, including our friend Prok, have consistently stated that *all* of the drugs were brought out of this warehouse…every time. There was never any of it that was brought from inside the city during trade negotiations. Always that warehouse!"

"Yet…there's nothing in this warehouse," said Horror Spreader, Vongvix. She scoffed. "If this is true…how did they get the drug…from inside the city…to this riddle of a warehouse?"

Chowsiyma shook his head. "Maybe that silly rumor… about teleportation…isn't quite so silly after all." He sighed. "Keep them digging. If you haven't found any tunnels by the time they're in a hole over their heads, then we'll have to assume that teleportation was the way they did it. That means that we're going to have a need to find some…any survivors and question them about their teleportation technology."

Susugam snickered. "We're going to have to do a lot of digging anyway. We still haven't figured out the code for opening those *pongfop* gates of theirs…the gates that open up the entrances that run under the city walls."

Vongvix frowned. "Why do we need the underground passageways opened? We have the giant wings those Teltermak showed us how to use. Why can't we just continue using them?"

"Sir, once we start harvesting all of those crops, flying them out is not an option. There'll be…just too much. It'll take too long to get the harvest out by using the wings. We have to have an avenue for the slaves to walk and pull the crops in carts… or else *we* have to give *them* the wings."

Chowsiyma scoffed. "Wings…for slaves? *That* is not an option. Yes, we'll have to have them dig their own passageway." He sighed. "Bone Breaker, Susugam…why do you smell like…?"

"It's the city, Sir." Susugam scowled. "The entire area, inside the walls, smells like an un-flushed, dirty urinal. They do have toilets in their bathrooms…but…it seems that they must all urinate freely…anywhere, anytime."

Vongvix snickered. "You don't think that…Owlam urine is an ingredient in the *Tuzine*, do you?"

Chowsiyma looked off to the side and shuddered. "I sincerely hope NOT. That would be…intolerable. Besides if it were an ingredient, they'd be collecting it…not just spreading it around…everywhere."

The depressing roll call was finally finished after six days. Several times during the roll, the person calling the role had to be changed. It just became too disheartening to continue. The final count showed that 218 Teams had been completely wiped out. 58 other Teams had lost one or more members. 249 males and 804 females had died in the attack. In prior attacks, after the change, they had lost a total of 1,031 people combined. This attack alone cost them 1,053 of their friends and colleagues. They were now down to 25,980 people…total.

In the High Staff, they had lost Holla and Chaza. This did a bit of a shake-up, however, they knew that they had to continue. Wilfadge was now the Supreme Officer. The new Sector 3 Commander, in his place, was the newly promoted Master Officer, Dwalooa.

Everyone was sent a message on the new High Staff. Supreme Officer, Wilfadge was now in command and the new *Voice of Power*. Master Officer, Ahandi was still the Sector 1 Commander, with Senior Officer, Antrong as the new Vice Commander. Master Officer, Teelila was still the Sector 2 Commander, with Senior Officer, Till as the new Sector 2 Vice Commander. Master Officer, Dwalooa was the Sector 3 Commander, with Senior Officer, Hoynama as the Sector 3 Vice Commander. Master Officer, Hadathoo was now the Sector 4 Commander, with Senior Officer, Shyshee as the Sector 4 Vice Commander. The chain of command was now rebuilt and intact at the top.

Wilfadge called the meeting to order. He was not his normal jovial self. "Is there any new business that we need to discuss…before we try coming up with a plan to retake the city of Owlam against those…Cacktash?"

Officer Grade 4, Akantini, one of the Team members of Wilfadge's, spoke up. "Sir, we have Officer, Bonarain from Team 7016." She looked around at the Staff members. "She says that she has information that is crucial towards defeating the Cacktash."

"I'm ready to listen to anything that's positive," said Teelila.

Akantini signaled to Bonarain and she came in looking a little sheepish.

Wilfadge leaned back in his chair and sighed. "What does our talented teacher have for us?"

Bonarain smiled. "Sirs, I was nearly a victim of those nasty Cacktash as well. When that…man…tried to take control of my mind…I ran in panic. I ran right through a wall. I was in Spy, he was in Home."

"Now is not the time to try to be funny," said Dwalooa bitterly.

"Sir, I'm not trying to be funny, I'm telling you what happened…and how we can use it." Bonarain looked around at the Staff a little disappointed.

Wilfadge nodded. "All right, please continue," he said calmly.

"Thank you, Sir. While he was trying to take over my mind, he was using his imagery to do a…telepathic intrusion. He was also *sending* that same imagery as he was doing it. When I ran through the wall, almost completely controlled by him, he slammed into the wall and it broke off the connection that he had with, and almost over, my mind. I don't remember doing it, when or why, but I ended up in Observation dimension. It was then that I discovered that they're incapable of reading our thoughts when we're in other dimensions, other than Home or Spy. I used their imagery to read their minds, involuntarily, from Observation… and now I can teach…everyone here…to do the same."

Hadathoo looked skeptical. "What's to stop them from getting back into our minds…if we try to get into theirs?"

"One: I've figured out a way to get past their blocks. Two: I've figured out how to block them…from us. Three: I figured out a way to read their minds, without sending them anything *from* us. I did this by having others, on my Team, try to block me and I broke in…plus I tried it on a couple of Cacktash…before we banished them to Stink. They thought that they were the only telepaths out there, and as a result, they had no problem transmitting the imagery while they were reading minds. They didn't know or they didn't care that they were transmitting while receiving."

Ahandi looked unconvinced. "Okay, so you're saying that…even if I block you, you can still get through?"

"Yes, Sir," said Bonarain with a smile. "Would you like to see it happen?"

Ahandi scoffed. "You're wasting our time."

Bonarain glared at Ahandi. "Try me, Sir!"

Ahandi was taken aback. She closed her eyes and concentrated for a moment. "Okay, you're blocked."

Bonarain smiled. "Think of a number."

Ahandi shook her head and gave Bonarain a condescending look.

Bonarain cocked her head to the side. "1200…uh…5555… uh…no it's 263, 264, 265…MAKE UP YOUR *CHOKWAD* MIND!"

Now Ahandi was looking shocked. "Okay…it…works… how…did you do that?"

Bonarain smiled. "I'll give it to the Supreme Officer first."

Wilfadge nodded. "All right."

Bonarain closed her eyes. She started sending the imagery to Wilfadge.

He sat there with his eyes closed as he received it. He frowned. "What about…?" He froze. "Oh…I see now. Okay, what about…?" He jerked his head a little and sat there like a statue. "Okay." Moments later he opened his eyes and shook his head. "That is…a huge pile…of information!"

"Yes, Sir, it is," said Bonarain with a slight smile.

Wilfadge sniffed. "And…you got all of that…in the time that you were…running from him?"

"Yes, Sir, he was sending it freely."

"You were panicking and…receiving all of that?"

"I received it as I was running. It took almost an entire day to figure it all out once I was safe…here at the gorge. Again, apparently, they don't know that they're sending everything when they try to read minds. They send out the entire thing…no matter what. They haven't learned how to properly control it."

He looked at Ahandi. "I'm going to try it." He smiled. "Think of a number…just ONE number…and don't change it."

Ahandi sat there looking a little guilty. She looked up at

Wilfadge.

"12,700,000," he said flatly.

Ahandi nodded looking a little stunned.

Wilfadge turned back to Bonarain. "Does it always have to be individual or can you teach...groups?"

She smiled. "Sir, the individual thing was just to show you how it can be isolated...completely from anyone else. That way, we can take over their minds without them being able to get help from anyone else because no one'll believe that they're being individually mind controlled...without anyone else noticing. I can teach groups."

"What would you say is the largest group...that you can handle at one time?"

She shrugged. "I suggest...twenty-five."

Wilfadge looked off into space with a big smile. "Then let's get it started and get to controlling some Cacktash minds."

Bonarain closed her eyes and started giving the imagery to the rest of the Staff, and any of their Team members that happened to be present. A few of them had some questions, however, she was able to respond to most of them before they were even spoken.

"Now, we'll be even more powerful," said Wilfadge. "Hopefully that'll stop anyone else from doing any more exterminations of the Owlam citizenry."

Prok was sitting in his luxury quarters in a rebuilt section of the city of Teltermak. He was fondling a totally unresponsive Shiganeea while he tried to think of how the Owlamites could have possibly escaped...without the use of teleportation. He could not think of any alternative. He was glad to hear that the telepathic problem was going to be taken care of by the Cacktash. It was their problem - not his. Now, he just had to try to figure out where the living Owlams were and get this information to the Cacktash...if he could figure out where they were.

The Cacktash had been doing some special remodeling, in the remnants of the city of Teltermak, under the rubble, so they could make the hang-gliders and be near Owlam for the assault. Now, that the assault had taken place, they were able to remove the rubble disguises and show their handiwork to the Algothon satellites.

The Algothon were not very busy watching the Cacktash in Teltermak, because they were having a hard enough time dealing with the Cacktash that had attacked Algothon. Though the Cacktash numbers were not large (in comparison to the Algothon), they were still a formidable army, with their mind controlling capabilities. Very few fights were won by the people of Algothon. Even if a fight was won, the Cacktash would show up quickly and destroy the victor.

The number of Investigators and military personnel that had been killed was devastating. Hashasee was still alive and very isolated. She had no idea how many other Investigators were alive, at any rank level, let alone functioning. She had no clue where to go or what to do to solve this crisis. She had seen the

Dara J. Carr

High Commander of the Military struck down. There were eight Vice Commanders and she was aware of the death of three who had died right in front of her. Of the sixty Side Commanders, she had seen twelve die. She knew that the military was suffering some bad blows to their upper echelon and there was nothing she could do about it...yet. She could only bide her time and hope that no one started picking her brain apart. She was not sure why she was not being mentally controlled by the Cacktash...yet, however, she was grateful that she still had her mind intact.

Wilfadge looked over the list shaking his head. "This is horrible! We had twenty Teams in Algothon, spying on those *Doovofts*. Of the twenty, I see that one Team was wiped out entirely. Six Teams lost one member and seven Teams lost two members. Eighty people that we had there...and now we've lost twenty-four of them. Only six Teams are intact."

Akantini looked at the other list. "There were ten Teams that were out there, previously, spying on Teltermak...a long time ago. Five of those Teams lost someone. Could we combine them...the experienced Teltermak spies...with the experienced Algothon spies? That's thirty-three of them...who are experienced in spying. That could replace the twenty-four...that were lost." She shrugged in a questioning manner.

Wilfadge clenched his teeth. "That makes a total of twenty-nine Teams...where we had thirty. We've lost Team 73 completely and we have eighteen Teams that are short."

"Yes, Sir...but that can't be helped...can it?"

"I am about to step on a lot of toes...but *that* can't be helped. I need to get the spies back in Algothon...just in case the Cacktash are taking over and trying to launch those firestorm weapons again. I need to find out if the Algothons have defeated the Cacktash and are planning on launching the firestorm weapons. I also need to find out where those wretched Cacktash have their bases...near us or their home. Do you get my meaning?"

"Uh...I get the part about...needing to get people back there...so we get information...but...*stepping on toes*? Whose toes are you stepping on?"

"So many people wanted to keep the partial Teams as they were. Don't forget the dead and don't forget why a Team is partial. Sorry, but I have to look at the greater good of Owlam. Let's find some partial Teams...that are not spies...combine them with the spy Teams to complete the Teams. This includes the two computer Teams that lost people. I also want two more computer Teams. We lost three people from the computer bunch...and that hurt. We need to get more people trained...and quickly."

Akantini pulled out the Team listings. "Yes, Sir. I understand. So now...we need to start filling slots."

Team 13 sat down and did some close scrutiny of the complete roll call roster, making every attempt at doing as little damage as possible.

The next day, Wilfadge called all of the Teams in to a meeting. All of the Teams that were involved in the new combinations were called in. He looked around the big conference room that had been redesigned to fit in the gorge. He did not like all of the columns that were in the room, however, he remembered the significance and need for them. He walked up to the podium and solemnly looked at the people that were assembled. He placed the papers on the podium. "People of the city of Owlam. We have suffered a tremendous loss in this newly found problem of the Cacktash. As the reports show, 218 Teams wiped out, 58 Teams lost some members and many saying that a total of 276 Teams were affected. NO! All of us were affected. I know that many of you are grieving over close friends that were lost…but right now, we don't have time to sit here licking our wounds. We have to fight back. In order to do this and get some new personnel trained in certain areas, I am going to have to put aside an edict made by a former Supreme Officer Neenatha. She did not want any partial Teams permanently combined. According to her, this would make us forget the ones who died in the line of duty. I'm not trying to forget anyone, I am trying to save what we have left. I am going to combine the Teams that are short on personnel with other Teams that have suffered losses as well. The experienced people are going to be training the new personnel and they are going to have to do it quickly. We don't know, at this time, if the Cacktash know about the gorge. If they do, all of our plans to make this place a safe haven are for nothing. I know that some of you may object, because you think that we will forget the dead, but…we can always etch their names in the walls that we will always be looking at…so that we never forget."

There were a few mumbles that went on for a moment or two.

"My Team member, Officer Akantini will read out the new

assignments. Get people moved in to their new quarters…quickly. Get used to your new Team members and assignments…quickly. We need to find out…anything we can on these…Cacktash."

Akantini walked up to the podium. She looked around nervously at all of the faces. "First of all…the new Teams that are being assigned new missions. Team 79, under Officer Leader, Yoobyool, your Team will be replacing Team 73, Officer Leader, Nachichi's Team…that was lost completely. Teams 257 and 258 will be getting with the other Teams that specialize in computers and get all the training that you need from them."

Yoobyool stood up. "Are you saying that my Team is now a spy Team instead of a bartering Team?"

Akantini smiled. "Yes, Sir, that is the decision…according to the statement that you made…quite a while back, when you said…"

He laughed. "When I said that I would rather be spying on and killing Galsino than bartering for *Tuzine* with them. Yes, I remember making that statement and I'm glad it was remembered… for this reason."

Akantini nodded. "Yes, Sir, your words are coming back to haunt you."

"It's not a haunt, it's a relief." He sat back down as several people chuckled at his response.

Akantini cleared her throat and continued. "Officer Leader, Ota. In that attack…you lost Officer, Tytay. To replace her, you will be getting Officer Grade 6, Hooloo from the incomplete Team

5051. Officer Leader, Blana. You lost Officer, Yoyasa. You will be getting the other member from Team 5051, Officer Grade 7, Tangga. That will complete both your Teams."

Akantini continued reading off the new assignments to all of the Teams. When she finished, she walked away from the podium with a tear running down her face.

Wilfadge stepped back up to the podium. "I know that a lot of you don't like these new intrusions. You might say that it upsets group dynamics. Remember that what is being done here is absolutely essential for the good of all Owlamites. If you have any petty squabbles...*get over it*. It's been sixty-eight years since that firestorm attack hit...so I know that you're all adults...all...a lot older than many of you thought you would ever live. Remember, if your age was thirty-two or older when the attack hit...you *are* now over one hundred years old. There should be some kind of maturity in there somewhere. Act like it, act on it, get used to your new Team members and let's get the ball rolling...preferably a great ball of granite that rolls over the Cacktash."

There was a round of applause.

Wilfadge continued. "For the moment...Officer Leader, Boneech and Officer Leader, Natsa...your two Teams did not suffer any losses. While the other Teams are getting acquainted, I need both your Teams in Algothon immediately...to assess what the Cacktash are doing in Algothon. Officer Grade 2, Kloob and Officer Grade 2, Ko...your two Teams were also spared the tragedy of losing anyone. I suggest that...in looking for a base of operations, by the Cacktash, near Owlam...since they arrived, flying from the east on those kites, start by looking over the city of Teltermak. Officer Grade 2, Nosk, Officer Grade 3, Izzanto and Officer Grade 4, Saskee - those three Teams did not lose any personnel. Those three Teams, get back to Owlam…now and find out what you can about what the Cacktash are doing there. Where ever you go, start causing the Cacktash as much misery as you possibly can. The rest of the Teams, get your acquaintances and moving of personnel done and wait for any information from the four Officers that I just mentioned." He swallowed hard. "Now, remember, this is for all of our fallen comrades…and if there are no questions…you are all dismissed."

All of the people in the room started vanishing. Some in groups, some individually. Finally the only ones left in the room were Wilfadge and his Team, Akantini, Oolooa and Chani. "We have work to do here," he said sadly.

"So…let's get to it," said Akantini with a sigh.

Natsa with her Team 82 and Boneech with her Team 67 made the Jump to Algothon. When they arrived they were somewhat surprised to see the mess that was being made by the Cacktash. There were areas where there were numerous unburied bodies. There were a few areas where the Cacktash had complete control and were mentally forcing many Algothons to do their bidding. There were a few other areas where the Cacktash were still attempting to control the local citizens, in mass groups.

Boneech shook her head. "Natsa, I'm the ranking one, but you're more experienced with this city. Where do we need to go, to make sure that we assure that there are no launches?"

Natsa snarled at what she was seeing. She looked at her Team members. "Osskood…Siy…take Noyee and Jojog over to the missile sites. Make sure that no one is attempting any launches. If they are, do some critical damage to the rockets. I don't want any launches…at all."

Noyee swallowed. "How do we destroy a…rocket…when we don't know anything about them?"

Osskood snickered. "Don't worry. They're highly sophisticated pieces of equipment. The more sophisticated something is…the easier it is to put it out of commission… permanently if you have to."

Natsa grabbed hold of Tooski. She looked at her other Team member, Eesteesee. "Boneech is going with you to Military Headquarters. See what kind of a mess is going on there. Tooski is coming with me to the Investigator Headquarters. We're going to assess there. Boneech, you and I will meet back here shortly to exchange information. Siy, if the Cacktash aren't launching anything, you be back here as well. If the Cacktash are trying to get anything launched…I want to know…immediately…unless you don't have time to tell me…and just destroy it. Everybody go!"

Natsa and Tooski arrived on the top floor of the Investigator Headquarters. Hashasee was alone on that floor. She was trying desperately to find anything on her computer that could tell her what was going on. The only thing that she was getting was frustrated. Occasionally she would look out one of the tiny slits of a window that she had to see the outside. That was no help either.

Tooski looked at Natsa. "Do you know who that is?"

Natsa snickered. "Yes. She's the number one, top of the heap, when it comes to the Investigative Services. No one outranks her. I don't know why the Cacktash haven't gotten to her yet…but she doesn't look like she's been able to do any fighting back."

"So…what do we do now?"

"We go down one floor and see what's happening there."

They Jumped down to where the High Investigators had their offices. It was a complete loss for the Algothons. The Cacktash were in control and were attempting to force any living High Investigator to give them the code to get the elevator to go all of the way up.

Natsa looked around and saw that there were only four Cacktash in this area. There were at least ten High Investigators who were being controlled by the enemy. She turned to Tooski. "Pick a Cacktash and hop the *h'oolyach* out of here."

Tooski picked one and Natsa picked another. Suddenly there were only two Cacktash on the floor while two other Cacktash were somewhere in Jahong's Death. Those two were torturing one of the Investigators at the elevator, trying to get the code for the upper floor.

Several of the Algothons fell to their knees. Three of them shook the cobwebs out of their heads, saw the torturing going on, pulled out their guns and opened fire. Now there were two bullet riddled Cacktash and the High Investigators were in control of their floor.

Natsa scoffed. "Those *Doovofts* are so sure that they're in absolute control...they didn't even take the weapons away from their enemies. How arrogant!" She looked around to see if there were any more Cacktash on this floor - none. "Let's go down another floor to the Chief Investigators."

Once again, it was a scene of a few Cacktash controlling many Algothons.

Tooski looked at Natsa. "Do we introduce a few more Cacktash out of here?"

"Yup!"

Four Cacktash disappeared and three more Cacktash were shot to death.

"Okay," said Natsa. "We've given the Algothons a few things to look over and the Cacktash have a puzzling setback. Let's get back to the meeting place."

Boneech arrived at the Military Headquarters with Imast. Boneech shook her head as she saw all of the dead bodies in the halls. "Do you recognize anybody?"

"Not really," said Imast. "Maybe we should go to the High Commander's office. See if anything is going on there."

Boneech shrugged. "You know this area...show me the way."

Eesteesee took Boneech by the hand and Jumped them

to the office. The usually neat office was a complete mess. There were six Cacktash in the room going through papers and attempting to find anything that they could on the computer. Just a few moments later, all six were in either Stink (for the rest of their life) or Jahong's Death.

Boneech looked around. "Let's wait a few…and see if any more of those *Bimyocks* show up. I don't mind sending a few more of them to…other places that they're not familiar with."

Eesteesee nodded. "Yes, Sir."

Osskood showed up at the launch control center. The Cacktash had a few of the technicians going over the final launch sequence for one of the rockets. He checked the monitor to see which missile silo was opening up for the launch and vanished.

Noyee looked around confused. "Where'd he go?"

Siy shrugged. "He didn't have time to talk. He's got to stop a missile from taking off."

Jojog scoffed. "So…what do we do?"

Siy snickered. "Make some Cacktash disappear."

Osskood reappeared in the control center. He looked at the other Owlamites. "DUCK!"

All four Owlamites squatted down just as the entire room shook violently from an explosion.

Jojog looked apprehensively at Osskood. "Was that any of…your doing?"

Osskood shrugged. "She did say that I had to stop any launch. I stopped it."

Siy looked at her fingernails. "So...what'd you do?"

"I ruptured a fuel line...which started a fire...in the fuel tank."

"Boom," said Siy lackadaisically.

"Yes, boom," said Osskood. He looked at several fights that were going on in the room. "What's all that?"

Jojog stood back up. "That's a bunch of Algothons, beating the *h'oolyach* out of a bunch of Cacktash...who thought they had complete control of everyone in the room."

Osskood nodded. "Why aren't the Cacktash able to retake the Algothons mentally?"

Noyee chuckled. "We kind of stunned them...a little. Now, the Algothons are stunning them...a lot."

Osskood smiled. "This room is now in complete pandemonium. It's going to take a while before either side can regain full control."

A Cacktash soldier came into the room and saw what was going on. He tried to mentally take over the Algothon combatants. He was clobbered over the head with a trashcan by an Algothon technician. Several other Algothons then started mercilessly kicking him and hitting him with chairs or anything else they could get their hands on.

"Yes, it's going to be quite a mess...for quite a while," said

Osskood.

Kloob with his Team 108 and Ko with his Team 119 made the Jump to Teltermak. At first, they were not surprised to see nothing but devastation. They were at the breach on the far west side of the large city. They could see nothing that was out of the ordinary from what occurred years ago.

Ko shrugged. "So…what do we do? We're here to find… what?"

"Anything out of the ordinary," said Kloob.

Xakisi looked at her Team Leader, Kloob. "What is out of the ordinary…in a huge mess?"

"Anything that's been cleaned up," said Kloob.

"Nothing's been cleaned up here," said Nelnee.

"All right," said Kloob. "Let's start Jumping around the wall…to different areas of the city. See if there's anything that's been cleaned up or is currently being cleaned…or used."

"We'll go south and you go north," sighed Ko.

Each one of them started Jumping around the wall around the city. They kept track of where they were Jumping to, in order to keep from covering the same territory. They also had to look further into the central part of the devastation. It was going to take a number of Jumps because Teltermak, like most of the other cities, had been a city of several million people. For the most part it was oval and when you are on the wall, you are quite a distance from the central part of the city.

After ten Jumps, Ko finally found an area that had been cleaned up. It also had several Cacktash military flying around using the hang gliders.

"Officer, Kloob, this is Officer, Ko, can you hear me?"

"This is Kloob, did you find something?"

"We found the Cacktash…in the southeastern part of the city. They have a big plant here for manufacturing the kites and teaching other Cacktash how to use them."

"The Cacktash were heard, saying that they have communicated with the Teltermak. Do you see any of those *Chogos*?"

"No, just Cacktash."

"Keep one of your personnel there. The rest of us will continue around the city and see if there's any more places that are being utilized."

"Good idea. See you on the east side."

When they finally met on the other side, Kloob decided they should go through the central part of the city and see if there was anything in there. It seemed strange that the only place that was being used, in a city this size, was one small area on the south side. The seven people Jumped all over the central part and found nothing but devastation. Finally Kloob gave up trying to find anything else and have everyone go to the kite school.

They walked around the area, in Observation, watching what was going on. There were all kinds of classes in making the frames, cutting the fabric that was used to keep it aloft, putting everything together and the actual act of flying.

Kloob looked up at five students who were gliding in lazy circles around the school area. He got an evil grin on his face and vanished. Two heartbeats later, one of the kites started falling. Then another kite fell. Then a third. Finally all five kites were falling and Kloob reappeared next to the other Owlamites. All five kites hit the ground with fatal results. The fabric that had been on each kite came down separate from the frames.

Ko was puzzled. "What did you do?"

Kloob smiled. "I Jumped up there, on top of a kite. I hopped the canvas, for just a tiny moment, into Ghost. After it was totally unhooked from the frame I hopped it back into Home. I then did the same thing with the other four kites."

Ipti scoffed. "What good is that gonna do?"

Kloob's grin got bigger. "Now, they're going to have to investigate why all of the kites lost their fabric, without any tearing of any of the fabric and no breakage in the clasps holding the fabric. That should keep them busy for a while…and not get any more students trained for a while."

Wanipi walked up to Kloob. "So what do we do now?"

"We don't have anyone to pit against the Cacktash because…"

Prok came out of his quarters after hearing all of the

shouting. "WHAT'S HAPPENING HERE? What's the problem with the training?"

One of the Cacktash walked up to him. "We seem to have developed…a fatal problem with the giant wings. All of them broke…while they were airborne."

Prok walked over to one of the accident sites. "Vithond, this is not good. What happened?"

Vithond scowled. "It seems that…something is amiss in the construction of the wings. All of them lost their fabric at the same time and now…we have five dead…and now we need some answers as to what happened."

Prok shook his head. "Well then, start your investigation… but do it a little quieter. I'm busy and I don't want to be disturbed." He walked back to his quarters.

Vithond glared angrily at Prok as he walked away.

Kloob smiled. "There is a little bit of a problem here. That *Doovoft* Prok, he needs to be dealt with. We need to let the Command Staff know that he's here."

Nosk, with his Team 119, Izzanto with his Team 122 and Saskee with her Team 276 all showed up at Owlam. They were standing in the north central area of the great wall.

Nosk was livid as he looked out over all of their crops. "Those thieves are trying to take all of our crops or at least the ones that were ready to be harvested. We grew these things and they want to take it away from us."

Izzanto sighed. "So what do you suggest?"

"Hinder them! Hinder them in any way that we can."

Toyee shook her head. "What is the best way to do that?"

Nosk was trying to think of some way of fouling up the system. He looked around and all that he saw was that the Cacktash were using all kinds of different races as slaves. They were gathering the crops that were ready to be harvested and getting them ready to be shipped out.

Saskee scratched her head. "How do they plan on getting them out? This gateway is still closed. We're the only ones who know the codes for opening them. What are they doing?"

"Start Jumping around," said Nosk. "They have to have a plan somewhere. Remember that there are eight different gateways under the wall. They might've actually stumbled onto the code for one of them."

Zoona looked at him. "You're saying that we randomly Jump around the wall checking on those nasty Cacktash?"

"Check near the gateways," said Nosk. "If they haven't opened one of them, they might actually try digging under the wall. They have enough prisoners here…they might just actually try something that stupid." He turned to the three Teams. "Go! Start looking."

It took a few Jumps, however, Shisha found the tunnel. **"They did it**," she sent. **"They dug a tunnel under the**

wall...near the trading area. They've got all of the stuff here for stealing all of our crops."

All of the Owlamites Jumped to the trading area in the northeast sector. They saw how a very large, crude tunnel had been dug under the wall. There were several empty carts that were being pulled in and full carts coming out of Owlam through this tunnel.

Nosk contemplated for a few moments. "We need to check the entire perimeter. I want to know if this is the only tunnel...or have they dug others. Someone do a complete circuit of the city and check."

"I'll do it," said Baya.

"Meanwhile," said Nosk. "Let's think of some way of fouling up their system...without hurting anyone but those wretched Cacktash."

Izzanto looked at the way the Cacktash were mistreating everyone. "No matter what we do...they'll probably take it out on their prisoners."

"We also have to figure out a way to close that tunnel... without destroying the wall," said Ahampi.

"We could Jump a few boulders in there," said Nootika.

"Not without raising a lot of suspicions," said Ichiy.

Nosk clenched his teeth while looking around. "There! Over there, I see a rather large tent. I see no one but Cacktash going in and out of it. If there's a place where only the Cacktash are, then only the Cacktash can be found guilty of killing another Cacktash. Let's see what's in that big tent."

They all Jumped down to just in front of the tent. Nosk led the way inside. Izzanto and Saskee followed. Then the rest of the Team members. They looked around in the tent at all of the activity that was going on. There were some canvas walls that had been set up so that there were different offices in there.

There was one large room where they had several desks set up. The papers on the desks were sections of the city, showing what crops were being grown where and what their status was as far as how soon they should be harvested. Another room had an inventory of all of the foreign prisoners that were being used as slave labor. Then there were the administrative offices and a conference room where they had a rather large map of the interior of Owlam. Finally a field kitchen with a dining room.

Nosk was slowly walking through the kitchen. He stopped suddenly with a big grin on his face. He grabbed hold of Izzanto's arm. "Didn't one of those Doctors say something…about the leaves of the *Shoonshook*…will make you…no force you to regurgitate?"

Izzanto frowned. "Uh…yes they did…why?" He then looked at two large cauldrons that had steam coming out of them and contained something rather aromatic. He grinned and chuckled. "You dirty, rotten…won't they get a little suspicious?"

"If they're the only ones in here, who else could sabotage their food? I mean…it's not like they're being forced to eat that… slop…that we saw out there that's been set up for the prisoners to eat."

Saskee looked at two of her Team members. "Zoona, Ahampi, do you think you could find a few…*Shoonshook* leaves, grind them up a little and…add them to this Cacktash porridge?"

Both women grinned and vanished.

Baya called in from the top of the wall. **"This is Officer, Baya. Officer, Izzanto where are you and everybody else for that matter?"**

Izzanto called back. **"We're all in the big tent. It's the Cacktash temporary headquarters…in the trading area. What did you find out?"**

"There's just this one tunnel. All of the trains of prisoners hauling carts are headed for this one tunnel."

"Good! That gives us a hard choke point and we can control things from there. Come on down to the big tent."

Baya did a Jump to the front of the tent and entered.

Nosk took everyone into the room with the map. They watched as one Cacktash was looking over papers and making changes to the large map of Owlam. There were two others who were sorting and filing other papers.

The one at the map looked up. "I need all the new information on the western section. We haven't updated that in three days."

The other two Cacktash left the room.

Nosk turned to one of his Team members, Nanina. "Go stand behind him and hop to Spy."

Nanina looked a little concerned as she walked over to the Cacktash. Nosk walked over, standing directly in front of the Cacktash. Nanina took in a deep breath and let it out slowly. She looked back at Nosk and shook her head. She closed her eyes and hopped to Spy. The Cacktash looked startled. He put his papers down, placed his index fingers against his temples, leaned his head back and closed his eyes. Nanina suddenly had a stunned look on her face. At that moment, Nosk took his knife and slashed the throat of the Cacktash from ear to ear. Now the Cacktash had a stunned look on his face as he dropped his hands to his throat and slowly sank to the floor, choking on his own blood.

Nosk looked at his colleagues. "Now, it starts. We isolate them...one or two at a time...and we give them some mysterious situations...here in the tent. We don't give them any reason to go after the prisoners, because we only kill Cacktash in areas where there are no prisoners. That should drive them a little crazy."

Izzanto smiled. "How about sabotaging some of those carts? That should slow them down...considerably."

Saskee smiled as well. "We could start by sabotaging some of them in that tunnel. That's their choke point. If we clog it...then we slow that part down...considerably."

Nosk nodded. "If you foul up a cart...make sure that there's no...prisoner...at that spot. Only a Cacktash...say a Cacktash that's walking next to a cart...and the wheel happens to fall off and...hit the Cacktash." He turned to all of his colleagues and grinned. "We need to slow their operations here...considerably."

2

Natsa and Boneech received a briefing on what that tremendous explosion was and the fact that the Cacktash no longer had full (if any) control of the rockets, Investigator Headquarters or Military Headquarters. There was complete confusion among both Cacktash and Algothons as to what did, was and is happening.

Kloob and Ko kept watching as the Cacktash attempted to come up with stronger lashings in order to keep the material attached to the frame of the giant wings. Of course there had been nothing wrong with what they had been using, however, Kloob and Ko were not going to let that stand in the way of further sabotage.

Nosk, Izzanto and Saskee kept up the problems in Owlam as the Cacktash were finding several more of their personnel murdered in the tent. After assigning some fifty Cacktash to guard the outside perimeter of the tent, in order to keep any enemies out, they finally determined that they had either a saboteur or serial killer among their own race. They were also having all kinds of further problems in attempting to get the crops out of the city of Owlam, because the wheels kept falling off of the carts and they always fell off in the middle of the tunnel, thus clogging the tunnel and adding to the frustration. Crops were rotting in the carts while they were waiting to clear the tunnel and another cart would fall apart.

Prominent King, Prok was getting tired of hearing all of the bickering by the Cacktash as to who was at fault over the bad lashings for the material on the wings. He decided to go back to Algothon, because there, he would not have to put up with any of these problems. Besides, the Cacktash in Algothon should have complete control of the city by now. He would be able to just walk in, declare himself the new Dictator for Life and start giving out orders that would be obeyed to the nth degree...especially by certain females that he was lusting for.

Prok took his current favorite slave women with him. He had obtained another woman from a race of Elf called Skirteer. Her name was Tabaseeska. She was right at six taja in height, had dark purple skin, black eyes and jet black hair. She had no more desire to be with Prok than the three Algothon women did, however, that nasty electric collar gave her absolutely no choice but to comply.

He got in his truck and set out for an eastern harbor. Three of the Cacktash went with him to make sure that there were no problems obtaining passage to Neopaure.

He also had half of the *Tuzine* that had been outside the walls at the time of the Cacktash attack. The Cacktash had the rest.

The search in Owlam went on to find the manufacturing plant for the *Tuzine*. Neither Prok nor the Cacktash were willing to admit defeat. The Owlams had to have hidden it somewhere in the city...but where and how did they keep it hidden? The secret location just had not been found yet. Prok left orders for them to continue looking. Several of the Cacktash were ready to kill him for making the order. The search would have continued no matter what he said.

If the Cacktash had had any capability at dimension hopping, they would have found all kinds of different things in (and under) the city. All of the living quarters and most of the underground vaults were in another dimension. The Owlam High Staff had decided that only the two upper levels of the underground vaults should be dimensionally hidden. If someone were to dig down that deep and not find anything, it was determined that they would probably give up and stop at that depth. If there were some hard-headed group who decided to dig deeper...the Owlam Staff would decide what to do at that time.

Three days later, Prok and his entourage arrived in the city of Blasinigan on the east coast of North Chilamte. Since the rediscovering of the *Tuzine*, all people from continents or islands that were east of this continent were coming through this harbor city in order to get the precious drug. As a result, it was one of the fastest growing cities in the world. The ships would come here for anchorage and the peoples from other lands would then need guides to take them to Owlam. Little did they know that the manufacture of *Tuzine* had been temporarily suspended... indefinitely.

Prok turned to one of his Cacktash allies. "Just think...in

a few more months…or maybe just days…we'll own all of this. We'll be the ones controlling all of this commerce. The harbor, the ships, the guides, the food and fuel for the trips…and the drug."

The leader of the three Cacktash, Throat Cutter, Fooloozh smiled. "Yes, that'll be nice. We've been waiting a long time to take our place as world leaders. Too long. I can hardly wait until the grand meeting to divide up the spoils." He looked at his colleagues. "**I can hardly wait until we drown this** *shongfop* **Algothon traitor in his own blood**."

Top Worker, Zhogvoth and Second Worker, Plundit both just smiled back.

Zhogvoth drove the truck up to the city gate and stopped. There was only one vehicle ahead of them, so the wait was not long. As soon as that truck pulled forward, so did Zhogvoth.

The City Guard personnel all looked in the back of the big ten wheel truck and saw the four naked women.

The current Chief of the gate walked up to the Zhogvoth. "What's this? Those women can't come into the city like that. If you want them coming in here…you'd better give them something to cover themselves up."

Prok leaned forward from the back seat of the cab. "Those women are my slaves and I'll dress them as I see fit!"

"Not in this city, Sir! I understand that they are your slaves, however, we do have some regulations here that make public nudity a crime…no matter what the status of the nude person is. Cover them up or you'll not be allowed to enter."

Plundit turned to look back at Prok. "Don't worry, Sir. I'll get some towels for them. They cover up while in the city. After we leave…on the ship…you rule."

Prok leaned back in his seat fuming. Disobedience to his demands was not to be tolerated, however, at this time he could not do anything about it…at this time.

Another Team of spies that had not lost a member, was called on to follow Prok as he headed back to Algothon. Officer Grade 4, Hadeetz, Leader of Team 333 and her Team members, Zhool, Lindaka and Hemchee were in the truck as well, watching the confrontation.

Lindaka looked at Prok angrily. "It's about time that *Doovoft* didn't get his way. Those poor women are getting badly sunburned…sitting back there."

Hemchee shook her head. "What's your problem? Three of those women are Algothons."

Hadeetz looked back at Lindaka. "You're the one with the correct opinion. No one should be treated that badly. Slavery is such a…horrid thing." She looked at the male member of the Team. "What's your opinion on this?"

Zhool just sat there looking forward. "The only thing that I'll say on it is that slavery is wrong and I can't condone it…even with Algothons."

Lindaka folded her arms. "So when do we get to send that *Bimyock* off to Jahong's Death?"

"As soon as we get word from Officer Leader, Boneech

that the problem is over in Algothon," said Hadeetz.

"I can hardly wait," said Hemchee.

"I've got a better idea," said Zhool. "We don't kill him. We make him suffer worse than what he's doing to these women."

Hadeetz cocked her head and eyed him suspiciously. "What did you have in mind?"

He snickered. "As soon as Boneech informs us that the problem is over in Algothon...I'll bring it up again. Until then... it won't be worth discussing because we might not be doing it at all."

Hemchee snarled at him. "Then why did you bring it up now?"

"To let you know that we could have fun with that *thing*... before we kill him."

"So..." said Wilfadge. "What is the report from Algothon?"

"Each individual Cacktash can only control so many people at one time," said Boneech. "If you find several Cacktash standing there, controlling several...others...you just take out one of the Cacktash and the newly freed prisoners start taking out the Cacktash who are still standing and...soon enough the Cacktash are all dead...in that location."

Wilfadge nodded. "Is that what you've been doing...in Algothon?"

"Yes, Sir. It seems now that the Cacktash are so badly outnumbered that the Algothons are rapidly retaking their city."

"Call back…to someone…somewhere! We need to get at least one Cacktash alive so that we can find out where they originated from. They are a…tremendous danger…and we need to get them under control…or get rid of all of them for good."

Boneech grimaced. "You know what you're saying Sir?"

He hung his head. "I am painfully aware of what I'm saying."

"Check those archives," said Wilfadge. "Somewhere, in all of that information, someone has to be able to find out where the home city of those Cacktash is located."

"I have," said Ahandi. "I found their city located on the southeast section of the Aerisau continent. I also found out that they left that continent just after the firestorm attack. They crossed over to the Cifpasica continent and were living there…until they figured out a way to launch an attack of their own against Algothon."

Wilfadge looked around. "Where's the map? I want to see…."

"One step ahead of you," said Hadathoo. "I found the two continents in question. Aerisau is east of Neopaure and Cifpasica is southeast of Aerisau."

Teelila scoffed. "That's an awfully long way to go…from Cifpasica to Neopaure. They left everything of theirs back in Cifpasica and headed out. Are all of their families…still back there in Cifpasica?"

Wilfadge leaned back. "That…is something that we need to find out. We need to find out as much as possible in order to be able to stop these Cacktash…from doing…who knows what."

Dwalooa cleared her throat. "Once we do that…what next?"

"We may have to…exterminate them…before they exterminate us," said Wilfadge sadly. "They seem to be a greater danger than any other that we've faced since the firestorm. They can read minds and they can mentally control others with it. Even the Sodle weren't this dangerous."

Kloob looked up at Xakisi. "What did you find?"

"I found the Cacktash," said Xakisi.

Ko looked startled. "What? You found them… somewhere…near here?"

Xakisi shrugged. "If you don't believe me, I can take you out there and show you. They have a massive encampment about fifteen kilotaja southeast of here."

Kloob looked around at the others on the Teams. "It's not that I don't believe you, I think that all of us should go there and take a look…and get a firm grip on just how large it is…the encampment I mean…and how many of them are there…before we give a full report to the High Command."

"That's fair," said Xakisi with a smile.

Zhool looked up as Hadeetz came in the stateroom. "Have you been in contact with Natsa?"

Hadeetz smiled. "Of course. I got the word that they've completely routed the Cacktash in Algothon. It seems that one Cacktash can only control...oh say...about twenty-five people. Anything more than that and they have some severe problems. All our people had to do was smack a Cacktash and spoil their concentration. Once the Algothons were no longer under their control, they would quickly dispatch the Cacktash. One leads to ten...and that leads to one hundred...and then that leads to thousands...and then the Cacktash are completely helpless against the Algothon overwhelming numbers. I hate to say it...but...we helped those *chogo* Algothons...retake their city."

Lindaka stood up with an expectant smile on her face. "Does that mean that we don't have to put up with this...garbage...here?"

Hemchee was just as expectant in her hopes. "We dump this...Prok and...the three Cacktash garbage...and we go home?"

Zhool had an evil grin on his face. "I think that it's about time I let you in on my plan for that piece of *h'oolyach*. It's a little complicated...so I've been thinking it over. It is a situation where the Algothons get rid of Prok...for us. Are you interested?"

Hadeetz sat down and sighed. She looked at the other three members of her Team 333. She nodded. "Let's hear it. We've got eight more days before we get to the harbor on Neopaure. As long as it doesn't take more than that to explain and execute your plan...I'll listen." She snickered. "We don't have anything else to do right now."

Lindaka grunted. "If it gives us a way to put him down... as painfully as possible...I think I'll listen."

Zhool smiled. "It's painful...and very...very...slow."

Nosk looked around at all of the bleary-eyed Cacktash. Most of the enemy had not been able to sleep for several days. They were completely baffled at all of the murders that had taken place against their own race without any evidence to support who was doing it or how – or why. "How many more bodies should we have strung out here...before we really start a Cacktash bloodbath?"

"Before we start a bloodbath, we'd better contact Wilfadge and let him know what's going on," said Saskee.

"I already have," said Izzanto. "I checked with him and according to the High Command, if we've done enough damage to the Cacktash to where the people that they've enslaved here can revolt and get their lives back...we should help them."

Nosk smiled. "How?"

Saskee shrugged her shoulders. "According to what we learned about that mind intrusion, from Bonarain, we should be able to get rid of a few more Cacktash and then start planting revolution in the heads of the slaves. They'll do the rest."

Izzanto frowned. "Do you mean...that we make those enslaved people do the fighting...for us?"

Nosk smiled. "Absolutely! That way, *we* don't lose any more people to these *chokwad* Cacktash. Plus, they'll be fighting for themselves as well."

Sarskatama woke up. Her knees were in pain – as usual. Being in a luxury stateroom on this ship was only beneficial in that fact that the floor was carpeted and she did not have her knees being constantly scraped by a concrete, metal or wood floor.

Prok was forcing his sex slaves to sleep with their knees up against their chest. They had to kneel down and sleep hunched over with straps around their bodies so that they did not, and could not, roll over and sleep in any other, than a kneeling position. When he released the straps, they should be able to do exactly what he demanded, otherwise all four of them would be punished. The only one that was allowed to sleep, laying down, was the one that happened to be in bed with him...at the time...servicing the master...sexually. Last night, it was Shiganeea who ended up in bed with Prok. Choya, Sarskatama and Tabaseeska had to be on the floor hunched over their knees.

The three Cacktash that were with Prok were taking turns doing mind control games on the four women. This assured their obedience.

Sarskatama tried to adjust her legs a little for some kind of comfort. She placed her hands against the floor for leverage and felt...moisture (?). She looked at her hands and in the dim light, she saw that the liquid on her hands was dark. She looked up and was very confused by what she saw at first. She had to blink her eyes and rub the sleep out before she was able to comprehend that what she saw was not changing. She slid the upper strap over her shoulders and to the floor. She sat up and looked around at the gory mess in front of her.

Tabaseeska was still sleeping next to her on her left side. Choya was not. Choya was laying in a very large pool of blood... on her back...dead...with a very large knife stuck in her chest. Two of the Cacktash were sitting in chairs with their heads hanging to the side in very unnatural positions with a gaping wound in their throats. The third Cacktash was on the floor. His throat had been sliced very deeply as well, however, he had been able to stab Choya to death before he died.

The three Cacktash were in the room because they enjoyed watching Prok sexually abuse the women. They were also using their mind control to make the women put on some kinky nude shows for their perverted desires.

Somehow, last night, Choya had decided that she had had enough, waited until the Cacktash and Prok were asleep...and killed the three Cacktash. Unfortunately she had been killed by the third Cacktash victim before he died from his slashed throat.

Sarskatama worried about how Prok was going to react when he woke up. Choya had not been able to take him out as well, so the situation would be very painful in the morning. She wondered if she should get one of those knives and take him out by herself.

Prok, somehow, had not been awakened by the obviously silent slaughter that had taken place in the room. He was laying next to Shiganeea sleeping peacefully. Shiganeea was sleeping, however, she had a pained look on her face.

Sarskatama was undecided as to what she was going to do until she saw that horrid little control box laying on the night stand…next to where Prok was snoozing. Usually that thing was kept in a safe when Prok was asleep. She could not understand how it had ended up out in the open while Prok was asleep. She did not know why, however, something seemed to be reaching into her mind, telling her to get the control box and use it to get the collars off of herself and the other two living women. She was terrified of the thought of what might happen, however, the urging seemed to get more desperate.

She slid the other strap off and crawled on weak and numb knees to the nightstand. She picked up the control box and looked at the small screen that was above a tiny keypad. She pulled the stylus out of the slot on the side. Immediately, the screen lit up. She gasped and held the box up against her chest, looking at Prok to see if he had noticed the bright light. She sighed in relief as she saw that he was still totally oblivious of what was going on.

She looked back at the screen. It had a prompt on it, asking for the password. 'Great,' she thought. 'Password protected. The password could be anything.' She was ready to give up and take one of those knives and slit her own throat…however…that strange urging was going on in her mind to try. She was at a loss as to what to feed in.

Zhool snarled. "What does it take to get to get the point across to her?"

Lindaka smacked Zhool on his back. "Quiet! Hadeetz needs to concentrate."

Zhool raised his hand as if he were going to backhand Lindaka. He just snarled at her. "We're in Observation. That Algothon can't hear us."

"No, but Hadeetz can."

Hadeetz was doing everything that she could to push Sarskatama into using the control box, however, she did not want that Algothon woman to know that she was getting any form of assistance.

Sarskatama was ready to put the box back several times, however, that strong urging kept telling her to try. The suggestion came in that Prok was not that brilliant. He had betrayed his own people, in order to get what he wanted, and did not seem to be smart enough to have masterminded the plot. That would mean that his password had to be...simple...from a simple-minded individual. What password could be the simplest? She used the stylus and keyed in the word: Password. When the screen switched to saying: Welcome King Prok – what is your bidding, Your Majesty? Sarskatama read it and wanted desperately to punch that idiotic fool in the most sensitive area that she could think of. Only the laziest or dumbest of fools would use "Password" as their password.

The screen started scrolling the prompts that had been fed into it. When she saw "Collar Maintenance", she highlighted it. A new list started scrolling. She saw "Removal" and highlighted that. Now it scrolled the names of the four female victims who were currently wearing the things. She highlighted her name.

Once again the box was asking for a password. She sighed and keyed in: Password. It came back as incorrect. She clenched her teeth in aggravation. Had he suddenly become intelligent on this one?

That strange urging pushed her towards… She keyed in her name. As soon as she hit enter there was a click from the collar around her neck as the clasp separated. She gasped and froze in surprise for a moment. She then had to fight, very hard, to keep from laughing out loud from the elation of having that *thing* off of her body. She triumphantly pulled the *thing* off of her neck. She then fed in the name: Tabaseeska. She watched as the collar on the Skirteer woman clicked when it released. The movement was so slight that it did not awaken her.

By now, most of the feeling had come back into her legs. She stood up with an evil smile on her face. She placed the control box on the nightstand. She stood up to her full height and brought her right elbow down on Prok's forehead as hard as she could. Prok's arms and legs bounced up from the impact. He opened his eyes momentarily, groaned and with a look of shock on his face, his eyes closed again and he was unconscious again…*knocked* unconscious, not sleeping.

The movement by Prok awakened Shiganeea. She looked back and forth from Prok to Sarskatama with horror and fear in her eyes. Her mouth was wide open and she shook her head. She did a whisper yell: "What did you do?" She looked at Prok again. "When he wakes up…he'll zap us…over and over. Why…?"

Sarskatama picked up the control box and showed it to Shiganeea. She wiggled her eyebrows with a big smile on her face. She looked back down at the screen and keyed in: Shiganeea.

Shiganeea, once again, had a look of complete surprise on her face as her collar unclasped. She slowly reached up and pulled the collar off. She looked up at Sarskatama and smiled. She tossed the collar on the floor and raised her fist to strike Prok.

Sarskatama held out her hand. "NO!" She shook her head. "Not now. He won't feel it."

Shiganeea grunted. "Okay, so what do we do now?"

Sarskatama grinned. "We put one of these nasty things on this *Shvok*."

Shiganeea grinned back. "Good idea." She looked down at the other victim. "Are you going to wake her up?"

"We can…if you want."

"Uh…where's Choya?"

Sarskatama sighed. "She died…attempting to kill all three of the Cacktash."

"Oh…no…are they…alive?"

"No! Choya gave her life…to save ours. She killed all three of the Cacktash though, so we don't have to worry about them."

"So…what do we do now? We're sitting here…with what…four dead bodies? How do we explain that to whoever is in charge of this ship?"

Sarskatama shrugged. "We explain it with what actually happened. Choya killed all three Cacktash. The third one woke up just as she was attempting the death slash on him and...he fought back...and both of them ended up dead."

"You're sure that that...is what happened?"

"You're an Investigator - take a look! What do you think happened?"

Shiganeea looked around at the gruesome sight. "As long as we don't touch anything...they can't really argue with it."

"I'm going to look through the tutorial on this control box. Then we'll put one of those *hongoth* collars on him...then we'll have to talk to someone on the crew...preferably someone in charge...and make sure that there's no problem with our passage to Neopaure."

"I'm going to wake up Tabaseeska and let her know the good news. Maybe she'll have some kind of other idea as to how we get away with this."

"Get away with what? WE didn't kill anybody. Choya killed the three Cacktash and was killed in self-defense by one of the Cacktash. We were on the side...asleep when the killing took place."

"I'm still gonna wake her up because that's such an uncomfortable position to sleep in. You can't breathe properly at all." Shiganeea got up, walked around the blood pool, knelt down and gently shook Tabaseeska. "Wake up, sister. The nightmare is over."

Tabaseeska stirred. She looked up in pain. "Wha...?" She looked at Shiganeea bleary-eyed and confused.

"Sarskatama got the collars off of us. She's trying to figure out how we put one on that *Shybeelan Ninyit*. Then we'll control him."

Tabaseeska sat there wide-eyed for several moments letting reality soak in to her mind. She slipped the straps off and raised up looking around the stateroom. The two Algothon women explained what had taken place in the last few moments. Tabaseeska got up on wobbly legs. She massaged some feeling back into her legs as she looked around the room again.

"So...we're free from being slaves to that...*poshonko?*"

"Yes," said Shiganeea with a smile. "We're free."

"So why isn't he wearing one of those pain collars?"

"Sarskatama is reading the instructions on the *installation* procedures. Once she's finished with that, we'll put one on him and...have fun zapping him."

Tabaseeska sighed. "While she's doing that, I'm going to get all of this blood off of me. I feel...horrible."

In Spy dimension, Hemchee frowned. "Are we going to help that Skirteer woman?"

"Of course," said Hadeetz. "That woman hasn't done anything wrong to us. We'll make sure that she's taken care of...unless she tries to pull something nasty against Owlam and

Owlamites."

Tabaseeska went to the bathroom and cleaned herself thoroughly. It was difficult for the two Algothon women to tell what was and was not clean on that dark purple skin. They just accepted it from Tabaseeska that she was satisfied with her cleansing.

"Got it," said Sarskatama. She pulled a new collar out of the box. She found a small extension wire in the collar and plugged it into the control box. She then hit the activation prompt. She smiled as she put the collar around Prok's neck. When she saw the request for a password for the collar, she grinned. She covered the small screen with her thumb. She closed her eyes and randomly hit twenty keys on the keypad. She opened her eyes and hit "enter". The screen showed a row of dots and that the password had been accepted. It then requested what level of shock the wearer was to receive. She moved the arrow to one line below the maximum. She then pressed the shock button. Prok's entire body went rigid and seemed to vibrate a little. She took her finger off the button. "Done," she said with a satisfied smile. "Now that *Hongoth* is ours to play with."

Shiganeea sighed. "So let's find some clothing for us, get dressed and then inform someone on the crew…about this mess."

Sarskatama grunted in agreement.

Tabaseeska took the control box and zapped Prok several more times. She enjoyed seeing him quiver. Now all she had to do was wait until he woke up, so that she could zap him and make him feel and remember it.

"Finally," said Hadeetz. "The situation is taken care of, those women have control of that *Bimyock* and we should be able to just relax for the rest of the cruise."

"I hope so," said Zhool.

Hemchee looked out the porthole. "Where are we headed?"

"The port city of Dandamira," said Hadeetz. "It's probably the most western spot on that continent."

Lindaka frowned. "That's the place they were going to… when our people sank that fleet of ships…wasn't it?"

"Don't forget," said Zhool. "That was a military excursion. This is just a small party of people who are passengers on a ship that doesn't belong to the city of Algothon."

Lindaka shrugged and looked off to the side blushing a little.

Hemchee scoffed. "So what do we do now…according to your big plan against that *Bimyock*?"

Zhool snickered. "Nothing. According to Natsa and Boneech, the Algothons have retaken control of their city from the Cacktash. Prok was the one who gave the order for the Cacktash to attack…in Algothon and Owlam. Prok doesn't know that the Cacktash have lost. We've got three credible witnesses here…who can testify to his betrayal of his own city. We let the Algothons put him on trial, convict him and execute him according to their law."

Hadeetz shook her head. "The only thing that we have to do is make sure that these credible witnesses give the correct answers at his trial."

Boneech stood on the top of the wall looking down at some of the devastation. "Now, these Algothons are experiencing some of the mess that they put us through. They actually had to attack and destroy part of their own city, in order to take it back from those Cacktash."

"Serves them right," said Tooski. "I just wish that the devastation had been worse. Then they'd have to rebuild a lot more."

Jojog scratched his chin. "They're having to go through a lot more. According to what I heard from Nosk, Izzanto and Saskee, all the rest of the world is blaming Algothon for a renewed loss of the *Tuzine* drug. They're being told that they'd better do something positive about it...right now."

Natsa sighed in satisfaction with a smile. "I'd love to hear some of the things going on in cities all over the world. They're all saying nasty things about the Algothons and they're wondering where we are and if the *Tuzine* will ever be manufactured again."

"We never stopped manufacturing it," snickered Eesteesee. "We're just storing more of it right now."

Sarskatama sighed. "We can't put it off any longer. We have to tell someone on this ship that Prok is no longer in command, the Cacktash are dead...and we're not slaves that are going to be paraded around for the pleasure of the perverts who were slobbering over us each time we were walked around out there."

"This stinks," said Tabaseeska. "It hasn't been that long since I wore clothing. Now it itches like mad."

Shiganeea scoffed. "Good. You're having that problem too. I thought it was just me."

Sarskatama looked at Prok with an evil grin. "Speaking of clothing...or lack thereof...." She yanked hard on the leash that was attached to Prok's collar. "If I hear any words come out of your mouth...you get zapped. You do not utter one word without the permission of whoever is holding that control box. NOTHING! We control you now you traitorous *ninyit!*" She looked at the door to the stateroom. "Let's go find someone in charge."

Prok looked back at her in fear. He showed fear now. He was sure that when they got to Algothon, his Cacktash friends would put things back the way they were supposed to be. He would be in charge again and all would be well for him.

The Leader of the ship was very surprised about the changes that had taken place in his highest costing stateroom. He was not too happy about all of the blood that had soaked into the carpet. It would have to be replaced. There was an investigator (of sorts) who was a part of the ship's crew. He confirmed the story that the three women told about Choya's revolt against the Cacktash. The crew and other passengers had to accept the fact that Prok was now the naked slave and the three women were actually high ranking personnel from their cities and had to be treated that way. Tabaseeska was treated as a diplomat and the two Algothon women were feared as high level members of the

Algothon Constabulary.

Sarskatama had not received any information over the radio as to the situation in Algothon, so she was very anxious about that. There was nothing she could do until they arrived in Dandamira and was possibly able to contact someone in Algothon.

Shiganeea was not that concerned with what was going on in Algothon as she was in torturing Prok for all of the sexual nonsense that he had put her through. She guaranteed that no matter what happened, he was not going to be in charge of anything. She would electrocute him to death before she would allow him to touch her again...even if it meant her own execution by some half-baked Cacktash tribunal. Her main fear was that she might still end up pregnant from all of that abuse.

Tabaseeska mainly wanted to get back home...possibly with some of the *Tuzine* that Prok had purloined for his own profit.

Kloob stood there in the Cacktash encampment looking around. "We've been given the order," he said. "Everything that we've heard about the Cacktash and everything that we've investigated here...these people are just too dangerous."

Ko shook his head sadly. "All those plans that they have in their main tent...call for world domination. All they had to do was take over Algothon, obtain full control of the firestorm weapons... they would have a threat of extermination to anyone who did not bow to them."

Wanipi gritted her teeth in anger. "Didn't these miscreants

learn anything? The world is, just now, starting to recover from that mass attack that the Algothons launched. The Cacktash wanted to…start that residual energy mess…all over again…why?"

Teeska huffed. "So where do we send these pieces of conquering trash?"

"I suggest Shogoot's Search," said Nelnee. "That was that area where the bodies were dissolved…by some kind of liquid acid. Send these *doovofts* in alive…and let them drown in that acid…since we have to kill all of them anyway."

Hathoya hung her head. "When do we start?"

"As soon as the other Teams get here to help us," said Kloob. "There's over 35,000 Cacktash in this camp. They brought *everything* with them. They were planning on a complete takeover here and Algothon. There's no encampment near Algothon so… they were planning on just keeping enough there…to launch a firestorm weapon or two. They were planning on living here, in Owlam, once they had completely taken over."

Ipti hugged herself. "I don't look forward to this."

"Yeah," scoffed Nelnee. "This is another city that we're going to finish the job of totally destroying them…a job started by Algothon. I'm getting tired of finishing their horrible task."

"Don't forget," said Kloob. "We didn't ask for any of this. Each time we've finished off someone - we were defending ourselves."

Nelnee stood there sulking. "That doesn't make me feel any better about wiping out an entire race…even though we didn't start the fight."

One hundred fifty of the Owlam Teams showed up. The massacre took only one day to complete.

Hadeetz did everything that she could to calm the anxiety of Sarskatama and Shiganeea. It was humiliating having to assist a pair of Algothon Investigators, however, considering the fact that the choice was between them and those Cacktash (most of whom were dead by now), the choice was made easier by virtue of the fact that they now had to deal with the traitor Prok.

When the ship finally docked at Dandamira, all of the anxieties of the three former sex slaves of Prok ended when they found out that the Cacktash had been routed completely in Algothon. There were people all over the port city talking about how the Cacktash had been beaten and in all probability slaughtered completely. The different races of people there all still blamed Algothon, because, for some reason, virtually all of them seemed to know that an Algothon Investigator had been involved in the plot and because of the attack, all trading for the precious *Tuzine* had stopped altogether. No one seemed to know where the Owlamites were or where any of the drug was.

Sarskatama looked at her colleague. "We need to get this *Hongoth* put on trial...publicly and make sure that the news gets out that he was the *only* Algothonian involved in the stoppage of trade for the *Tuzine*."

Shiganeea scoffed. "So we put him on trial and he gets hanged. How is that going to start the trade for *Tuzine* again?"

"Don't you remember all that stuff about how the Owlams bypassed the jamming system by those Sodles? If they could override that system, I'm sure that if it gets out that the Algothon traitor has been executed, they'll know…in a very short time."

Tabaseeska walked up to them chewing on some kind of food that she had obtained. "Do you really want me there, in Algothon, to testify against that *fonkothok?*"

"It'd help considerably," said Sarskatama. "Once you testify that you were…sexually mistreated…the same way that we were then there'll be more credibility to the fact that he operated outside, not only Algothon law, but he violated you and yours as well."

Tabaseeska nodded. "All right. I'll go…but I will have an escort of my people with me. They want to protect me from any further illegal abduction or incarceration."

"That is *not* a problem," said Sarskatama with a big smile.

"I just wish that we had some way of contacting the Owlams and letting them know that we didn't have anything to do with that plot by Prok," said Shiganeea.

Hadeetz snickered. "We know, darling. We're just going to make you Algothons sweat for a while."

A member of the Constabulary of Dandamira came up to the women. He looked at the predicament that Prok was in. "I'm afraid that you can't leave him naked while in this city. There are children running around here and…that's not quite what is done… in a civilized city."

Sarskatama smiled. "I understand, Sir. Don't worry, we'll get something on him as quickly as possible."

The Constable looked around. "It's not that I'm trying to tell you how to run your life, but…we don't really care for slavery and slaves in this city."

"He's not a slave," said Shiganeea with a smile. "This is the man who is being taken to Algothon to be put on trial for treason. He's the one who launched the attack against Owlam and halted their trade for *Tuzine*."

The Constable raised his eyebrows. "Oh…so he…is a prisoner!"

"Yes, Sir, he is our prisoner," said Sarskatama.

The Constable looked at Tabaseeska inquisitively. "Are you part of this as well?"

"I'm a witness for the prosecution against that traitor," said Tabaseeska with a friendly smile. "I was there when he made the call to launch the attack. I was there trading for *Tuzine*…and all of a sudden, after he made a radio call…those nasty Cacktash were everywhere…and treating him like some kind of…deity."

The Constable smiled. "Good! Eyewitness accounts are *very good* for the prosecution. If you'd like…while you're waiting for your ride to Algothon…we could put him up for safekeeping… in our prison."

Sarskatama smiled. "That won't be necessary. I've received word that our escort to Algothon will be here before midday. They want to get here and get him back…and up on the gallows…as soon as possible."

"Fine! But until then…keep him covered up."

Prok was on his hands and knees at Sarskatama's feet. She draped a cloak over him to obey the Constable's order. Prok tried to wrap the cloak around himself. Sarskatama gave him a painful zap with the collar.

"Don't think that we're allowing you any modesty, you traitor! As soon as you're on the truck to Algothon, I get my cape back."

Prok scrunched closer to the ground sniveling. He was hoping that all of the reports from Algothon were incorrect and that it would be Cacktash people coming to Dandamira to rescue him and put him back in control.

Hadeetz looked at her Team. "I'll be glad when they pick that *doovoft* up and we can turn him over to Natsa and wash our hands of him. I'm getting pretty tired of him and his…I'm just getting tired of him."

"I like watching him suffer," said Lindaka. "I think of all of the Owlamites that are dead because of him and those Cacktash. It's a shame that they can only execute him once."

Zhool snickered. "I've got another idea about that. I'll discuss it with Natsa when she gets here."

Hemchee raised her eyebrows. "Another idea?"

"You all liked the last one," he said with a leering grin.

"We'll see what happens when Natsa gets here," said

Hadeetz.

"Yes," said Zhool. "Maybe they'll let us help."

At midday, a team from Algothon showed up at Dandamira coming from Algothon. There were two High Investigators leading the team: Segger and Quay.

Segger greeted the two Algothon women. "I understand that you have that traitorous fool in your custody?"

"Yes, Sir," said Sarskatama. "He was working with the Cacktash and started that violent and bloody mess at Owlam...that has caused us no end of grief."

"The Cacktash also attacked our home city. We're still counting the dead."

"Sir, I don't know the situation back at Owlam. I know that the Cacktash had to have had a forward base somewhere near the city of Owlam and they were doing a lot of work, trying to obtain the *Tuzine* manufacturing plant in Owlam, but..."

Segger held up his hand. "We have word from that area that the Cacktash have been routed and...if there are any still alive...they're on the run."

Shiganeea smiled. "Outstanding! That plot didn't work at all."

Segger shook his head. "It did, however, upset a lot of people, all over the world. All of the people who were freed when they revolted against the Cacktash at Owlam have gone home and told what happened and who was responsible."

"Shiganeea frowned. "Are some of them coming to Algothon for the trial of Prok?"

"Yes, we have many that are already there. They can hardly wait to testify regarding what they saw."

Tabaseeska walked up to Segger. "I'm going to testify as well. He…that monster used me…as a sex slave. It was humiliating and…I want him punished."

Segger smiled. "My Lady, the sooner we get him back to Algothon, the faster it'll get done. Shall we depart?"

Sarskatama and Shiganeea were ready to go now.

Tabaseeska had to get her escort (which did not take long) and she was ready.

The Owlamites were having their own conversation off to the side.

Ota and her entourage greeted Hadeetz as soon as she found the Owlamite Team that had been following Prok. "Why weren't you able to find out anything prior to the attack?"

Hadeetz shook her head despondently. "He did not do any face-to-face with any of the Cacktash prior to ordering the attack. He and the Cacktash…apparently made several arrangements… prior to the order being given and…they didn't meet after that. He did most of the arrangements prior to becoming a person of interest. All of the transmissions between them were short and blunt. There was nothing that we could follow up on until the attack occurred."

Ota glared at Prok. "My good friend and Aide...Officer Tytay is dead because of him."

"Yes," said Yoobyool sadly. "She was one of over a thousand."

Hadeetz chuckled. "One of my Team members...Officer Zhool...he has an idea of what to do with the traitor...once he's been convicted. Would you like to hear the details?"

Ota looked suspicious. "Will it make him...suffer... longer?"

"Oh, yes," said Hadeetz. "He'll be begging for death."

Yoobyool smiled. "Where is Zhool? Let's hear this plan."

Hadeetz signaled Zhool to join the group.

After hearing the plan, all of the Owlamites Jumped back to Algothon, rather than having to take the long ride in dusty trucks.

The Algothon group was not so lucky. They had to ride in the trucks. They did, however, make haste in getting to Algothon in order to start the trial of the traitor Prok. Many peoples all over the world were very interested in it and were hoping that it would bring the Owlamites out of hiding.

3

On the way to Algothon, the three (former sex slaves of Prok) took turns hitting the shock button on the control box. They punished him for anything and everything that they considered, even slightly, as an act of disobedience.

Segger watched the way Prok reacted and did not have any pity at all, especially after hearing the stories of the three women. He even was thinking of taking a few turns on that shock button as well.

Prok was sitting in the back of one of the trucks still hoping that his nightmare would end. He was positive that the Cacktash should have been able to take over Algothon completely and that once he was back there he would be rescued and those three women (plus a few others) would be naked on the end of leashes that he would be holding on to. He held on to that hope… until they got to the main boulevard that led to the west entrance of the north section of Algothon. The entire road was lined, on both sides, with trees. There were at least three dead Cacktash, hanging by their necks from every one of those trees. The smell of all of the rotting flesh was very thick in the air. That was when he finally had the devastating revelation that he had lost…everything.

The five Officer Leaders who were in charge of spying on Algothon were on that boulevard watching as the traitor was driven through the entrance.

"I can hardly wait to do that plan that Zhool came up with," said Ota. I just hope that we can make him REALLY suffer. Tytay was a good friend and…I'll miss her."

"I lost Yoyasa," said Blana. "We all lost Team 73. Nachichi, Lasska, Oostaya and Tetch…all of them were…good friends."

"I can't even look at that list…without crying," said Natsa. "I wish I could get through it…just once…but…I just can't."

"*Don't* forget," said Yoobyool. He looked at the faces of the women he was with. "Don't ever forget. We worked with them… for so long…and now…we'll never see them again. Don't…ever forget."

Boneech waved a hand at all of the others. "Hey! Getting on to another subject, for the moment, did we do enough damage to all of the missiles?"

"Yes," said Ota with a smile. "It's going to be a *long, long* time before they'll have a chance to ever launch any missile again."

Blana frowned. "What's the major thing that's slowing them down?"

Yoobyool laughed. "They have to get cranes in there that are large enough to lift all of the damaged missiles out. Those cranes are so large that they have to be moved one piece at a time. Each silo will take at least two months to clear out. Then they can start rebuilding. That takes, at the very least, another month. Nobody has to fear any launch...for quite some time."

The procession with Prok headed for the Great Hall of Justice. The streets were lined with the citizens of Algothon who glared at the man in the back of the truck with hatred, malice, anger, sadness and many other melancholy emotions. This man was now the most infamous citizen of Algothon that had ever existed. The book publishers in Algothon were rewriting the dictionary to include a new synonym for traitor - Prok. Anyone else in Algothon whose name was Prok were going to the courts to legally change their name.

Sarskatama looked up and saw that Tabaseeska had arrived first. She was a little surprised by this, however, she did not concern herself with the how or why. She was just glad that there was another witness who had been personally victimized by Prok and would testify against him.

All four of the Prominent Investigators were standing at the top of the stairs at the entrance: One old and three new. Hashasee was the only one of the four to survive the Cacktash attack. Since the victory over the Cacktash, Quoybaton, Nindeebee and Skokom had been promoted to Prominent.

When High Investigator Awndool had been assigned as part of the group that went to trade at Owlam, he had been number 29 of 30 High Investigators. Now, because of all of the fatalities, he was number 13 in seniority.

Sarskatama wondered where her standing was among the

Chief Investigators. She had been very low on the list. She really did not want to check that new list to see where she was…yet. The number of dead would be completely disheartening.

Shiganeea had heard of several promotions in order to fill slots left vacant as a result of all of the fatalities. Since she was almost last on the list of Second Investigators, she knew that it was probably a very slim chance that she had been promoted.

The truck with the prisoner was taken to the side of the building. They decided that it would be safer for all concerned if he were not taken up the front stairs. There were too many angry people who wanted to get a piece of him. They also knew that there would be those who would be throwing all kinds of foul smelling garbage at him and they did not want the front area of the Justice building littered with all kinds of unknown, rotting and possibly toxic substances. They had to show all of the people that everyone in Algothon would get a fair trial…even a miserable turncoat like Prok.

Prok was pulled out of the truck and hauled into the building. Three times he fell down screaming as he was shocked by the collar. There were those who thought that he might be faking, however, when the guards who were dragging him were shocked as well, they realized that he had been shocked.

Segger turned to Sarskatama. "Why are you shocking him?"

"I'm not," she said with a frown. "I haven't touched the shock button. I think…maybe the collar is malfunctioning."

"So, how do you get it off of him?"

She fought to keep from laughing. "I don't know."

Segger stopped the entire procession to face Sarskatama. "What do you mean?"

"I mean that it takes a password to get the thing off and I don't know what the password is."

"You forgot?"

"No, Sir, I never knew."

Segger scoffed. He closed his eyes in thought for a moment. He stopped and looked at her sternly. "Explain yourself!"

She sighed. "When I found out how to put the thing on... or off, I just did a crazy little manipulation. I figured if I put the shock collar on him and the Cacktash wanted it off...they would just read my mind and get the password, take it off of him and I'd be punished...horribly for what I did. When I put the collar on him and it asked for a password I closed my eyes, randomly hit twenty keys...I think...and then without looking at what I had fed in, I hit enter. The control box accepted it. I have no clue what the password is. I only know that it might be...19...or 20...or possibly 21 characters. The only way to find out what the password is... find someone who's a lot smarter than I am, when it comes to programming, and maybe you'll find out what the password is. This way there was no way I could tell any Cacktash *Hongoth* what the password is...because I don't know it. The collar is on him...until someone can figure out what I entered."

Segger scratched his head and cleared his throat. "And you say that you...are *not* shocking him?"

"No, Sir, I haven't hit the button once."

What she did not know was that the Officer Leaders of Owlam were taking turns hitting the button. They were having fun watching Prok fall to the floor screaming in pain when they shocked him.

Segger shook his head. "I hope he survives to see his trial. I'd like to see him hanged. But I'd like to see a live body make that fatal drop. I don't want to have to handle a corpse."

Prok screamed in pain and hit the floor again.

Segger growled. "Give me that stupid control box."

Sarskatama handed it to him and held her hands up in surrender with a smile on her face.

The guards were tired of being shocked. They placed the limp, moaning and panting Prok on a cargo truck and pushed him into the courtroom. They did not care whether he was awake or not, they all wanted the official proceedings to get under way.

Hashasee walked up to the prone Prok, just as he cut loose with another scream of agony. "Is there any way to get that thing off…by cutting it?"

Sarskatama shook her head. "That would cause a fatal shock."

Hashasee sighed. "Let's hope that it stops malfunctioning. We can't have him screaming through his trial."

Yoobyool scoffed at his colleagues. "Stop shocking him! Let these *Doovofts* get the trial started and finished…so we can execute Zhool's plan."

The four women looked at Yoobyool with guilty grins and snickering. They looked at each other and all nodded in agreement while still giggling like little girls. Prok would now have to sit and listen to all of the trial before he would get his next shock…from an Owlamite.

Ota shook her head while chuckling. "The only reason that they're going to have a trial - show off to all of the other peoples that it was Prok and not Algothon who caused all of the problems. They're just doing it to save face."

"Everyone knows that," said Boneech. "They still want to see that parasite squirm. The world wants to see if he's going to come up with some kind of explanation for what he did."

"It wouldn't be anything but arrogant waffling," said Natsa.

"It'd still give the people of the world more reason to accept his execution," said Yoobyool.

Boneech frowned. "Why does anyone want to question his execution?"

Yoobyool scoffed. "There are still some people on this planet who…no matter how nasty or horrid the criminal or his crime…they don't believe that anyone should be executed."

Natsa huffed. "That's dumb!"

The trial started three days later. There was a defense attorney who did not do much of a job at defending the traitor.

Why should he? He did not care for the life of his client and neither did anyone else in the world. If Prok was going to try to claim that he did not get a fair trial, his appeal would be put off until after the execution. The Algothon Councils agreed to change a law about appeals…just for this case. If execution was the final verdict – nothing would stop the execution. Any appeal would be considered at a later date – much later. Prok was not aware of this law, however, no one, including the defense attorney cared.

There was an enormous list of witnesses for the prosecution. All of the witnesses for the defense were hanging from trees on that main boulevard or off somewhere in Jahong's Death or Shogoot's Search. No matter where they were, it was assumed by most of the peoples of the planet that all of the Cacktash were dead. It was absolutely known by the people of Owlam that the Cacktash were definitely all dead.

The trial dragged on. Day after day there were witnesses from the attack at Owlam who all testified as to what they saw Prok do when the Cacktash came in. The witnesses were a huge variety of races of Elf and Heyyah from different parts of the entire world. There were twenty-seven different Elf races that had been enslaved by the Cacktash at Owlam. There were Heyyah from sixty different neutral cities in the mix. There were peoples from all of the continents and most of the island chains.

No matter what the enslaved people said, the most devastating testimony came from the three surviving sex slaves. To the people of Algothon, the fact that he enslaved two of their own was bad enough. When they found out that he had gone outside of his race to commit some acts of promiscuity with a woman of another species, this was considered bestiality. He had committed yet another unspeakable act.

Over three thousand witnesses gave testimony. They gave testimony about enslavement. They gave testimony of people they knew who were now dead as a result of what happened. By the time they had finished, the people adding up the figures were astonished to find the death toll was over two million souls…that they knew about. The vast majority of the dead had been Algothon citizens. The military had been hurt badly, the investigative services had been hit very hard and the scientists were down to a bare minimum. This made a death sentence a mandatory outcome of the trial – if the verdict was guilty – which no one believed it would be anything else other than guilty.

The prosecution finally rested. The defense attorney stood up and said that the defense was resting as well. When Prok tried to protest the complete lack of defense, his attorney backhanded him and told him to shut his mouth. No one wanted to hear anything that he had to say. Less than half a day later the verdict came in as guilty and the sentence of death was given by the Judge, with no emotions at all.

Prok started screaming for an appeal, because he was not properly represented. It was then that he was informed about how his appeal would be put off until a date eight months away. His execution was scheduled for only four days from now. The execution would not be delayed, because of the "Prok law". He could appeal in eight months…if he was still in the mood (or condition) to do so…at that time.

Ota sat there with a smile on her face. "I can hardly wait to try Zhool's plan."

"You're becoming quite sadistic," said Blana.

Ota stretched. "Only where that piece of *h'oolyach* is concerned."

The other Owlamites sat there snickering.

The day of the execution arrived. The four Prominent Investigators were personally taking part in the execution. The execution was going to be done outside the walls of the city of Algothon. One reason was because there was no way that all of the spectators could fit in any open square anywhere inside the city walls (plus the Algothon Council was adamant that they would not allow that many foreigners inside the walls at one time…for any reason). The other was because they determined that Prok did not have the right to die inside the walls of Algothon. His last moments were to be lived in complete shame outside the walls of Algothon.

Hashasee, even though she was getting up in years, was determined to be there. "Maybe I should have retired ten years ago, but, I wouldn't miss this for anything."

Nindeebee helped Hashasee up the stairs. "Be glad that you're here to help execute the worst traitor in the history of Algothon."

"I wish that I had never lived to see that monster."

"Well, you did, so be glad that you're going to outlive him."

Hashasee sighed. "Yes, there is that satisfaction."

Quoybaton and Skokom waited at the top of the gallows for their two female counterparts.

"Don't worry about how hard it is to pull the handle," said Skokom. "We'll help you."

Hashasee smiled. "We are going to ALL pull it together. I can hardly wait until I see that...*thing*...swinging."

"I wonder if he'll do any...dancing in the air," said Quoybaton.

"I hope he does," said Nindeebee. "That'll make him suffer a little longer."

Ota was at the top of the gallows in Spy. "How did she hear about Zhool's plan?"

Blana snickered. "I don't think she did. I think she's just as hopeful that he'll suffer an extended time while hanging from that rope...before he finally dies."

Boneech frowned. "You're sure that they won't cut him down?"

"No," said Yoobyool. "Their law states that he hangs until he dies. If it doesn't snap his neck when he falls...he dies slowly from exposure and starvation...no matter how long it takes."

"And we're going to make sure that it lasts as long as possible," said Natsa.

"Or until we get bored with it," said Ota.

"I don't think that I'm going to get bored…soon," said Yoobyool. He then Jumped down below the trapdoor.

All of the people on the gallows heard the roar of the crowd as the condemned was brought out. He was standing in an open cart, bound up in a manner where he could not move at all. There were manacles around his ankles and knees. There was a brace hooked to these manacles so that he could not squat down to avoid any of the garbage being thrown at him. The brace went all the way up to a chain around his jaws. It had been carefully placed to make sure that he could not choke himself to death before arriving at the gallows. There was a belly band that had manacles around his wrists. He had a gag in his mouth so that no one would have to listen to anything that he had to say. His motion was extremely limited.

They made sure that he would be seen by all peoples gathered. There was a sign on either side of the cart with a statement on them: This is the traitor who murdered over two million souls.

Ota scoffed. "Hypocrites! How many people died when they launched all of those missiles…sixty-nine years ago? We lost more people in our city alone than any two million."

Yoobyool shook his head. "A lot of these people gathered here…seem to have forgotten that particular piece of history."

"I don't think that any of the Elf races have forgotten," said Boneech. "I can't think of one single new race that, for some reason, it extended all of our life spans. None of us know for how long…but it does look like all of the Elf races live a lot longer now."

Natsa chuckled. "While the Heyyah inside the walls of Algothon live their abbreviated lives, suffering for the failures of their parents and grandparents…we live longer, remember what happened and can still wreak havoc and vengeance on these *doovofts*."

The procession continued from the gate to the gallows that had been built just for this event. Prok was being spat on by the ones who were closest to the cart, while others were tossing all kinds of rotten vegetables and feces…and other miscellaneous trash. Most of the people throwing things were very accurate with their aim. By the time Prok arrived at the gallows, there were cuts and bruises all over his exposed skin and he was covered with all kinds of unrecognizable and smelly debris. The guards that had to drag him to the top of the stairs on the gallows were all wearing full body, rubber suits, including gas masks. The bombardment of debris continued until he was about half-way up the stairs.

At the top of the stairs, he was taken to the railing to face the crowd.

Quoybaton went to the microphone. "Here is the monster who betrayed…everyone. Peace was coming to our world. Trade and commerce were starting to become the way of life…instead of war. This traitor stopped the manufacture of the best cure for all bacteriological diseases that we know of. We can only hope that with his execution, the Owlams come out of hiding and start manufacturing it again. Today, we see the extermination of one of the most hideous creatures that ever stunk up our planet."

"Hypocrite," said Yoobyool.

Quoybaton continued. "Normally, we would ask the condemned if he has anything to say. Normally! This is not normal. This is a necessary task, getting rid of this thing. I don't think that anyone cares what he has to say, so we won't let him comment."

There was a loud, long lasting cheer.

Ota looked around at her people. "Everybody…get ready."

Quoybaton continued: "Without further ado, we will put the rope around his neck…and do that what we all came here to see."

Prok tried to resist as the rope was placed around his neck and tightened. Because of the brace it was impossible. They only had to make one small movement with the chain around his jaws, to remove it for a moment from the brace, slip the loop over his head and then re-hook the jaw chain to the brace. He stood there breathing in and out very rapidly in fear.

Quoybaton and the other three Prominents took hold of the handle.

Hashasee took the microphone. "Let him rot in the lowest level of the 666 punishments."

With that, the four Prominents pulled the handle, the trapdoor opened, down went Prok…and there was no snapping of the neck. At first a cheer went up as he fell. It was suddenly silenced as the observers all saw him squirming at the end of the rope. They could hear him trying to scream behind the gag in his mouth as he swung back and forth.

Hashasee chuckled into the microphone. "It seems that the Great Maker doesn't want him either. It seems that the Great Maker wants him to suffer a little longer...in his mortal body. That's all right...we can wait. According to our law, he was sentenced to hang by the neck...until dead. He's not dead yet... so there he hangs...until he does die...from whatever reason he happens to die from. If you're going to continue throwing garbage at him, please make sure that it is nothing...fatal. We wouldn't want the Great Maker to be cheated of the visible punishment that we're witnessing. Also, please wait until we've descended the stairs before throwing anything else at him. Thank you."

The reason that Prok was screaming was not because he had survived the hanging, it was because of a voice that he heard, very clearly, in his head.

"No, no, no, no, no, no...you're not going to die right now. I'm Officer Leader, Ota of the Owlam military. I'm here to tell you that we prevented you from your death at this time. We want to play with you a little longer. We're going to make you suffer as long as we can...until *we* get bored with you. You're going to stay here swinging until we allow you to die. Don't think for one heartbeat that we did this out of any kindness. No, no, no, no, no, no, no, no, no. We're going to remind you of all of the people that should still be alive. They're not here...because of you. I'll even say that this includes the Cacktash people. If you hadn't done what you did - they'd still be alive as well. Don't think for a moment that we're going to leave you alone while you're hanging here. We're going to take turns having all kinds of fun with you."

The ten men who were standing under the high platform waiting for Prok to drop were now all standing there looking a little proud of themselves.

"We did it," said Yoobyool. "I don't know how...but we did it."

Goloomo snickered. "I never figured that we would... but...I guess we got lucky."

Natsa huffed at the men. "What are you talking about? You sound as if you didn't think it was going to work!"

"I didn't," said Yoobyool.

"I didn't either," said Osskood.

Eelok shook his head. "None of us have ever attempted anything like that before...and you think that we were going to be professionals at it! What made you think that?"

Gagan huffed. "We caught him at the right moment...by *fool luck*!"

Ota looked at the men. "Are you seriously saying that none of you thought that catching him would work?"

Yoobyool scoffed. "Absolutely!"

"Name one time that that sort of thing has ever been tried before," said Nosk.

"The only reason we caught him without a hitch...divine

guidance," said Yotonjo.

Yoobyool crossed his arms and gave Ota a nasty look. "Can you name one person who *is* a professional at catching somebody who is being dropped through the trapdoor from the gallows?"

Ota cleared her throat nervously. "Uh…no." She looked off to the side fooling with her hair. She looked back at Yoobyool and stuck her tongue out at him.

"So don't criticize us because we weren't sure that it would work." He then stuck his tongue out at her.

Ota looked off to the side and sighed. "Okay. By either luck or divine guidance…you caught that piece of *h'oolyach*." She shook her head. "We control the rest of his useless life. What we do now is play with him until we get tired of him. Then we let him rot."

Natsa chuckled nervously. "Uh…excuse me…but…how are we going to keep him alive? After four or five days, you starve to death and have that…uh…renal shutdown…I think they call it. What do we do…to keep him alive?"

Ota grinned. "We can always hop some…nourishment into his stomach. We can keep him alive that way…indefinitely."

"That's mean," said Blana.

"So what," said Gagan. "He deserves every bit of suffering that we can dish out to him."

Ko snickered. "So…what're we going to do…as far as torturing him? You must have something in mind for us to do…

for the next few days."

Ota smiled. "We're going to tell him everything. We're going to tell him about how we're the ones who've been causing the Algothons all of their misery. We're going to tell him about how we're using the Galsinos as puppets. We're also going to read off the names of all of the Owlamites that he murdered." She looked down at Prok through the trapdoor. "We might also give him a few nasty shocks with that collar."

"I think that the collar should only be used to keep him awake," said Sankiki. "If we do much more of it…they might get suspicious."

Kloob laughed out loud. "Suspicious of what? They have no idea that we're here. They already think that the collar is malfunctioning. A few more shocks won't make that much difference."

Ota stretched. She sniffed as she looked around at all of the people who were jeering Prok and throwing garbage at him. "I think that you men should go get yourselves decontaminated. There's no telling what kind of *h'oolyach* those people were and are throwing at him. Even though all you did was reach through the dimensions to stop him from getting a snapped neck…no telling how much of that stuff you got on your hands."

The men all looked at their hands in a disgusted manner. They all vanished.

Natsa snickered. "I get to go next."

Wilfadge huffed. "It only took those Algothons…what…a year? All the time that they wasted on that trial…when everyone knew what was going to happen. Utter nonsense!"

"True," said Ahandi. "They did take a long time, but I think that they were trying to get the message across to us…that he was the only conspirator working with the Cacktash."

"Meanwhile," said Dwalooa. "Have you finished all of those reassignments that you were talking about?"

Wilfadge hung his head and nodded. "It…hurt. It really hurt a lot of people. We had to break up several partial Teams and spread them out to other Teams…in order to make complete Teams. We tried to keep that ratio that we have…three women to one man. As it turns out…we have eleven incomplete Teams… three women and no men. All other Teams…that are left…are complete."

Till cleared his throat. He was still trying to get used to this new promotion and was nervous among the Command Staff. "What did you tell them…when you broke up some partial Teams…in order to complete other Teams?"

Wilfadge sighed. "It is for the good of all Owlamites."

Hadathoo looked a little confused. "How much longer are we going to stay in hiding?"

Wilfadge shook his head. "I guess that it's about time to show ourselves again. That *doovoft* is still swinging…even though he's not dead, so I guess that we can accept the word of the Algothons that the mess is over and we can get back to trading."

Shyshee snickered. "Are all of those people still taking care of the crops...inside the walls of Owlam?"

"Yes," said Wilfadge. "There are thousands of outsiders who are tending the crops. They're even taking care of the *Shoonshook*...because they think that we used it as some kind of border to mark the areas off...between crops...even though everyone else thinks that it's just a useless weed."

Hadathoo leaned forward. "What're we going to tell them when they ask...where were we hiding and how did we get out of Owlam so fast?"

Wilfadge gave him a nasty look. "We tell them...because that sort of thing might happen again...we're not going to let them know any of our secrets."

"Good plan," said Ahandi with an approving nod.

The Owlam Teams that were spying on Algothon kept Prok alive for fourteen days before they grew tired of torturing him. They would hop some kind of mush and water into his stomach. They constantly harassed him about all of the people who had died because of his failed plot. They would shock him any time he started looking as if he were going to sleep. The only reason they stopped torturing him was because they were no longer sure of his sanity. They were not sure if he could understand any of the taunts or torture that they were inflicting on him. He did not seem to be listening, so what was the point of continuing? After the Owlamites departed, he lasted for four more days before finally expiring from starvation.

Hashasee walked up to the body of Prok holding her nose. "Are you sure that he's finally dead?"

"Yes," said the Coroner. "I am absolutely baffled as to how he lasted as long as he did though. He should have been dead…at least twelve days ago. I guess that the Great Maker did want him to suffer…greatly…before he departed his mortal home."

Hashasee scoffed. "At least now…we won't have to smell him anymore. This whole area still…stinks…so badly. Throw his body on the staircase of the gallows and…burn the whole thing down."

The doctor signaled the workers to move Prok's body. "Once he's been burned…we won't have to worry about any more stench from him."

"Let's hope that those Owlams have heard about this situation," said Quoybaton. "Maybe…they'll show themselves… and we can start getting more *Tuzine*."

"I'm sure that they know," said Skokom. "I read, in the history books, that they have some kind of…highly sophisticated communications system that completely foiled that highly sophisticated jamming system by that bunch that originally built the Turgon Wall. No one has or had ever designed a jamming system like those people had. If the Owlams still have their system…and there are any Owlams left…believe me…they know."

Hashasee stretched and sighed. "The way that traitor was hanging on…still breathing after all those days…I was wondering if he would outlive me. I'm not getting any younger and…he just…wouldn't *die!*"

"That's no longer a concern," chuckled Skokom.

Quoybaton looked off towards the east. "I still wonder about our missiles. For all those years…we were wondering as to whether or not it was the Owlams or Galsinos that were destroying our launches. Now…we won't know a thing…until we can get all of the debris cleared out of the silos and…rebuild a missile and then attempt to launch it."

"Yeah," said Skokom. "All that time…it just might have been the Cacktash…all along. Here we are with all of that damage in the silos, in every last silo out there. If it had been the Owlams or the Galsinos…I'm sure that the damage would have been much worse…before. Since the Cacktash were here…it's going to be quite some time before we have a full force of working missiles again."

Hashasee grunted angrily. "The problem that we're looking at now is…it might not have been the Cacktash. Consider the possibility that…it was someone who has been making us follow the Owlams and the Galsinos…and then tested us with the Cacktash…to check our resolve. They could be learning all kinds of ways to counter anything that we did against their puppets… and in the long run, we end up as their puppets as well."

"Oh, I hope not," said Skokom sadly.

Three days after the world was informed of the death of the Algothon traitor, the Owlamites returned to their home city and the trade for *Tuzine* was back on. The Owlamites were back in business and they were letting the world know that seed was not the only thing that they wanted now. They would trade for bolts of cloth (or any kind of fabric), farming equipment, electrical equipment, vehicles and (if the others were so inclined) weapons.

The people who had stayed in Owlam and tended to all of the crops throughout the city were rewarded generously with one hundred cases of *Tuzine* – each. The ones who received the gift were extremely grateful.

Dwalooa stood on top of the wall watching all of the outsiders as they departed with their treasured drugs. "Weren't you just a little bit too generous with those people?"

Wilfadge scoffed. "They kept everything as we left it...or should I say that they repaired the damage done by those invaders. The Cacktash wanted all of it and nearly ruined everything. Those people...they rebuilt and replanted everything. The land inside the wall looks wonderful. Why shouldn't we thank them?"

"Yes," said Ahandi. "We are grateful...but...one hundred cases each! I think that was just a little bit too much as well."

Wilfadge shook his head. "Understand this...I don't care. I thanked them...they're happy...and the rest of the world will realize that we have plenty on hand...if we're going to be that generous. Now, they might be a little bit more generous with what they bring for trade as well."

"I hope you're right," said Teelila.

Wilfadge chuckled. "You hope? I hope! Maybe...now with those Cacktash and the traitor out of the way...things will settle down...and we can finally hope for some kind of peace.

I've been in the military…all of my life and I've seen war between us and…all of our neighbors. This might actually be the start of something…wonderful."

"We hope," said Hadathoo.

Boneech walked up to the Leader of Team 333. "Officer, Hadeetz, you…killed that one Algothon woman…when you performed that crazy little stunt against Prok."

"Yes, I did, Sir," said Hadeetz.

"Why?"

"Why…what?"

"Why did you kill her? You could have killed those Cacktash and left her alive. Why did you feel that you had to kill her?"

"First and foremost…if I hadn't killed her…when the others asked her what happened…she would have denied killing those Cacktash. Where would we have been then? Second…she was a lot smarter and much more observant than any of the other personnel who were at the scene of the Cacktash attack. I used that new mind game we have and read her thoughts…as to what her plans were once she got back to Algothon. She saw Afa-Ee hop in, grab two Cacktash and then commit suicide by dragging them off to Jahong's Death. She also observed someone else – an Owlamite – who appeared but was transparent, who killed two other Cacktash. She had mulled all of that over in her mind and figured that we were the real puppeteers and not the Galsinos or the

Cacktash. She had made a mental note of that and she was going to bring that up with the Prominent Investigators. Where would we be then? She was a lot more dangerous than we originally thought. If she had ever obtained the rank of Prominent…that could have been a real calamity for us."

Boneech shook her head. "Okay…you did think it through. Thank you for…that explanation."

Once it was announced in Algothon that the Owlamites were once again trading for *Tuzine*, they got another team together to go there and trade more kwatha for the antibiotic. It still irritated them that they had to beg for it, however, the drug was just that valuable.

Now that the trial and execution were over, Hashasee decided to retire. The new Prominent Investigator was named Atkisk.

4

For thirty-three years there seemed to be an uneasy, but welcome, peace between all of the peoples of Hardooth. The trade for *Tuzine* went on and the Owlamites found that they were going to have to increase production...radically. The need was becoming tremendous. They had to teach more of their Teams the process of manufacturing and they had to step up the amount of crops that made up the ingredients. Of course most of the special fields for the ingredients were kept in other dimensions so they would not attract that much attention.

The Algothons were constantly trying to determine the exact ingredients for the drug, however, no matter what they did it still eluded them no matter how much they increased their technology. The fact that there were some Owlamites in the laboratory doing all kinds of funny things to corrupt the tests did not help any, however, the Algothons were still not aware of the uninvited guests.

The Algothons were also attempting to rebuild their arsenal of missiles and were finding it extremely difficult to obtain the raw materials needed and the rebuilding never seemed to go well. The rockets just did not seem to be holding together at all. The Owlamites were zealously willing to lend a hindering hand to that process as well.

Most of the other races and cities were doing what they could to increase commerce and trade. This new peace was making all kinds of new opportunities for everyone. Most of the peoples were happy with this kind of peace and trade. Most people…then, of course, there are always the unhappy and ambitious ones who are only happy if they are conquering or abusing.

The Owlamites had to keep a close watch on their forest – at first - the one that covered the Zee-Althan massacre area. Numerous races were coming to that area and taking seeds and cuttings from the strange trees that were growing there. People who were familiar with botany were confused about these new species of trees they had never seen before, however, they all attributed it to that residual energy that had plagued the entire planet for several decades after that massive attack by Algothon. The presence of all of the Elf races backed up the entire story of strange new plants. If it can affect the Heyyah, it can affect plants as well. Every new plant (of which now there were numerous trees and plants) that the Owlamites had brought from Forest and Beasties was allowed this belief and this made all of Owlam breathe a sigh of relief: All new anomalies were because of that residual energy that had changed just about everything on the planet.

The time of the residual energy was over – for the most part. The entire planet started recovering and getting new green plants all over the place. Many plants were familiar and many of them were strangely different, however, again this was shrugged off as some mutation that resulted from that energy. Only the Owlamites knew that these new "unknown" plants were coming from other dimensions.

The current four Prominent Investigators of Algothon were having a meeting. Voothoko, Ilbaskon, Shoshako and Vixom were in their top floor sanctuary.

Ilbaskon looked up from the latest report on how much *Tuzine* had been brought back from Owlam. "Why do we always put women in charge of these trade missions?"

Shoshako snickered. "It's a firm belief...and has been a firm belief by all of the last four Supreme Leaders...the other side takes us more seriously...as to the fact that we come in peace... when we send the group with a woman in charge."

Voothoko looked at Ilbaskon suspiciously. "Do you have some kind of...reservations about the abilities of High Investigator, Saskeema?"

"No," said Ilbaskon. "I just wonder how our senior ranking High Investigator, Chapshok feels about being left behind...or out of this picture completely."

"He's got plenty of work to do here," said Voothoko.

"Yes," said Vixom. "Especially since we still haven't figured out why we can't get one single *hongoth* missile launched."

"Let those women keep on doing the trading," said Voothoko. "We haven't been short changed yet...and we know that those silly Owlams are still absolutely mad about that nasty kwatha. Keep on growing and trading that stuff to them and we can keep on getting generous supplies of *Tuzine*."

Vixom scoffed. "We really need the *Tuzine* now...since the doctors have discovered that new STD: *Koovanchat*! Some of our people have been...fooling around with other species...and as a result...this new STD popped up...and this disease requires a much larger dose of the drug."

Ilbaskon shook his head. "I've always wondered how a new disease can just...*pop up*...seemingly out of nowhere. No one has ever heard of it before...no one has ever suffered from it before...and *poof*...there it is."

Vixom laughed. "Everything that comes up as new...it's always being attributed to that residual energy. The changes that were seen immediately weren't questioned. Why should some of these later changes be any different?"

Ilbaskon simply grunted. "It still doesn't make sense."

Vixom sighed in frustration. "Look at it this way...when the bombs went off, there was some...person in one of those cities who had an STD. When the bombs went off and that person survived and was changed...the disease inside the person was mutated as well."

Ilbaskon grunted again. "That makes more sense than anything else you've said so far."

Voothoko looked at one of the other reports. "What's this stuff about this bunch called...Perfor? We're getting reports that they're starting their own little type of conquering. What do you think about their uprising on the South Chilamte continent?"

Vixom looked up confused. "Should we worry about them? They're not on the North Chilamte continent and they're not on our continent. Why should we concern ourselves at this time? They don't affect the *Tuzine*...or us."

"Those wretched Cacktash weren't on our continent... or the North Chilamte continent either," said Voothoko angrily. "Look at the trouble that they caused."

Ilbaskon grunted. "So how do we recognize this bunch of...wanna-be-world-conquerors?"

Shoshako looked at his documentation. "They have − believe it or not − skin that is shimmering blue. I don't know exactly what is meant by shimmering, but, that's the information that we have on them."

Vixom started keying information in on his computer. "Don't we have some kind of pictures of them...from the archives?"

"If we had archives that were that old," said Ilbaskon bitterly. "Ever since the archives disappeared...years ago, we haven't been able to retrieve a lot of that information...from anywhere."

Vixom shook his head. "Don't we have anything on our current hard drives?"

"Nothing," said Voothoko. "Our new batch of scientists still haven't been able to figure out the problems with the spy satellites. They can't seem to get the things to look at anything we want them to. They're telling me that there is one array...it does nothing but scan outer space…looking for…well they have no idea what it is looking for. It does seem to be on some kind of search pattern though."

Vixom frowned. "Is someone controlling it?"

"No one that we know of," said Shoshako. "We sure aren't in control of it."

Vixom scoffed. "Is anyone in Algothon trying to find out?"

Shoshako scoffed back angrily. "Do you think that we're just sitting around feeling sorry for ourselves? Of course someone is trying to fix the situation."

Senior Officer, Till was still a little disgruntled over the fact that he was now one of the top echelon people. He did not really want to be one of the top personnel, he wanted to continue his searches. Being the Vice Commander for Sector 2 meant that he did not have to be out on the bartering tables anymore, however, it did still mean that he was going to be interrupted, at any time, day or night, with some meeting or other emergency that would require his attention and take him away from his obsession with outer space and the possible existence of extraterrestrials. Numerous times he would try to send his ranking Aide – Officer Grade 3, Ababi, however, Wilfadge did not like to be dealing with anyone lower than an Officer Leader at a Staff meeting. Still he did find some time to do his scans of the heavens because of the fact the Owlamites needed virtually no sleep…unless they had overworked themselves into complete exhaustion…which did not happen very often – even with a large amount of hopping or jumping.

Wilfadge looked at the reports on this new bunch of conquering scoundrels – the Perfor. "Why is it that whenever there is a chance of peace, here comes some upstart group that thinks they're so important that everyone should bow to them? What do we know about these *Doovofts*?"

"We don't find much information on them in the Algothon archives," said Dwalooa sadly. "We just have a location on the continent where they lived and were targeted for a firestorm attack by Algothon. The Perfor were hit and now they can be recognized by their shimmering blue skin. They can't hide at night…just like the Zee-Althans. They can still be trouble though."

Teelila looked confused. "Aren't they in the southern part of the continent?"

"Yes," said Dwalooa. "But they're trying to make their presence known…all over the continent."

Teelila was still confused. "Our area…in the gorge…is in the northern section. It's surrounded by some tremendously high cliffs…on all sides. On the north, east and west…nothing but ocean. On the south, those cliffs make a very formidable obstacle for anyone to try to overcome…as far as any conquering of the continent. Do we really need to worry about them?"

Ahandi scoffed. "We were growing our own kwatha… on the east side of the gorge, just above our hidey-hole-homes. Once all those traders found out that we *love* our steaming hot kwatha…some *bimyock* let it be known that kwatha was growing wild, all over the place, up there. Now everyone, from even other continents and islands went there, ravaged all of OUR kwatha plants and brought it there to the trading tables at Owlam…where we end up trading *for our own* kwatha." She sighed. "We stopped growing it up there…because we have no way of protecting our kwatha fields…without giving away our location."

Dwalooa grunted in disgust. "Those…Perfors…want to get control…so that they have more kwatha…than anybody else… for trading. How do we stop *them*…without giving ourselves away?"

Wilfadge sighed. "We have to stop planting kwatha up there…at least in Home dimension. Can't we plant it…in Spy or Observation?"

Ahandi shook her head. "We have no convenient way of watering the plants in those dimensions. We have to have the plants in Home dimension…or we have to hop…gargantuan amounts of water to Spy…or Observation…in order to keep the plants properly watered. We have enough trouble keeping the plants that are part of the *Tuzine* watered. We don't need the headache of having to water an entire huge area of kwatha."

Wilfadge hung his head. "So the only option is to stop planting kwatha up there."

"Right," said Hadathoo. "We keep all of the kwatha plants…our kwatha plants…inside the city walls of Owlam. That's the only way that we can keep our plants…without having to trade to keep them."

"Irritating," muttered Wilfadge.

Teelila shrugged. "We'll just have to keep an eye on them and make sure that the only thing they wanted up there…was the kwatha. If they want more…then we may have to do something drastic."

Ahandi frowned. "Drastic? Drastic…like what?"

"Depends on the situation," sighed Dwalooa.

Wilfadge shook his head. "Very irritating."

"I've got something that may be even more irritating for you," said Hadathoo.

"Oh wonderful," said Wilfadge. "More good news. What now?"

Hadathoo smiled. "There's more information about someone hording kwatha. One of my Aides found a race called the Maka-Or…on the Lusaratia continent. They've started some of their own…minor takeovers…at first. Then they became a little braver. They're trying to corner the market on kwatha on that continent. They got all of the plants. Usually you can harvest some of the root…and more plant will grow from the partial root. On Lusaratia, they're taking everything and moving it to a place in the Cheelsyels Island chain. It seems that they're causing several different groups of Heyyah, in those islands, a lot of grief…as they take over a lot of some rather limited territory."

Ahandi shook her head. "It's a shame. We have something that everyone needs…and can put to good use. Now, here's someone who wants to keep others from getting it…by trying to take over all of the plant that we like the most for trading. I think that we need to take a different look at how we trade...especially for the kwatha. If someone is willing to try to steal all of the kwatha worldwide...in order to get more *Tuzine*...we need to rethink our trading practices...or something."

Teelila looked off to the side and snarled. "No matter what you try to do to make things better...it seems that there is always someone who figures out a way to turn it to evil...and use it for their own greedy purposes."

Wilfadge nodded. "Everyone go home. Let your Vice Commanders know about this and...let's do some thinking about what we need to do...in order to curb this kind of activity. We'll meet at a later date...in order to determine if we have to collectively come up with something usable."

Dwalooa sniffed. "Or at least...make it clear to everyone that we have nothing to do with any of these people committing these thieving acts."

Teelila stood up. "Meanwhile we have to keep an eye on everyone else to determine whether or not these two...are the only ones who are currently trying to do something nasty to all of us."

Wilfadge snickered. "Why don't we leak the information about these...Maka-Or...to the Algothons? That way we can make them think about this as well. Maybe they'll give us some clues as to what the Maka-Or want. Other than that...meeting adjourned."

They all departed, heading for their separate domiciles.

Wilfadge stared around at the empty room thinking. 'Now

I know what Neenatha, Jahong and the others felt like…when they got this…*power.*'

Voothoko looked at the new report. He shook his head and frowned several times as he looked it over. He looked up at the other three Prominents. "Who are these…Maka-Or? Where did they come from…and what are they doing?" He looked over the document. "Where did this report come from? The silly thing is unsigned."

Shoshako shrugged. "I see…a race of the Elf people… who are either trying to get all of the kwatha for trading…or they think that it is a major ingredient in the making of *Tuzine*."

Ilbaskon looked puzzled. "Do we think that kwatha is one of the main ingredients?"

"No," said Vixom. "Our scientists and botanists have ruled it out completely. Whenever we trade the kwatha seeds for *Tuzine*, all of our traders have said that the Owlams were all licking their lips when they saw it. We've had too many observers telling us that they eat way too much kwatha for it to be one of the ingredients. If it were one of the ingredients…they'd need three times as much as they're getting now…in order to devour as much as they do *and* use it in *Tuzine*. No, if the Maka-Or are thinking that it's a main ingredient, they're in the wrong chamber of the house altogether."

Ilbaskon scoffed. "So we just let them waste their time trying to cook it up as an ingredient. If they're trying to conquer anyone or take over the *Tuzine* trade…neither we nor the Owlams have anything to worry about."

"Let's hope so," said Vixom.

Ilbaskon let out another one of his grunts.

Wilfadge looked at the report. "This seems so...sketchy and incomplete and...unprofessional...compared to what we used to get from the Algothons."

Teelila gave a helpless smile and a shrug. "It's because the older ones that we dealt with at first, they were trained by the real professionals. The ones that are popping up now...they were trained by the leftovers...that we allowed to live. The fact that we got rid of the real professionals and others have died off, we're getting a herd of partially trained Algothons that are doing their best, but were never given a chance to learn from the best."

Hadathoo shook his head. "So do we allow this bunch to live...or do we finally get rid of all of Algothon?"

"We might still learn something from them," said Dwalooa. "Every now and then a good one pops up. There's still the chance that...we can still learn from them."

"Meanwhile," said Hadathoo. "They're still trying to build more new firestorm weapons. They didn't learn from that first batch...the problems that can result from it...like that residual energy."

"I wouldn't worry about that," said Ahandi. "From what we're hearing from our spies all of the great brains, of the past, who built those things…no one new has come up who can match them…plus we've corrupted the textbooks that showed the proper sequence on making the warhead."

Hadathoo had a disgusted look on his face. "So far! We never know when another one could pop up." "That's why we keep watching them," said Wilfadge.

"I still think that we should just get rid of all of them," said Hadathoo.

Wilfadge giggled. "Not when we can set one of our enemies against them. It helps us…watching them get in a fight with the Algothons. That helps us in the long run."

Ahandi shook her head. "It helps if they have the intestinal fortitude to go after some city with a population as numerous as the Algothons. Otherwise, they come after us. Even after all this time…there aren't that many Elf races with enough people to go after the Algothons…and of course with those other races…we are talking about ones who can procreate. Even after that mess with the Cacktash, the Algothons are back over 22,000,000 in population."

All of them hung their heads for a few moments.

"It would be nice…to hear the sounds of some children playing again," said Dwalooa sadly. "Our children…that is."

"Let's stick to what is at hand," said Wilfadge. "I am going to send a few Teams to this…Cheelsyels Island chain…and do a little reconnaissance. See if we can figure out what these people are up to. See if they're trying to manufacture their own *Tuzine* and compete with us."

Dwalooa gave him a half-hearted smile. "And what if they are?"

"One step at a time," said Hadathoo. "Find out what they're doing…and how far along they are."

"Exactly," said Teelila.

Officer Leader, Natsa and her Team 82 were taken off of the Algothon list and became the lead Team for Team: Maka-Or. They were joined by Teams 802 and 881. First they had to find this island chain. Then they had to find which island the Maka-Or were attempting to execute their plot from.

They started with the northern most part of the chain - Curov Isle. After doing as rapid a search as possible they then had to head south. Trice Isle was directly south of Curov. Nothing there either. Next east southeast to Hul Isle. They found nothing there. They headed back southwest to the island that was the most central island in the entire chain – Satroco Isle. Here they finally found the Maka-Or. They went ahead and searched the other four main islands of Lokver, Inlychik, Gommont and Mol-Mol. There were signs of the Maka-Or causing trouble on all of the main islands. There was no sign of trouble on any of the smaller (mostly insignificant) islands in the chain.

Natsa sighed as with some relief as they found the large fields of kwatha. They had received a briefing that the Maka-Or people were usually just over seven taja in height and were covered, from head to toe, with dark fur. They found the fields and there were Maka-Or tending them, however, there seemed to be another race that was there as well and they were not being treated as slaves. Everything looked as if they were equals. These people were slightly shorter, had shiny brown skin with no hair and what appeared to be some very long, nasty looking fangs.

After reporting the description of this other Elf race, the computer personnel were able to locate them in the Algothon archives and identify them as Yagalom-Ayin. They had originated in an area near the Maka-Or and now both races were here on these islands cooperating with each other in raising kwatha and driving all of the regular inhabitants out of the area to the smaller islands. This cooperation did not seem to raise any emergency flags at first, because there were several different races of Elf who were starting cooperatives. The Turgon Wall was an excellent example.

Officer Grade 3, Coycoy, of Team 802 frowned as she looked at the massive fields and...*two* compounds. "Why do they have those different facilities? I don't understand why they would need two...that seem to be so far apart."

Officer Grad 3, Kooami, the leader of Team 881 shrugged. "Maybe they found out that one facility was just not big enough."

Natsa scoffed. "Big enough for what? You don't build a second facility...until you have the first one completely overwhelmed with work." She shook her head. "Coycoy, you take the facility on the left and check it out. Kooami, you take the one on the right. We'll find out what they're doing in them and go from there. Meanwhile, I and my Team will do some inventory on all of these fields and see what else they're growing here...just in case it looks like a *Tuzine* crop."

Officer Grade 3, Osskood scoffed. "I'm no botanist! The only reason that I recognize that *Shoonshook* plant, is because I've had to spend an inordinate amount of time peeing on the smelly things."

Officer Grade 6, Siy smacked him on his shoulder. "Don't worry…I know all of the seven plants and how to identify them."

"I'm glad you do," said Officer Grade 6, Eesteesee. "I can't recognize one plant from another…unless it has a pretty blossom."

Natsa looked at her Team with a little bit of disgust. "Do any of you *bimyocks* know how to recognize kwatha?"

Eesteesee blushed. "Yes, I can recognize kwatha…and that smelly *Shoonshook.*"

Osskood grunted and shrugged.

"All right, let's start looking over these fields and see what we've got," said Natsa. "See if there's any of the actual ingredients for *Tuzine.*"

Team 802 hopped to Spy dimension and walked through the walls of the facility. Coycoy did an initial glance at the activity. "Okay, Umeso, you go forward, Didazee to the left and Nashasi to the right. I'm going upstairs and see what I can find up there. Let's go."

They all headed off to their respective areas.

Coycoy walked around the upper floor. All she could find were personnel who were, for the most part, sitting around gossiping. The Maka-Or and Yagalom-Ayin all seemed to be getting along rather well with each other. The conversations were all about things back home, minor accomplishments, some hunting feats and…children. She felt some bitter resentment about the children, however, she knew that she could not concentrate on things beyond her control. She kept on walking around through the offices, trying to glean any kind of useful information. The offices all seemed to have some kind of organization, however, none of them were talking business. She gave up after going through every single office and obtaining no information at all.

Umeso, Didazee and Nashasi were standing at the place where they had entered the building.

Coycoy looked at them expectantly. "Did anyone get anything useful? I sure didn't."

Umeso shrugged. "Everything down here…it's the same thing. There are all kinds of laboratory technicians, all at identical work stations, trying to determine the ingredients for *Tuzine*. I didn't see anyone doing anything else."

Didazee nodded in agreement. "It's several hundred Maka-Or and Yagalom-Ayin who are all doing what they can to unlock our secrets. I saw a few of them comparing notes, but… not much else."

Nashasi yawned. "They've got determination, but whatever our people are doing to hide the ingredients, in the manufacturing process…it is working."

Coycoy sighed. "All right. Let's go back and find Natsa."

Team 881 arrived in the other facility and were immediately confused by the fact that there were very few personnel, of any type, in the building.

Coycoy shook her head. "Okay, Zozz, you go off to the right and see what's over there. Yasimika you go to the left. Twana…you go through to that other room. I'm going to check upstairs and see if it is just as vacant as this floor."

Yasimika slowly started walking along through several areas that looked like something from a slaughterhouse. There were large long tables for cutting or carving meat and at the end of each one was a set of meat grinders. No one was currently working on any of the tables and they were all sparkling clean. The thing that really confused her was the fact that there were four different table areas and they seemed to be color-coded. One set of red, one brown, one yellow and one white. Each set had four lines for processing…something. Red, brown and yellow were virtually identical – except for the color. The white had some special tools that she was completely baffled as to what they were used for.

There were also sets of ovens for cooking…something. The ovens in each section were different. They all seemed to be the same size, however there were different dials and knobs on them depending on which section they were in. Whatever was being cooked up, in each section, required some kind of different treatment in the oven.

She took another closer look at each one of the areas. In each one, there were marks on the stainless steel tables where someone had been doing some carving. The other three, in each set, were pristine indicating that they had never been used at all. They had been preparing something, however, the facility was much larger than whatever they were cutting, cooking and preparing. They were ready for a large load – which they currently did not have any of…whatever.

She shook her head and went back to the meeting place.

Zozz was walking through a storage area of row after row after row of containers. There were red, brown, yellow and white containers. There were large containers, the type that you would put something in to ice it down and keep it chilled. There were small ornate bottles that were color-coded along with the ice chests. All of the ice chests were in neat squared stacks. The crates that contained the boxes appeared as if someone had taken *some* of the bottles and left the crates open for further use of more bottles later. All of the containers were sectioned off by color and left him completely puzzled as to the purpose for each set.

Twana found herself shivering in an enormous freezer. There was currently a lot of wasted space in here. The freezer was sectioned off in color coding. Red, brown, yellow and white areas in the freezer. Each section had several dozen small ornate bottles that were color coordinated with the shelves. She was not sure what to do about the bottles so she left them alone and headed back to the meeting place. Decisions on what to do with the bottles was definitely above her pay grade of Officer Grade 7. She just wanted to get out of the freezer and warm up.

Kooami walked around the upstairs area and saw a few

people there who seemed to be very bored. There were no conversations going on – at first. She figured that gleaning any information would be rather difficult – at first. She heard one conversation going on and headed that way…it was something… hopefully.

Two Maka-Or and two Yagalom-Ayin were sitting around a desk looking at paperwork.

One of the Maka-Or shook his head. "We're finished with all of the supplies we had in stock. Everything has been mixed and cooked. It's a question of supply and demand. We have all of the supply and the demand is great." He had a huge grin on his face. "We can charge anything that we want to for the elixirs."

One of the Yagalom-Ayin smiled. "Oboko…which one can we charge great prices for?"

Oboko laughed. "All of them Chachak! Until there's more supplies…which I don't see happening any time soon…we have a complete monopoly on the elixirs."

Chachak looked at his Yagalom-Ayin partner. "Bifonok, do you think that those Teltermaks will try to get some of the elixirs back?"

"Of course they will," said Bifonok. "They're the ones who taught us the recipes for the elixirs. We got all of the ingredients, we did the cutting, the mixing, the grinding, the cooking and the storing. If the Teltermak or those Axswain want any share in the profits, they'll have to supply more of the prime ingredients. Until then…we have full control of all of it."

Kooami stood there in shock. She knew that there were still some Teltermak that were…somewhere in the world. Axswain? How did they get back in the picture? She wanted to send all of them into Jahong's Death, however, she could not justify it to herself - at the moment. She also felt that she needed more information – a lot more information from them that she could get back to the Command Staff.

The meeting broke up. Kooami headed back downstairs to find her Team.

Zozz was waiting, feeling rather bored at not having found any kind of fantastic evidence of *Tuzine* theft or research. He saw Kooami headed toward him with perspiration dripping down her forehead and cheeks and a look of horror on her face. He looked to see if either of the other two Team members was heading back. "Uh…Kooami…what's the problem?"

She stopped and swallowed. "It's not…just the…whatever these people are. It's also…the Teltermak…and Axswain. They're all involved here…but…I don't know how or why…or what they're doing."

"They've got a bunch of bottles…of something…in a big freezer," said Twana. "They're color coded…for some reason. They got them preserved here for something."

Yasimika came back and joined the group. "What do you mean by color coding?"

"There's all these bottles in a big freezer," said Twana. "There are no labels of any type. They're just stored by color in the freezer."

Yasimika chuckled nervously. They've got a bunch of tables over there. They're all set up for…processing…something. They have them set up in different colors. They're the type of tables that look as if they're used to process meat. I don't know what kind of meat they're processing but…they haven't used all of the tables yet. They're prepared to process a lot of it, but…they haven't yet."

"This whole place is color coded," said Zozz. "They have a bunch of ice chests and empty bottles…color coded. They're processing something here that…it seems very important to them. Now…you're telling me that the Teltermak and the Axswain are involved…with these people. What is in that freezer?"

"It's a bunch of bottles…they're all sitting on shelves that are color coded…the same color as the bottles," said Twana.

Zozz huffed. "I think that we need to get a few of those bottles. We need to get them back to Owlam and see if our doctors can analyze what's in them…and do a better job than these people are doing at examining our *Tuzine*."

Kooami sighed. "I can't disagree with that. Let's get…oh say…five of each color. We'll take them back to Owlam and… keep an eye on these *Doovofts*."

Twana had been the one to find the freezer, so she was the one who got to pull five bottles of each color and take them to the doctors in Owlam for analysis…along with taking the message to the Command Staff in regards to the Teltermak and the Axswain.

Wilfadge listened to Twana's report silently. He then called a full meeting of all of the Command Staff.

"We've found where the Teltermak are running their business from. They hid themselves in an island chain and they now have some allies...possibly. Why anyone would ally themselves with cannibals...I am completely baffled about that one...but...they did and are. They and their allies are attempting to analyze *Tuzine* and then they'll probably try to take over with the manufacturing and distribution thereof."

Ahandi shook her head. "So how do we fight it?"

"We wait," said Dwalooa. "We find out what they know and go from there."

Teelila was confused. "Why do we wait? Why don't we go after them now?"

Hadathoo grunted in disgust. "We need to know what they know. Haven't you learned that yet?"

Hoynama sighed. "We found them. We needed that. Now we know where they are and...at least one of the things that they're doing...we can investigate and get all of the big picture before we act."

Shyshee leaned back. "Yes, we know where they are. We knew that the Teltermak still exist...and now we know that the Axswain are still around. That helps us with something...at least."

"I wish we had learned something else about what...exists in the world," said Antrong.

Wilfadge sighed. "At least the report does not show that they found any of the seven plants, which make up the *Tuzine*, are being cultivated there."

"Right," said Ahandi. "It just states that there are three of them, the Mychelik herb, the Fendelik plant, the Poolhatha vine, that grow wild on the island and it seems that they're being ignored...for the most part."

Soolchakan grimaced in anger as he found out that Team 7016 was going to be temporarily assigned as part of Team: Maka-Or. He looked at the report with a disgusted feeling and saw that they were going...where? He saw that (of course) his Team was the last one on the list (as far as rank). The nice thing about being the lowest ranking one – his Team was the only one listed as "temporary". The other twelve Teams were a little more permanent and would be there a lot longer. He sighed as he prepared himself to tell the three women (who were currently taking long soaking baths) that they had to get ready to go to another destination...that he had never heard of.

Once all of the Teams that made up Team Maka-Or were present on Satroco Isle, Bonarain was informed that she was there to assist and/or lead in any training that any personnel would need as far as espionage against the four allies that currently inhabited the island.

Soolchakan, Kiyalee and Chyning were just...*there*. They decided to do some of their own exploring and see if they could come up with anything useful...like the exact location of the

Teltermak and Axswain...where ever they were hiding on this island. There had been absolutely no information in regards to the exact location of their longtime enemies...only that they seemed to be a part of this project.

Kiyalee looked back at the area where the main briefings took place. "I wonder...if we headed to one of the other islands...I doubt that any of those *bimyocks* would know...or care."

"I agree," said Chyning in a disgusted manner.

Soolchakan shrugged. "Okay...which one?"

Kiyalee looked up. "Which one...what?"

"Which one of the other islands do we go to in order to look for the Teltermak?"

Kiyalee flushed and closed her eyes.

Chyning looked out over the water. "Which island is supposed to be the closest?"

"Gommont is the closest," said Soolchakan. According to the map, due south of the island that we're on right now."

Chyning shrugged. "That's as good as any place to start."

Kiyalee picked through some pictures. "Do any of these have a landmark that we're supposed to look for on that... Gommont Isle?"

Soolchakan yawned. "Look on the back of the photo."

"Here it is," said Kiyalee. "They labeled it as...a major meeting place for the Heyyah that lived there."

Chyning grunted. "Lot of good that does us. We're looking for Teltermak."

Soolchakan shrugged. "It's as good a place as any to start."

The three of them concentrated on the photograph and performed the Jump. They found themselves in an area that looked as if it had been a somewhat large city…at some previous time. The tall building in front of them looked as if it had not been used in years. There were several broken and boarded up windows. The only thing that they heard was the wind.

Chyning sighed. "Now what?"

Kiyalee looked around. "Has anyone else noticed…it's not as hot here…like it is back at the gorge? I mean…it doesn't seem to be as hot and humid as it is in the gorge."

Chyning shook her head. "The gorge is located a *lot* closer to the equator. Here…we're *way* south of the equator. We're not as far south as the city of Owlam is north, but we're far enough away so that we don't have that constant high humidity and heat."

Kiyalee nodded. "Makes sense."

Soolchakan looked up at the top of their landmark building. "Why not go to a high point and take a look. The further we can see…the more we know about…what is not here."

There was a balcony that completely surrounded the top floor of this fifteen story structure. The three of them Jumped up to the balcony and looked out over the city. Again, the only thing that they could hear was the wind and the only things moving were branches and leaves.

Kiyalee looked down at her compass. "The way that we're facing is east. I wonder if the other directions are equally boring."

Chyning scoffed. "Only one way to tell."

Kiyalee snickered. "Has anyone else noticed that there are no buildings…that are anywhere near as tall as this one?"

"It might be, or might have been the central part of the city government…and some high muckity-muck decided that he didn't want any buildings blocking his view of other portions of the city," said Chyning mockingly.

Soolchakan scratched his chin as he contemplated. "I'll go right…you two go left and we'll meet on the other side of the building."

Chyning shrugged. "Sounds good."

He went to the south side of the building and looked out. They were closer to the water line than he had originally thought. He could see, what at one time, had been a good sized port for the commerce and trade that had originated from this island. Now it was only six docks that were badly in need of repair. The only ship that he saw was nothing more than three masts sticking out of the water with a few remnants of sails slowly moving with the wind. He sighed and shook his head. He wondered if the Algothons had any capacity to realize how much damage their previous generation had done to the entire planet.

He continued to the west side of the building. He looked out over the city and shook his head. Most of the structures in that direction had completely collapsed. Nothing but ruins as far as he could see.

He was a little confused over the fact that he did not see the women. He felt a little concern and hastily headed for the north side of the building. As he rounded the corner, he saw the two women, staring off to the northeast with their mouths hanging open. He followed their gaze and…off in the distance he saw those wretched kites…the same ones that the Teltermak had used to fly over the walls of Owlam. They were making those lazy circles that indicated the pilots were all in training and getting used to the kites.

5

Soolchakan slowly walked to the women while still staring at the Teltermak kites. Just to assure himself, that no enemy could see them, he quickly hopped to Observation dimension. The two women disappeared. He hopped back to Spy dimension and was once again with the women. He sighed. "I think we found… something," he said quietly.

Neither woman moved for several moments.

Kiyalee looked at him and nodded. She turned her gaze back to the kites.

Chyning swallowed hard. "Should we go over there…and investigate?"

Soolchakan rolled his eyes. "No! We should just continue to stand here, looking stupid and accomplishing nothing."

Kiyalee gave him a dirty look. "No need to be snippy!"

He huffed. "No need for stupid questions."

Chyning stuck her tongue out at him.

After three Jumps, they were at the kite school. The only ones that they found there were Teltermaks. There was no laboratory for testing *Tuzine*, there was no form of a school for espionage. Nothing but manufacturing and the practicing of flying those kites.

The reason that the school was in this location of the dead city was because it was the only area of the city that had buildings that were not falling apart. There was an area where they could take the kites up high for a takeoff and a good sized plaza for landings. They also had a large warehouse where they assembled the kites.

Kiyalee cocked her head to the side. "They assemble those kites…here."

Chyning gave her a dull look. "So?"

Kiyalee huffed. "Where do they manufacture the PARTS?"

Soolchakan shook his head. "Good question. Those fabrics and the frameworks. Those things don't just grow out of the ground. They have to have someone who makes those parts and then ships them here."

Chyning shook her head. "How do we go about…finding out?"

Soolchakan sighed. "We start by reporting this to our illustrious Team Leader – Natsa."

Kiyalee looked a little skeptical. "Should we…do some more exploring first? I mean…if we tell her right now…the report will be rather incomplete."

Soolchakan smiled at her. "Finding any Base of

Operations for the Teltermak is information that the higher ups would want to know now…quickly. They'll determine just how many more personnel will be sent here to do further exploring and investigation."

After some mental communication with Natsa, Team 1290 and 2559 were immediately dispatched to Gommont Isle in order to do some more of the exploration.

Officer Grade 3, Voolala was the Team leader for 1290. She looked at all of the kites that were circling overhead. "They told me that the reason that we didn't see those things, the last time that we were here, was because it was too windy…at that time."

Officer Grade 4, Yondi, the Team leader for 2559, scoffed. "I think that someone is making some excuses. They missed it and they want to save face…by blaming the wind."

"I'd say that's a pretty good excuse," said Soolchakan. "Those things can be blown about by the wind. I've flown one of those things and the wind can do some really nasty things to mess you up badly. No point being up there…if you have no control of where you're going."

"That's all beside the point," said Voolala. "They've been spotted and we know that they are here now. That takes care of step 1. You say that you can find nothing here that even hints at the manufacturing the parts from raw materials. Okay, that takes care of a step 2…in this area. Step 3…find out what else is here and do some more checking around to find the manufacturing plant and any other Bases that the Teltermak have here in these islands."

Yondi looked around. "Who does what?"

Voolala pursed her lips while thinking. "My Team will do some more close examination of this city. Yondi, you take your Team and start doing some quick explorations of the rest of the island. Soolchakan, you and your Team…go ahead and do some quick explorations of the other three islands."

Soolchakan cleared his throat. "Which one do we start with?"

Voolala smiled. "Your choice."

Soolchakan looked at the photographs of island landmarks. He turned to Kiyalee and Chyning. "Let's start with Lokver."

Chyning folded her arms, looking a little disgusted. "Why that one?"

He wanted to slap her. Instead he gave her a friendly smile. "Why not?"

The three of them closely studied the landmark for Lokver.

Soolchakan looked at the women. "Ready?"

The three of them Jumped to Lokver.

They found themselves standing near a huge obelisk. The trio stared up, all a little awed at how tall the thing was.

"I wonder why they build something like this," said Chyning.

"I think that those are some kind of holy symbols…they go all the way to the top," said Kiyalee.

"Kind of stupid," said Soolchakan. "*Who* is going to be up at the top…reading those lines?"

Kiyalee scoffed. "Supposedly…the god or gods that they were worshipping."

Soolchakan sighed. "We've got a big island to explore… let's get to it."

Chyning snickered. "Aren't we going to investigate this giant pole?"

Kiyalee scoffed again. "What for? We're not here to investigate their religion. We're here to see if the Teltermak, or Axswain, have another base of some type here."

Chyning nodded and shrugged. "Okay, where do we start?"

Soolchakan looked at the map of the island. "We can start by going around the shore areas. We Jump around there and… when we get back to this…holy pole…we start going inland."

Yondi and her Team were Jumping all over Gommont Isle. They found a few places where there were some small communities of Heyyah that seemed to be hiding from someone. She could only guess that they were original inhabitants of this island and that they were probably hiding from the Teltermak…or one of their allies. The people were living in totally primitive conditions, without any of the technological luxuries. She guessed that this was also because of the Teltermak.

Her Team members: Toosooa, Yindool and Fayfa were all getting a little bored with the fruitless searching.

Yindool shook his head. "How much longer are we going to continue counting the Heyyah?"

Yondi looked at the notes that had been taken so far. "Until we're sure that there are no more Teltermak on this island."

Fayfa sat down on a log. "Don't you think that we would've found something by now? Look around! All eight of the larger island cities are in ruins. The Heyyah have been forced to live in...grass huts...covered with camouflage netting. The only Teltermak that we've found are at that flight training school."

Toosooa shook her head. "Yeah...those two harbor cities... complete mess. No one has lived in those places...or done any docking for trading...for decades. They're not using the Heyyah ports...to receive the parts for their kites."

Yondi nodded. "I wonder just how long the Teltermak have been here. We'd have to check our archives...and find out just how long ago they fled from our area."

Yindool chuckled. "Maybe we should get that guy...you remember, the one who was always finding and destroying the Teltermak tunnels. Maybe they did a lot of tunneling here...and that's where the majority of them are hiding."

Fayfa shook her head. "Nah! If they were living underground...we'd have found some smokestacks...or some other kind of sign...like tunnel entrances or other stuff like that. There'd have to be a working power plant...somewhere."

"Probably," said Yondi. "We're going to keep looking until we're sure."

Toosooa hung her head and sighed. "Okay…which way do we go next?"

Yindool snickered. "Any place that we haven't been yet."

Voolala stood in front of her Team. "Find out anything?"

Jinsami shook her head. "The only thing off in that direction is more ruins. They didn't build…or rebuild anything over there."

"Same thing in my direction," said Tatawava. "All I found was rubble."

Moolkooz cleared his throat. "It looks like…at some time…someone tried to do some rebuilding, just south of here. It also looks like they gave up…a long time ago as well. I guess that either the original Heyyah, or the Teltermak, wanted that area…but it didn't get very far. The only power plant or water purification… just in the local area around the kite school."

Voolala sighed. "So we have nothing new to report here. All we have is the school. We may have to wait until the next shipment of parts comes in…and follow those people back to their home of operations."

Jinsami groaned. "How long could that take?"

"I shudder to think," said Tatawava.

"Lokver Isle is boring," said Chyning.

"So we didn't find anything here...that helps us locate the Teltermak," said Soolchakan. "We go on to the next island."

"Oh what fun," said Kiyalee sarcastically.

Soolchakan looked at the photographs of landmarks. "On to Inlychik Isle."

They made the Jump and were shocked by what they saw. The landmark, a large building that was pictured, was just enough for them to arrive there safely. They quickly updated the landmark building in the computer system. The area around the building was almost gone. The only reason that the building was still there was because, being concrete and brick, it had not burned when a lava flow came up against it. Most of the other structures in the area were completely gone. The only thing that could be seen was the lava flow that was devouring everything in the area.

The Jumping on this island had to be done very carefully. A massive volcanic eruption had changed the face of the island to such an extent that virtually nothing they had obtained from the archives was accurate any more. The entire northern portion of the island was gone. Apparently there had been some massive earthquake associated with the volcanic eruption that had sunk a major portion of the northern area. There had been several towns and harbors in that area that were now completely submerged. Perhaps someday someone could come here and reestablish working communities on the island, however, it could be sometime before that particular migration of sentient people would take place. Any population that was here now was doing everything they could to build levees that might redirect the lava flow. The communities were not really prospering...just surviving.

Next the trio from Team 7016 Jumped to Mol-Mol Isle. Apparently there had been another volcanic eruption there, however, it devastated the island in a completely different manner. There were thousands of holes all over the island from which some kind of smoke was either wafting or spewing up from the ground. The buildings were dilapidated from longtime lack of repair or use. The ground was littered with the bones of...possibly...millions of people and animals and birds.

Kiyalee swallowed hard. "What happened here?"

"If that smoke...or gas that's coming up from the ground... is poisonous...I'd say that everyone here died from some kind of suffocation...from lack of oxygen," said Soolchakan.

Chyning chuckled nervously. "I think that we'd better stay in Spy dimension while we're here. Fortunately, because we're still alive, it seems that the poisonous gases are all still in Home."

Soolchakan sighed. "It's going to be sometime before this island is usable again."

"If ever," said Kiyalee.

"We did see some Heyyah still living on the southern end of the island," said Soolchakan.

Kiyalee shook her head. "Some? Didn't look like very many to me."

Chyning shook her head. "Me either. Are there any more islands to explore…in order to find the Teltermak?"

"No," said Soolchakan. "Those islands are being explored by other Teams. The only thing that we could possibly do is…go to the continent that is the closest to this island chain."

Kiyalee looked at her map. "Is that…Ficara or Lusaratia?"

"Lusaratia," said Soolchakan.

"Okay…let's go," said Kiyalee.

Chyning looked puzzled. "Should we go check on Bonarain first?"

Kiyalee huffed. "For what?"

Chyning shook her head. "I'd think by now…those people have learned just about all they can from her. It's been three months since they started all of this stuff here. Maybe…if we're going to Lusaratia, we should collect her to help with the search."

Soolchakan shrugged. "Why not? It couldn't hurt to find out. Let's go check."

Back on Satroco Isle, they found that Bonarain had been sitting around doing virtually nothing for over one month. She was more than happy to depart this boredom and see if they could find any trace of the Teltermak or the Axswain.

Bonarain looked at the landmark photographs that they had for the western tip of Lusaratia. "Why are we going to the continent…now? I mean…aren't there a few hundred smaller islands in this chain…where the Teltermak could hide?"

"They could hide," said Soolchakan. "They couldn't really exist. The main eight islands are the only ones that could support entire communities. Most of the other islands would only be capable of supporting one or two families. There are maybe five that could support a community...and not a very big one at that. There just isn't enough resources available on any of those islands for...any kind of long term living."

"Still," said Bonarain. "Why couldn't they do that? Have a family or two here and the same thing on another island."

"We could do it," said Kiyalee. "We can Jump from one island to another. They'd have to use their kites. If the wind were to kick up, like it was the other day, they'd be stuck and couldn't use anything other than a motorized boat. Totally unfeasible."

Bonarain shrugged and sighed. "Onward and forward...to the continent."

Wilfadge looked at the reports. "Several hundred of these...Maka-Or and Yagalom-Ayin...all trying to chemically analyze the *Tuzine*...and not one has been able to isolate any of the seven ingredients."

"I'd say that's pretty good," said Antrong. "I guess the cooking process just completely ruins any singularity of any of them."

"True," said Hoynama. "There are several though...who have been able to eliminate...at least fourteen different plants. That is definitely one way of narrowing it down...and I can't think of any way we can stop that."

"Other than mass murder," said Hadathoo dryly. "I've seen enough of that for the time being."

"We need to find the main nest of the Teltermak," said Wilfadge. "Maybe that'll also lead us to the main nest of the Axswain."

Dwalooa shook her head. "I think it's puzzling...that we've found some Teltermak...but we haven't found the Axswain yet. Don't you think that if they are allies that...they'd be equally represented...in that kite school?"

Shyshee spoke up. "Remember that attack pattern back at Owlam? The Teltermak came from one side and the Axswain from another. The Axswain were tired of being slaughtered in the Teltermak tunnels. They might still be allies, however, they're living in different communities, doing different types of training... and...let's not jump to conclusions...until we find the Axswain camp."

"Good idea," sighed Wilfadge.

Team 7016 arrived on the most western tip of the Lusaratia continent. Off to the north they could see what appeared to be a thriving community...unless the Teltermak had ruined that area as well. They could not see any form of large community to the south. Just a few scattered beach houses or small fishing villages.

They performed three Jumps in order to get to the larger city. There they found a huge harbor with a large city that appeared to be a very thriving center of commerce.

Kiyalee groaned. "Where *DO* we start now?"

Bonarain shook her head. "It looks like there are several plants...that are manufacturing or processing something. Let's take a look at each one and...see if anything looks familiar."

Chyning looked a little concerned. "Do we go together or separately?"

Soolchakan chuckled. "Since we're in Spy dimension... and that means that we're not in danger, we can go ahead and split up. Each of us checks a different plant and then we get back together and compare notes."

Bonarain frowned at Soolchakan. "A...plant? There are at least fifteen...that we can see from here. Which...A...plant are you talking about?"

He muttered something under his breath. "We don't have to take on all of them today. We each pick one...preferably in the same area...we each check one out...rejoin the group...compare notes...and then check another one. If any of us finds one that appears to be...*really* interesting...then we all go and give that one a thorough looking at."

Kiyalee shrugged. "Sounds good."

Chyning chuckled nervously. "So...if we do find something...when we go to report it to the Command Staff... where do we say that we are? I mean...what's the name of this city?"

Dara J. Carr

Bonarain checked her pad. "According to…what I can find here…this city is called Shashkanit."

Chyning giggled. "Sounds like something that needs to be mopped up off of the floor."

"Not according to the people who live here," said Soolchakan. "Let's pick a place and go. We're not accomplishing anything just looking at the outside of a building."

They mapped out the plants on their pads and each picked one. They all then Jumped to the appropriate manufacturing plant and started their preliminary scrutiny.

Soolchakan found a vehicle manufacturing plant. He looked at some of the vehicles that were coming off of the assembly lines and snickered. He mentally contacted Kiyalee and asked if she wanted to trade places. He gave her a landmark in the building and she quickly Jumped there. She looked like a child in a candy store as she ogled all of the vehicles. She started to go towards the lines to check them closer.

Soolchakan grunted in exasperation. "Kiyalee…would you please give me a landmark in the one you were originally in? I need to get there and do a closer look."

She looked back at him a little confused. She grabbed his hand, Jumped him to the other location and then vanished.

He just stood there snickering for a few moments. He sighed, sniffed and then started exploring what turned out to be a plant that was putting out different kinds of fabrics. One of these fabrics looked very familiar. He nodded. If you cut this stuff into large triangles…you would have the fabric that they attach to the Teltermak kites.

He walked around looking for any other type of familiar fabrics, maybe for uniforms, however, he found nothing else that was…interesting.

He made a mental recall to his Team and Jumped back to the rendezvous point. Chyning and Bonarain showed up almost immediately. Kiyalee suddenly appeared, grinning and sitting in a big pink truck.

Chyning stood there gawking at the truck. Bonarain rolled her eyes. Soolchakan was fighting off the desire to punch Kiyalee.

Bonarain shook her head. "Where…did you find…that?"

Kiyalee giggled. "It was in the plant I looked at. It's a truck manufacturing plant."

Chyning snickered. "So you grabbed one…for…the Team?"

Kiyalee nodded merrily.

Soolchakan groaned. "Why did you pick…that…one?"

Kiyalee looked affronted. "Because it's the only one that's pink!"

Now Bonarain groaned. "The…*only*…one that is pink?"

"Yes," said Kiyalee proudly.

"Put it back," said Bonarain. "If it's the only one that is pink…it's a special order. Someone is going to notice that it is gone…and…maybe might just start an investigation…especially if someone is mad because their pink truck is missing."

Kiyalee looked hurt. She opened her mouth as if she wanted to say something. Her shoulders sagged. She looked back at her Team members.

"I agree," said Soolchakan. "Put it back before they notice it missing."

Kiyalee sighed sadly and then truck and all disappeared.

Bonarain shook her head. "She does like being a mechanic…and taking care of the trucks that we have."

Chyning scoffed. "So what do we need with another truck? Where would we put it?"

Soolchakan hung his head. "There are…several of the new homes…in the gorge…that are…not being used."

Kiyalee reappeared standing there akimbo. "Can I swipe a red one?"

Soolchakan closed his eyes, shook his head and groaned. "Maybe later." He opened his eyes and smiled. "Okay, ladies… reports! Obviously, Kiyalee was in a vehicle assembly area."

"Yeah," said Kiyalee. "They make some small trucks… probably for personal use…or for a small business. They also have some light and heavy duty utility trucks."

Soolchakan nodded. "So it's all trucks…in there?"

Kiyalee nodded.

"I got a plant for different kinds of cloth," said Soolchakan. "All kinds of cloth. Anything from light and frilly to heavy canvas...including the stuff that looks like the material for Teltermak kites."

Bonarain smiled. "I'm glad that we can't smell anything... from Home while we're in Spy. I was in a plant where they're processing and canning fish. The smell in there...must be... horrid. Fish heads and fish guts are everywhere."

Chyning shrugged. "I got a food plant as well. They were canning vegetables though."

"Okay," said Soolchakan. "Next set of factories."

When they finished the inventory they had four factories that made clothing, one for children, one for men, one for women and one for utility clothing and uniforms, along with the plant that manufactured all of the fabrics for all four. There were four vehicle assembly plants, one for trucks, one for sedans, one for farming equipment and one entire plant just for luxury vehicles. There was the fish processing plant, the vegetable processing plant and a meat packing plant. One plant dealt with all kinds of furniture, one dealt with all kinds of plastic products (including the frameworks for the Teltermak kites). There were four smelting plants that processed steel, iron, aluminum and tin. There was a massive building where they built some very large ships. Another place where they build fishing boats and pleasure yachts. There was a plant that dealt with all kinds of glass products. Of course, a distance from the city was a paper mill that had been built with the prevailing winds in mind. All of the smells of these places blew inland and the city itself did not smell...too badly.

Soolchakan stood there looking over the list. "We found where the Teltermak are getting all of their equipment for building the kites. We haven't seen any of it moved yet, but we do see several crates that were marked for Gommont Isle."

Bonarain shook her head as she looked at the list. "Where do they get the animals for...meat packing?"

"They probably have some kind of domesticated herding beasts that are farther inland," said Soolchakan. "You have to have a lot of open land...in order to keep animals like that...in sufficient numbers for selling them to a meat packing plant."

Chyning looked around, slightly disgusted. "You think maybe the Teltermak get their meat from there now?"

Bonarain shook her head. "One would hope so."

Wilfadge read the report from Team 7016. "I don't know what they were doing on the continent...but I'm sure glad that they went there and took a look-see. That city could supply...just about anybody...with anything that they need."

Hadathoo grunted. "Everything except weapons... personal or military grade."

Teelila looked up. "They don't make weapons, but with all of the metal and plastics that they make...you could probably talk them into manufacturing parts for...anything you want."

Dwalooa frowned. "One entire vehicle assembly plant...

for nothing but…luxury vehicles. I don't get it. Is there that big a market for the things?"

"Rich people do like to show off," said Shyshee.

"Especially if they're rich leaders," said Hoynama. "We've seen some of the vehicles that they have in Algothon."

"We still haven't found what we really wanted," said Ahandi. "We got the kite school of the Teltermaks on Gommont Isle. We got a hotbed of Maka-Or and Yagalom-Ayin on Satroco Isle. Where are the homes of the Maka-Or, the Yagalom-Ayin, the Teltermak…and what's left of the Axswain?"

Wilfadge sighed. "Don't forget that we still have this pestilence of the Perfor here on South Chilamte. They do seem to be making a lot of headway."

"Yes," said Antrong. "They're chasing a lot of the Heyyah refugees up onto the high cliffs that surround our gorge. If someone goes down into the gorge…and discovers our hidden sanctuary… what do we do then?"

"We may have to make some hard decisions about what we do with some Heyyah," said Wilfadge sadly.

Till shook his head. "Or…we can do some major hindering…to the Perfor."

"I hope we don't have to," said Wilfadge. "As near as we can figure…from the size of their military…and what's still left back at their home city…there's over a million of those *bimyocks*."

"I didn't say wipe them out," complained Till. "I just said

that we should hinder their progress. Maybe then they'd get the idea that their undertaking is just too monumental to continue."

Wilfadge huffed. "Yeah, some kind of harassment could buy us some time. I just hate to dedicate too many Teams to that kind of an undertaking."

Teelila snickered. "It's just harassment, not a major invasion."

Hadathoo shrugged. "They say that an army marches on its stomach. Cut off their supply lines...and..."

"And they start ravaging the countryside," said Hoynama sharply.

"We've got to do something," said Hadathoo.

Dwalooa looked around. "Cut them off from *Tuzine*. They have traders come to Owlam as well. Tell them if they're going to start conquering...we don't trade with aggressors."

"That might make them attack just like the Cacktash did," said Antrong. "I suggest that we foul their vehicles and other equipment that they're using. That'd give them headaches that they can't blame on others...like being cut off from *Tuzine*."

"I like that thought much better," said Wilfadge. "That would keep them from blaming anyone else. Plus it could slow them to a crawl...or maybe it might get them to turn around completely...and forget the whole thing."

Some fifty kilotaja southeast of Shashkanit, Team 7016

stumbled onto a rather large nest of Teltermak. They had been able to find them because of a huge number of kites that were seen flying overhead. They had heard a few rumors about the kites from eavesdropping on conversations in taverns. It had not taken long to find them, once they got all of the rumors (and slurred drunken speech) figured out.

Bonarain shook her head chuckling. "If you want to stay hidden, you don't advertise where you are with those *chokwad* kites."

Kiyalee scoffed. "A lesson that they haven't learned."

The Team headed into the heart of the Teltermak nest, looking to see if they could figure out some numbers, find out any intelligence information and see if they knew where the Axswain were hiding.

Kiyalee snarled and clenched her teeth. "Over a hundred years since those firestorm weapons hit us…and this garbage still has pulse weapons."

The Team observed several of the Teltermak soldiers cleaning and repairing their power weapons. They were also cleaning trucks and doing some close order drills of younger looking Teltermaks in very new looking uniforms.

"This stinks," said Soolchakan. "They are getting ready for some kind of…large invasion…or intrusion into someone's lives."

Bonarain grunted. "Let's see if we can find…some kind of headquarters…in this convoluted mess."

They walked for some time before they finally found an area that was heavily guarded by fully armed military personnel. They brazenly walked past the guards in the knowledge that they could not be seen or noticed...until Chyning put her hand in Home dimension long enough to yank on the hair of one of the guards. He swung around trying to find the perpetrator and was thoroughly confused at seeing nothing. His colleagues looked at him as if he had lost his mind.

Bonarain huffed. "You ought to be slapped for that."

Chyning just giggled, Soolchakan rolled his eyes and Kiyalee shook her head.

They found a conference room with several charts and chalkboards.

Kiyalee looked at one of the chalkboards. "If I'm reading that scrawl correctly, I think that it says that there's going to be a briefing...in about three days."

Soolchakan sighed. "Sounds like something that we need to be in on and take some notes. We're going to just have to sit here and wait."

Bonarain and Kiyalee just nodded in agreement.

They looked through papers in the room to see if there was any information that they could glean from it. There was nothing that was very useful. They all four stood around now, bored, wondering what to do until the briefing took place.

Chyning walked out into the hallway. "I guess we'll just have to wander around the offices here...and maybe pick up some little tidbits as we go."

"We don't have anything else to do," said Kiyalee.

"No," said Soolchakan. "We report this camp to the Command Staff and let them know about that briefing. Any decision other than that…is above our ranks."

The three women shrugged.

He smiled at them. "I'll notify Wilfadge…you start… wandering around the building."

The Command Staff had an emergency meeting and their decision was that Team 7016 continue gathering information in the Teltermak camp until some information came along that warranted more personnel.

Team 7016 did as they were told. They found virtually nothing that was of any value. They could hardly wait until this mysterious briefing and why no one was doing or saying anything about it prior to the meeting taking place. The day came and Team 7016 was there early – too early. They spent most of the day being bored stiff.

Finally some of the Teltermak started coming in. It did not take very long before there were thirty of them in the room mostly sitting at the conference table drinking some kind of dark hot liquid.

Bonarain looked in one of the mugs. "What do you suppose they're drinking?"

"I don't want to know," said Soolchakan flatly.

Chyning huffed. "Considering the diet that they had… when they attacked us, I don't want to know anything about their cuisine."

They saw that familiar dark green uniform. They also knew that the more gold bands that appeared on the uniform, the higher the rank. The highest rank had ten bands and was called the Ultimate Leader. The primary person giving the briefing here had eight gold bands on his uniform.

Kiyalee sniffed. "If I remember correctly, that guy is called a Section Leader."

Bonarain frowned. "There's one over there…with zero bands."

Chyning snarled. "That's a Brass Standard. His rank is equal…to mine. He's an Officer Grade 7."

"Let's discuss their ranks later," said Soolchakan. "That horn eared *bimyock* is about to start the briefing."

The briefing started. The one with the eight bands looked around. "Is everyone here that is supposed to be here?"

The Brass Standard stood up. "Section Leader, Pirbako, I've taken roll. All are in attendance at this time."

The Section Leader grunted. "All right. It seems that those *mombik* Maka-Or have double-crossed us…in more ways than one. I can't say that it's worse than what the Cacktash did… but it is up there in that area nonetheless. While the Cacktash were able to get a rather meager amount of the proper ingredients… now that they're mixed, the Maka-Or, along with the Yagalom-

Ayin have taken control of the elixirs. Now, since neither of them have figured out how to properly fly the great wings, we're going to do an aerial assault on their compound...and get back what is ours. The Cacktash gathered it and tried to control it. They spread themselves just a little too thin and as a result, the Algothons and the Owlams kicked them into...apparently...into extinction."

A man with three gold bands stood up. "Section Leader, Pirbako, are we sure that the Cacktash are...completely wiped out?"

"Yes, we are Gold Standard, Honkoshk. We've heard nothing from them...and considering what the elixirs are worth and that they're the ones who gathered the primary ingredients... we're sure that they would want some and would be ready to work with us to take back the elixirs."

A woman with six gold bands stood up. "Section Leader, Pirbako, I and my flying unit are ready to attack at a moment's notice."

Pirbako smiled. "Thank you, Icon Supreme, Jinjaja. I'm sure that we *all* are ready to go back and take what is rightfully ours." He grunted. "We discovered it, we nurtured it, we found the way to brew it, we shared our secret...and now those thieves want to keep it from us. NO! We're taking it back."

Everyone applauded.

Pirbako continued. "We have the forward base on Gommont Isle. We should be able to get about six thousand more great wings to Gommont, within ten days. We'll rest for two days...and then attack."

A man with four bands stood up. "Section Leader, Pirbako, what do we do…with any prisoners?"

Pirbako smiled. "Icon Second, Honnklook, we always have a need for more slaves. If they don't want to work with us…we can always enslave them…or even sell them as slaves… to some of these Heyyah."

A woman with two gold bands stood up. "Section Leader, Pirbako, why would we want to sell them to…Heyyah?"

Pirbako grinned. "Silver Standard, Idyising, the Heyyah that we're going to sell them to…are *not* Algothons. One of these days, we're going to figure out a way to attack and destroy that city…and all of the inhabitants…for what they did to us. Until we have enough forces…and allies…we can't. Any slaves that we obtain…Heyyah or Elf, we sell to…anyone who'll buy…except the Algothons."

The rest of the briefing covered some of the tactics and strategy that were going to be used. Soolchakan told the three women to get as much information as possible in regards to times and dates while he left the briefing room to send a mental communication to the Command Staff.

Wilfadge called an immediate Command Staff meeting. The decision was made to wait until the attack started and then grab as many of those strange little bottles as they could, get them away from Satroco Isle and get them to either Owlam or the South Chilamte gorge. Then they could do some real studying on these elixirs and try to figure out what they were.

Team 881 had to go back to the processing plant and set up giving tours to all of the other members of Team – Maka-Or. When the Teltermak attacked, the Owlamites would be there, ready to clean *all* of the bottles out of the freezer. The architects had to set up one of the vacant apartments as a rather large freezer in order to keep the elixirs frozen. Since the Maka-Or were keeping them frozen, for the moment, it was determined that until it was known exactly what was in those bottles, the Owlamites might as well keep the stuff frozen as well.

Wilfadge was getting a little impatient in regards to the testing of the elixirs. He contacted Team 227 and requested an initial report – even though it might be incomplete.

The Team Leader, Doctor Thongola came to the briefing room with Doctor Hoonsi in tow. The two women smiled as they walked in.

Wilfadge stood and smiled. "What can you tell me…if anything?"

Thongola sighed. "At this point…not much. Our first step was to narrow it down between animal, mineral or vegetable. It is not vegetable. As far as the other two…it may be a combination of animal and mineral."

He nodded. "Is that important?"

Hoonsi shook her head. "At this point in time…we're not sure what is significant. We know that it has grease floating at the top of the bottle…when thawed out. We know that there is some kind of organic material…that is not vegetable. It appears that there is some kind of mineral oil as an ingredient."

He closed his eyes and grunted. "What I am wondering… have you found out anything significant yet?"

Thongola hung her head. She looked up and smiled. "We don't know what is or is not significant at this time. The only thing that we have figured out, so far, is that none of the four are toxic. Other than that…we don't know whether you drink them or rub them…on a certain part of your body."

Wilfadge sighed. "Would it help if you had more people working on it?"

Thongola shook her head. "We've solicited suggestions from all of the other doctors. There have been several suggestions and we've tried them all. So far…this stuff has been as elusive to us…as *Tuzine* is…to everyone else."

Wilfadge nodded. "Would it help…if we had someone… there on Satroco Isle watching…as they mix and brew this stuff?"

The two women both perked up.

"Oh…yes, Sir," said Thongola. "That'd be a great help."

He nodded. "Okay, we'll have to keep someone there, waiting and watching…"

Hoonsi interrupted. "The best thing to do would be to call us…when they start mixing and brewing. Our spies might not be able to figure out what's going on. If we are notified…we could Jump straight there and…we could do the watching…and probably figure it out a lot faster and easier."

Wilfadge nodded. He cleared his throat. "Then that's the

way we'll do it…when we find them mixing it…whatever *it* is."

The day of the Teltermak attack came. Natsa was standing outside of the giant freezer looking around at all of the members of Team Maka-Or. "Are we ready?"

Coycoy snarled. "Ready to start our thieving ways again."

Kooami joined her in her anger. "Seems like the only thing that we've ever produced is the *Tuzine*. Everything else…we've stolen from somebody else."

Natsa nodded. "Yes, but in each case, it seems that it wasn't really our fault for starting any fights…except that fiasco against the Axswain…when Nagasoom went crazy."

Coycoy huffed. "I wish I could forget that."

"Well you can't," scolded Natsa. "NOW…as I said before: Is everybody ready?"

"Yes," said Kooami. "We all have those coolers. We're going to put as many of the elixir bottles into each one – color coded of course – and Jump the whole mess back to the gorge."

"Good," said Natsa. "Does anybody have any questions?"

Voolala raised her hand. "Why don't we get started now?"

Natsa shook her head. "No, the Command Staff was adamant that we wait until the attack starts. That way, all of the Maka-Or and the Yagalom-Ayin will have all of their attention on the Teltermak…and we should be able to get all of it out of here…

basically unnoticed."

Yondi scoffed. "I can't believe that we're actually looking forward to a Teltermak attack."

There was a loud round of laughter over that comment.

Team 7016 was outside looking to the south, yawning while waiting for the sighting of massive amounts of the Teltermak kites.

Shortly after the sun came up Kiyalee sighed. "Finally… there they are."

Soolchakan looked up. "Where…oh…there they are."

"Sure is a lot of them," said Bonarain.

Soolchakan sent the mental communication to Natsa. Then he turned to his Team. "We've been allowed to go home. They're grateful for all of the information that we found out for them."

Kiyalee looked at him. "Home? Are we going home…to Owlam or the gorge?"

Bonarain looked thoughtful. "Where do we have that fresh batch of kwatha stored?"

"In the gorge," said Chyning.

Soolchakan smiled. "Home to the gorge…some hot kwatha…and a hot bath."

6

No sooner had Team 7016 arrived at their gorge home, a summons came from the Command Staff. They all hung their heads in exasperation.

Bonarain huffed. "What did we do now?"

Kiyalee gave Bonarain a nasty look. "Maybe they want you to teach somebody something else."

"If they do," said Chyning. "I'm not sticking around there again. I'm coming directly back here and taking a bath."

Soolchakan grunted. "Shut up, the lot of you! Let's go find out what they want so we can get it over with."

They Jumped to the hall where they would meet the Commanders.

Officer Grade 4, Akantini was there to meet them. She smiled at them. "Welcome to Headquarters." She frowned a little. "When was the last time…any of you took a bath?"

Soolchakan spoke slowly through his teeth. "We were all about to bathe when all of a sudden we had to come here. Any more stupid questions?"

She wrinkled her nose and cleared her throat. "This way." She led them to the conference room. She walked to the doorway. "Team 7016 is here, Sir."

Wilfadge called for them to enter. The four of them filed into the room all still wondering what was going on.

Soolchakan closed his eyes. All of the Command Staff was here. The Supreme Officer, all four Sector Commanders and the four Vice Commanders as well. This did not look good.

Wilfadge looked down at a paper then back up. "In this report...you say that you wandered around that Teltermak encampment for...three days...before listening to that briefing." He shook his head and put the paper down. "Why didn't you just do some mind reading? Wouldn't that have saved a lot of time?"

All three looked directly at Bonarain. She gave each one of them a dirty look and then turned to Wilfadge with a blank face. "Sir, we found out...we cannot read the minds of the Teltermak."

Wilfadge raised his eyebrows. "Why not?"

"I don't know, Sir. We tried to read their minds...but nothing came through."

Teelila looked as if she had a bad taste in her mouth. "How is that possible?"

Bonarain huffed. "I don't know, Sir," she said through her teeth. "I just know that we could not read anything in *their* rotten little skulls. I don't know whether their skulls are made of granite or their brain is made of granite, I just know that no matter what we did, we *could not* read their minds."

"That's astounding," said Hoynama. "If we can't read their minds…I wonder if the Cacktash could."

"I doubt it, Sir," said Bonarain. "I think that the main reason the Cacktash allied with the Teltermak, was to keep an eye on them. If you can read other minds…but not the Teltermak, you would want to get close and watch them."

Wilfadge looked around the table smiling. "Can anyone else think of a better reason?"

There were several grunts and huffs, however, no one could come up with a better reason.

Hadathoo leaned forward. "Did you get anything from reading the minds of the Maka-Or or the Yagalom-Ayin?"

Soolchakan smiled. "Sir, we weren't part of that group. We struck out on our own and that's how we found the Teltermak."

Wilfadge nodded. "All right, we've found out something about the Teltermak. Nothing can penetrate their thick heads."

"Except a pulse pistol or a sledgehammer," said Antrong.

After the laughing subsided, Wilfadge wiped his eyes. "Did you find out anything about the Axswain?"

Soolchakan shook his head. "The Teltermak Commander talked about the Axswain, but we never saw any of them in the Teltermak camp."

"Pity," said Wilfadge. "At least we have some idea of where they might be located…somewhere in the western part of Lusaratia." He looked around the table. "Does anyone have any more questions for this Team?"

Ahandi clicked her tongue. "Did you find out anything about those elixirs?"

Soolchakan shook his head. "Again, Sir, we weren't part of that group."

Wilfadge nodded. "Very good then...dismissed."

Team 7016 was back in their gorge home.

Soolchakan scratched his chin. "You women go ahead and get bathed. I'll heat up the kwatha."

The three women did not argue. They all headed for a bathtub.

Officer Leader, Natsa walked into the Command Staff conference room. She smiled. "Good day, Sirs."

Everyone nodded to her.

Wilfadge clicked his fingernails on the table, licked his lips and looked up. "Is there anything that you can tell us...about these *chokwad* elixirs? I'm getting so tired of hearing nothing... except...I don't know."

Natsa smiled and sighed. "We did find the recipes for the elixirs. Unfortunately, the information is sadly...incomplete. I did take this information to Doctor Thongola along with some of the captured elixirs. She got together with a couple of other doctors and...I think you need to talk to them, Sir."

Wilfadge nodded. He made a mental call to Thongola, telling her to bring which ever colleagues were assisting her in examining the elixirs.

Moments later Akantini led three women and a man into the conference room. The three women were introduced as Doctors Thongola, Hoonsi and Initaya. The man was Doctor Wasoosk.

Wilfadge smiled. "What can you tell us about these infernal things?"

Thongola smiled back. "We've learned a few things... however, even though it has answered some questions...it has raised a few more."

There were several groans from the Staff.

Thongola continued. "I've been looking more closely at the *red* bottles. The recipe that our spies found...well...step one says: Remove any excess matter from the prime and do not remove the blood."

Teelila looked up. "Prime...what?"

Thongola sighed. "I don't know, Sir. It's just...what... ever the prime ingredient is."

Teelila sighed. "Continue please."

"Yes, Sir. Step two: Run the prime through the meat grinder. Step three: Thoroughly mix the ground meat with... ingredient 2."

Ahandi looked a little sick. "Ingredient...2?"

"Yes, Sir…and that we can identify."

All of the Staff looked hopeful.

Thongola smiled. "I don't know what it means, but, ingredient 2 is actually the heart of the Chookon fish…ground up and mixed with a vegetable oil."

Dwalooa frowned. "What does this oil do…other than preserve?"

"That's all it does, Sir. It's not toxic…nor does it do you any good…as far as nutrition is concerned. It just goes through you. Some people…it softens their stool…but other than that…it is useless."

"Okay," said Wilfadge. "Step…4?"

"Yes, Sir. Step 4: Pour the mixture into a square plate and refrigerate it until it turns to a gelatin. After it is gelatinous, you cut it into sixteen equal sized squares. You take one square and mix it with ingredients 3, 4, and 5." She chuckled. "Number 3 is the ground up heart of a crustacean called a Nasask. Number 4 is the ground up heart of a Lindisi Eel. Number 5 is the ground up heart of a Zazakimi fish."

Wilfadge sat there dull-eyed. "You are sure…of these ingredients?"

"There is no secret to these, Sir. The Teltermak allowed their…friends to do the butchering of the sea creatures in order to obtain what they needed for the elixir." She waited for another question. She heard none so she continued. "You put all of these ingredients into a blender along with…" She cleared her throat.

"...five *kosik*...of pure water."

Wilfadge raised his eyebrows. "*Kosik*?"

"Yes, Sir...I think it is some kind of...Maka-Or measurement. We know all of the Teltermak measurements...and until I saw this recipe...I never heard of that word. I don't think that it is very much...because when you look at the bottle...the mixture does not take up very much space. A *kosik*...is probably measured with a small spoon...I mean...if you have five *kosik* mixed with five other ingredients...and all of it fits into this little bottle..." She held up one of the elixir bottles. "...it can't be very much."

Wilfadge nodded. "Continue."

"You pour all of this into a blender and liquefy it." She sighed. "Are you ready for some more strange words?" She smiled. "You then bake the mixture...in an oven for...nine *skays*...at a temperature of...150...*teelow*."

All of the Staff leaned back and looked around or at the ceiling.

"*Kosik, skay* and *teelow*," said Wilfadge. "Are these more...Maka-Or measurements?"

"Obviously, Sir." She sighed again. "You remove it from the oven and allow it to cool for...fifteen...*skays*. You put this in a blender again and liquefy it. You pour the mixture into the bottle and freeze it." She shook her head. "The last step states: When you sell the product, make sure that the customer knows that they have to heat it up to room temperature and consume the entire contents of the bottle."

Hadathoo looked around at the other Staff members. He then turned to Thongola. "Do you have any idea…what it does… to you or for you?"

Thongola sighed. "None of us have had the courage to try it."

Wilfadge hung his head. "Next."

Doctor Wasoosk stood up. "Thank you, Sir. I have been looking at the recipe for the contents of the brown bottles. This one starts out the same as the red. Step one: Remove any excess matter from the prime. Again…we have no idea what the prime is. Next you run it through a meat grinder. The next step is to mix it with ingredient 2. Ingredient 2 is from the same Chookon fish, however this time, it's the liver. You place both together in a blender and liquefy. Add three…*kosik*…of pure water and liquefy again. You refrigerate it for one day. The next day you add ingredients number 3 and 4. 3 is the liver of the Nasask crab and 4 is the liver of the Zazakimi fish. You liquefy this mixture as well. Next step is to place it in a flat plate and bake if for… fifteen *skays*…at a temperature of 100 *teelow*. Remove it from the oven, liquefy it again and pour this mixture into a brown bottle… and freeze it. The last step, just like the red bottle, you make sure that you tell the customer to heat it up to room temperature and consume the entire contents of the bottle." He looked at each of the members of the Staff. "This one, just like the red bottle, no one has had the courage to drink this stuff either."

Wilfadge nodded. "And there is nothing anywhere…in

writing that describes what it is or does?"

Wasoosk shook his head sadly. "No, Sir…nothing."

Wilfadge sighed. "Next."

"Sirs, I am Doctor Initaya. I've been working with the yellow bottles. This one is just as enigmatic as the other two. The first step is to remove any excess matter from the prime. You then run it through a meat grinder, and add four each of ingredient 2 as you grind it. Ingredient 2 goes back to the Chookon fish…only this time…it's the brain. You then grind up three of ingredient 3 – which is the brain of the Nasask crab – and stir it into the mixture. You then grind up three of ingredient 4 – which is the brain of the Lindisi eel – and six of ingredient 5 – which is the brain of the Zazakimi fish. You add this to the first mixture. You pour all of this into a blender, add three *kosik* of pure water and liquefy in the blender. You place all of this into a small pot and cook it on the stove top until it boils. You pour this into a yellow bottle… and freeze it. Just like the other two, you make sure that the customer knows that they have to heat it up to room temperature and consume the entire contents of the bottle."

Wilfadge grumbled at them. "And no one has had the courage to try it."

"No, Sir…no one."

He looked at the last of the three women. "I suppose that we're going to hear the exact same thing on this white bottle?"

Doctor Hoonsi stood up and had a nervous smile on her face. "Well…not exactly, Sir. The contents of the white bottle…

very different and…the mixing is very different as well."

Teelila rolled her eyes. "Oh my, we get to hear something new and exciting," she said sarcastically.

Hoonsi gave Teelila a dirty look and cleared her throat. "One of the differences that we noticed…first…the white bottles are marked. The markings show…male and female."

Wilfadge raised his eyebrows. "A…different mixture… for the genders?"

"Yes, Sir. This one also starts out with the step of removing any excess matter from the prime. Step 2…says that you carefully peel off the outer skin and remove all of the… *bulbous* glands. You then run the glands through…the *fine* meat grinder. You then thoroughly mix the meat with…four *kosik* of…ingredient 2." She closed her eyes and took a deep breath. "According to the instructions…the way you obtain ingredient 2, you…scare a…Mofallak Eel." She opened her eyes. "It states that…when you scare this eel…it will secrete a brown slime…as a defense against predators." She looked off to the side and took several deep breaths. She turned back to the Staff. "Use a small fishnet and scoop out the slime. You measure out four *kosik* of the slime and then seven *kosik* of pure water, put it all in a blender and liquefy. This mixture is poured into the appropriate gender-marked container…and frozen. On this one, you tell the customer to thaw it out before consuming the entire content. No one has tried it…yet…so we don't know the…affect…or consequences."

Shyshee was sitting there horrified. "EEL SLIME? You mix eel slime into this…*h'oolyach*?"

Hoynama was not pleased either. "And someone is supposed to...drink that...goo?"

Hoonsi nodded. "Yes, that seems to be the plan."

Ahandi looked like she was going to be sick. "You said that this...eel gives off...that slime when...scared. How does... giving off a bunch of slime help the eel?"

Hoonsi gave her a wan smile. "When it gives off the slime, it then flees. If a larger predator fish follows...well...fish breathe by opening their mouths and sucking in water...to wash it over their gills. If the slime gets caught up in the gills then...it would be like us having a...chunk of food go down the windpipe. If the fish cannot clear the slime out of the gills...it dies."

"I thought you said that the stuff is not toxic," said Hadathoo.

Hoonsi huffed. "The slime is *not* toxic...it...is more of a clog."

Wilfadge leaned his head back. "I'm even afraid to ask for volunteers...with this stuff." He looked at the doctors. "Some of it has fish and crab guts...and brains...one has...eel slime...and... you're supposed to...consume each one of those messes?"

All four doctors nodded.

Hadathoo looked at them in a deadpan manner. "And we still have no idea what the prime is...for any of the four...messes?"

Thongola shook her head. "We haven't been able to isolate it at all. We've tried to identify...the ingredients that we know and use some process of elimination...but so far nothing has been successful."

Wilfadge nodded. "Thank you…keep on trying…it can't hurt."

All four doctors nodded, smiled and vanished.

Wilfadge cleared his throat. "Officer Leader, Natsa, we still need to talk to you."

Natsa stood up with a smile. "Yes, Sir."

He blew his breath out. "How goes the battle…between the Maka-Or and the Teltermak?"

Natsa closed her eyes and grunted. She opened her eyes. "Sir, it is a…*horrible* blood bath. When the Teltermak attacked, the Maka-Or and the Yagalom-Ayin all headed for the freezers to defend the elixirs. When they found all of the bottles gone…they thought that the war was a punishment for something the Teltermak had already obtained. The Maka-Or declared something that they call…an 'eternal blood feud'…between them…and the Teltermak. What this means…the Maka-Or are saying that…the only way that you can stop us from killing all of you…you have to kill all of us. It's a fight that will not end until one race is exterminated."

Hadathoo chuckled. "Should we choose a side?"

Ahandi spoke up. "Do the Yagalom-Ayin feel the same way?"

Natsa shook her head. "I don't think so, Sir. They are… however…still fighting alongside the Maka-Or. It appears that the Teltermak have the strength of numbers, but…the two allies are putting up a fierce battle."

Dwalooa leaned forward. "Any word on the Axswain?"

Natsa shook her head. "They're still as elusive as ever. We thought we had a few good leads...but...nothing. We still have no idea where they are."

Antrong started laughing. He looked at all of the other faces as he snickered. "Maybe we should send that Team 7016 back out there to look for the Axswain. They're the ones who stumbled onto the Teltermak camps. Maybe they can foul up... again...and find the Axswain."

Wilfadge sighed. "That may not be such a bad idea."

Teelila huffed. "The last time they were here...they stunk badly. You think maybe they've taken a bath...in the last six days?"

"I hope so," said Wilfadge. He leaned back and mentally summoned Team 7016 to the conference room.

Moments later, Akantini led Team 7016 into the room. All four members of the Team were holding steaming hot mugs full of kwatha...and looking a little upset.

Hoynama cleared her throat. "Why didn't you leave the kwatha behind?"

Soolchakan gave her a dirty look. "It was ready, I'm hungry, I brought it with me. I'm not going to let it cool down, I'm going to eat it while it's hot...Sir."

Chyning took a spoon and started eating the big lumps

from her mug.

Kiyalee did some rather loud slurping from her mug.

Wilfadge smiled. "You've had a little while to rest. We would appreciate it if you would go back to Lusaratia and see if you can find…any more Teltermak bases or…see if you can find where the Axswain are hiding. We've had two Teams going all over the western part of Lusaratia and they've found nothing. Maybe… with your luck, you can find…something…of the Axswain…or other Teltermak bases."

Soolchakan had spooned a large lump out of his mug and was chewing on it. "Do you mind if we finish our kwatha first?"

Wilfadge chuckled. "Not at all…dismissed."

Team 7016 Jumped back to their abode in the gorge.

Chyning plopped down in a chair and continued spooning for lumps.

Kiyalee sighed. "I'm going to go take another bath."

Bonarain scoffed. "You just took one…why again…so soon?"

"Because I can…right now," said Kiyalee with a snarl.

Soolchakan headed for a tub as well. "A bath sounds good…right now."

Bonarain hollered at Soolchakan before he left the room. "Where are we going to start our search?"

Soolchakan stopped and shrugged. "I guess we'll start at

that camp…that was just southeast of Shashkanit."

Bonarain sat down and started spooning for lumps. "Good a place as any." She shook her head.

Team 7016 stood in the middle of the Teltermak encampment. There seemed to be a flurry of activity as they saw more kites coming in from the north that were landing, the crews were getting something to eat, they had a quick nap and then on to the battle front on Satroco Isle.

Kiyalee grunted. "So where are we supposed to start? They send these people to Satroco to reinforce their flying legions there…what've we got here?"

Bonarain watched another fifty kites come in for landing. "Why don't we try to find out where those people are coming from? There's a huge number of them coming in…from somewhere."

Chyning laughed out loud. "Those people have already departed from whence they came…how are we supposed to turn the clock back and watch where they took off from?"

Soolchakan was busy checking his small handheld pad.

Bonarain bumped him. "Hey, are you listening to us…in trying to figure out where these fliers are coming from?"

He glared at her. "No, I'm trying to figure out something from what THEY said…as far as where they came from. Listening to you is getting us nowhere…listening to them…might help." He went back to his pad.

Chyning giggled. "What...figuring out that two plus two equals four...how's that going to help us?"

He closed his eyes and shook his head. He looked up at Chyning. "The information isn't in here. I have to go back to the gorge." With that he vanished.

The three women all three stood there gawking.

"He went back," said Bonarain.

"Yeah," said Kiyalee. "If he's gone back...so am I." She vanished.

Bonarain and Chyning looked at each other and both shrugged. Then they vanished.

All four of Team 7016 was back at the gorge. The three women saw Soolchakan busily entering something into the computer. He had already opened up the stolen Algothon archives and was in the geography section.

Bonarain looked over his shoulder. "What are we looking for?"

Soolchakan did not look up. He kept on typing. "I heard one of the Teltermaks call himself...some high rank from...'Team Drib'."

Kiyalee looked puzzled. "What is...Drib?"

The screen on the computer changed.

"There it is," said Soolchakan. "Drib Isle." He looked back at the women. "That Teltermak came from another camp on

Drib Isle. That's why they're so hard to find…they're scattered. I also heard another one of them say that he was part of 'Team Zorab'. There's another island in that chain…called Zorab Isle."

Bonarain got interested now. "Where?"

"It's another island chain," said Soolchakan. "Only this one is north of the Lusaratia continent. It's the…uh…Gardigoecia chain. There're eight main islands and several hundred insignificant islands. I think the Teltermak are putting bases all over these island chains. That way, if someone finds one of their bases…and just happens to massacre them…they still have all kinds of assets in other places."

Bonarain blew her breath out. "So…on to Drib Isle."

"No," said Soolchakan. "Drib is in the middle. We start with the island that is closest to Lusaratia…Livel Isle."

They all checked their pads for the landmark on Livel Isle.

Soolchakan looked up. "Ready?"

The three women nodded and all four of them Jumped to Livel.

Four days of searching Livel came up with nothing other than an abandoned camp. It appeared that this had been a very active base, however, because of the Maka-Or battle, all personnel from this base had gone to join the fight. No families were left behinds. They put a few new landmarks into their pads for this location and then Jumped to Iratam Isle which was the next island heading north. On Iratam, they found a base that was not quite abandoned. Here they found a few families that were taking care of a lot of young Teltermak. They landmarked this area and headed to the next island in the line: Drib Isle. Once again they found a base that seemed to be completely abandoned.

"That must be some nasty war going on with those Maka-Or," said Kiyalee. "These *doovofts* have departed...without leaving anyone behind."

Bonarain shook her head. "We'll probably find out... soon...who won or lost."

Kiyalee snickered. "Should we care?"

Soolchakan sighed. "Has everyone landmarked this place?"

The three women nodded.

He smiled. "Onward to the north...the next island is Kaha Isle."

Kaha was no different than Drib. Next they went to Jinzem Isle and found the same thing.

"This is getting very boring," said Chyning.

"I know," said Soolchakan. "They still want us to keep looking."

Kiyalee sighed. "What's next?"

Bonarain looked at her pad and shook her head. "Balikibodon Isle."

Chyning snarled. "Who named these places?"

"These names probably go back for more millennium than we could even comprehend," said Soolchakan. "Their history was lost a long time ago…otherwise we'd know…or maybe find something in the Algothon archives."

They Jumped to Balikibodon. After a two day search, they stood there amazed.

"We found them," said Soolchakan.

"I don't understand," said Chyning.

Bonarain frowned at her. "Don't understand…what?"

Chyning shook her head. "Of the eight main islands in this chain…this one is the smallest. Why would they…settle…on the smallest?"

Soolchakan scoffed. "The Axswain, except for the name of their city, like a lot of syllables. Of all of the islands in this chain, this one has the longest name."

"That's dumb," said Kiyalee. "I don't believe that."

Soolchakan gave her a dirty look. "Then why don't you go ask them?"

Kiyalee blushed and turned away muttering.

Bonarain looked around. "Well…we haven't found any Teltermak here. It seems that…though they both ran at the same time…they don't live together."

After sending a mental report to the Command Staff Soolchakan opened his eyes. "Only two more main islands to check."

Zorab Isle and Omahan Isle both turned out to be more abandoned Teltermak bases.

"I wonder why the Axswain base...is so small and...so few of them...compared to the Teltermak," said Bonarain.

"Good question," said Soolchakan. "Do you want to go ask them?"

"Not really."

"Okay," said Kiyalee. "We've looked at all of the main islands. All of the Heyyah were displaced...and the Teltermak own seven of these islands while the Axswain own one. Can we go back home and take a bath?"

"After we report all of our findings...good idea," said Soolchakan.

The plan to go back was short lived. The Command Staff asked them if they had made any attempt at reading the minds of the Axswain. The four of them stood there rather embarrassed and realized that they were going to have to go back and take a closer look at one of their long-time nemesis. With heavy hearts they headed back to Balikibodon to try reading some Axswain minds.

Soolchakan stared into the small compound. "Where does anybody suggest that we start?"

Bonarain snickered. "Let's see if we can figure out who the leader of this place is. Then...we see if there is any hierarchy."

"I don't think there'll be...any chain of command," said

Kiyalee. "They...are all just...living and...existing. I don't see any...weapons or...plans for any attacks. They're just...here."

Chyning snarled at her Team. "We're not going to figure out anything by sitting here guessing...let's go!"

Soolchakan pointed to a group of men. "I'll start with them. See if that is some kind of...council meeting."

Bonarain gave him a dirty look. "What makes you think that it's going to be the men in charge? This place could be run by the women."

Soolchakan closed his eyes and snarled to himself. "So you go listen to the women! You check the women, I'll check the men. Either way, we should find out something...eventually... hopefully...whoever is in charge and why."

Kiyalee giggled. "Yeah...like if *anyone* is in charge."

"Or if anyone cares," said Chyning.

"Pick up any information that we can get...meet back here at midday and compare notes and see if there's anything that sounds particularly interesting," said Soolchakan.

They all walked off in different directions. Not one of them wanted to really be here. These were still Axswain and some old prejudices die very slowly.

Team 7016 was standing in the Command Staff conference room, with all nine of the ranking personnel in attendance. Wilfadge called the meeting to order and Akantini was in there ready to record the proceedings.

Soolchakan smiled. "Sirs, we have found out that we most definitely are able to read the minds of the Axswain. Trying to control them to do something…or pick up a specific thought…is rather difficult, however, we can still get just about any piece of information that we want. I was surprised to find out…their total population is only 212. When we attacked them…in the gorge near Owlam and at their city wall, we killed many thousands. There were only twelve who were able to escape because they were in a meeting with the Teltermak…in the Teltermak city at the time. There were nine men and three women. This does *not* make a…very large gene pool…and they're rather nervous about procreation. Their main concern is…four or five generations… from now…what will their children be like?" He stopped and cleared his throat. They do have the original twelve…still alive. It seems that they have extended longevity…just like us…so they're able to give account of what used to exist in their city…to their young. Since these twelve were in the center of Teltermak…when the Teltermak decided to abandon their city, they have no idea of how they lost everyone in the city or that gorge outside of Owlam. They only know that every attempt at contacting anyone in the city or the gorge came up empty."

"That is all somewhat interesting," said Wilfadge. "Do you have anything that we can…use…in any way at all?"

Soolchakan looked at Bonarain. She smiled back and stepped forward.

She looked at the Staff. "We know a few more things

about those mysterious elixirs. The Axswain were waiting to buy some of the last batch…before we purloined all of it. They seem a little discouraged and despondent over the fact that there's a battle going on and…in reality they don't know that the stuff is missing. They're hoping that whoever wins this battle will still sell some of the elixirs to them."

"So they want to buy some of the elixirs," said Wilfadge. "Any particular reason why?"

She cleared her throat. "It seems that the red bottle contains some kind of cure all. Unlike *Tuzine*…it will cure *anything*. While *Tuzine* is a powerful antibiotic and will cure any known bacterium…whatever is in the red bottle cures anything and everything. They do know, according to the Teltermak…there is a drastic shortage of the prime ingredient. They don't know what the ingredient is…but they're certain that it is extremely rare."

Wilfadge growled. "Well if that isn't a load of *h'oolyach*! We now know what the stuff in the red bottle does…but we still don't know that *chokwad* prime ingredient."

"Yes, Sir," said Bonarain. "We also found out that the stuff in the brown bottle is a magical elixir of either life or youth. According to what we could glean from them, it seems to make one…either feel…or look…or maybe even *be* younger. They're very hopeful…in the possibility of obtaining some of the brown bottles."

Teelila scoffed. "An elixir that makes one younger? Where did they come up with that superstitious fiction?"

Kiyalee responded. "Sirs, it seems that they've observed

a few Heyyah drinking the stuff…and within half a day, that same individual was a lot more youthful looking. If someone pulled off some silly illusionist trick…they did a good job of convincing the Axswain…that it is true."

Hadathoo scoffed. "I suspect that we could…slip it to some… unsuspecting elderly Heyyah individual…and see if it works."

Dwalooa chuckled. "That could make things very interesting."

Wilfadge looked up at Bonarain. "Anything else?"

"Yes, Sir. The yellow bottle contains some kind of… intellect enhancement. According to what we heard, if you drink the yellow bottle, you can concentrate better, you can figure certain problems out faster and you are able to learn more things faster… and retain them."

Ahandi shook her head. "All that from eating ground up fish brains? It's once again that prime ingredient…that makes the difference."

Wilfadge looked up expectantly. "Anything about those… gender specific white bottles?"

All four of Team 7016 looked away from Wilfadge.

Soolchakan finally decided to act as the Team leader and take any flak that might come out of the situation. "We never heard one thing from any of those Axswain about the white bottles. No one mentioned…or even talked around…or thought about…the white bottle. That one is still as mysterious as ever."

Wilfadge looked at the rest of the Staff. "Why are all of

you looking so glum? We have new information. Okay, so we don't have all of the information...yet. I'm not going to sit here and pout over the fact that we don't have it all...I'm going to sit here and gloat over the fact that we found out *something*...about those bottles and their contents...and none of the Teltermak are any wiser that we know anything."

Hadathoo laughed. "You're right, Sir. Each little tidbit of information that we obtain is a positive. We still have a ways to go...but we're making progress."

Wilfadge stood up. "Team 7016, I'd like to thank you for the excellent work you've done. Very valuable information that...now, we'll have to decide what we're going to do with it." He scratched his chin. "The four of you have earned some time off for all of that work so go ahead and take about ten days rest for yourselves." He gave them a big smile. "Unless you have something else...you're dismissed."

All four of Team 7016 Jumped back to the home for some fresh kwatha.

Hoynama grunted. "I guess that was it."

Wilfadge sat down. "I like that idea...about slipping it to some Heyyah...without their knowledge of it. Don't let them know...that way, whatever we see happen...will be an honest manifestation of what that stuff does."

Antrong huffed. "So where do we go to find some lab rodents?"

"Algothon," said Shyshee with an evil look on her face.

Wilfadge chuckled. "Why not? All of what we've been through...because of them...I like that idea...very much. Start experimenting with their lives. Good idea. Contact Ota, as soon as possible, and start the experimentation."

Natsa stood in the conference room. "The war is over. The Maka-Or have been completely obliterated. The Yagalom-Ayin are down to some very low numbers. The Teltermak and the Yagalom-Ayin are now arguing over...where the elixirs are."

Wilfadge snickered. "I take it that there's lot of finger pointing going on?"

"Accusations are flying all over the place," said Natsa. "Oh...one thing that we noticed about the...Yagalom-Ayin... those...fangs of theirs. We watched some of the fighting and...they have...venom in those fangs. We saw them bite several Teltermak during hand-to-hand and...after being bitten, the Teltermak victim went into convulsions and died. After biting one of the Teltermak, the Yagalom-Ayin that did the biting didn't stick around to watch the death. He...or she...just went on to fight another Teltermak... with fangs at the ready."

All nine members of the Staff stared at her in shock for several moments.

Teelila cleared her throat. "That...is good to know...in advance...about anyone who could...possibly be an enemy."

Dwalooa shook her head. "Some of these...characteristics that've cropped up are...WOW!" She leaned back in her chair still shaking her head.

Hadathoo clicked his tongue. "In case we have to face off against these Yagalom-Ayin…I suggest that…we avoid any…face to face. I don't like the possible results."

Ahandi looked at Wilfadge. "What do you suggest that we do now…in regards to the locations of the Teltermak?"

Wilfadge looked confused. "What do you mean?"

Ahandi shrugged. "Now that the battles are over…I don't think that they're going to need all of their military power on Satroco Isle. Many of them are going to redeploy back to their particular home base."

He still looked confused. "So?"

She scoffed. "So send someone to each of those island bases…and maybe we can get some accurate numbers in regards to how many Teltermak we may have to face off against…if that should ever arise again."

Shyshee chuckled. "Team 7016 is the most familiar with the locations. Why don't we send them?"

Wilfadge smiled. "Wonderful suggestion. Whoever their Sector Commander is, go ahead and inform them immediately. Anything else?"

"Yes," said Hadathoo. "Have they gone back to… analyzing the *Tuzine*?"

Natsa nodded sadly. "When they did all of their fighting… the battle never raged into the analysis facility. All of the fighting was outside or in the elixir manufacturing plant. Almost immediately after the battle was over, there were Yagalom-Ayin… and some of the Teltermak who went back to the analysis."

Soolchakan was sitting in a bathtub cleaning the back of his neck when he received the marching orders. He sighed. "I'm beginning to hate being in the military," he muttered. He finished his bath, dried off, got dressed – in uniform - and headed down to the main room. As soon as he walked in all three women looked up. When they saw him in uniform they all three groaned and hung their heads.

Bonarain was the first to look up. "Now what?"

He gave them a half-hearted smile. "It seems that the battle between those Makas and the Teltas is over."

Kiyalee looked suspicious. "So?"

He sighed. "They want us to go back to the home bases of the flying teams and do some head counts."

Chyning flopped back in her chair. "Do they want us to count the Axswain again?"

He chuckled. "I doubt that, but, they do want a head count on the Teltermak at each location…or at least a good estimate of their numbers."

Bonarain sighed. "So back to Satroco Isle."

"No," he said. "If Officer Leader, Natsa and twelve Teams can't handle *that* job there on Satroco, I'll put in for her job…and rank."

"I'm going to take another bath before we go," said Chyning.

Bonarain huffed. "We're supposed to get going…you don't have time for another bath right now."

Chyning gave Bonarain a dull look. "It's going to take some time for all of the Teltermak teams to redeploy. Then we have to count them. It's not like all of the counts will be done in one or two days."

"Good point," said Kiyalee. "I'm taking a bath too."

Bonarain stood there in thought for a few moments. She shrugged and headed upstairs, unbuttoning her shirt.

Soolchakan shrugged. He walked into the kitchen. He turned the stove on and pulled a large container of freshly chopped kwatha out of the refrigerator. He filled a pot with water and put the kwatha in the pot. By the time the three women were finished bathing, the mixture was ready for the table. All four of them enjoyed another meal of kwatha while planning out where they were going to go first. They determined that it could be rather lengthy depending on which Teltermak team deployed back first to where. That thought was rather discouraging, however, it was decided that since the kites could not really fly at night, for lack of being able to see a lot of landmarks, they would all Jump back to the gorge at night (at Lusaratia) and do their counting during the days. They took their time deciding on their full plan of attack.

"This stinks," said Natsa.

Coycoy snickered. "Which part?"

"No one is working the processing plant...for the elixirs."

"Apparently they can't find any of that...prime ingredient right now."

Both women sat there trying to think of what it could possibly be.

Coycoy sighed. "I hope that our doctors can get...some kind of better results than what these *bimyocks* are getting."

Natsa simply grunted.

7

Forty-one days after starting the counts, Team 7016 was finally finished. Soolchakan went to the Staff conference room by himself and presented the report to the Command Staff. He looked around at each one of them as they all sat there looking it over. After several moments of not hearing anything but some breathing he Jumped back to the home in the gorge.

He saw that all three women were at a table eating some kwatha. They all had damp hair and were wearing bathrobes. He smiled. They are finished bathing so now it was his turn. He headed to his room to change. No sooner did he start the water running in the bathtub, he received a mental summons from Wilfadge – for the entire Team to show up at Headquarters. He growled to himself and relayed the message to the women.

Team 7016 showed up at Headquarters, all looking a little upset and once again each one holding a steaming hot mug of kwatha.

Dwalooa gave the Team a disgusted look. "Do you all get a mug of kwatha every time we call you?"

"No, Sir," said Soolchakan dryly. "It seems that we're eating every time you people call us."

Wilfadge waved his hand at Dwalooa. "Leave it alone, they can have their kwatha and still talk." He picked up the main page of the report. "So according to this, you found twelve more Teltermak bases on the continent itself."

"Yes, Sir," said Soolchakan without any emotion.

Wilfadge nodded and stroked his chin. "Each base ranges from…6,000 to 30,000." He nodded. "What's this annotation here…you say that there are…about 22,000 Teltermak on Kaha Isle and then there's this annotation of…minus 1." He looked up confused. "What's with the minus 1?"

Chyning grimaced and her face turned bright red. She opened her left eye and noticed that everyone in the room was looking directly at her – including the other members of her Team. She looked off to her right and her face appeared to glow an even deeper red. She scowled at her Teammates.

Soolchakan loudly and purposefully cleared his throat. "Officer Grade 7, Chyning, the Supreme Officer wants a response."

Chyning quickly spooned a large lump out of her mug and popped it into her mouth. A sudden look of shock and pain came across her face as she realized that the lump was extremely hot and was scalding the inside of her mouth. She opened her mouth wide and tried blowing air in and out rapidly to cool it off. When that was unsuccessful she spit the lump back into her mug and had her hand over her mouth…with her eyes closed. She once again did a one-eyed look-see to check out the situation. All of the people at the conference table were leaning forward and still staring intently at her. The rest of her Team were standing around her with accusing looks on their faces. She sighed, dropped her shoulders and hung her head. "He deserved it."

Wilfadge started drumming his fingers on the table. "Who deserved what?"

She raised her head up a little, looking like a hurt child. "He peed on me!"

Wilfadge looked as if he had been slapped. He closed his eyes and shook his head. "Somebody had better start explaining... and don't start in the middle...start at the beginning so that we are all up to date."

Bonarain shook her head. "It was near midday. It was hot and we had been counting in a certain area, trying to keep track of who was moving where. We all decided to take a break." She looked down her nose at Chyning. "And..."

Chyning looked back as if she were confused. "Go on, you're doing fine."

Bonarain leaned closer to Chyning with her eyes widening as if in accusation of something.

Chyning sighed. "I went...and sat in the shade...under a tree. Some Teltermak *bimyock*...landed his kite...and came over to the...same tree." She sniffed and gave each one of her Teammates a dirty look. "He...opened his pants...and he...started peeing on me."

Ahandi scoffed. "Weren't you in...Spy dimension?"

"We were," said Soolchakan.

Ahandi put her hand to her forehead. "So why didn't you just move?"

Chyning huffed. "I did...I...got up...and..."

Kiyalee interjected. "And kicked the *h'oolyach* out of him." She turned away snickering.

Wilfadge sighed. "I may be sorry for asking this...but... where did you kick him?" He nervously cleared his throat.

Soolchakan shook his head and sighed. "Where do you *think*?!"

Wilfadge closed his eyes and groaned. "So...you... *neutered* him...with a kick. I remember....Nagasoom having those...contests...and if I remember correctly...Team 7016 was... never defeated."

Teelila looked up at the ceiling. "And we heard of one of the Team...who had a broken arm...and was able to use some pretty nasty kicks...to defeat her opponents."

Hadathoo was having a terrible time trying to not laugh. Till lost that battle completely and nearly got others to start laughing as well.

Wilfadge looked at the two men with some disdain. "So what was the final outcome...of the...kick?"

Chyning shrugged and looked around trying to make no eye contact with anyone. "He...got this...funny look...on his face...grabbed his...crotch...and...fell down."

Bonarain sighed. "A few moments later he was dead."

She turned to face the Staff. "Some Teltermak doctor took a look at him and, fortunately, did not do an autopsy. He determined that the man had…suffered some kind of fatal cardiac…episode from…too much exertion."

Wilfadge closed his eyes and sighed. "So you got away with it."

"Yes, Sir," said Chyning cheerfully.

Shyshee looked back at the paper. "If that's the case…who made the annotation on the report?"

Kiyalee turned away sniggering with a hand over her mouth.

Shyshee rolled her eyes. "Uh-huh!"

Wilfadge grunted. "In the future…if you're going to…do something like that…or you make an annotation like that…please supply some narrative or instruction…so we don't have to have another…episode…like this."

Soolchakan smiled at Wilfadge. "Yes, Sir."

Wilfadge shook his head. "If there are no other…strange or…outside or…extracurricular stories to tell…Team 7016… you're dismissed."

Team 7016 all vanished. All nine of people at the table – along with several of their Aides – broke down into gales of laughter that lasted several moments before anyone could regain any of their composure and return to reading the report.

Finally Wilfadge held up his hands. "That's enough of

that. I know that every now and then we all need a good giggle and…we got a good strong one there. Back to business! Now, I think…since they found all of these other Teltermak camps, we're going to have to give Natsa a lot more Teams. We need to keep an eye on those people."

"I don't think we need to panic yet," said Ahandi. "Let's just have Natsa determine which camp is the High Command camp and…then see if they plan on doing any conquering. If they're satisfied to stay there…and leave us alone…then why don't we leave them alone for a while?"

"Good point," said Dwalooa. "We might end up spreading ourselves too thin if we try to keep a lookout on all of them."

Wilfadge pondered for several moments. "Let's go ahead and give her a few Teams…initially. Find that Command camp while keeping a close watch on the manufacturing plant."

Hadathoo frowned. "Don't we have eight partial Teams?"

"Yes," said Wilfadge.

Hadathoo shrugged. "Why don't we send those Teams to Satroco Isle and keep an eye on the two plants while Natsa does the searching?"

"I guess we can do that," said Wilfadge. He turned to his Aide. "Akantini, call those Teams up and give them the details."

"Yes, Sir," said Akantini.

Back at the gorge home, Soolchakan snickered as he walked into the main room on the first floor. "I just got a mental call from Officer Grade 4, Zayzay of Team 4331. She said that they're headed for Satroco Isle and they wanted a heads up on what they would be looking at."

Bonarain chuckled. "I got a call like that as well. Only I got it from Officer, Vinsa of Team 5091 and Officer, Imjatsa of Team 5421."

Kiyalee frowned. "So did I…get a call, I mean. The one who called me was Officer Grade 4, Shyshina of Team 4850."

Chyning was looking around rather puzzled. "They're sure sending a lot of Teams there. I got a call from Officer Grade 5, Oymami of Team 5709. How many people are they sending to keep an eye on those…Yagalom-Ayin?"

Soolchakan shrugged. "Who knows what the higher ups are thinking? Maybe they…" He shook his head. "I don't know." He looked around. "I'm going upstairs to beat the *h'oolyach* out of a practice dummy."

Bonarain stood up growling. She closed her eyes tightly.

Kiyalee backed away from Bonarain cautiously. "What… is the matter?"

Bonarain finally opened her eyes and looked at the rest of her Team angrily. "They want me to go to Satroco Isle and train some of those people in…how to watch the Yagalom-Ayin do their testing of the *Tuzine*."

Soolchakan scoffed. "Why don't you tell them to send the students *here*? We'll set up a classroom in the unoccupied home next door and the students can bring their own lunches."

Bonarain looked at Soolchakan in shock. She closed her eyes and did a few mental communications back to the Command Staff. She opened her eyes and grinned. "They bought it! They're going to send the students here and we have full run of the home next door." She giggled. "Thank you for that idea."

Soolchakan smiled and shrugged. "You're welcome."

Natsa looked at the list of the new people that were joining her – temporarily. "I don't know what they told you initially… but I don't need this many people…just sitting around here… watching those tables in the manufacturing plant…when no one is doing anything. I also don't need that many people keeping an eye on all of the ones that are testing the *Tuzine*. What I need is some people who can go out and do some scouting and see if we can find any more Teltermak camps."

Officer Grade 4, Zayzay gave Natsa a smile. "So…who goes and who stays?"

Natsa smiled back. "Since you're the ranking one of the eight Team Leaders…you get first choice."

Zayzay shrugged. "I'll stay and…watch the manufacturing plant. We'll go around among those people and see if we can find out…anything."

Natsa nodded. "Who is next in line?"

"Me," said Officer Grade 4, Vooskani. "I'm Team Leader of Team 4737."

"Okay," said Natsa. "You and two other Teams will stay in the *Tuzine* plant. Keep an eye on as many of them as you can and see if any of them have a breakthrough. If they do, see if you can foul the results...somehow." She smiled at the other four Teams. "You'll be joining us in searching out there for more Teltermak camps."

Oymami placed her fists on her hips emphatically. "Just how are we supposed to find them?"

Natsa smiled sweetly. "The same way that Team 7016 found them - look UP! Those Teltermak love flying in their kites... especially when the weather is good."

Oymami blushed and started doing a cursory scan of the sky. "I forgot about that *h'oolyach*."

Six days later Natsa received a mental communication. **"This is Officer Grade 4, Yeebtay, Team Leader of Team 5482. Can you hear me**?"

Natsa sighed. **"Yes, I hear you...what did you need**?"

"We found something that is...flying...but... they...are not using kites. They seem to have wings of their own."

Natsa stood there stunned for a few moments. **"Can you come and get me and...take me...wherever you are**?"

The next moment Yeebtay was standing in front of Natsa. "Are you ready?"

Natsa took her hand. "Yes, I am."

Yeebtay Jumped the two of them to an area that was almost three hundred kilotaja from Shashkanit. Natsa looked up and was totally amazed at what she saw. These people appeared to be (semi) normal Heyyah, with ebony skin, standing about six and one half taja in height, however, they had a set of wings with a tremendous wingspan.

Natsa looked at Yeebtay. "Have you attempted any… communication with these people?"

Yeebtay chuckled. "They live up in those cliffs. If we suddenly appeared up there…without flying in…what do you think they'd do…or say?"

Natsa looked back up, shaking her head. "Those wings… look like…"

"Yeah," said Yeebtay. "We did go up there…in Spy. Those wings are just like those tiny little flying mammals that we used to see at night around Owlam. The difference here is…they don't have wings that are covered with fur. They don't have feathers either. They're just…skin and bone…and they fly very well."

"Do we know what they call themselves?"

Yeebtay shook her head. "We're going to have to…figure out some way of contacting them…and see if they're friendly."

Natsa did some thinking. She decided that it would be best if she got some instruction from the Command Staff before doing anything rash. She did some mental correspondence with Wilfadge to inform him of the situation. A little while later, Master Officer, Ahandi was standing there trying to decide what would be the best way to contact these people.

Ahandi finally shook her head and gave up. She sent a mental communication to Bonarain and the rest of Team 7016. A little while later, Team 7016 was standing there (all with nasty looks on their faces) staring up at the strange winged people.

Soolchakan spat on the ground in disgust. "Did any of you people do any reconnaissance on the ground...before calling us?"

Ahandi blushed. "Uh...no...why do you ask?"

He pointed to a place at the bottom of the huge cliff area. "It looks like they have some kind of greeting area...you know... like the *Tuzine* trading area that we have...just outside of the city of Owlam." He shook his head and growled. "Do you need me to hold your helpless little hand while you go up there and try to talk to them?"

Ahandi turned even redder in the face. "NO!" She stood there with her teeth and eyes clenched tight. "Just wait here... until we determine whether or not they're friendly. If they are... friendly...then you can leave. If not...help us do some damage and try to get out of here...with as few casualties as possible."

Soolchakan shrugged and sat down. The rest of Team 7016 sat down with him.

Ahandi took a deep breath. She sent a mental communication to the rest of her Team 20. She called for them to join her in this isolated area on the Lusaratia continent. A few moments later, Officer Grade 5, Nashisi, Officer Grade 5, Kiykay and Officer Grade 6, Koolong joined her.

Koolong snarled as he looked at the cliff. He shook his head. "What's the possibility of us getting out of here alive?"

Nashisi gave him a dirty look. "Why are you being so pessimistic?"

He snarled. "I'm not pessimistic, I just don't like taking stupid chances."

Ahandi stomped her foot. "Stop that nonsense! We're going to attempt to communicate with these people...and...hopefully... we'll make a new ally...instead of seeing the Teltermak get new friends."

Koolong just shook his head and snarled.

Ahandi looked around. "We're going to go...about two kilotaja away from the cliff...and we're going to hop to Home... and then we're going to come here...in peace."

Koolong rolled his eyes. "Oh, joy, joy, joy," he said sarcastically.

Team 20 Jumped to a spot that was approximately two kilotaja away. Ahandi sighed and gave the order. All four of them hopped to Home and they started walking in the direction of the cliff.

Kiykay saw some shadows on the ground and looked up startled. "Look...they've already seen us."

"They don't mess around," said Nashisi.

Ahandi looked up at them. "They seem to be just... watching us. They don't look hostile."

"Yet," said Koolong bitterly.

Ahandi looked back at Koolong and snarled. "Shut up!"

They continued walking. The ones that were flying above did not come down any closer. They maintained their altitude and continued circling as more of the fliers joined the group. Both sides eyed each other nervously as the Team got closer to – what appeared to be - the greeting area.

They got within shouting distance and some of the fliers started landing. Team 20 could now see that they had some rather large projectile firearms and had no qualms about showing them.

Ahandi sent a mental note to her Team to make no form of hostile moves.

Koolong just snarled, looked at the fliers and smiled.

They also noticed that when the fliers landed they were able to fold their wings up against their bodies to a point where you could not even tell that they were there – other than an appearance as being somewhat hunchbacked. There were several of them who were landing on both sides of the Team and following them while keeping a close eye on them.

The greeting station was gaining a lot of other personnel as well. Many of them – unlike the ones who had been flying – had shirts on and the shirts appeared to be uniforms.

Nashisi had been the most adept, on this Team, at reading minds. She found that these people were rather suspicious as to where these four strangers had come from – without transportation. She sent a quick mental message to Ahandi and Wilfadge and pleaded for help.

Wilfadge sent out a message to all Owlamites everywhere, wondering if there was anyone who could get a vehicle from somewhere and get it (or them) to Lusaratia and help out with Team 20.

Kiyalee groaned as she heard and answered the message. Now she had to explain to Team 7016 just where she had obtained four trucks and why she had not told them of this multiple acquisition. After a quick explanation, Team 7016 was headed, once again, to Lusaratia (after taking a quick side trip to Owlam itself). This time, however, they had to Jump in approximately three kilotaja away from the cliff and then drive the four trucks up to the cliff area.

Ahandi had finally walked close enough to the station to do a nervous greeting. "I greet you…as a representative of the City-State of Owlam. I am Master Officer, Ahandi and these are my Aides."

A man walked slowly towards her, scrutinizing her as he approached. He folded his wings against his back. "I am Tenhonok, Brybron. I greet you in the name of all of the Kafal-Rooak…in friendliness…I hope."

Ahandi smiled sheepishly. "Is…Tenhonok…your name or…rank?"

He smiled. "Tenhonok is my rank…Brybron is my name."

She finally got close enough and held out her hand. "We definitely want it to be in friendship. We have seen enough of enemies…especially those…Teltermaks."

He frowned. "Are those the ones…who fly with false wings?"

Ahandi nodded. "Yes, they are…and they are…or at least have also been cannibals."

Brybron nodded. He reached out and the two shook hands. "I am wondering why…someone from Owlam…is this far from home…without transportation."

She chuckled nervously. "We left our vehicles a ways back. We decided that if we came in on foot it would appear more…peaceful."

Brybron frowned. "Risky…but it worked."

Ahandi looked back at Koolong. "Go ahead and call up the trucks."

Koolong was almost ready to panic. He did not have any radio of any sort on him. He reached into his pocket and found a small bottle of his favorite spice. He pulled it out and attempted to keep as much of the bottle hidden as he could. He put the bottle up to his mouth. "You may drive in now." He mentally sent out a desperate plea for any kind of truck at all. He was very relieved when he received a mental response from Soolchakan and was even more relieved when he heard the sound of truck engines.

Team 20 had to remain straight faced as they watched Soolchakan drive up in a red truck, Bonarain in a blue truck, Kiyalee in a yellow truck and Chyning in a green truck.

Brybron nodded. "I see that you've been trading with the city of Shashkanit for some new trucks...good choices."

Ahandi tried to hide her bewilderment. "Thank you, kind Sir."

He looked at some of the boxes in the back of the four trucks. "Since you're here on a peaceful mission and...there is only one thing that the people of Owlam are trading with...right now...is it possible that you have some *Tuzine*...to trade...while you're here?"

Soolchakan got out of his truck smiling. He opened up one of the boxes in the back of his truck and pulled out a bottle of the antibiotic. "Of course, Sir. It is the best peace offering that we have."

Ahandi breathed a deep sigh of relief when she saw the bottle. She turned back to Brybron with a big smile.

They spent the next few days getting to know the Kafal-Rooak people. While they stood only six and one half taja in height, their wingspan was fifteen and one half taja in width. It was no wonder that they were able to get airborne rapidly, without really needing a high point to take off from.

They found out that the Teltermak had been on this continent (and surrounding islands) for about fifty-five years. They had been meddling in the affairs of just about everyone on the continent. The only way to stop them from expanding further west on the continent was for the Kafal-Rooak to ally with many other peoples and let the Teltermak know that enough was enough. The fact that they could fly, without the aid of any devices, made the Teltermak back off.

Ahandi was also able to find out that Kiyalee had purloined all four of the trucks that her Team were driving. She had parked all four in the same garage. One truck had been parked in Home, one in Spy, one in Observation and one in Ghost. That way, all four could fit into one garage. After a few mental communications with Wilfadge, it was decided that any more acquisition of vehicles, would be done through legitimate trading. As long as Team 7016 was able to keep their four trucks, Kiyalee did not care who obtained what, when or how.

Kiyalee did not find out until later that Wilfadge also gave the people of Shashkanit four hundred bottles of *Tuzine* in trade for the four stolen trucks. She also found out that she might be spending a little time at the Turgon Wall – as a prisoner – if she ever stole another vehicle from anyone – without the knowledge or permission of the Supreme Officer.

Wilfadge was reading a new report. He was amazed at the fact that Kiyalee had somehow obtained four vehicles and had not stirred up any panic or hostilities from the people of Shashkanit.

Teelila looked up from her copy. "Are we going to try to come up with some…trade agreement for new trucks with these… Heyyah of Shashkanit?"

Wilfadge chuckled. "Better a trade agreement, rather than Officer, Kiyalee going in there and stealing mass amounts of vehicles."

Hadathoo almost choked. "You...don't know the full story...do you?"

Everyone at the table looked at him.

Wilfadge closed his eyes. "I...I'm almost afraid to ask... but...what are you talking about?"

Hadathoo gave them a big friendly smile. "It seems...that our mischievous little Officer Grade 6, Kiyalee, has more than just those four...purloined trucks. Do you remember that...load of trucks that we got from that Algothon Naval convoy?"

Everyone nodded.

"Hers is still in good working order."

There were several groans and a few shocked looks.

Hadathoo again smiled at everybody. "Do you remember that attack against the Axswain...where we used...OUR vehicles?"

Again everyone nodded.

"She still has a fully functional 161 in her garage."

Antrong scoffed. "Oh...*h'oolyach*! That's impossible! The last one of those trucks...it rusted away into complete disrepair...over fifty years ago."

Hadathoo sniffed. "Not all of them. Kiyalee has a fully functional, One hundred and six year old 161. I didn't believe her until she showed it to me...and gave me a ride in the truck. It still *works*...as if it were brand new."

Wilfadge flopped back in his chair. "I think that maybe...

we've had the wrong individual in charge of the motor pool...all of these years."

Hadathoo shook his head. "No. We had the right person in charge. We just didn't have the right worker...in the pool. When it comes to leadership...I wouldn't trust Kiyalee with anything." He snickered. "She barely knows how to follow. She finds a new truck that she likes...so she steals it. She *was* given the responsibility of taking care of that truck...and has done a wonderful job...for over one hundred years, but she still needs to know when and why to obtain a new one."

Hoynama looked sick. "Has it been...that long...since that attack on Axswain?"

Wilfadge nodded. "Yes, it has. One hundred and six years ago...Nagasoom led us out of Owlam...on that silly, useless attack against Axswain."

Dwalooa sighed. "All of that stuff put aside...what about the way that we found a new friend on Lusaratia? Is there a possibility that we could find new friends on each continent?"

"I don't think that we'll have a problem on Neopaure," said Shyshee. "Most of the people on that continent hate the Algothons anyway. Anyone who is not an Algothon, on that continent, could be our friend."

"Okay," said Ahandi. "What about the other continents? Do you think we can find someone on those other continents that we can trust as allies?"

Hadathoo snickered. "Anyone who doesn't like the Perfor

will definitely be an ally."

Dwalooa looked thoughtful. "The way it's going…it seems that all we have to do is find some troublemaker on a continent… and side with the others. That's a real good way of finding new friends."

"I agree," said Wilfadge. "So far we have friends of North Chilamte, Lusaratia and Neopaure. All we have to do on South Chilamte is find someone who doesn't like the Perfor. That leaves us with finding someone on Aerisau, Cifpasica and Ficara."

Teelila sighed. "We may also have to do the same thing on some of the larger island chains."

Wilfadge nodded. "You're right." He sighed. "Make sure that everyone gets a good update on all of the landmarks…for all of the islands in those chains." He shrugged. "We may be sending people out there…sooner than they think."

Wilfadge came into the Headquarters area. Akantini was there to greet him. She handed a report to him and then beat a hasty retreat. He looked at her quick escape with a bit of a frown and then looked very apprehensively at the report. New reports from some personnel who were doing some scouting that the Teltermak might be on some of the islands in the Slantati chain. The rumor was unconfirmed, however, there was a strong probability that they were there.

He chuckled a little to himself. "Akantini? Where is this…Slantati island chain?"

She peeked out of her office looking somewhat apprehensive herself.

He smiled. "What *is* the matter?"

She cleared her throat. "Sometimes you can be... overemotional, Sir."

He sighed. "Where is this Slantati island chain?"

"East of South Chilamte...Sir."

"That would put it in the South Talanka Ocean."

"Yes, Sir."

"Thank you."

She quickly pulled back into her office.

He stood there and pondered a moment. 'Overemotional? About what?' He shook his head and went into his office to read the full report. After he finished he called the four Master Officers in for a quick meeting. Each one of them read the report.

Soolchakan was sitting in the tub cleaning the back of his neck when he got the call. He finished cleaning and got out of the tub. He pulled out his pad and started looking up the Slantati island chain. Six major islands, eight significant islands and over three hundred insignificant islands. He shook his head. 'What is the difference between a major island and a significant island?' He looked it up in the lexicon. A major island usually has several large villages or even cities on it. A significant island usually can support three or more villages. An insignificant island is usually very small and cannot support a village – two or three families at most.

He started checking the map for the major islands and found that on three of the major islands, the inhabitants were at odds with each other as what the name of the island actually was.

He finished drying himself off and went down to the main room on the first floor. The three women were looking over a catalog of new designs in clothing.

He huffed as he looked at a dress that they were ogling. "Is that another outfit that you want…that you'll never wear?"

All three women gave him a dirty look.

Kiyalee pointed at the printer. "Is that something that you're printing up or is it coming from Headquarters?"

He sighed as he looked at the computer. "I'm getting several maps."

Bonarain frowned. "For what?"

He gave them a big smile. "For our next excursion."

All three women groaned.

Bonarain looked up. "Where?"

"The Slantati island chain."

Chyning glared at him. "What's so special about *this* island chain?"

He sighed. "There are rumors that…the Teltermak have been spotted…on one or more of the islands. Since we're the ones who discovered the Teltermak bases in those other chains…they want us to go take a look at these islands."

Chyning hung her head. "Do you think this is gonna take longer than those other searches?"

"Yeah…a lot longer. There are six of the islands in this chain that are…massive compared to what we saw in those other two chains." He looked at the printer. "Let's go take a look at the maps and you'll see."

Bonarain scoffed. "Look at the name of the northern most island. It sure is long."

"No it isn't," sighed Soolchakan. "The people who live there can't make up their minds what the actual name of the island is. Some call it Doolrak and some call it Zhuseed."

Kiyalee grunted. "Why?"

He closed his eyes. "I don't know, I've never been there." He opened his eyes and gave her a sarcastic smile. "That one isn't the only one where they have that problem. There's also the two largest southern islands…one of which is either Nistava or Shamshau and the other large island is either Setotoon or Zintanala…depending on which faction you talk to."

Bonarain shrugged. "We really don't have to communicate with these people, do we? All we're going to do there is look for Teltermak."

Kiyalee sighed. "Right. We don't have to communicate with anybody. Are there any more arguments over names of islands?"

He shook his head. "No, just those three."

Kiyalee looked at the report about the rumors of Teltermaks in this island chain. "Doesn't it give us any clue as to which island they're talking about?"

He shook his head sadly. "None."

Chyning looked at the map. "The sooner we get started, the sooner we get this bunch of *doovofts* out of our way."

Bonarain scoffed. "So…let's get ready and go."

They did several Jumps that finally took them to the southeastern part of South Chilamte. As they made each Jump they continued looking for Teltermak. On this continent, however, all they found was the presence of the meddling Perfor race. They indeed did have blue skin, which even during the day, seemed to shimmer and glow. This was another race of Elf who could not hide during the night.

They found themselves geographically as close to Folnor Isle. They checked their landmark and Jumped. They were now on the northern tip of a rather narrow island that stretched quite a ways north and south. Most of the time you were on the island, if you look east or west you could see ocean. This was an island, however, it was so far south that it was nowhere near being a tropical island. There were mostly deciduous or evergreen trees and very few of the tropical variety. After a long, boring trek due south they had found nothing.

Chyning stood on the beach looking south. "You didn't expect to find those Teltermaks on the first island didja?"

Bonarain scoffed. "Even if we had, we'd still have to explore all the other islands anyway."

Chyning fluttered her lips. "You're right. What's next?"

Soolchakan looked at his map. Mala Isle is east of here. It's one of the three smallest islands that we're going to have to explore." He held up a picture. "Here's the landmark."

Now they found themselves on another island. This one was less than one sixth the size of Folnor so it took considerably less time to explore. There was nothing flying here.

The next island to explore was northeast of Mala. It was called Chiwass Isle. It was slightly larger than Mala and still no signs of anyone flying those telltale kites overhead. Another boring two weeks of exploring and finding nothing interesting.

Next was Kukami Isle. This one was almost the same size as Folnor. It was another island that stretched from north to south and was very narrow east and west. It was just as boring as the other three islands they had inspected.

Slightly southeast of Kukami was Ro Isle. It was a little larger than Chiwass and had nothing there that was interesting.

Soolchakan looked at his maps. "East of here…is one of those double-named islands. This end of it…the people call it Setotoon. The largest city, on this western end, is called Moonta."

Chyning looked at him dull-eyed. "Is that supposed to be interesting?"

"No, just informative."

They made the Jump. They found a rather curios situation in the city of Moonta. The Perfor were present here, however, they were not trying to be the conquerors on this island like they were on South Chilamte. All four of them annotated this conundrum in their part of the report.

The Setotoon half of the island was larger than all five of the previous islands. They were ready to settle in for a very lengthy search of this island – until they saw something flying high off to the east...and heading east. It took several Jumps, looking for minor landmarks, in order to make a quick move east.

They found themselves at the foot of some high cliffs that stretched as far as they could see to the south. In the northern section, the cliffs went right up to the water line and the only way around them was by boat.

What the Team was seeing left them all confused. It appeared as if there were numerous Elf people flying around, however, from their vantage point it also appeared as if they had different kinds of wings.

Soolchakan looked down and rubbed his neck. "Not comfortable doing that. Why don't we go all the way up top and see what we can find up there?"

"Good idea," said Bonarain.

They made the Jump and found themselves on a somewhat rugged and very large plateau, that just like the cliffs, stretched as far to the south as they could see.

Here the Elf people were walking around and they could

see that there were some very different races, who seemed to be living rather well in complete harmony. It took almost thirty Jumps before they reached the southern tip of the cliffs on the southern side of the large island. Everywhere they looked they saw the same three different races of Elf, all living peacefully up here on the cliffs.

Chyning snickered as she looked around. "How do we report this? Is it just one…very diverse race or…three…who can get along?"

"We start doing some mind reading," said Soolchakan. "Bonarain, you check out the ones with…feathered wings, Kiyalee you get the transparent wings and Chyning you get the skin wings."

Chyning looked affronted. "What're you gonna be doing… while we're working?"

"While we were going along, I noticed something…at the foot of the cliffs. I'm going to go check on that. When we're finished…we'll meet back here. Hopefully this won't take too long."

The next day, the Team gathered together to compare notes.

Bonarain folded her arms. "So, Mister Leader, what was so important at the foot of the cliffs?"

He gave her a nasty look. "The Heyyah on the island… even though they can't agree on the name of the island, have carved four, very long tunnels under the cliffs. This way they can go back and forth easily…for the purposes of trade. Each one of the tunnels is a toll-way. Each side of the island has their own currency and you have to change money at each end of the tunnels. There doesn't seem to be much bickering at either end so…I guess that even though they don't agree on the name of the island…they still get along peacefully." Now he folded his arms and looked smug. "What did you find out?"

Bonarain wrinkled her nose. She glanced at the other two women then back to him. "It *is* three definite races. They're getting along pretty good as well. The *feather wings*…as you called them…are called the Kawneff-Ebraw. They're pale skinned, the parts that are not covered with feathers that is. They're just under six taja and they seem very friendly to the other two races. The ones with feathers seem to be the most prevalent. When the Algothon launched their attack, the Kawneff-Ebraw had a walled city on the west side of the cliffs."

Soolchakan nodded. "Okay…Kiyalee…what've you got?"

She glanced off to the side at some of the fliers as they landed. "The ones with the transparent wings…I don't know how they fly. Those wings look…so fragile. They had a walled city on the west side of the cliffs as well. They got bombed by the Algothons and…now they can fly as well. They're just under seven taja, their skin is a light brown and…from what I've seen – as well as reading a few minds – they seem to be a little mischievous. They do pull a few pranks, but, they still get along with the other two races."

Soolchakan nodded. "Chyning?"

She scratched her chin. "Those…leather-winged people… are about seven taja in height and their skin is a darker brown than the bug-winged bunch. They have an attitude where they can be pranksters as well, but, they don't have the really playful attitude that the others do. They had a city on the west end of the island… before the Algothon bombing and now…like the other two races… they live all the way up here so that they'll have a nice place to live without Heyyah interference."

Soolchakan nodded. He took another look around at all of the three races that seemed to be living very well…peacefully. He grunted. "I wonder if this is the fliers that were rumored to be the Teltermak."

All three women shrugged.

Chyning scoffed. "When all of our spies were originally sent out…just after the firestorm attack…why didn't they annotate anything about these flying people at that time?"

Soolchakan chuckled. "We were testing some newly acquired capabilities at that time. Maybe these people were doing the same. Now that they're more familiar with flying…and with each other…things have become more peaceful."

Kiyalee grunted. "So that's why they didn't find fliers… back then."

Bonarain sighed. "We still got the rest of this island to explore and several others to go as well."

Soolchakan sighed. "Don't remind me."

Kiyalee stretched. "We done here?"

Soolchakan nodded. "Yup! Westward we go."

The Zintanala end of the big island came up with nothing interesting.

They moved on to the next split island of Nistava/ Shamshau. This island was divided by a series of cliffs as well, however, those cliffs were not near as tall or rugged.

Ketill Isle was a smaller island just east of Nistava. It was rather boring as well.

Next it was north to Exow Isle. They noticed two more races of Elf on Exow, however, nothing that was flying. They left that one and headed further north.

Yelwok Isle was one of the smaller ones and did not take that long to explore. It was nothing but Heyyah.

Further north to Jornbas Isle. This was another one of the larger islands and took a while to explore. They did not notice anything flying here, other than some birds that they had never seen before. They wondered how these birds had survived the residual mess, when very few others were still around.

Mingool Isle was next. It was the last of the small islands and only had three villages of Heyyah. Another boring trip.

They went on to the last island in the chain. The northernmost, the largest and another split island. The Zhuseed Heyyah people were in the majority and controlled a larger portion of the island. They did not have such a peaceful coexistence with the Doolrak people on the western part of the island. At a certain point, both factions had built a rather large wall that stretched completely across the island. There was a no-man's-land in between the walls that showed no signs of having ever been developed. There was a rather large bay, right at the northern end of both walls. If someone wanted to set up a harbor city it would have been the perfect spot. As hostile as the two sides were to each other, it did not seem likely that either side would accept the other one actually building a city there, so it remained virgin territory.

Chyning looked around at the capitol city Sabalitan on the Doolrak side. "Okay we're done with this bunch. On to the next island."

Kiyalee looked horrified. "I thought that this was the last one!"

"It is," said Soolchakan. "That next island north of here is part of the Ficara Separation chain. We're not going there... because no one told us to and I'm not in the mood to commit to any initiative at this time. I'm tired of exploring...what we could probably investigate from those flying cameras."

Chyning looked at her pad. "Okay, let's go dump all of this *h'oolyach* on the Command Staff and go home."

"I agree," said Bonarain.

Wilfadge looked at the reports. "So there are three other races of Elf with wings...and all three were on the same island... when the firestorm weapons hit."

Ahandi shook her head. "First time I heard of...similar changes...in close areas."

Hadathoo looked up with a smile. "No telling what caused all of the different or similar changes is there? Those Algothon just launched the things and...everybody is still trying to contend with all of the changes."

Teelila looked up from her copy. "I wonder how long it's going to take before we get all of the different groups and places cataloged."

"Look how long it has taken so far," said Shyshee.

Dwalooa shook her head. "And we're still no closer to determining what those crazy elixirs are made of...at least that prime ingredient."

Antrong smiled. "The Teltermak aren't any closer to determining the ingredients of the Tuzine either. Look on the bright side."

"Funny thing," said Wilfadge. "They don't seem to be in too much of a hurry to obtain their prime ingredients either."

"We'll always have someone watching them in case they do," said Shyshee.

After all of the Staff finished reading the reports, Team 7016 returned to the home in the gorge...hoping that they could sit down and relax for a while.

8

The Heyyah woman woke up. She remembered when she would wake up and cry…because she was still alive. She had prayed daily for death to take her from this prison. She had no idea how long she had been here. She had no mirror in the small area where she was allowed to exist…that she had not been allowed to leave…since being dragged in here…so long ago.

She knew that he would be coming back. He came every day. He came in here and forced himself on her…every day. He would bring food – which she did not want and make her eat it, so that she would live another day…in this prison. He claimed that he loved her and was protecting her. She huffed. If he loved her he would allow her to leave the room. He would allow her to go out and experience life. What was he protecting her from? The only thing that she could really remember was her brother, his wife and that two-year-old son of theirs. Was he protecting her from her brother?

She looked up at the light shining in that big hole in the high ceiling. A million times she wished that she had a ladder that she could use to climb out that hole. She had tried to build one. She made it in sections so that she could hide it. He found the ladder and destroyed it. Then he put a chain around her ankle so that she could not even get out even if she were able to build a ladder.

He had her completely trapped in here and she was clueless as to how long it had been. Years...decades? She did not know. There was no mirror for her to look at herself and see how much she had aged...if at all.

Every time he came, he would take those manacles and chain her to the bars in the brass bed. He would then force feed her and have sex with her. He would lay there sound asleep while she could not move out of the bed because of the manacles on her wrists.

A while back she had come up with the idea of making her own key for the manacles. It took a while – quite a while, however, again, with no clock or calendar, she had no idea how long it was. She had a key that could open the handcuffs. She made a key that could open the painful thing on her ankle.

She made a key that would open the big chest in the corner. She was amazed at the weapons that she had found in the chest. She was trying to figure out a way to use them against him. Maybe use one of those handheld bombs to blow the door off. Maybe. She had nothing but time here in this room and she used it to make keys and plot a way out.

She could not figure out how to make a key for the door that he came in. She was going to have to wait until he was here. She had everything settled in her head and was ready to execute her plan. The only thing that might be a problem – do not act like there is anything different going on. He might get suspicious and…all her plans would or could be dead.

She waited for him to arrive. What else was she going to do?

She looked up at the shelf at the two little brown bottles that had been sitting there…how long? They were covered with layers of dust. He said that someone named Teltermak had sold him those bottles. He made her drink one of them. He drank the other one. She did not remember ever tasting anything that had been as foul as that thick glop in that bottle. According to him, whatever was in those bottles was supposed to prolong their lives. She did not want her life extended – unless she could get out of here.

She sat down on the bed and waited. She looked up at the big hole in the roof. Whenever the rays of the sun were shining on that one place, through the hole, that was when he came and abused her.

She sighed. Maybe today…she would be able to do it… and get rid of him…and get out of here…and be free.

The rays of the sun hit that one board – and she heard him fumbling with the chains on the outside of the door. She always heard three chains drop when he was coming in. He would then unlock four different locks on the door. Then he would come in with something for her to eat. He would make her eat and then he would cuff her to the bed and sexually abuse her. It never changed.

He came in and locked the door from the inside. He placed the keys in an area that she could not reach, because of the chain attached to her leg. He brought the food to her. She always tried to fight him, however, he was very good at inflicting pain and forcing her to eat. She wanted to regurgitate it back up, however, he had an answer for that as well. She still fought him because she had nothing better to do.

Once again he was the victor in forcing the food down her throat. He then placed her wrists in the handcuffs and had her chained to the bed. He took the manacle off of her ankle, forced her legs apart and had his way with her…again.

She hoped that she had not been different…or not different enough that he would notice something peculiar going on.

She did what she always did while he was copulating with her. She lay there like a rag doll. She refused to act or sound like there was any pleasure on her part. Why should she act like it was pleasant – it was not pleasant at all – for her?

She heard the familiar grunts and moans that told her he was nearly finished. Those last three moans and then that big stupid grin on his face. Then he would fall off to the side and go directly to sleep. She could follow the rays of the sun down the upper boards, telling her how much longer he was going to be asleep.

She cautiously reached into a small crack in the wall just at the head of the bed. Her keys for opening these handcuffs were in there. She had to be careful not to drop either of them because if she did then she would have to wait until tomorrow to go through with the rest of the plan. She got both keys out and scooted her way up to where she could work. He had always left these handcuffs attached to the head of the bed. They were always easy access so it had been simple to file down a key that would open up the cuffs. Simple but time consuming. She put one key in her mouth and worked the cuff on her left wrist first. She nearly panicked when it did not open the cuff. She frowned and switched the key to the right wrist. It snapped open easily. She let out a sigh of relief. She opened the other cuff.

She carefully placed his wrists inside the cuffs and snapped them closed. She was thinking of doing something really nasty to him now. No, that had not been part of the plan. Stick to the plan and get out of here.

She eased her way off of the bed and nearly laughed out loud. This was the first time in…who knows how long…she had been off of the bed without any form of a shackle on ankle or wrist. She almost felt naughty about it…almost.

She retrieved her other hidden key and opened the big chest. She pulled out one of the handheld bombs. Her brother had shown her one of these things…a long time ago. It looked that same and if it operated the same, she was going to use it to her full advantage. She laid the bomb on the nightstand.

She went to his clothing and looked through it to see if she could possibly make something fit. The clothing was full of his sweat, however, that could not be avoided. She was going to have to fold the bottoms of the cuffs on the trousers up quite a bit in order to keep them from dragging on the ground. A rope would suffice as a belt in order to keep the pants up. Buttoning the bulky shirt on would not be a problem. She was not going to worry about shoes. She had been barefoot ever since she had been imprisoned in this room and now, the bottoms of her feet were tougher than any shoe bottom.

She picked up the little handheld bomb. She squeezed the armature towards the body of the bomb until it clicked. She remembered that you have to keep the pressure on the weapon constant. Push the black button, where the armature adjoins to the ball of the bomb. When you push it, the armature will click as it goes closer to the ball. You then throw the bomb and after a four count - it goes off. She had no intention of throwing it. She was going to place it under him and set it. When he moved, he would set it off himself. He was shackled to the bed and would not be able to get away from it.

She walked over to the door. She picked up the keys and saw that big silver one that he always used to open the door from this side. She placed the key in the door, unlocked it…and opened it. It was exhilarating being able to be here and be able to get out. She propped the door open so that there would be no accidental closure.

Time to set the bomb. She squeezed the armature until she heard the click. She reached down and pushed it under his back. She pulled her hand out carefully. She reached in and pushed the activation button. She saw his back lower slightly as she heard another click. It was done. The moment he rolled off of the bomb…four count and…boom.

She turned and tiptoed to the door, slowly closing it behind her. She did not know how long it would be until that uncomfortable thing would make him move, so she decided that she needed to get some distance between her and that bed as quickly as possible.

She closed the door and found herself in a yard that was surrounded by a huge hedge. She was smelling things that she had not smelled in...how long? She followed a well beaten pathway through the yard. There was an archway in the hedge that appeared to be the only opening. She went through to take a look and see if she could, in any way, shape or form, figure out where she was.

There was a road just outside the hedge. She saw that she was high up on a hill. She walked to the other side of the road and was ready to scream. She was looking down on the seaside village where she had been born and raised. That monster had never taken her away from the village, he had kept her right here...at home... all this time. Time to go down the hill and find her brother.

She took about twelve steps and heard a loud explosion behind her that made her jump in fright. She looked back at the hedge. She saw a plume of smoke coming up out of...what must be the exterior side of that hole in the roof.

She scoffed. "He moved," she said. She shrugged, turned and continued down the road. She heard birds that she had not heard since... She heard sound coming up from the village that... Tears ran down her face as she went further down the road.

She wondered if she could still remember the way to her home. She stopped. Her home? What if...? She could not think of the bad right now. She had to concentrate on something good. She had been in that room for so long and without a clue as to how long it had been.

She entered the village and there were so many things that looked familiar and…she saw things that were rather strange. That butcher shop…used to be run by two brothers. They were both tall, fat and a little temperamental. She looked in the window and saw at least three men in there and not one of them was fat.

There were those three taverns that competed with each other. The one that had put that bright yellow and red awning up in order to look a little more sophisticated…now the awning was badly faded to orange and…bird droppings. The one with the metal tables outside…the tables were gone.

The baker shop was still there and the smell coming out of it was heavenly. She looked inside and once again, did not recognize anyone in there.

She stopped as she looked in the window and noticed that…for the first time in years, she could finally see her reflection. There had been no mirrors in the prison room and here…was a reflective surface where she could finally see her face again. She felt a little better about herself in that she did not notice very many changes in her face. Other than the fact that she looked a little haggard and rather pale, she did not see many differences.

She continued down to the waterfront. The house that she had been raised in was very close to the fish processing plant where her family had worked for generations. She had hated the smell when she was growing up. Now, it would be…a wonderful memory.

She fretted over the thought that her brother, Eeshak, would not recognize her after all these years…however many it was. The sister-in-law, Mosska, was she still there? The nephew, Fenteth, how old is he now? How many more children were there in the family now?

Anticipation was tearing at her as she finally came to the familiar street that was home. She slowed her walk a little and looked around at all of the homes. Trees that had been saplings were now towering shade trees. The parts of the street that had been nothing but dirt were now worn cobblestones. A house that had been surrounded by a wooden fence, now had a high brick wall. She swallowed hard and continued towards the...home?

Then she was there. Almost everything was the same. The only thing that was really different was the height of the trees. The two trees that she and Eeshak had planted as almost just twigs. When they were planted you could put one hand around the trunk. Now, it would be impossible to get her arms around the circumference of either one.

She held on to the bars of the tall wrought iron fence, not just to get closer, but to keep from falling over. She felt a little dizzy when she realized that those trees told her that she *had* been a prisoner in that room for...decades.

Someone tapped her on the shoulder and she yelped in surprise as she backed away and fell down.

A man was standing there looking a little stern. "May I help you with something?"

She got up and steadied herself against the fence. She was not sure what to say. She saw a look of shock come across his face and then she felt a shock of her own. This was her brother, Eeshak.

But it could not possibly be him. The brother she remembered had thick, unruly brown hair. She had been nineteen and he had been twenty-two when she was abducted. This man was old and wrinkled. He had mostly gray hair with a few patches of brown. He had a thick gray moustache that covered his upper lip. He was still a lot taller than she, however, he was not as muscled as he had been…how many years ago?

He grabbed hold of her arms and looked deeply at her face. "You…look…like my sister…Menya…you look like she did… when she disappeared…some…forty years ago."

Her strength failed her completely. She collapsed to the ground. He slowed her fall, still holding her arms, however that was all he could do. He knelt down as she collapsed and still stared at her.

His voice sounded desperate. "Do you…know anything about my…sister?"

There were several strange sounds that came out of her throat as she was trying to think of something, anything to say that could alleviate the shock of…*FORTY YEARS AGO.*

"You…must be her daughter…but…if you are…where has she been and…where have you been?" He shook his head helplessly. "Talk to me…please!"

The daughter bit sounded good. She remembered her reflection and from what she saw there she should only be about four or five years older. Looking at her brother and hearing…*forty years ago*…that meant that she was at least fifty-nine years old. She decided to stick with the daughter thing…at least for now…

until she could figure out what was going on.

"My...mother...she was...Menya.   She...and...me...
we...were kept in a room. We were kept there...by the man...
he...would come in there every day and..." How do you describe
the sex act...from an ideology of ignorance? She swallowed. "He
would feed us and then...stick that thing...between his legs...in
my mother and...bounce on top of her. Then he would stick it...
between my legs...up inside me...and bounce on top of me."

Eeshak was looking horrified.   "Where...where's your
mother?"

Good question. How do you respond to that one? "She...I
don't know. She figured out a way...to get those...shackles off
of us and used...some funny looking little rock...that made a
horrible, loud noise...to make him stop...hurting us."

Eeshak looked around searching faces to see if he could
find his sister. He pulled Menya to her feet. "You...you've got to
show me...show me where she is...please!"

The pleading in his eyes nearly made her cry. How could
she continue with this fabrication?

He stopped suddenly and looked down at her. "What...did
Menya...name you?"

Oops! Good question! Now what? "She...called me...
Sinisa...when the man wasn't there. When he was there...she
called me...daughter."

He hugged her close and started crying. "Sinisa...that was
our mother's name." He wiped his nose on his sleeve. He wiped

his eyes with his hands. He turned to the house. "MOSSKA! MOSSKA! Come quick!"

A very fat woman came out of the house. Menya recognized her as Mosska, however, she...was four times the size she had been, the last time they had been in contact. The woman came out looking rather concerned.

"I saw that woman standing there," said Mosska. "I wasn't sure what to do."

Eeshak nearly broke down into tears again. "This...is Menya's daughter...Sinisa!"

Mosska's eyes went wide in shock. She looked closely at Menya's face and she put her hands over her mouth. "It has to be." She dropped her hands as she came closer. "She...looks exactly like her mother did...at that age."

Once again Eeshak was pleading. "You've got to show me where your mother is. I need to find her. Please show me!"

Menya looked up to the hill. "It...was up there." She pointed. "When I came out...of that room...for the first time... in my life...I was looking down from that hill." She was at a complete loss as to what she was going to tell him when they got up there. She looked as if she were still nineteen...or maybe twenty...or twenty-one, while he looked his age of being over sixty. She would have to do some thinking as she was riding up the hill with him.

He got his truck and headed out as quickly as he could. He did all kinds of illegal passing of other vehicles because he wanted to get there quickly and find out anything that he could about the situation.

She was getting rather sick because this was the first time in over forty years that she had ridden in a vehicle. It was somewhat unnerving.

He finally reached the cutoff to head up the hill and sped up the narrow road. They came upon several emergency vehicles as they neared that horrid prison room she had been kept in for so long.

A Constable signaled him to stop.

He hit the brakes and leaned out the window of the truck. "I'm looking for my sister! She's been missing for a long time… and I just got a clue as to where she is."

The Constable shook his head. "I'm sorry, but there's a situation up here and I can't let you in…unless you have something to do with the incident."

Menya looked at the Constable as innocently as she could. "Do you mean that big bang…that happened a little while ago?"

The Constable raised his eyebrows. "Do you…know something about it?"

She smiled sheepishly. "My…mother may have…set it off…I was here…when it happened."

The Constable cleared his throat. "Don't move!" He turned around and put a handheld radio to his mouth and spoke rather quietly. He looked back at the two people in the truck as he pressed on an earpiece in his left ear. He once again whispered something into the radio and listened to what was coming in on the earpiece. He narrowed his eyes as he looked at Menya. "The Detective...will be right here."

Another man, dressed in the same uniform as the Constable came walking towards them. The difference in their uniforms appeared to be some kind of markings on the collar. "What is going on here?"

The Constable pointed at Menya. "She says that she was here when the bomb went off."

The Detective looked down his nose at her. "Would you step out of the truck, please?"

She got out and tried to look scared...on purpose.

"Now," said the Detective. "You say that you were here when the bomb went off...did you set it off?"

She looked at Eeshak and then back at the Detective. "If you're talking about that loud bang...I think my mother did it... with that funny looking rock."

"Why would your mother do that?"

"So I could get away."

The Detective frowned. "Get away from...what?"

"The Master."

He stood there with his eyes closed and his mouth open. He shook his head and opened his eyes. "I feel like I just came in on the middle of the story."

Eeshak got out of the truck. "Then let me give you a preface!"

The Detective looked a little irritated. "Only if it is relevant."

Eeshak huffed. "Forty-one years ago, my sister, Menya, disappeared. We never had a clue as to what happened to her... until today...when this girl..." He pointed at Menya. "...she appeared in front of my house...and she looks exactly like Menya did, when Menya was that age."

The Detective looked at Menya suspiciously. "And who is this...Menya...to you?"

Menya sighed. "She's my mother."

He nodded. "And your name is?"

She nearly slipped. "My name is...Sinisa."

He nodded again. "Okay, this...Menya is your mother... and...today you decided to go...to your...Uncle's house." He narrowed his eyes as he looked closely at her. "Where have you been all this time...if your mother was being kept...here?"

Menya shrugged. "Today...is the first time in my life that I ever got out of that room."

The Detective looked back and forth from Eeshak to Menya. "If today is the first time...in your life...that you ever left that room...how did you find your way to your Uncle's house?"

Her heart nearly skipped a beat. She had to think quickly. "She...my mother was...always talking about the house. She described it to me...every day. She told me...every day...where it is...in the village."

The Detective looked skeptical. "She must have done a masterful job of describing it...appearance and location...if you've never seen it, but found it...so easily."

Menya shrugged. "Like I said...she described it...every day. The only thing that she was wrong about...was the size of the trees."

The Detective licked his lips. "What were you doing in that room...all of your life?"

Eeshak interjected. "They were being sexually abused... all of that time."

The Detective nodded slightly. "By whom?"

Menya shrugged. "The Master."

The Detective frowned. "The...Master? Don't you know his name?"

She shook her head. "No, that's what we had to call him."

A look of shock came over the Detective's face. "You say...you were in that room...all of your life! You were born... and raised in that room! The only man...that you saw in there... was this Master?"

She nodded.

"That would...make him...your father...and...you say that he was sexually abusing *YOU*...as well?"

She feigned ignorance. "I don't know what that means."

Eeshak grunted. "Tell him...what you told me...about... bouncing."

Menya shrugged. "Every day he would come in there and bring us some food. After we ate, he would stick that thing... between his legs...in between my mother's legs and then bounce on top of her. Then he would stick that thing up inside me... between my legs and bounce on top of me."

The Detective looked at her horrified with his mouth hanging open. "He...was your father...and he..." He looked off to the side and spat. He looked back at Menya. "How long...has he been...bouncing...on top of you?"

She cupped her breasts. "Ever since...these things grew out of my chest."

The Detective covered his face with his hands for a few moments. He dropped his hands. "I wish that thing...was still alive...so I could kill him." He took a deep breath and let it out slowly. "So...how did you...get out of there...today?"

She shrugged. "My mother has been working on these little pieces of metal...for a long time. She made...what she called...keys. She used them to open up those shackles that he had on our wrists and ankles. After he finished bouncing on me and fell asleep, my mother used her...keys and unlocked the shackles from me and her. She put them on him. Then she got this funny looking shiny rock…and told me to get out of there…and don't look back." She looked up the hill. "A little while later…I heard that loud bang. She told me to not look back…and find my Uncle's house."

Eeshak looked at the Detective terrified. "Did…my sister die…in the explosion?"

The Detective shook his head. "No…she got out in time. There's only one body and…it is male…minus most of his chest cavity." He shuddered.

Eeshak looked all around him. "Where…could she have gone?"

The Detective sighed. "Look, I need to get a few things straight. We need to go over the story again…make sure that we have all of the facts lined up…in good order. Some of what has been said has answered a few questions…but raised a few more. Let's talk this out…see if we can figure it all out…to everyone's satisfaction."

Eeshak had to go over the abduction story only twice.

Menya had to go over what had happened in the room four times before the Detective was satisfied with the entire story.

They had to show Menya one of the handheld bombs, to see if that was what she was calling "the funny looking, shiny rock". It was.

After the Detective was satisfied, Eeshak still was not. "So where is my sister? Why did she just disappear?"

The Detective sighed. "I think that the reason she's gone...she thinks that she's in trouble. She got her daughter out of there...and killed *him*. She probably thinks that we're going to pursue her...for murder."

Eeshak leaned forward. With a sinister look on his face he said: "Are you?"

The Detective shook his head. "No. No Judge, who is worthy of picking up a gavel would think of allowing charges to be pressed against her. She was abducted and abused...you said for forty-one years. She ended up giving birth...to a daughter and then saw her daughter being abused by the same monster. She fought back...and won. The whole thing...for her...is self-defense." He sighed and nodded. "If...your sister...ever shows her face here again...you may inform her that no one is going to think of pressing charges against her." He sighed. "She is free... completely free."

Menya sighed inwardly. She was now confident that she got away with it. She thought of those dusty brown bottles that were still in the room. When the Master had made her drink that nasty glop, he had said that according to Teltermak, it was supposed to prolong their lives. Here she was at sixty years old, looking as if she were only twenty. The stuff was working. She could not think of any way of telling her brother that she was a sixty year old woman, when she still had her youth and her brother who was only a few years older than her was old, gray, father of five, grandfather of fourteen and about to see the birth of his fourth great-grandchild. Since she was sixty while looking and feeling twenty, she wondered just how long that glop was supposed to work and keep her youthful looking. Only time would tell…and it appeared that she had a lot more of it than she had originally thought possible.

Several times during the first days of her freedom, she would stand in front of a mirror naked. She would look at herself and have to remind herself that she was sixty years old. What was in that brown bottle?

Wilfadge and Hadathoo were sitting on a balcony overlooking a field of *shoovaline* melons in the city of Owlam. They were each enjoying a steaming hot mug of kwatha as the sun was setting.

Wilfadge blew on a hot lump that he had pulled out of the mug to cool it. "I was doing some thinking about those silly elixirs."

Hadathoo chuckled. "Really?"

"Yes…I'm still wondering…just how we're supposed to find out if those things can really do…what they say."

Hadathoo took a sip of the broth. "Which one is bothering you the most?"

Wilfadge grunted. "That…youth stuff. If one of us drinks it…how are we supposed to know…if it worked? I mean…look at the situation. It has been over a hundred years since that firestorm attack…and all of us…still look like we're in our late twenties or early thirties. So…how would we know…when to look for some…sign that the stuff…has actually done something…to prolong or…restore…youth?"

Hadathoo chuckled. "That one would definitely require some…unsuspecting Heyyah to be used as a lab rodent."

Wilfadge huffed. "Right! We give it to someone…and then we have to follow them…for…how many years before…we find out if it worked or not." He shook his head. "Too much time…too many people devoted to…a maybe."

Hadathoo snickered. "How about that…brain elixir. They say that it makes you smarter. The problem I see with that one…does it make you more intelligent? Does it give you more common sense? Does it give you better clarity? Does it give you better focus? Does it change a clumsy person into someone who can…do incredible things with their mind? Does it change a… dull normal to a genius?"

Wilfadge scoffed. "That's another one where…you'd have to follow someone…for a long time to determine whether it worked or not."

"Now the cure-all…that one…we might be able to see instant results. Find some poor old fool…who is stricken with… some horrid disease…and…give him a snort. That one just might give us something that we can see…quickly…if not instantly."

"But who do we want to find to try it out on?"

Hadathoo chuckled. "Some other unwitting Heyyah rodent."

Wilfadge grunted. "Then…there's those…white bottles. They're marked by gender. What…does that mean?"

Hadathoo just shook his head and took another sip. "So far...we've all been pondering this puzzlement. So far...none of us have come up with much that is new as far as experimenting with those things."

"Yeah, and no one had or has been able to find any notes on...that stuff...in the Teltermak files. So far, the doctors have tried some of those things on some Heyyah but...we may have to wait for years before we see results."

"Yeah, those *doovofts* sure know how to keep a secret."

"Very irritating!"

"Yeah, especially since they...don't seem to have any more of that...prime ingredient...that they're bringing to that processing plant."

"Very strange."

Hadathoo looked up. "Have you heard anything new... about those headaches in South Chilamte? Those Perfor people. Are they still causing a lot of grief...around the gorge?"

Wilfadge shook his head. "Unfortunately...yes! And not just the gorge. They're becoming a real pain...everywhere on the continent. I'm going to have to send...several Teams out there to...follow them and see what we can find out about them."

"Why can't...some of these people...just...leave everyone else alone? Why do some of them have to...go out and try to conquer? It's so...*rude*!"

"It makes one wonder - were they that way...before the

firestorm attacks…or did they become…greedy and ambitious…because of the attacks?"

Hadathoo popped a lump into his mouth and chewed on it slowly. "Seems that all of this warfare has changed drastically…as well as making peace with others."

Wilfadge frowned. "What do you mean…on either?"

He sighed. "How long…had we been holding off the Axswain, the Galsino, the Kalash, the Teltermak and Zee-Altha…prior to that attack. We never had any new territory. Neither did they. Now…we…seem to be global. We go…anywhere we want to go and…no one knows any better. We've made friends out of peoples that we never met…and we have enemies…of peoples that we never met before."

"Okay, I can see those points."

"Yeah. The Turgon Wall…how many new friends do we have? Going global…how many new enemies did we acquire?"

Wilfadge snickered. "The Algothons, the Cacktash, the Sodle, now very possibly the Perfor. I wonder how long the list will end up being."

Hadathoo grunted as he spooned through his kwatha looking for another lump. "And we still have the pleasure of those wretched Teltermak and Axswain."

"The Galsino haven't been exterminated."

"They haven't attacked us in a long time."

Wilfadge laughed out loud. "They learned a very expensive

lesson when we killed a whole bunch of them by blowing up their own weapon in their faces."

"I wonder if we'll ever see peace in our lifetime."

"As long as there is as much as one ambitious *bimyock* out there who can raise an army…no."

9

Teelila looked at another report. "What are those Perfor doing now?"

"They're getting uncomfortably close to the gorge," said Dwalooa.

"Very uncomfortable," said Ahandi.

Wilfadge shook his head sadly. "I think that we need…to make another large Team of spies…and get a much closer look at these people. All of their movement…it just gets them closer to us and…they've taken just about everything that we planted up above our hidden homes…in the gorge."

Hadathoo shook his head. "We don't have to make another large Team of spies. We have…probably several hundred of our people who…spend a lot of time in the gorge. All we have to do is tell some…if not most of them to go up top and take a look."

Wilfadge shrugged. "That is definitely worth a try. They can get an estimate of how many of the Perfors are up there…and just how much damage they've done to the crops."

"Even if it is nothing but a minor reconnaissance, we still have to have someone in charge," said Teelila. "We need someone for all of them to report to…in order to keep things organized."

Wilfadge sighed and leaned back in his chair. He made a mental call out to all Officer Leaders. The question was: Is there an Officer Leader who is currently in the gorge with their Team?

A response came back from Officer Leader, Skalix of Team 37. He was currently in his gorge abode of apartment 1-9. He and his Team were doing some furnishing and decorating in the apartment. He heard the instructions, sighed and called his Team together. "Omika, Shirfaya, Beskeen…we have some orders… since we're already here." He shoved a table into position and smiled at the three women. "It seems that the Perfor are doing some massive damage to our crops…here above the gorge. The Command Staff wants us to get everybody up there and do a full check on them to find out just how much damage…and how many of those *bimyocks* are up there."

Omika wrinkled her nose. "Does that include…everybody who is here…in their gorge apartments…at this time?"

Skalix smiled. "According to Supreme Officer, Wilfadge… yes." He leaned his head back and made a mental call to anyone who was currently in their gorge apartments. He opened his eyes. "That's…incredible!"

Shirfaya frowned. "What's the matter?"

He chuckled. "There are only twelve Teams…who are currently here in the gorge. Most of the other Teams are…back in Owlam…taking care of crops."

Beskeen shrugged. "That's forty-eight. That's a start…

and we don't have to have anyone…crowding anyone else…when we go up there."

Skalix nodded. "Hold on, I'm going to inform Wilfadge of who the Teams are…just in case he wants to send someone else… somewhere else." He sent the mental message of Teams 37, 347, 906, 2017, 3033, 4167, 4270, 4541, 4707, 5194, 6337 and 7016.

Chyning growled in disgust. "Why is it always us?"

Bonarain sighed. "At least this time, it was a call out to all Teams who are currently in the gorge. It wasn't a thing where we were singled out."

Kiyalee scowled. "So now we have to get up top and start counting perverts?"

Soolchakan snickered. "Perfors." He shook his head. "And yes, we have to count them."

Kiyalee. Sighed. "At least this time…we didn't have any kwatha boiling on the stove."

"Right," said Soolchakan. "Let's get up there."

Team 7016 Jumped to the top of the gorge on the eastern side. They looked around, somewhat shocked, at seeing hundreds of the Perfors walking around and doing some kind of inventory on all of the plants that were there.

Kiyalee grunted in disgust. "Are we supposed to try to read their minds?"

"It would help," said Bonarain. "It might…accidentally… give us a complete count of all of these…" She snickered. "…

perverts."

Skalix was staring at the strange Perfor people. They did have blue shimmering skin that glowed even in the day. He was rather confused as he saw hundreds of them wandering among all of the plants that were above the gorge homes. They were all walking around sniffing the air. There was no reason for them to try to smell anything up here because there were no unusual plants in the area. There were virtually no animals, wild or domestic, in the area either, thanks in part to the residual energy from the Algothon weapons. He stood there trying to determine what it was that they were attempting to smell.

Shirfaya sent out a mental communication that the Perfors, which were close to her, were all walking directly towards her while sniffing the air.

Omika and Beskeen were sending the same information.

Team 7016 came up to the top and noticed that all of the Perfors in their area were advancing towards them…sniffing the air.

Kiyalee shook her head as she looked around confused. "I wonder what stinks so much. There aren't any *Shoonshook* plants here."

Chyning shrugged. "Kwatha doesn't smell bad and… neither do the melons that are growing in this area."

"They're getting…awfully close…to us," said Soolchakan. He decided to move away from his current position. He walked forward a few paces. He noticed that all of the Perfors close to him

changed directions and all were still headed directly towards...
him. He looked over at Bonarain. "Could they be...smelling...
US?"

Bonarain shrugged. "Let's...try to read some minds."

Chyning looked as if she were about to panic. "I...can't
concentrate. They...keep following me. What are they...? How
are they following me? I'm in Spy dimension...and...they can't
see us...but they keep following me."

Bonarain clenched her eyes shut and did everything she
could to concentrate on reading minds. At first she was frustrated
because all she could get was the minds of her Team members.
She blocked them out and went for other minds in the area. Her
concentration was broken when the Perfors finally started talking
to each other.

"I can smell them...here...but I can't see them," said one
Perfor.

"It is...as if they *are* here...but I can't see any of them,"
said a second Perfor.

"That's ridiculous," said a third Perfor. "No one can turn
invisible...and even if they could...we should still be able to touch
them."

Bonarain concentrated on these specific ones. She was
aghast when she realized that the Perfors were talking about smelling
her...and other Owlamites in the area. "They ARE smelling us!"
She sent out the mental communication to all Owlamites above
the gorge homes. **"These monsters can smell...US! Even**

though we're in Spy dimension. Somehow…they can smell…US!" She stopped to wait and see what they were going to do.

Five of the Perfors came directly up to her and they were sniffing through her and around her.

"It smells…like there's a female Owlam…right here… right now," said one Perfor.

"I can smell her…but I can't…touch…or see her," said a second Perfor.

"She…must have…been here…just before we got here," said a third.

A fourth one scoffed. "If she was here…what direction… did she go when she left? I don't smell any…departing path."

"Something is very strange here," said a fifth.

Bonarain Jumped to a spot that was fifteen taja to her left, just to check the reaction of the five Perfor who were sniffing her armpits. All five looked up surprised and started sniffing again. It was not long until all five were slowly walking towards her… sniffing away. **"This is ridiculous**," she sent. She did not realize that she had sent it until she received several different sendings from other Owlamites. **"I'm going to go to Observation dimension and see what they sniff at…from there**."

Skalix was curious about that experiment. "**I did the same thing…and these blue beasts are…still sniffing at me…except now…I don't know what they're saying**."

"**Then read their *chokwad* minds**," sent Soolchakan.

"**Hard to concentrate**," sent Skalix.

Soolchakan snarled.   "**Then Jump back to your apartment and call Wilfadge...or someone else in the Command Staff**."

Skalix was a little upset over the fact that an Officer Grade 5 was staying calm and giving him advice on what to do. He did the Jump and called the Command Staff. When they responded that they were having a difficult time believing him, he sent back a very nasty message that they should come and see it for themselves...since they were so sure that he was fabricating the situation. A little while later, all of the Command Staff and their Team members were all in the area above the gorge in South Chilamte.

After wandering around for quite a while and being sniffed where ever they went, Wilfadge called for all of the present personnel to go to the gorge conference room and they would all compare notes.

Wilfadge called the meeting to order, once everyone was there. "We now know that these...Perfors...can smell us...in Spy and Observation. I wonder if...they can smell us anywhere else."

Till stood up. "I found a tree...and I went inside it...in Spy. I hopped to Ghost dimension and...they were still surrounding the tree...still sniffing away and thinking that they could smell me... even through the tree and even though I was in Ghost."

Kiyalee scoffed. "What's so rancid about our armpits...

that these *doovofts* can smell us…no matter what?"

Wilfadge snarled. "Keep the comments relevant."

"That is relevant, Sir," said Kiyalee. "What part of us are they smelling?"

Bonarain stood up. "They were even able to determine gender."

Hadathoo stood up. "We'd have to know a lot more about their olfactory capabilities…before we can determine…what part of our anatomy male and/or female, they can…smell!"

Wilfadge looked around. "Was anyone able to…do any kind of mind reading before we all came down here?" He looked out over a field of red faces. "Is there anyone who could…look past…a bunch of them…sniffing…your armpits and…try to read their minds?"

Ahandi stood up. "Why don't we send that teacher from Team 7016?"

Bonarain rolled her eyes and groaned. "I'm on my way up there, Sir," she said sadly.

Wilfadge nodded. "The rest of Team 7016 should go up there to protect her."

Chyning scoffed. "Protect her from what?"

Wilfadge glared at Chyning with clenched teeth. "Just go!"

Team 7016 reluctantly Jumped back up to the top. They

saw hundreds of Perfor walking around sniffing the air.

Kiyalee scoffed. "Don't they get tired of that *h'oolyach*?"

"Apparently they're used to it," said Bonarain.

Soolchakan sighed. "So…Team…we protect her…while she tries to read a mind."

At least four dozen Perfor started heading for their position…all sniffing at the air. Soolchakan, Kiyalee and Chyning made a ring around Bonarain. The Perfor crowded around, all frowning as they were attempting to isolate where Team 7016 was located. Bonarain clenched her eyes shut and tried to concentrate.

Bonarain stomped her feet. "There's too many of them! I can't isolate…any one of them. It's just a bunch of…jumbled thoughts."

Soolchakan shook his head. "Let's…all Jump to the edge…of where they're all located. They have to have…some… home place…somewhere around here."

The four of them Jumped to an area that was nearly ten kilotaja to the south. There were only three Perfor in this area. As soon as the Team arrived the three Perfor started sniffing and slowly moving towards the Team.

Soolchakan looked at Chyning. "Get your foot ready."

Chyning stood there confused looking back and forth between the other two women.

The three Perfor came up to the Team sniffing.

"I smell Owlams here," said one Perfor.

"So do I," said another.

Soolchakan smiled. "If Bonarain wants to read a mind without any distraction, we need to have only one that is awake." With that he slugged one of the Perfor. The Perfor man momentarily wobbled on rubber knees and then went down.

Chyning shrugged and then kicked another Perfor in the chin. This one went down like a rag doll.

The third Perfor was standing there sniffing with his eyes closed. Bonarain closed her eyes and concentrated while the rest of the Team watched for any other Perfors that might end up in the area...accidentally. The third Perfor got a strange look on his face and then was just standing there dull-eyed and slack-jawed. Bonarain moved her head around several times as she was concentrating, trying to get into different parts of his mind and figure out exactly what was in this mind. Bonarain finally opened her eyes and had sweat beading all over her forehead. She took several deep breaths...and then did a spinning kick to his head, knocking him out.

Bonarain looked at her Team members. "Let's get back to the Command Staff. There's some things that I need to tell them."

Soolchakan shrugged. "Okay. Off we go."

The Team Jumped back to the gorge conference room.

The Staff all looked up as Team 7016 walked in.

Wilfadge smiled. "Do you have something worthwhile to

tell us?"

Bonarain shook her head. "These people...are nasty. They...have a sense of smell that...puts canines to shame. They can find us...anywhere. We now know that they can also smell us in...other dimensions as well. There's no way that we can hide from them...not as long as they can smell us out. One of the main reasons that they're up there...above our gorge apartments...they can smell...that we've been here...in mass."

Ahandi looked skeptical. "Do we really need to hide from them? Isn't there some way that...we could talk peace with them?"

Bonarain wiped the sweat off her forehead. "They feel that we, the Owlamites, are one of the most dangerous races on the planet." She cleared her throat. "There are others they think are dangerous...to their survival, but we're the worst...according to their thought process."

Hadathoo leaned forward. "Are you saying that they are planning on exterminating us?"

She shook her head. "No, Sir, they want to enslave us. They plan on finding all of us and putting something like those... electric collars on all of us...so they can control all of us. Once they have control of us, they have five other races that are on their list of primary conquest." She bit her lip. "The rest of the list...of necessary conquests is...ridiculous. They're planning on controlling at least thirty different Elf races...in order to achieve world domination...using all of the enslaved Elf races as the ones doing all of the fighting...while they sit in the background...

controlling."

Wilfadge sat there pondering. "Why…are WE so dangerous?"

Bonarain crossed her arms. "They want our technology. One thing that they *really* want is that…multi-fat-headed thin-lick communicator…that *goolywoggled* the Sodle jamming devices."

Wilfadge rolled his eyes. "Oh…they want that. How cute."

Bonarain shook her head. "Yes, Sir."

Wilfadge grunted. "So…who else is…a top priority?"

"The Teltermak…because they have an airborne military. There's another race called the Gabeesh-Or. Why they want them…I don't know. There's a race called Twakon. That's another one…I'm not sure why. The Kalash are on that list. Another one is called…P'Lalfan. I don't know why they want that group either."

"Any word on…the secondary ones that they want?"

"All I can remember of that list…is a race called Mountarn. It seems that they are very good at hand-to-hand combat…because they have four arms. The rest of them that they want…are wanted because of their numbers…it seems that they can…procreate rather…rapidly."

Wilfadge sighed and shook his head. "It sounds as if…we are going to have to do away with another race of Elf. I hate… finishing the job that the Algothons started."

Hoynama huffed. "Why can't these people…just leave us

alone? Why can't they...live and let live?"

Dwalooa grunted. "Greed! It's all a question of greed. Always has been."

Wilfadge gritted his teeth. "Let's try...something different." He looked at Bonarain. "Is there anything...that you got from that...mind job...where you can identify some...top leader? Maybe...if we talk to the ranking one...then we could avoid a whole lot of...unnecessary deaths."

Bonarain snickered. "I'll have to find someone...other than that *bimyock* that I was reading. It seems that he's a very low ranking enlisted...called a Second Follower...and the only higher ones that he knows about...are his enlisted supervisors. He's not even allowed to know the names of the officers...or even who is in charge of his unit."

Shyshee scoffed. "So...what's your suggestion...as to finding a top echelon officer?"

Bonarain shrugged. "We're going to have to start grabbing some...Perfors who look like they're...giving orders...and go from there."

Ahandi looked around. "Isn't there some kind of Command Center...somewhere in that bunch of *doovofts*? Someone has to control it from somewhere. They have to report...to someone...somewhere."

"Unfortunately, every time we go up there and start looking around...they all start crowding around us...sniffing our armpits," said Skalix.

"That's only part of the problem," said Soolchakan. "Once we grab one and pull the *chokwad* down here...what do we do with them...once we find out that they're...a low enlisted or a nothing officer and...no use to us whatsoever?"

Wilfadge sighed. "I suppose that we can afford to...drop a few of them off...in Jahong's Death." He shook his head. "They'll have to accept a few casualties. Even if it does turn out to be one or two high ranking officers."

Skalix snickered. "So...who starts the...abductions?"

Wilfadge smiled at him. "Since you're the ranking one... we'll let you get the ball rolling."

Skalix looked back at his Team and got three nasty glares back at him. He motioned with his thumb for them to go up top. All four vanished...and reappeared a few heartbeats later with a very surprised looking Perfor.

Wilfadge turned to Bonarain. "You've done this before... find out...who and what he is."

Skalix, Omika and Shirfaya held the man down while Bonarain concentrated. The Perfor suddenly stopped squirming and laid there limp.

Bonarain shook her head. "This one is enlisted...a Fifth Follower. He's just a few grades above that one I questioned before."

"Sit on him for a while," said Wilfadge. "Who's the next Team in line?"

Officer Grade 4, Myasana chuckled. "That would be me… and Team 347, Sir."

Wilfadge smiled.

Myasana sighed. "Choonbon, Nebenema, Yeesatsi…let's go."

Team 347 vanished and reappeared a few moments later with a female Perfor.

Bonarain started concentrating. She opened her eyes. "This one is lower than that other Perfor."

Wilfadge sighed. "Team 906?"

It did not take long until they had a collection of fourteen Perfor in the room. All of them were enlisted. Only one of them was a high ranking enlisted and he only knew who was in charge of his unit…not where those personnel were located.

Wilfadge growled. "All right…everybody who is in this conference room, including all of the Command Staff and their Team members…we're all going to the top. Look for…an area where there is a group of those *bimyocks* and see if you can determine which one is giving orders."

Skalix pointed at the current prisoners. "What about them?"

"Tie them to a chair and knock them out," said Wilfadge dejectedly.

After the prisoners were all sleeping (involuntarily) and tied to some seats, Wilfadge gave the order for all twenty-one

Teams to go up top and find...someone.

In a very short time, they were all back in the conference room with twenty-one new prisoners – nineteen men and two women. To make sure that they could not get much, in the way of reconnaissance in this room, they were all held face down on the floor until Bonarain could mentally question each one.

Bonarain finally found an officer. He was a Group Controller. It took a few more bits of mental manipulation before she was able to find out that his rank was a fifth level officer in a hierarchy of eleven officer grades. She was able to glean the information that the High One was at the top and the Exalted One was the rank just below that. The really bad piece of information was the fact that Group Controller was the highest ranking Perfor... within two thousand kilotaja of their current location.

Wilfadge hung his head. "This...thing...will have to do. Let's start questioning him...to the full extent."

Hadathoo looked at the other prisoners. "What about them? They all know that they were yanked out of their work areas...by means that...they can't comprehend. They're going to say...something...to their superiors...if we let them go."

Wilfadge did not look up. "Then let them go...in Jahong's Death. When we're finished...with that officer...same thing."

"They're going to have over thirty unexplained disappearances up there," said Teelila.

Wilfadge looked up. "Tough!"

After dispatching all of the other Perfors, Bonarain sat

down behind the Perfor officer while Wilfadge sat directly in front of him. She did everything she could to not dig too deep into his mind. They wanted to question him and she needed him to be thinking clearly. Wilfadge would ask the question, the Perfor would think of the answer and Bonarain would relay the information to six of the Command Staff Aides who would write the information down as quickly as they could.

The first thing they found out was that all of the higher ranking personnel were not here in the gorge area. This sniff-hunting was a job for underlings. This man was one of five Group Controllers in the area. They ruled with an iron fist. He had memorized all of the other faces that he had seen in captivity here and was going to punish all of them severely if any Perfor secrets got out.

Bonarain snickered at that. Those underlings were not told anything and therefore did not know anything. They had been told to gather crops and sniff out the Owlams. They did not know why or what the crops would be used for.

The Perfor were just as arrogant as the Beetsik had been. They thought that they were something very special. Because of their incredible olfactory capabilities, no one could hide from them. They had determined from this that they were the superior race on Hardooth and that everyone should be subservient to the high and mighty Perfor.

They wanted the Owlam technology badly. They were confused as to how the Owlamites were able to hide all of their secrets and this made them dangerous. They had to be captured and enslaved at all costs. If they refused or fought back, extermination was the only answer. No one was to be allowed to defy the great and mighty Perfor.

The Perfor were confused as to how the scent of so many Owlamites could be present on the giant plateau in the northern part of South Chilamte. They had not been seen here so how were they able to hide so easily? The fields of kwatha were very prevalent here, so why were they Owlamites not here cultivating the fields...even though their scent was all over the place? The Perfor were going to answer these questions. As soon as they had all of the Owlamites in captivity, the answers would be tortured out of them, the Perfor would have all of their spectacular technology and world conquest could really begin.

The Perfor thought that the Owlamites were such silly people because with all of their technology and the sole ownership of *Tuzine*, they were not conquering. They needed to be incarcerated and controlled since they had no ambition.

Wilfadge leaned back in his chair. He did not know whether he was more tired or disgusted. Here was another pack of conceited monsters who had decided that they were special and because of *their* decision, everyone was supposed to kneel in awe at their feet. He decided to let this snobbish Perfor know the complete truth – before he was condemned to one of the nasty dimensions.

"First of all...Group Controller Yugyug..."

The Perfor snarled at him. "My name is Yooyog! You will address me as befitting my status! Is that clear?"

Wilfadge smiled. "Here's the thing…Yugyug…I outrank you. I am equivalent to…what you perverts call…High One."

"You're less than a First Follower. You are NOT a Perfor, therefore your rank means nothing…to me or to any other Perfor. I can see that you are going to need a lot of discipline in order to be properly utilized."

Wilfadge hung his head and sighed. "Somebody…keep this pervert's mouth shut. He needs to listen…and find out the real truth."

Hadathoo walked up and hopped to Spy dimension. He hopped his right hand into Home dimension and held Yooyog's mouth shut. He used his left hand to slap Yooyog in the back of the head every time the Perfor tried to interrupt and spout his delusions of superiority.

Wilfadge smiled. "Now…*pervert*…we the Owlamites… have been instrumental in the annihilation of the Beetsik, the Neksheth-Or, the Towlayaw-Or, Zee-Altha, Sodle and the Cacktash. We are also responsible for the near extinction of the Axswain. One of our actions *caused* the extinction of the Maka-Or. Because of us, the Galsino and the Teltermak are on the run and have no home of their own…anymore."

Yooyog remained defiant. He sat there looking bored.

Bonarain made a mental communication with Wilfadge. Wilfadge agreed to the little trick. Akantini quickly set it up and communicated when it was ready.

Wilfadge smiled at Yooyog. He reached off to his right

and hopped his right arm into Spy. Akantini was standing there with a mug of kwatha and gave it to him. He pulled his arm back into Home dimension and started stirring the thick broth with a long spoon. Yooyog looked as if he had been slapped...again.

Wilfadge sipped the broth. "We...don't have technology. We have...some very strange...natural abilities...that came about...after that firestorm attack. We can, without the use of technology...hop...into other dimensions. We can..." He held the mug up. "...retrieve things...from other places...without actually going there. This mug...was just heated up...in my kitchen... back in the city of Owlam. The city that sits in the northern part of North Chilamte. I was informed...by my Aide...through mental communications...that the kwatha was ready, I reached through the dimensions to the stove...in Owlam and picked it up. I did not have to take any other part of my body to the city of Owlam...just my arm." He held the mug a little higher. "Here it is...hot and ready to eat. Prepared in North Chilamte and now I have it here in South Chilamte."

He leaned back, hopped to Ghost dimension and took a sip of the kwatha. He looked up and hopped back to Home dimension. "You were able to see...right through me...for a few heartbeats. That is another dimension. We call it...Ghost. We can...at will...hop from one dimension to another. We can Jump...from here to North Chilamte...to Ficara...to...wherever we want to go." He snickered. "This is how we move around." He looked down at the mug as he spooned a lump out of the mixture. "We can also read minds." He looked up. "When we asked you those questions...we didn't expect you to answer...and you didn't. That was meaningless. When I asked you a question, you thought of the answer…and I had one of my Aides read your mind. We got an answer to every question that I asked you… without you opening your big, fat, arrogant mouth once. We got it out of your mind." He chuckled. "If you don't believe me…think of…a number…or a friend…or a favorite place. Don't speak it out…just think of it. We know it already." He laughed and smiled in a friendly manner. "The number was 176. That is where you stand…in seniority among the Group Controllers. The friend… is your lover…Laksheema." He got a sinister look on his face. "You're never going to see her again." He took another sip. "The favorite place…is a small cottage…that you secretly share with Laksheema…on a lake…a place where you have a rendezvous with your lover…a place that her husband doesn't know about." He shook his finger in Yooyog's face. "You naughty boy… fooling around with someone who is already married." Wilfadge chuckled again. "Do you see? We already know your secrets. You've given us all the information that we need…and because of the snobbish attitude of you…perverts…we're going to have to exterminate you…and your people…just like we did the Sodle… and the Beetsik." He leaned back in his chair. "We're going to kill all of the perverts…starting with you." He looked up at Hadathoo. "Start with Stink and then send him to Shogoot's Search. Once his body is dissolving in acid…I think that he'll finally get the message…that he and his kind…are finished."

Hadathoo let go of Yooyog's mouth. He grabbed the back of the Perfor's head and hopped him, from the neck up, into Stink. They all watched as Yooyog's abdomen convulsed while vomiting. His breathing became rapid, which did not help the man, seeing as how he was breathing nothing but air from the Stink dimension. He convulsed several more times, however, everyone there knew that he could not possibly have anything left in his stomach.

Hadathoo brought his head back into Home dimension. "Do you see...pervert? You cannot have our technology...because it is NOT technology...it is US! You can't have us! Now...I'm going to kill you...and then find your precious Laksheema and get rid of her as well." With that he hopped Yooyog into Shogoot's Search.

Wilfadge sighed. "How many...of the Perfors...are up there on the plateau?"

Ahandi shook her head. "Somewhere between 25,000 and 30,000...I think."

Wilfadge nodded. "Then we'd better get to work."

Dwalooa grimaced. "What about all of the peoples...that they're using as slaves...who are on the plateau...as well?"

"Try to keep them from seeing the...disappearing acts," said Wilfadge. "Try to make the...overseers disappear...while the unfortunate ones are busy looking down...while digging. That should solve...some of the problem...I hope."

Shyshee shook her head. "What if it doesn't?"

Wilfadge huffed. "Then let them be confused!" He grunted loudly. "Let's get to work!"

Wilfadge called over one hundred more Teams to come to South Chilamte and start getting rid of the Perfors. It took the better part of a full day to get rid of all of the Perfors that were on the plateau. When they were finished, Wilfadge decided that he wanted to know the exact count of how many Perfors had been... removed from Hardooth.

When everyone was finished reporting in, Akantini looked up at Wilfadge helplessly. "It turns out...Sir...there were a lot more up there than we thought. We just got rid of 32,669 Perfors. Of course...that was just what was on the plateau...around the gorge."

Wilfadge grunted. "That's right. We've still got a bunch of those *doovofts* on the rest of the continent."

Ahandi grunted right back at him. "According to that exploratory trip that Team 7016 took...they're on a couple of the islands...in that Slantati chain."

Wilfadge groaned. "We're going to have to get rid of them...without making the people on those islands...or the rest of this continent suspicious."

"That's a pretty tall order," said Dwalooa.

"I'm painfully aware of that," said Wilfadge.

A mental call came in to the Command Staff. "**This is Officer Grade 4, Hakani of Team 3033. Can you hear me**?"

Wilfadge frowned and responded. "**Yes...is there something new from somewhere on the plateau**?"

"**Yes, Sir, there's a call coming in on a radio...from**

someone who says that he's a Principal Leader. He's demanding that one of the Group Controllers respond to his call."

Wilfadge looked around the room. "Does anyone know what a Principal Leader is?"

Bonarain shrugged. "From what I got…from those mind readings…that would be equivalent to an Officer Grade 1."

Wilfadge grunted. **"Hakani, tell that *h'oolyach* that we'll only respond to the High One."**

Hakani shook her head snickering. She gave the response. **"Sir, I just learned how to cuss in Perfor. I learned a lot of cuss words, Sir."**

"That's very rude of him," thought Wilfadge while snickering. **"Repeat the message and tell him to clean his mouth up. Tell him that the message comes from the Supreme Officer of the Owlam."**

A few moments later a response came in. **"He said that there's no rank among slaves…or *koofkup*…whatever that is."**

Wilfadge sighed. "Such impudence." He looked around at the rest of the Staff. "It appears that there will be no peace with these monsters." He sighed again. **"Tell that…*koofkup*… that…because of the puerile arrogance of the Perfor lowlifes…all of the perverts that were on the plateau have been executed. Inform him…that if any more perverts dare to stink up the plateau with their rancid** presence...they will be exterminated as well and used as fertilizer."

Hakani called back. "**I just learned a bunch more Perfor cuss words. They sure have a lot of them**."

Wilfadge hung his head. "**People who are abusive... usually have all kinds of demeaning words in their vernacular**." He looked around the room. "**These people don't know when they're defeated. We're going to have to...do a full search and destroy**."

Hadathoo grunted angrily. "Again!"

Ahandi leaned forward. "Why don't we get...as many of our people to the south part of the plateau? Find out where those Perfors are coming up and just...urinate all over the area so that they can't smell anything...but urine. That should give us an easier time at getting rid of them."

Wilfadge frowned. "Which Team...is it?" He bit his lip. "Oh, yeah." "**Team Leader, Team 4167...are you at the south part of the plateau**?"

"**Yes, Sir, Officer Grade 4, Tsogoma here. We're watching the perverts...send all of their...captured people up to the top of the plateau. The perverts don't have the guts to fight their own fight**." She looked at her Team. "The Command Staff is going to have to make a decision here."

The rest of the Team just shook their heads.

Officer Grade 5, Yoolanaya looked down to the bottom

of the cliff. "It seems that we're going to have to take the fight to them. They're sending those others...to do the fighting...at gunpoint and giving their...puppets...nothing but clubs."

Officer Grade 6, Vovox snarled as he looked at the elevator system that had been installed. "Even if we bust up that elevator... all it would do is hurt the slave...not the master." He grinned. "We'll have to allow the slaves...safe passage and then...take out the pervert overseers."

"Good idea," said Officer Grade 7, Kipa. She grinned at the rest of the Team. I see a good place to start. Down there... they've got a big collection of perverts...right near that one outcropping of rock. That stuff...would make a nice landslide... that they couldn't blame on the slaves...or us."

Tsogoma nodded. "That'll make a big mess." She pondered a moment. "Vovox, you sabotage the elevator electrical system...while we drop a few thousand rocks on those perverts."

Vovox wiggled his eyebrows and smiled. "I love screwing with wiring systems." He waited until the elevator had reached the top. He hopped a junction box into Spy and placed a handheld bomb in it. He hopped to Observation and waited for the bomb to go off. When he saw the elevator stop, on the way down, he hopped back to Spy and saw the junction box completely destroyed. He hopped the tangled mess back to Home. He looked down the cliff. "Figure that one out you perverts."

The fact that the elevator was completely stopped was only an irritating distraction for a few heartbeats. The spot where the massed Perfor officers were shading themselves suddenly became their tomb as three boulders, each one about the size of a small house, came crashing down on their position.

Kipa scoffed. "Look! Even their blood…glows blue!"

"You can even see the glow during the day," said Yoolanaya. "That is…weird!"

"Don't worry about weird," said Tsogoma. "Let's see what their reaction is…to this disaster."

The Team watched as several injured Perfors crawled away from the landslide. One Perfor started shouting orders for the enslaved people to start helping the injured Perfors. Another Perfor was arguing that the slaves should continue going up by climbing the scaffolding for the outside elevator shaft. The first Perfor decided to split the slaves up and have some help the injured while others started the climb.

Kipa growled. "What do we do now? They're going to make them climb up that outer part. That's not very safe."

Vovox shook his head. **"You start taking some of the bars that they're climbing on…out…down there. I'll start busting some of them out…up here**."

"Good idea," said Tsogoma.

The three women started hopping the connections for the bars into different dimensions. It did not take long before the entire thing started to collapse. There were several Heyyah and Elf people who were high up, who were able to grab hold of some of the rock ledges and then slowly climb back down.

On the top, Vovox removed numerous braces that were holding the elevator shaft in place. He finally found the critical ones and the shaft leaned away from the cliff. It leaned slowly at first and then crashed down completely.

Vovox looked at all of the different ones who had been brought up so far. He noticed that they were all wearing some kind of collar. He snickered and started going around, hopping the collars into Spy dimension and throwing them off to the ground. As he pulled each collar off, each victim noticed immediately that they no longer had the collar on. Each one looked around confused…but very happy.

After removing all of the collars Vovox did a little mind reading. **"I don't know if any of you have noticed before… but I just found a new Elf race…or at least it's a race that I've never seen before. They call themselves…Aree-Pawneh. They're a little over four taja…their skin is a little darker than ours…and they appear to have…feline faces. They're actually…quite handsome."**

Tsogoma shook her head. **"Are you finished sight-seeing up there**?"

Vovox sighed. **"Yes, Sir."**

"Are there any Perfors up there?"

He looked around. **"No, they were sending up only the…slaves first.**"

"Good! Get down here and let's see how much more damage we can cause to these *bimyocks*."

Vovox sighed, chuckled and Jumped to the bottom of the cliff.

Kipa looked over at one of the Perfors. "Isn't that the one who was giving all of the orders?"

Tsogoma looked at him. "Yes, he's the one...why?"

Kipa smiled. "Now that he's standing over there...keeping his big mouth shut while everyone else does the work...why don't we Jump him to the Command Staff and see what they can do? He has to be someone...who's higher than an O-5."

Tsogoma nodded. "Take him!" She cleared her throat. "Make sure that Wilfadge knows you're bringing that pervert... before you go."

Kipa stopped and closed her eyes. After a few moments she opened her eyes and smiled and wiggled her eyebrows at Tsogoma. She then grabbed the Perfor and both vanished.

Wilfadge and the entire Command Staff looked at their new (very surprised) prisoner with big smiles.

"Just for the record...pervert...state your name and rank," said Wilfadge casually.

Bonarain sat behind him reading his mind.

The Perfor looked around angrily. "I don't do anything that I am told to do by Owlam trash!"

Wilfadge received Bonarain's information. "Oh...listen to this...mister high and mighty. He's just a Primary Leader. He's not the High One...not even an Exalted One...or even a Great

Leader. He's just a Primary Leader and he thinks that he can give me orders…in my headquarters."

The Perfor swallowed hard. "How did I get here?"

Wilfadge grunted. "We used our technology, stupid!"

"Who are you calling stupid?"

Hadathoo chuckled. "Since you won't state your name or rank…for the record…your name is stupid. Any other questions… stupid?"

The Perfor looked as if the top of his head was about to blow off. "My name is Thoddock! YOU…trash…will address me as Master!"

Wilfadge grunted again. "Too late…stupid." He cleared his throat. "By the way, you're addressing the Supreme Officer of the Owlam Military. You will address me as Supreme Officer or Sir. I will NOT address an underling like you as Master. Is that clear…stupid?"

Thoddock looked even angrier. "I am a Primary Leader and you will address me according to my rank!"

Wilfadge sighed. "When you start acting like a mature adult…I'll treat you like one. As long as you continue to act like a child…you'll be treated as one…stupid."

Thoddock glared back at him. He looked around at the different people in front of him attempting to size up the situation.

Bonarain shook her head in disgust. **"This _Bimyock_ is trying to figure out a way to get out of here. He seems to**

think that by bullying us and bragging about his Perfor superiority, we should all cringe in fear and awe."

Wilfadge belched. "Up until a little while ago, we had never heard of you Poofers. We were wondering…what makes you think that we should fear…something that we know nothing about? The Algothons…they bombed us…and you…we have a respect for them because they…might do it again. You…who are you and…what makes you think that you're…superior…to anything….including those blue trash beetles that we could never seem to get rid of?"

Thoddock tried to give Wilfadge a sinister look. Bonarain rolled her eyes and shook her head in disgust.

"We are called PERFOR! We ARE the superior race," said Thoddock. "You're ignorance of us is of no consequence. We will own all of you as slaves, in a very short time. Then we'll force you to bathe regularly…so we don't have to smell you as much. We were made the superior race…when that explosion went off. We will control the entire planet…very soon."

Wilfadge shook his head. "That Algothon attack was just over one hundred and seven years ago. You…Poofers…haven't done a thing…in all that time. In that time…we have exterminated the Beetsik, the Towlayaw-Or and the Sodle. We have made friends with the Kalash, the Rahanan-Sar and several others. We have scared off the Teltermak, the Axswain and the Galsino. What makes you think that you're going to do anything that…should frighten…or even…maybe get our dander up?"

Thoddock shook his head. "All too soon, you will see our

power..."

Wilfadge leaned forward. "Oh...by the way...we're the ones who killed *all* of you Poofers that were up on that plateau... in South Chilamte. You were trying to get up there...to find out what happened. All Poofers that were up there on the plateau are dead. That's why you can't contact any of them."

Thoddock tried to look as if he were not impressed. Bonarain let Wilfadge know that the Perfor had been stunned by the news that no Perfor was still alive on the plateau.

Wilfadge continued. "We are also the ones who caused the collapse of that elevator...and caused the landslide that killed... many of your friends. If you don't stop this ridiculous nonsense... of trying to conquer us...we will add you Poofers to the list of garbage that we have exterminated. Any questions...stupid?"

Bonarain tried to keep from laughing. "**You scared him. He's trying to keep from wetting himself. He is also trying to figure out a way to get out of here and inform the High One. He hasn't lost much of his conceit, but he is scared...for his own preservation**."

Wilfadge leaned back in his chair. "We're going to send you back to the cesspool that you were hatched in. You can deliver our message to that king of feces that you call the High One." He looked back at Hadathoo. "Get this piece of manure out of here."

Hadathoo looked at Wilfadge. "**Where**?"

Bonarain smiled. "**It seems that the original location of Perfor is in the central part of Ficara. Check your**

landmark application on your pad and you can find it easily...under Perfor."

Hadathoo grunted. He sent a message to his Team to look up the landmark for Perfor. Officer Grade 5, Yoytay looked up at him and smiled. The entire Team – with Thoddock – Jumped to the city of Perfor. They arrived at one of the main gates to the city.

Thoddock broke away from his captors and started screaming at the gate guards to take these marauders prisoner. He could not understand why none of the guards were paying any attention to him. He tried to slap one of them in the head and his hand went through the man without any contact at all. He looked back at Hadathoo in shock.

One of Hadathoo's Aides, Officer Grade 6, Leelaka walked up to the man that had been the intended victim of the slap. She smiled at Thoddock. "This is how you do it." She backhanded the unsuspecting guard.

The guard flinched from the slap and looked around trying to figure out who hit him. He saw no one that was close by. He rubbed the left side of his face still looking very confused. He did a little sniffing in the air while frowning.

Officer Grade 7, Wees, nudged Thoddock. "Now, Mister Poofer...you either deliver the message...or we mess with you... just like we messed with that guard."

Hadathoo grabbed Thoddock by the arm. "Let's go talk to this...High One." He got close to Thoddock's ear. Very quietly and in a sinister manner he said: "Now!"

Thoddock swallowed. "How am I supposed to...talk to anyone...when they can't see me?"

Hadathoo chuckled. He touched Thoddock and hopped the bewildered Perfor into Home dimension. The guards on duty, now saw Thoddock and all of them snapped to attention.

Thoddock saw their reaction and pointed at the Owlamites. "Take these Owlam trash into custody...NOW!"

The guards all looked around confused.

When Thoddock saw their reaction he turned to where the Owlamites had been standing and saw no one. He rolled his eyes. "Oh...*thpokot*!"

10

Thoddock glared at the guards. "Get me a vehicle. I need to get to Prime Headquarters…as soon as possible."

The guard swallowed hard. He ran into a small alcove in the gateway. Another Perfor came out.

The new Perfor looked at his guard unit. "Who's demanding a vehicle?"

All of the guards pointed at Thoddock.

The new one snapped to attention. "Yes, Sir, Detachment Controller, Kykog at your service, Primary Leader. Sir, may I ask where you need to go?"

Thoddock walked up to Kykog. "I need to get to Prime Headquarters…NOW!"

"Yes, Sir." Kykog turned to his guards. "Go…Third Follower! Get the truck!" He looked a little confused and started sniffing the air.

One of the guards ran inside the gate. He drove back out in a truck. He jumped out, opened the door for Thoddock and saluted. Thoddock got in looking a little irritated and still suspicious as to where the Owlam contingency had disappeared to.

Hadathoo and his Aides, who of course were in Spy dimension, got in the truck as well.

Hadathoo chuckled. "This thing isn't much to brag about is it?"

The three women snickered.

Thoddock turned to the driver after he got back in the truck. "Third Follower, do you have a siren on this thing?"

"No, Sir and this is the only vehicle, at our disposal, at this time, Sir."

Thoddock sighed. "All right, get to Prime Headquarters as quickly as you can."

"Yes, Sir." He put the truck in gear and headed into the city.

Hadathoo looked around as they rode through the streets. "It appears that they've done some rebuilding…since the firestorm attack."

Yoytay grunted back. "They…seem to have sufficient people…to do it."

Leelaka scoffed. "They…have military formations… drilling…everywhere!   Is this entire society…built around military?"

Wees was looking at the uniforms of the Perfor. "I see… the only difference between the officers and enlisted…the right sleeve…for the officer has gold stitching and the enlisted has… black stitching. What I don't see…how do you tell the difference between the ranks…of officer or enlisted?"

Yoytay grunted. "It appears…that the longer the stitching goes down the sleeve…the higher your rank."

Wees shook her head. "Okay…but…shouldn't there be some lines…that mark the different ranks?"

Hadathoo looked at the sleeves on the light blue uniforms. "Apparently…you have to learn by looking…or get punished."

The truck driver was sitting there sniffing.

Thoddock noticed the sniffing. "What's the matter?"

"Sir…if you don't mind…my saying…you seem to…"

"Smell of Owlam?"

"Uh…yes, Sir." He cleared his throat. "How…uh…what could…cause that, Sir?"

Thoddock grunted. "Being too close to that bunch…for too long. It seems that the smell gets all over you…whether you like it or not."

Leelaka looked at Hadathoo. "Can I kill him…now?"

"Patience," sighed Hadathoo. "Let's see what this piece of *h'oolyach* does when he meets the high *h'oolyach*. If he does as he's been told…we may have to let him live."

The three women sat there sulking.

Hadathoo looked thoughtful. "He said that he's…a Primary Leader. Do any of you know…what he's equivalent to…in our ranks?"

"I think he's an Officer Leader," said Wees.

Hadathoo grunted. "Still doesn't give him the right to degrade our Supreme Officer. Even enemies should have some consideration for the ranks of others."

"That depends on how conceited you are," snarled Yoytay.

The truck arrived at a very tall building near the center of the city. The driver pulled up to a place near the front and stopped. One of the attendants was ready to admonish the driver…then he saw Thoddock. He saluted and opened the door.

Thoddock got out of the truck. "Sixth Follower, do you know if the High One is in his office at this time?"

The man quickly looked off to his left. "Sir, the High One's vehicle is here. He is somewhere in the building…at this time, Sir."

Thoddock started up the stairs to the front door while several of the guards for the building stood there sniffing at Thoddock as he passed by.

"I'm getting very tired of that," said Leelaka.

"Don't do anything about it," said Hadathoo. He looked at some of the Perfors who were all sniffing while looking confused. "Yet!"

Yoytay looked at Hadathoo. "Does that mean we can slap

the *piddleeyanks* out of him later?"

"I hope so," said Hadathoo flatly. "For right now, stay close to him so that they'll think he's the one...with...smelly Owlam armpits."

Yoytay just snarled.

They went up the stairs to two enormous doors that were part of a rather elaborate entrance to the building.

Leelaka snickered. "Showy...aren't they?"

Hadathoo just shook his head.

Two enlisted personnel opened the doors as they saluted. When Thoddock walked by them, they both started sniffing.

Wees shoved one of the doors back into the face of one of the doormen. He would not be smelling anything for a while...not with a nose full of shattered cartilage and a fractured cheek and jaw.

Thoddock heard the man yelp as he was hit. He looked around doing a little sniffing of his own while looking very suspicious.

An officer at a reception desk stood up. "Primary Leader... may I help you, Sir?" The business like look on his face turned to confusion as he started sniffing.

Thoddock leaned close. "Controller...I spent a little too much time near the Owlams. I can't seem to get the smell off of me...yet. Right now, I have some very important information for the High One."

"I'm sorry, Primary Leader, but you'll have to go through Great Leader, Pitchpon before you could possibly see the High One."

Thoddock snarled. "All right...where is Great Leader, Pitchpon?"

The Controller turned to one of his Aides. "Grand Follower...take the Primary Leader to Great Leader, Pitchpon."

A man saluted. "Yes, Sir." He pointed towards an elevator. "If you'll follow me, Sir."

Thoddock motioned the man to go. The Follower walked to the elevator, pulled out a key and plugged it into a slot. The elevator door opened up. The Follower waited until Thoddock was inside and followed him.

"Great Leader, Pitchpon is on the twenty-first floor, Sir,"

Thoddock nodded.

The Follower entered the elevator and keyed a code on a pad. The doors closed and the elevator started moving.

The Follower started sniffing. He turned around and looked at Thoddock with a frown on his face.

"I spent too much time around Owlams," said Thoddock.

The Follower nodded. "Yes, Sir." He faced forward and cleared his throat. He continued to sniff the air until the elevator stopped. "Twenty-first floor, Sir." The door opened and the Follower continued sniffing. After Thoddock left the elevator, the Follower started leaning over as he sniffed.

Thoddock walked up to another receptionist. "Primary Leader, Thoddock, here to see Great Leader, Pitchpon...I believe they called from the first floor to announce me."

The receptionist stood up. "Yes, Primary Leader, they did. I am the Great Leader's Aide, Force Controller, Okton." He looked at the elevator suspiciously. "Grand Follower, you may take the elevator back down!" He frowned as the door of the elevator was still open. He looked at Thoddock helplessly. "Excuse me a moment, Sir." He walked over to the elevator. "Grand Follower, I told you that..." He looked around confused. "Primary Leader... there was...a Grand Follower...in the elevator with you...when you came up...wasn't there?"

"Yes," said Thoddock. "There was...why?"

Okton looked all around the room. "Where'd he go?"

"I don't remember seeing him leave the elevator."

Okton shrugged. "He's not in there now...and...I don't remember seeing him leave either."

Hadathoo looked at Wees. "Where's that elevator man?"

Wees looked up at the roof. "He leaned over...and was... getting a little too personal. The moment he got his nose...near my crotch...that was too much."

Hadathoo folded his arms and leaned closer to Wees. "Meaning?"

She scowled back at Hadathoo. "I grabbed him, hopped him into Spy, shoved him through the floor, hopped him back to

Home...and let go." She smiled.

Hadathoo groaned as he put his hands over his face. He dropped his hands and sighed. "Let's try to keep that stuff to a minimum!"

Okton picked up the inter-office communicator. He punched in a code. "Yes, first floor, this is Primary Leader Pitchpon's Aide. The man that brought the elevator up here to the twenty-first floor...seems to have pulled a vanishing act and... WHAT?"

Thoddock flinched as Okton shouted. "What...what's the matter?"

Okton looked at Thoddock in shock. "He...fell to his death...in the elevator shaft!"

Thoddock looked back in the elevator. "But...the floor... is intact...how...?" He looked at Okton rather concerned.

Okton could do nothing but shrug as he put the communicator down. "This is...uh rather disturbing." He straightened his shirt. "The Primary Leader said for you to wait until he is free." He pointed to a row of chairs. "If you'll have a seat, please, Sir."

Thoddock sighed. "Thank you." He dejectedly walked to a chair and sat down.

Okton got back on the communicator. "The elevator is still here...on the twenty-first floor...and the floor of the elevator is intact! How did he...I don't know...well I think that this elevator should be flagged as nonoperational until someone can figure out what happened." He put the communicator down...and started sniffing.

Thoddock groaned. "I was too close to too many Owlams for far too long!"

Okton cleared his throat and nodded. He took one more sniff, shook his head and went back to his work.

The wait to see the Great Leader was mercifully short. When Thoddock heard the loud rasping noise that the communicator made, he was sure that it was for some other reason. When he was signaled by Okton to go into the Great Leader's office he was very pleasantly surprised and relieved. He got up and marched to the door. He opened the door, made the instant assessment as to the location of the desk and marched up to the desk. "Primary Leader, Thoddock, reporting. I am here to supply the Perfor Empire with some very important intelligence information in regards to the technology of the Owlams...and how we may have to act against them...sooner than we thought, because of these capabilities."

Yoytay squawked. "That's not what that *bimyock* was supposed to say!"

"I know," said Hadathoo flatly.

Leelaka cracked her knuckles. "Do we execute him now?"

Hadathoo shook his head. "Let's hear this out. Find out what he's going to say and then we'll decide on how we have to react to it."

Pitchpon leaned forward and started sniffing. "Is that... Owlam...that I smell on you?"

Thoddock hung his head. "Unfortunately, yes, Sir."

Pitchpon scoffed. "The amount of time that it takes to… get from South Chilamte to Ficara…and you haven't cleaned that smell…off of you…yet?"

Thoddock cleared his throat. "Sir…that's part of the information." He looked at his chronometer. "Less than four kasska ago…I was on the continent of South Chilamte. The Owlams…destroyed one of the cliff elevators that we'd built… to get up to the great high plateau. They caused a landslide… that caused the deaths…of at least…forty Perfor officers. They abducted me…at the base of the cliff on South Chilamte…took me to…some place and asked a few questions. They brought me here and told me that I should give the High One…this information, Sir."

"How long…did it take…to get you from South Chilamte… to Ficara?"

"I…think that it…was almost…instantaneous, Sir."

Pitchpon took a few more sniffs. "I can hardly wait…to obtain this technology. You're right! We need to get to work and… capture all of those Owlams. I'd love to have a few of them as my personal slaves. Maybe…we can all get some good advancement out of that."

"Yes, Sir," said Thoddock proudly with a smile.

Leelaka looked at Hadathoo sternly. "Do we execute him now?"

Hadathoo cleared his throat. "Wait until we have that…

number one *bimyock* in our sights."

Leelaka stuck out her lower lip and gave Hadathoo a dirty look. "Yes, Sir."

Pitchpon started punching in information on his computer. He waited for a few moments until the computer beeped. He nodded. "Let's go upstairs, Primary Leader, Thoddock!"

"Sir, did you hear about the elevator incident?"

"No, why?"

"I think that we'd better take the stairs."

Pitchpon leaned forward. "WHY?"

"Sir, the man who brought me up...somehow...went through the floor of that elevator...and fell to his death...in the elevator shaft. Until they figure out what happened...that elevator is...not to be used."

"We'll take the stairs."

"Yes, Sir."

They went to the stairwell and proceeded up two floors. They arrived in the area of the highest ranking military individuals for the Perfor. There were fifteen offices on this floor. Eight of them were offices for the rank of Exalted One. Eight of them were for the primary Aide of each Exalted One. The one at the end of the long hall was the office of the High One.

There was another Great Leader standing at the doorway to the office of the High One, beckoning them to speed up their pace. They did and were ushered into the office. They walked up to one end of a long conference table and reported in.

High One, Nooskoonim stood up. "I understand that..." He started sniffing. "Is that...Owlam...that I smell?"

Thoddock closed his eyes and his face turned red. "Yes, High One...I was...in too close a contact with the Owlams...and I haven't been able to get the smell off."

Nooskoonim grunted. "Well, this had better be important if you're going to stink up my office with...Owlam."

"Yes, Sir," said Thoddock. "The technology that the Owlams have...is much greater than we previously believed. About four kasska ago, I was on the continent of South Chilamte. They abducted me, asked me a few questions and then told me that they wanted me to come here and talk..." He snickered. "...peace. They want us to make peace with them and treat them as equals."

Nooskoonim huffed. "What arrogance!?" He then scoffed in disgust.

"Yes, Sir. Anyway, as I said, their technology...is unbelievable. One moment I was on South Chilamte...I think... well I was on South Chilamte, they abducted me and then sent me here from...where ever it was that they were talking...peace. It took...less than a millikasska for me to be transported from that conference room of theirs...to the main gate of the city of Perfor."

Nooskoonim nodded. "It seems that we must hasten the attack on Owlam. We may have to postpone that attack on the

Teltermaks…in order to achieve this end."

One of the Exalted Ones stood up. "That is impossible, High One…the attacks on the Teltermak positions…began…" He checked his chronometer and shrugged. "It has begun…four decikasska ago. We're already attacking the Teltermak positions in those island areas."

Nooskoonim sighed. "You are sure of this, Exalted One, Zilzoono?"

"Absolutely," said Zilzoono. "I just received the message from the main battle areas."

Nooskoonim shook his head. "All right then…that can't be helped. Now, we have to start setting up for an all-out attack… with what we have left…on Owlam."

"There is a problem there, High One," said Thoddock. "When we had our people on the plateau, they said that the scent of Owlam was too fresh. The Owlams have been or were there… or still are there…hiding. This may be more than one battle front."

"Unfortunate," said Nooskoonim. He looked around the table. "Exalted One, Palij…where are your forces?"

Palij shook his head. "All are engaged against the Teltermak."

"Exalted One, Teffet, what about you?"

She shook her head. "All of my forces are backing up Palij, High One."

"Exalted One, Zilzoono, what about you?"

"Fully engaged against the Teltermak, High One,"

Nooskoonim frowned. "Are there really that many Teltermak positions?"

Zilzoono nodded. "Yes, High One, they're scattered over numerous islands and some of them are on the Lusaratia continent as well."

Nooskoonim snarled. "Exalted One, Prookasikatem... what about you?"

He shrugged. "High One, All of my forces are currently doing the reconnaissance on South Chilamte...looking for the Owlams and their positions. We're having a hard time isolating exactly where they are."

Nooskoonim turned to another. "Exalted One, Finzaskit... what about you?"

"High One, my forces are currently scouting all of the positions of the Twakon."

"Exalted One, Olba...your forces?"

Olba shook his head. "High One, the majority of my forces are engaged in training all of the new troops that are coming up now. If we took them...we'd have no one doing the training and the troops that are currently in training are too new to be taken into any battle."

Nooskoonim blew his breath out in frustration. "Exalted One, Bashakana?"

"High One, we are currently scouting the P'Lalfan."

"Exalted One, Reebrono?"

"High One, we're scouting the Kalash, and they have spread themselves all over North Chilamte."

"Exalted One, Dolikon?"

"High One, all of my forces are involved in training as well. It'll be at least three months before we can have the trainees battle ready."

Nooskoonim hung his head. He looked at the last of his Exalted Ones. "I know that you're troops are currently pre-staged in that...abandoned city called Galsino. Do you have enough intelligence data to...start an attack on the city of Owlam?"

She nodded. "High One, we could start the attack...in about twenty days."

Hadathoo hung his head. "I'm really hating these perverts now."

Yoytay looked at all of the people at the conference table. "They haven't given the order...to attack Owlam yet. The only order that they've given...is to attack the Teltermak."

He looked up. "And...soon they're going to give that order?"

Leelaka huffed. "They said that they would be ready in twenty days."

Hadathoo scowled. "How long have you been in the military? Don't you know that when someone says that they'll be ready in twenty days, the first thing that the Commander does is cut that in half. Have you ever heard of it ever being done differently?"

Leelaka clenched her eyes shut. "No."

Wees smiled. "So don't give him the chance."

Hadathoo gave her a confused look. "Don't...give him... how?"

Wees shrugged. "There's four of us...there's thirteen of them. How long does it take for four Owlams to dump thirteen *bimyocks* into Jahong's Death?"

Yoytay shrugged back with a smile. "If he's not here... he can't give the order. If all of them disappear...it should have a definite impact on their chain of command."

Hadathoo sniffed. "That *doovoft*...Thoddock...he's last. That way...he knows that they're all dead...because he refused to cooperate."

In a rather short time, Hadathoo and his Team 24 were standing in front of a wide-eyed Thoddock as the Perfor looked around the room trying to figure out where his comrades had disappeared to...so quickly. "This is an outrage! Who do you think you are...coming in here...and...?" His visage changed to looking baffled. "What...did you do...with...them," he asked meekly?

"They're dead," said Hadathoo grimly. "We told you... we want peace. We are tired of fighting...all of these different peoples and races. If you and your ilk...are going to attack and attempt to enslave us...this is your future...nothing!"

Thoddock headed for the door. "Well I'm going to sound the alarm!"

Leelaka got to Thoddock first. Thoddock was now somewhere in Jahong's Death.

Yoytay sat down. "What do we do now?"

Hadathoo looked around the room. "I wonder…how fast this place…could burn down." He nodded. "Someone…go get something that is extremely flammable and let's turn this room into an inferno."

Wees smiled. "We don't have to get anything like that. Remember that one dimension…everything burns up."

Hadathoo raised his eyebrows. "Your point?"

"Grab one end of the conference table…hop the other end into…what was it…Ninka's Death…and whoosh…the table is on fire. We then get out of here before we get fried."

A few moments later, Team 24 Jumped back to Owlam to talk to Wilfadge, leaving a very hot burning conference room.

Wilfadge and the rest of the Command Staff listened to Hadathoo's report. He looked around the table sadly. "Do we have confirmation…of the attack on the Teltermak by the Perfor?"

Dwalooa nodded. "According to Officer Leader, Natsa… the Perfor have started a blood bath. She reported that…even though the Perfor executed a perfect surprise attack, the Teltermak already have the upper hand."

Wilfadge nodded. "So we should execute a surprise attack

on the ones hiding in Galsino." He sighed. "That way…we're sure that we have the upper hand…from the start."

Ahandi bit her lip. "How do we start?"

"We start by sending a few Teams to Galsino to get their exact positions and an estimate of their numbers," said Teelila.

Wilfadge nodded. "That sounds good." He sighed. "Master Officer, Teelila please take care of the scouting."

Hadathoo snarled. "I don't know if we'll ever be able to live this down."

Wilfadge frowned and looked at him. "What *are* you babbling about?"

Hadathoo shook his head. "We're going to be in…an alliance with the Teltermak in a fight against the Perfor."

Shyshee looked sick. "They don't have to know that…do they?"

Wilfadge groaned and covered his face with his hands. "Please…let as few people as possible…know that that…unholy horror…has happened."

Officer Leader, Jeejow of Team 41 and Officer Leader, Yim of Team 44 were standing on the wall at Galsino – in Spy dimension. The two men were a bit confused as to how they were going to be able to sneak into a Perfor camp, find all of the positions, count the Perfors and get out…without being smelled by the Perfors. So far, the Perfors had shown that they could smell an Owlam in any dimension.

Jeejow looked through his binoculars. "They seem to be isolated to the western part of the ruined city."

Yim scoffed. "From what we can see here…yes. From what I understand of how they rebuilt their own city on Ficara… that could be meaningless. They could have built…all kinds of disguised structures…and we wouldn't know a thing unless we get in there and let them sniff our armpits."

"Have we received any intelligence…from the battle front between the Perfor and the Teltermak?"

"Just that last report…that says that the Teltermak are beating the *h'oolyach* out of the Perfors. They just were *not* ready…to take on any airborne army."

Jeejow grunted. "Some of the High Command are of the mindset that…if the Teltermak continue smashing that invasion… the Perfor just might pull some of these personnel out…to go fight the Teltermak."

"I'm not holding my breath on that one."

"Neither am I."

"So…my best idea…wait until dark…when hopefully… most of them'll be asleep. Then we go in, take out any guards that are awake and…do the count."

"You know that once the killing starts…we can't just stop and…let them regain any form of upper hand. We have to get them confused and keep the chaos going."

"Then the other option…get about a thousand Teams in here and just start slinging them into…somewhere else."

"A thousand Teams…makes four thousand personnel. If they have…thirty thousand Perfors here…that makes it about seven or eight perverts that each one of us has to get rid of. That shouldn't be taxing on anyone."

"One advantage…if we wait until the sun goes down… they'll have a light on in all of the inhabited buildings. That'll make it easier to find them."

Jeejow sighed. "Let's put that idea in front of the High Command. Let's put all of our ideas in front of the High Command. Let them make the final decision."

"I wonder if they're going to want a body count…after we're finished."

"I don't know. They might."

"That would mean that everyone would have to keep track of how many they send…to wherever."

"Yeah, it would."

Officer Leader, Skalix of Team 37 was given the task of finding the Perfor encampments on the South Chilamte continent. The personnel that were under his current control were getting very adept at finding and flinging Perfors into Jahong's Death or drowning them in the Water dimension or dissolving them in Shogoot's Search or even leaving them to die, vomiting in Stink dimension. Just to keep in practice with the different dimensions, they were also flinging some of the Perfor victims into Kiymee's Search, Naka's Search and Sesqua's Search.

Skalix looked at the figures that he was getting from the twelve Teams that were creating all kinds of misery for the Perfor on South Chilamte. After three days they had sent 1,680 Perfors into other dimensions. From what he was seeing, they had made only a small dent in the Perfor population.

One of the Team members, Shirfaya looked at the information. "Sir, shouldn't we be asking for some help? These numbers are…getting bigger…but…we keep on finding more Perfors that are enslaving…anyone and everyone on the southern part of this continent."

He sighed. "We do need help. The problem is…the Perfor that are hiding in the city of Galsino…they're way too close for comfort. We have to get rid of that problem first. Then we can worry about the ones that are on a different continent."

"But…Sir, they got close to the gorge."

"Got! Past tense. There's not one single Perfor that's still alive…up on the plateau. Plus, we've destroyed all sixteen of those elevators that they built."

She giggled. "Yeah and every time they try to climb up the cliffs…we have someone up there cutting the ropes."

He sighed. "No, we're just going to have to make do with what we have until they get rid of the pestilence in Galsino. Once that's accomplished then we can get some help…a lot of help…in getting these perverts off of this continent."

She huffed. "North Chilamte, South Chilamte, Ficara... and some islands. I wonder if they've established themselves on other continents as well."

"I hope not."

Natsa walked through a battlefield of bodies. She hopped into Observation so that she did not have to listen to the moaning of the wounded ones. There were Teltermak and Perfor everywhere. She got tired of what she was seeing. She hopped back to the facility where they were still attempting to identify the ingredients of the *Tuzine*.

Officer Grade 3, Coycoy greeted Natsa when she arrived at the facility.

Natsa looked inside. "Are the Yagalom-Ayin still analyzing...or are they fighting?"

Coycoy shook her head. "There's probably...one fifth of the number of both Yagee and Teltas doing the analysis. Most of the rest of them are off in the battlefields trying to keep this place out of the fighting."

Natsa frowned at her. "Yagee?"

Coycoy shrugged. "It's only two syllables versus five."

Natsa snickered. "That is where ethnic slurs come from."

"If they were friendly to us...I wouldn't do that."

Wilfadge gave the order and 1,500 Teams were sent to Galsino.

The Teams went in, checking the wind direction before they entered the city of Galsino. The wind was blowing in from the west, so they had to get to the Perfor area by going through the untouched ruins. They had as much information that could be gleaned from watching the Perfor through binoculars.

The guards were in teams of three. The first few teams that were sent to other dimensions had absolutely no clue what had happened. A system of checking in at set intervals soon gave the Perfors the idea that something was dreadfully wrong…for them.

An alarm was sounded and soon all of the Perfors were up with their weapons at ready. They were all sniffing and smelling Owlams. They just never saw them. All that the Perfors saw was a lot of their comrades suddenly disappearing…and then they were on the missing list as well…if there had been anyone left who would have made that list.

One thing that irked the ones who were cleaning the Perfor pestilence from Galsino was that they had brought their families with them. They were there for good. They were going to rebuild Galsino and rule the Owlams and probably all of North Chilamte from that location.

Any rule and reign for the Perfor, on North Chilamte, ended in fourteen days of Owlamites tossing them into various dimensions. The total, as far as the people who were counting their victims could remember, ended up as 35,629…give or take a thousand.

Hadathoo looked up from the report. "It is just…disgusting. Why do these others…who can procreate…always want to come after us?"

"Because they can," said Wilfadge sadly. "It seems that the only way to…stop them…is total annihilation."

Teelila dropped her copy of the report. "Do we now send all of those personnel to South Chilamte…to do the same there?"

Wilfadge sighed. "Send a different group of 1,500 to South Chilamte. Having to kill off the families as well…because the minds of their children were already polluted…could be a bit much for some of our people. If that bunch, which we send to the south, gets in any trouble…we send…more…until we get rid of all of the perverts on South Chilamte."

Nineteen days later Natsa showed up at Headquarters with a new report. "Sirs, it seems that…the Perfors…are no longer a problem in Lusaratia or the island chains. The Teltermak have… massacred…all Perfors that were there and…" Her entire body shuddered in disgust. "The Teltermaks are now…dining… heartily…on the carrion."

Wilfadge looked at the report. "It seems…according to this that…the Yagalom-Ayin are still…analyzing the *Tuzine*. Is there any indication that they've made any headway in their investigations?"

"They've decided to encrypt their findings. I've told

numerous people in my group to read their minds and see if they can decode their secret notes. What we've decoded so far...shows the same results as before...they're still baffled."

Teelila looked up from the report. "Is this accurate?"

Natsa smiled helplessly. "Uh...Sir...which part?"

Teelila held the document up. "The Perfor lost over 120,000 personnel in those island battles?"

Natsa nodded. "That is what we have obtained from their reports, Sir. The Perfor sent a large contingency to each island... in order to take over quickly. It didn't work. Plus, that also includes a few thousand that were...fanged...by the Yagalom-Ayin. Whatever venom those people have in their bite...it seems to be very deadly...to anyone who has been bitten so far."

Hadathoo growled. "All those casualties and we haven't made a dent in their numbers."

Ahandi frowned. "What do you mean?"

Hadathoo huffed. "Yes, they've been defeated in North Chilamte. Yes, they've been defeated in Lusaratia and those islands near that continent. Yes, we've kicked them off of the high plateau in South Chilamte. Big deal! They still have a contingency on the southern part of South Chilamte, they still have their home city on Ficara...and they also still have someone scouting out those others that were on their primary list."

Wilfadge looked up. "Yes...the others. The Kalash were on that list weren't they?" He turned to his Aides. "We did send a message of warning to the Kalash didn't we?"

Oolooa smiled. "Yes, Sir, we informed them of the Perfor problem a long time ago."

Akantini gasped. "Oh…Sir…we need to inform the Kalash…that we found that bunch in Galsino…and have dispatched them."

Wilfadge grimaced. He looked around the conference table with a red face. "I believe that we should inform the Kalash of that incident…quickly."

Akantini jumped up and ran out of the room.

Wilfadge cleared his throat. "Okay…as for those others… that the Perfor considered important…does anyone remember that list?"

Shyshee picked up her pad. "It was us, the Kalash, the Teltermak, the Gabeesh-Or, the P'Lalfan and the Twakon."

Ahandi scoffed. "No point in telling the Teltermak…they already know…and have done a pretty good job of…"

"Adding to their cuisine," said Antrong in a disgusted manner.

"Be that…as it is," said Wilfadge. "We have to find out… where these others are and…why the Perfor want them…and if they might be a threat to us."

Dwalooa smiled. "If we can warn those other peoples… we might just make some friends…and keep them as friends…if at all possible."

Hoynama sighed. "That would be nice…to be able to

make friends…instead of having to fight more enemies." She smiled.

Teelila was looking at the report again. "You show here that the Teltermak did actively chase down any stragglers…from the Perfors. They took all of them prisoner. Are you sure that… none of the Perfors got away?"

Natsa rolled her eyes. "Uh…yes, Sir…very sure. It seems that…" She cleared her throat. "Some of our people were following the stragglers…to see if they could or would get away… and…when the stragglers…smelled us…they would stop and try to find us…and…that's when they got caught by the Teltermak."

Till snickered. "Are you saying that…we were in part…responsible for…none of the Perfors escaping from the Teltermak?"

Natsa shrugged. "It appears that…was what happened, Sir."

Dwalooa thumbed through a few pages of the report. "Didn't those Perfors have any kind of…retreat plan…in case things went badly?"

Natsa shook her head. "They beached all of their boats… because they are so arrogant that…they didn't think that they could lose. There was no retreat plan. If anyone had been able to get back to where the boats had been beached…I don't know if they would have had the strength to push a boat into the water. The boats were designed to hold about fifty troops and…" She shook her head and shrugged.

Wilfadge sighed. "Ahandi...why don't you start looking up this...bunch called the Gabeesh-Or? Teelila you look up the P'Lalafan and Dwalooa...you look up the Twakon. Let's see what we can find on them and...try to make some friends."

Hadathoo looked up. "Is there any information from Officer Leader, Skalix...on South Chilamte?"

Wilfadge shrugged. "Search and destroy. Those perverts are all over the continent and he's kind of...spread thin. Now that the ones in Galsino are gone...and the only ones that we have to worry about on North Chilamte are the ones who are scouting the Kalash...we might be able to give Skalix some more help."

Hadathoo stood up. "I think that I'll go visit our friends. The Kalash need to know and...I'll be the one to tell them of the Perfor."

Wilfadge nodded. "You all have your assignments. We have some work to do so let's get to it."

All of a sudden Skalix had all kinds of personnel at his disposal. They were all there for the purpose of getting the Perfor out of South Chilamte. When the indigenous Heyyah learned about the task that the Owlamites were doing they were more than willing to lend any assistance that they could. It took nearly five months, however, the Perfor that had not been flung into other dimensions were getting on boats and heading for the city of Moonta on Setotoon Isle.

Now they might have to deal with the Perfor on Setotoon.

The Command Staff was having another meeting.

Hadathoo stood up. "It seems that the Kalash knew about the Perfor. They did know that they were being spied upon...and I very quickly gave them all of the information that I could find... and now...the Perfor – that are still alive - are getting on boats and heading back to Ficara...before they end up as prisoners at the Turgon Wall."

Dwalooa looked up at him. "Did they believe you... without proof?"

He snickered. "They'd been suspicious. Some of the things that they were observing...in the actions of the Perfor were confirmed by my information. Now...I think that...the Perfor and the Algothons...might be at the throats of each other...because both...want to rule the world...and be the lone masters of all of the races. If they ever become an alliance...we could have some trouble."

"We could always ask the Teltermak to go chase them down," said Teelila in a droll manner.

Wilfadge grimaced. "Let's try to avoid...any contact with the Teltermak."

Hadathoo chuckled. "We have started some rumors in Moonta...and the rest of Setotoon. We've informed the inhabitants of Setotoon...what kind of people the Perfor are...and that they'll probably try to take over that island...in order to have a base of operations to re-invade South Chilamte. The Heyyah of Setotoon were very eager to believe this information because…they've been having a few problems with the Perfor for a long time. Our first observations of the Perfor on Setotoon was that…everything was peaceful. Now…the local Heyyah seem to have some proof of the nastiness of the Perfor and are willing to give them all a strong *shove* off of the island. The other half of that island…called Zintanala…they'd already given the Perfor the shove."

"The main point being…the Perfor are losing ground… everywhere," said Wilfadge.

Hadathoo just smiled.

Wilfadge blew his breath out. He looked at Ahandi and smiled. "Now…what about these…Gabeesh-Or?"

Ahandi snarled. "A bunch of *chokwads*! They're located in the northeastern part of Ficara. This is another bunch…with strange skin. These, however, don't glow. Have you seen some of these…seashells…that some of our people are bringing back… from some of their trips to some of the equatorial islands?" She watched while several of the Staff nodded. "It seems that these… Gabeesh-Or…have skin that looks…like the part of the shell where the animal touches the inner part of the shell. Their skin doesn't glow…like the Zee-Althans or the Perfor…but it is… rather attractive. It has a pearlescent quality. It seems to shimmer but it really doesn't. They are very pretty people…but they have a very nasty attitude. They're about six and a half taja in height, they have…absolutely no hair at all. They acted as if…I should be…subservient to them. They know that the Perfor are watching them and…they kill the perverts…every chance they get. We tried a little spying on the Perfors in the area and we found out...they are waiting for orders from the...Exalted One who...is in their specific chain of command. Since they have received no word from...whichever one it is...they're not sure what to do other than continue what they are doing...even though they're losing several of their people to the Gabeesh-Or...every single day."

Wilfadge grunted. "Do you think there is any chance of becoming friends with them?"

Ahandi shook her head sadly. "I don't know if we want to...they are very snobbish and...if they had...half the assets that the Perfor have...they'd probably be trying to take over...as well."

"This is beginning to sound redundant," said Hadathoo.

"Don't remind me," grumbled Wilfadge. He sighed. "Teelila...what's the report on these...P'Lalfan?"

Teelila scoffed. "You wanna talk about nasty attitude? Let me give you a clue...to a really nasty attitude. It's called...P'Lalfan people. They are...probably seven taja...in height...or maybe I should say...length. They have pale brown skin and...they have no arms or legs - they have flippers. They can outswim most fish. From what I have found out...their city of origin...is well inland... in the south central part of Aerisau. When the firestorm attack hit, they became...like some kind of aquatic mammal. They couldn't live in their city. They had to abandon it and move to the water. They originally tried a lake that is near their city...but fresh water didn't suit them. They had to...crawl...all the way to the ocean. They now have control...or mostly have control of virtually every fishing village on the southwestern shores of Aerisau. As their population increases…they have a tendency to take more beach area…both directions from their central location. I think that the Perfor want them…as slaves…to make them take over any and all shores…any place in the world."

Wilfadge frowned. "Have the Perfor approached them with this…idea?"

Teelila giggled. "I wouldn't use the word…approach. The Perfor attacked and tried to take control. It seems that the P'Lalfan can hold their breath for…a very long time. They just grabbed a Perfor and pulled the *chogo* under…until they drowned. The Perfor are sitting there…sulking…trying to figure out a way to conquer these people without getting their feet wet."

Wilfadge looked up sadly. "Is there…any chance…of us making friends…with *these* people?"

Teelila sighed. "I doubt it. They're very nasty to anyone… who come near them. They demand…tribute…from all of the people in the fishing villages…regardless of race."

Wilfadge shook his head. "Two down…one to go." He looked at Dwalooa. "What have you got to report?"

Dwalooa shook her head back at him. "These people… the Twakon…are nastier than the other two. They're another race…with an exoskeleton. These people are gray instead of the black like the Sodle. They're about seven and a half taja in height. This exoskeleton of theirs…they have…random hairs…or maybe tendrils…or *something*…growing out of that skin. They found the Perfor…and have…brutally killed every single one that they found. They never talked to…anyone…they just kill…anyone who is dumb enough to get…anywhere close to them.'"

Wilfadge narrowed his eyes. "Where…are these people… located?"

"They're living near the southwestern coast of Ficara."

"And they don't like anybody."

She shook her head. "I was afraid to come out of Spy dimension. I saw two Heyyah children…get too close…and…" She looked off to the side and cleared her throat and shook her head. "What they did to those children…there was no reason for it."

Wilfadge huffed. "So these are three peoples…who are just as hateful and nasty as the Perfor…and they don't want to be slaves of the Perfor…they want to do their own damage." He shook his head. "I wonder how many other hateful peoples we'll find on the planet." He leaned back in his chair. "So far…the only reason that none of these people…get along…or will form an alliance…they all just…hate! They hate everybody else, so they don't form any alliance. That works for us. At least they won't get together…voluntarily. If one of those races…does conquer the others…they'll have a real *chogo* of a time…trying to control their…slaves."

"I doubt that any of them would or could stand being slaves…to someone else," said Hadathoo.

"Their mutual hatred and distrust for everybody…is our greatest weapon against them…if we ever have to use one…on any of them," said Wilfadge. "Are there…any other new races of

Elf...that we've not discussed yet?"

Shyshee smiled. "Yes, there is one."

Wilfadge closed his eyes. "Is this good news...or bad news?"

Shyshee giggled. "It's good news. While Hadathoo was talking to some of the Kalash...at the Turgon Wall...I had a chance to meet with some other new friends of the Kalash. They're called...Wokig. They're a little over seven taja in height, they have pale skin, bright straw colored hair...and both sexes...have a large mane that completely encircles their entire head."

Wilfadge looked up hopefully. "So...they are now... friendly with the Kalash...and so they are...friendly...with us?"

"Oh, yes, Sir, I had a lovely conversation with several of them," said Shyshee. "I found out that they have a large contingency at the Turgon Wall. They're extremely good at being guards there, because they take no guff from anyone and they are very, very good at hand-to-hand combat...which makes them very good at handling any unruly prisoners."

Wilfadge sighed with a smile. "At least we can end this meeting with one very nice and positive piece of information... for once. Are there any other new Elf races that anybody knows about?"

"Yes," said Hadathoo. "They're another new bunch at the Turgon Wall. They're called Towtoo. They're just under five taja, they have dark brown skin and they have multi-jointed arms and legs. We have one elbow...they have two. We have one knee...

they have two. The way they walk looks rather awkward, but if any of the prisoners give them any backtalk, those extra joints make them extremely flexible and very tough to beat in a wrestling match. They're also...very picky when it comes to the letter of the law." He grunted. "The law is everything to them."

The Command Staff of the Owlam Nation continued to receive reports of battles with the Perfor. It became rather apparent as to why the Perfor wanted to get other peoples to do their fighting for them. The Perfor were not very good at fighting. After two years, there were no more reports of any sightings or battles with Perfors. Another race had become extinct.

11

Team 7016 was in their gymnasium area getting ready to beat the stuffing out of the big bags. Soolchakan had already finished his warm up and was punching and kicking a well-worn bag.

The three women were stretching on the mat getting ready to start doing some punching and kicking.

Chyning stopped for a moment. "I know that the Perfor were run out of Lusaratia and the islands by the Teltermak. We got rid of them…here on South Chilamte. The Kalash did some heavy damage to them on North Chilamte…what happened in Ficara? How did they get thrown out of their own city?"

Bonarain let out a loud squawk. "Don't you ever read any of the after action reports? Maybe if you did, you wouldn't have to ask these dumb questions."

Chyning smiled back. "I don't read the reports because you're always so eager to talk about them."

Kiyalee snickered. "Maybe you should keep your big mouth shut and then she'd have to read them."

Bonarain sighed. "When the Perfor were thrown out of

all of those places, most of the Heyyah tribes on Ficara saw…a bunch of defeated Perfor headed back to their home city. Those tribes were very tired of being harassed by the Perfor…on their own soil. So they followed them and…about twenty tribes of Heyyah…attacked in full force. Most of the Perfor that were left, inside the city, were nothing but trainees…*basic*…trainees. Most of them hadn't received any training on handling weaponry and the ones who had received training were still not proficient. It was a complete slaughter. There were a few more Perfor stragglers that wandered back into the city, but…as soon as they did, the Heyyah were all over them. The Perfor were completely done in because they irritated everybody. All of those people they were spying on…killed them. All of the Heyyah on Ficara were tired of them. When you irritate everybody, you don't have any friends. That…is a deadly mistake."

Kiyalee sat there giving Bonarain a nasty look. "I thought I told you that you should keep your mouth shut. That'll *make* her have to read the report."

Bonarain looked up despondently. "I can't keep my mouth shut. I like talking about the defeat of *h'oolyach* like the Perfor."

Chyning just giggled as she stretched.

Wilfadge felt a little uncomfortable about the visit that Hadathoo had taken to the Turgon Wall. He decided that it was time that he visited the big prison. It had been the Owlamites who had a big hand in demolishing the Sodle and turning the Turgon Wall into a great international prison. He felt guilty about not visiting more since…he could not remember when he had last been there. A visit by the Supreme Officer would be a good thing…he hoped.

He took his Team 13 to the Turgon Wall with him. He, Akantini, Oolooa and Chani were a little surprised when they pulled up to the wall in one of the trucks that had been supplied by Kiyalee. They remembered the wall being further away from the place that they had just driven up to.

Akantini frowned. "Is this…the right place?"

"I think so," said Wilfadge. "Unless…they've done a few changes around here…that no one told us about."

They drove up to a gate. Chani was driving. She leaned out and smiled at a guard who was of the T'Mor race. "Hello, Sir. I'm here with the Supreme Officer of the Owlam nation. We're here to see…whoever is in charge."

The guard stood there for a moment with a shocked look in his eyes. "The…leader of…Owlam?"

"Yes, Sir."

The T'Mor got on a radio and started talking so rapidly that none of the Owlamites could understand him. A response came back over the radio that was in the same strange dialect…or accent…or whatever the T'Mor was using for language.

He seemed to be quivering with excitement as he looked at all of the inhabitants of the truck. "I…remember those days… when the Owlams…come to our rescue. I remember that we… were almost food for those Turgons. We remember the Owlams.

We…forever thank you…for saving us.   Saving us from…
Turgon…and Sodle."

Wilfadge smiled. "Yes, I remember those days as well.
You are quite welcome."

He held up the radio. "My supervisor…he say that I take
you to main building. I drive truck…I know the way and I drive
and show you."

Another guard came out. He was one of the Rahanan-Sar.
The green shock of hair on top of the yellow skinned man still
looked as if it were some kind of strange costume. "I remember
the days when we first met as well. I'm so glad that we were able
to be friends with you…and so glad that those nasty Sodle were
exposed…and defeated completely. I'm also very glad that you
shared the information about those nasty Perfor."

Wilfadge smiled back. "As always, it is best to share
any information with your allies. I don't know what those pesky
Perfor were trying to pull, but, I'm glad that everything worked
out for the better…for us all."

The T'Mor man got in the driver's seat. He started
chattering on his radio again in a language that left everyone there
just looking around in confusion. He drove for quite a ways before
Wilfadge got a little suspicious.

"I thought that the main building was a little closer to the
main gate," said Wilfadge.

"Oh, that change," said the T'Mor excitedly. "New wall…
on the east side…change gate location. Main building still there,

but new gate because of new wall."

Wilfadge nodded with a bit of a strained smile. "Maybe I should come here more often."

The T'Mor nodded his head. "Oh that would be nice…but you have big responsibility. You find nasty Perfor and help stop them. You make *Tuzine* and spread it around. No one else do that. You help us all."

Wilfadge smiled with a little more conviction this time. "Again, my friend, you are quite welcome." He sat back and enjoyed the rest of the trip.

Oolooa sent Wilfadge a mental message about checking the fuel gage. He returned a message that they could always hop back to Owlam and get some more – if needed. Oolooa shrugged and leaned back as well.

They finally arrived at the main building and everything looked familiar to Wilfadge. He had taken a few trips out here before, however, that was a long time ago. The building of a new east wall intrigued him as to why it had been deemed necessary.

They were greeted by an old friend – Milthiy of the Great River. He was a Principle Officer in the Kalash military. "So good to see you again, Supreme Officer, Wilfadge."

Wilfadge narrowed his eyes. "Have you received a promotion since the last time I saw you?"

"Oh, yes, my friend. Last time I was a Lead Officer. It seems that each one of my counterparts received a promotion… so I did as well. It doesn't mean that much now, however it still sounds nice."

Wilfadge chuckled in agreement. "What is this…east wall? I don't remember that from the last time I was here."

Milthiy nodded. "That was an idea from one of our Argaman-Or friends. They saw that the prison population was growing rapidly and…we only had the wall itself…as far as housing prisoners. There was ample opportunity for them to escape. So…a new wall was built." He snickered. "We used prisoner labor to build it. They thought that they were going to be getting newer nicer quarters." He shook his head. "Now they know that it was built just to keep them in."

Wilfadge nodded. "Are there still that many attacks… from the Turgons?"

Milthiy shook his head. "Daily! Somewhere along the wall…every day…there is an attack somewhere. Those Turgons must be…procreating at an incredible rate. According to the reports we kill at least fifty per day."

"Every day…that…is some…staggering figures."

"It certainly is." Milthiy frowned. "I…hope you don't mind…my observation but…your ears…look as if they've… grown."

Wilfadge looked at his Aides. He paid careful attention to the size of their ears. "It…is…possible. I hadn't thought about it. I'll have to see…if there are any pictures of us…from right after the firestorm attack…and see if our ears have…grown."

Milthiy huffed. "At least if your ears *are* growing…they

didn't just...shoot up like ours did. Your change is happening slowly."

Wilfadge nodded. "So slowly that we haven't noticed." He looked to the east. "Do you have a map of this...new wall and...the area in between?"

Milthiy snickered. "Of course. Come on in and I'll give you a grand tour of what has been accomplished in the last few years."

As they walked inside, Wilfadge could not help himself. "I must apologize for not assisting at the Wall...with my personnel."

They went to the office area where the Kalash had their area. They went into an office to sit, relax and converse for a few moments before the tour.

Milthiy shook his head. "Oh, think nothing of this...lack of assistance. The intelligence information that you have supplied to all of us...along with assisting in the defeat of the Cacktash and the Perfor, plus continuing the manufacturing of the *Tuzine*...no one is upset with the Owlam people at all. Your contributions are so valuable no one has any complaints...except maybe for any Cacktash or Perfor that might still be lurking about."

"Yes, it's a shame that we've had to...finish a job that the Algothons started, but if it takes putting someone down...to make sure that we survive...I'm afraid that it is painfully necessary."

Milthiy nodded. "You are correct." He looked down sadly as he shook his head. He gave Wilfadge an inquisitive look. "One thing...I've been meaning to ask...is why...did your people come here…to the Wall…and tell only us – the Kalash – about the Perfor? There are many other races here…but…you warned us… alone."

"The intelligence that we uncovered…us – the Owlamites, the Kalash, the Gabeesh-Or, the P'Lalfan, the Twakon and the Teltermak…were all listed as primary targets. They listed those six races as the most important…in enslaving all six of those… first." He shook his head. "They wanted us because of the *Tuzine* and some of our other technology. They wanted the P'Lalfan… because those people now…have no arms or leg, just flippers. They can take over…any fishing village…and then they'd have owned the coastlines. They wanted the Teltermak…because no one else has an airborne army. The Gabeesh-Or and the Twakon… are brutally nasty…just plain mean. Why they wanted those two races…I don't know. I also don't know…why the Kalash were on the primary list as well. Why would they have wanted you?"

Milthiy smiled. He turned to his intercom and hit a switch. "Bring that disobedient Fastern in here."

Wilfadge and his Team all looked confused. "Fastern… what is a Fastern?"

Milthiy pointed. "That…is a Fastern."

A prisoner was being brought in with a Kalash guard holding each arm. He had an arrogant look on his face. He was over seven and a half taja in height. He had dark brown skin…and fangs.

Milthiy stood up and slowly walked towards the belligerent prisoner. "I understand that you don't like the tasks…that have been assigned to you…when there are no Turgon attacks."

The prisoner looked off to the side, doing everything he could to show no interest in what was being said by Milthiy.

Milthiy shook his head and sighed. He raised his hands up to shoulder level and out, almost as if he were surrendering. He started rubbing his thumbs against his fingers. A soft crackling noise started emanating from his hands. The noise got louder and it appeared as if there were electrical sparks arcing from one finger to another. The crackling became even louder and now it appeared as if there were small blue lightning bolts coming off of all of his fingers.

Chani closed her eyes and started concentrating to see if she could read Milthiy's mind, in regards to this strange magical, electrical act.

The prisoner was now looking at the electric show with some trepidation. Milthiy grabbed the shoulders of the prisoner. The Fastern man let out a piercing scream and fell to his knees. The Kalash guards did not let go of the prisoner and showed no sign that they were being electrocuted. Milthiy had his eyes clenched shut as he continued holding the shoulders of the screaming prisoner. The prisoner now fell prone on the floor.

Milthiy stood up straight and smoothed his hair back a little. "Get up, prisoner!"

The Fastern man looked up in horror at Milthiy.

"I said GET UP!"

The two Kalash guards helped the prisoner to his feet,

roughly. The Fastern man was now panting and looking at Milthiy without being able to hide any of his fear. Milthiy stepped back and started rubbing his hands together. The electrical show became even louder as larger bolts of electricity shot out of his hands.

The Fastern prisoner fell to his knees again. "I...behave... Prison Leader...I...do what you want! Please...no more...Prison Leader...I do...tasks!"

Milthiy smiled. He walked over to a table in his office. The only thing on the table was a large metallic globe. He placed his hands on the globe and it started glowing as the electrical crackling subsided. He walked back to the prisoner. The globe continued to glow for several moments after he had depleted his charges on it.

Milthiy looked sternly at the Fastern. "So we don't need another...disciplinary session?"

The Fastern shook his head violently. "No...Prison Leader...no...problems. I do tasks!"

Milthiy smiled. "Good boy."

He patted the Fastern on the cheek. The prisoner flinched as the Kalash hand came in contact with his face. He looked up in terror. The two guards pulled him up to his feet and hauled him out of the office.

Milthiy turned back to the Owlamites. "When...there are no enemies...pestering you...it is easier to find out things...about yourself. We have found...that we can produce electrical charges from our bodies...at will. The...Perfor...just might have wanted to utilize that…for their benefit."

Wilfadge nodded. *"That*…is a definite possibility."

Another Kalash entered the office, pushing a cart full of refreshments. All four Owlamites started doing their own sniffing as they were hit by the smell of hot kwatha coming out of a small steaming pot in the middle of the cart.

Milthiy looked at the other Kalash. "Thank you, Fossatayn." He smiled at the Owlamites. "Something to eat… before the big tour."

Fossatayn used a ladle to fill four mugs with kwatha and then handed the mugs to the guests who took the mugs gratefully with huge smiles.

Milthiy took a cup of some other liquid from the cart. "I… wonder…if…you have discovered anything…about yourselves… like my electrical show. I understand that there are some unusual manifestations…coming from some of the Elf races…and… other than your technology…have you noticed…anything about yourselves?"

Wilfadge sent a quick mental message to his Aides. Just this once, he was going to let someone know one thing. He hopped to Ghost dimension and walked over to a shocked Milthiy. He waved his arm through Milthiy's chest with a big grin on his face. He backed off and returned to Home dimension. "We have found…that we have a capability of…turning ourselves…to an untouchable state. It is a good…defensive weapon."

"Very impressive," said Milthiy with wide eyes. "I can

understand how someone would want to…utilize that. It does have the drawback…that…you can still be seen. You can't be touched, but…you can still be seen. Not much for…sneaking up on someone."

"Unfortunately, no," said Wilfadge. "It is strictly… defensive." He looked at Chani.

Chani smiled back while chewing on a lump of kwatha. She stood up, hopped to Ghost, walked over to the wall, walked through the wall and came back. She hopped back to Home dimension and went back and sat down.

Milthiy chuckled. "I like that. You can escape from any enemy without…having to have some elaborate plan. The unfortunate thing, they can still follow you."

Wilfadge looked at Oolooa and smiled.

Oolooa sighed. She hopped to Ghost dimension and sank through the floor. She came back up smiling and hopped back to Home.

Wilfadge grinned. "You turn untouchable…go into the ground…and they have no idea which way you've gone."

Milthiy chuckled again. "You can get away from anyone that way." He frowned. "Could you…spy on someone that way?"

Wilfadge shrugged. "Unfortunately, again, we can be seen. Plus, when we turn, the sounds are…a little distorted. Very difficult to tell what was said and what was not said. It does have that strange drawback."

Milthiy snickered. "I wonder if the Algothons had any idea...what would happen...once they let all of those horrid weapons loose."

Wilfadge snarled. "I don't think that they had a clue. They just thought that they could scare the *peewodon* out of everybody and anyone who was left would...surrender. I don't think that if they knew that they would make Elf races that...are superior in many ways to Heyyah..." He shook his head. "I don't think that they were thinking."

Milthiy grunted. "I think you're right." He stood up. "Is everybody ready for a tour of the newer part of the facilities?"

Wilfadge smiled. "Why not?" He looked at his Aides. "Let's go see what we have here."

Chani looked up from her mug in consternation. She looked back down at the mug.

Milthiy smiled. "You may bring that with you."

She flushed, got up and walked behind the two men happily sipping at the steaming hot broth.

They spent half the day looking at all kinds of new buildings and the inner section between the walls. The new east wall was approximately five kilotaja from the old west wall that the Sodle had built. It gave them a massive amount of room for expansion within the walls. They could build several cities inside the walls seeing as how both walls stretched from the north shore to the south shore at the eastern end of the peninsula.

After the tour they were back in Milthiy's office.

Milthiy looked around merrily. "Well...what do you think?"

"You've...done quite a bit...in making sure that the prison can expand...without having to add another wall," said Wilfadge.

"We're going to start building on the east side of the east wall though."

Wilfadge was shocked. "But...why?"

"Consider...right now, all of the prisoners are housed in the west wall. They still have...some access to the inner area between the west and east wall. That means that they could possibly get to the administration building and to the homes of the guards." He shrugged. "So, we build all of the homes and administration buildings...on the outside of the east wall. Then...we have guards who stay on the east wall and make sure that no prisoners can get...east...out of here."

After spending two days at the Turgon Wall, Wilfadge said his farewells to the friends and allies at the Wall. They got in their truck and departed.

Chani scowled at Wilfadge as they departed. "How far do we have to drive before we can Jump back to Owlam?"

Wilfadge sighed. "I'd say...at least fifteen kilotaja. That way no one should be watching from the Wall."

"That sure was something impressive...that he did with his hands," said Oolooa. "I wonder if...we could ever do anything like that."

Chani giggled. "I read his mind while he was doing it. I got some imagery...but I can't figure it out. Maybe if I give it to you...we could all figure it out and...we could start shooting sparks out of our hands."

Wilfadge glared at Chani. "You...read his mind?"

Chani looked back defensively. "I didn't...interfere... with anything."

Wilfadge huffed. "Okay...so you got the imagery. Let's wait...until we get back to Owlam. Talk to that Officer, Bonarain. If you can't figure it out...maybe she can." He gave Chani another dirty look and shook his head as he grunted in contempt.

Chani huffed. "What's wrong with what I did?"

He snarled at her. "To spy on...friends like that Kalash... it...just isn't very polite."

Oolooa looked at the odometer. "We've driven nineteen kilotaja."

"So let's Jump," said Wilfadge.

Bonarain listened to Chani. She sat there frowning the entire time listening to the explanation. Chani gave the explanation five different ways as to what she saw when the Kalash did his little electrical trick with his fingers. Before Chani could give a sixth long winded oration about the trick Bonarain held up her hands.

"Just give me the imagery," said Bonarain. "I'll study it...

and see what I come up with."

Chani looked a little hurt. She cleared her throat, closed her eyes and started sending the imagery. She opened her eyes, smiling at first she looked at Bonarain and saw a frown. "What… what's wrong?"

Bonarain held her hands out. "That's it?"

"Yeah…that's all of it."

Bonarain looked off to the side a little perplexed. "Okay, if that's all of it…I'll think about it and see what I come up with."

Chani smiled, nodded and Jumped back to her office.

Bonarain looked over at Soolchakan. "Were you eavesdropping in on that?"

He scratched his head. "It does…seem rather…*minute*… for something like the electric show that she said came out of his hands."

Bonarain sighed. "Why do all of these people keep coming to me? Why can't they figure it out for themselves?"

He chuckled. "Because then they'd have to do some work. If they can dump it off on you, they don't have to work, or even think about working."

She stuck her tongue out at him. "Why don't you do some of the pondering on some of this stuff?"

He smiled. "Because right now…I'm going to heat up some of that stew that Chyning made last night. Did you want a bowl of it?"

"Yeah...that's some good stuff. I didn't know there was any leftovers."

He rolled his eyes. "She used that big, steel pot when she made the stew...and she filled the thing."

Bonarain giggled. "That means that we'll have plenty... for at least five days."

"Right," he said as he went into the kitchen.

She did some deep breathing to clear her mind. She started running the new imagery through her mind slowly. It still seemed that there was not enough information in the imagery that Chani had shared. She started running her thumbs across her fingertips. She heard the crackling and was both excited and puzzled at what was happening. She placed the middle finger of her right hand against a table...and blew a hole right through the table. She looked through the hole in shock.

She stood up, holding her crackling hands out. She looked at the small little bolts of electricity that were arcing between her fingers. She (without thinking) placed her hands on the table and tried going over the imagery in her head again. Then she smelled something burning. She looked down. The wood of the table was starting to catch fire. She pulled her hands off of the table and saw two charred handprints on the table surface.

She hopped to Spy dimension and Jumped to the area above the gorge on South Chilamte. She looked around to see if anyone was around. She saw no one. She walked over to a boulder and placed her hands on the boulder in an attempt at depleting the electrical charge in her hands. All she did was blast the boulder into millions of tiny fragments. The energy in her hands seemed to be getting stronger.

She looked up to the sky. "Think, think, think! Where did…Chani get this imagery? She got it from a Kalash Officer…at the Turgon Wall. I…gotta get to the Turgon Wall…find a Kalash… and see if…I can figure out how to turn this…power off."

She Jumped to the Turgon Wall. It took her half the day and several Jumps around the wall before she found a Kalash that was using the power. She closed her eyes and read his mind. She looked for the imagery that he was using to do the electrical hand trick. She found it easily and followed along with him. When he turned the power off, she grabbed hold of that imagery and used it. The crackling and arcing in her hands stopped immediately… however her hands kept on steaming for a little while. She sank down to her knees in exhaustion. All of that electrical display and Jumping had taken a toll on her.

She sat there panting for several moments. When she regained a little bit of her strength she Jumped back to her private chambers in the gorge, flopped down on her bed and slept for the other half of the day.

When she woke up, she felt nasty. She went to the tub and scrubbed her entire body. When she finally felt clean, she got out, dried off, put on a clean uniform…and went looking for Chani.

Chani was in the Headquarters Offices in the city of Owlam. She was doing some of the work assigned to her by Wilfadge.

She was a little surprised when Bonarain walked into her office… with a very sinister look on her face. Chani chuckled sheepishly. "Can…I help you?"

Bonarain put her fists down on Chani's desk. "The next time you get some kind of imagery…from anybody…get *all* of it!"

Chani's eyes darted around in confusion. "What…are you talking about?"

Bonarain leaned further forward and was talking through her teeth. "You got all of the imagery…on how to turn that power on. You did NOT get the imagery on how to TURN IT OFF!" She stood up straight. "Yuh *bimyock*! I ruined a perfectly good table…because I didn't know how to TURN IT OFF!"

Chani flushed and smiled helplessly. "Uh…how did…you finally figure out…how to turn it off?"

"I had to Jump to the Turgon Wall and find a Kalash that was doing it…and follow him until he TURNED IT OFF!"

Chani shrugged and smiled again. "Well…then… everything…is okay…then."

Bonarain bared her teeth. She lowered her head and looked at Chani from underneath her eyebrows. She held up her hands and started rubbing her thumbs across her fingers. The crackling started up again.

Chani got a look of sheer terror in her eyes…and Jumped… somewhere. She went to any location…where Bonarain was not.

Bonarain took a deep breath and shut the power off. She stood there a few moments trying to calm down. She smiled and turned the power back on. After burning two steaming handprints into the middle of Chani's desk, she Jumped back to the gorge. She then taught the rest of Team 7016 how to perform the electric hand trick…and how to turn it off.

Wilfadge had to send out a message to all Owlamites. He wanted someone to check and see if they had a picture that was taken shortly after the firestorm had hit…or at least had a photograph that was at least fifty years old. He wanted to check the size of the ears at that time versus the size of the ears now. If for nothing else other than to satisfy his own curiosity. He wanted to know if the Owlamite ears were growing…even at a slow rate, he wanted to know if they were growing.

There were at least two thousand who had pictures for him to look at. After seeing just twenty of the pictures he had the confirmation that the Owlamites ears were growing. They seemed to be growing up with a point at the top. He remembered some of the older men, when he had been a young boy, whose ears grew out in every direction. Things had changed completely since the firestorm attack.

Hadathoo looked at the new report. "I don't see anything here…about us doing anything…about purloining any Perfor stuff…from their home city."

Wilfadge snickered. "There wasn't anything there…worth

taking."

Ahandi scoffed. "Are you saying that we couldn't find… anything? What about their underground storage?"

Wilfadge shook his head. "Those people didn't have any underground storage. Everything that they had…they stored above ground."

Hoynama flipped through a few pages. "What about… that bunch with flippers? They had to have left a bunch of stuff behind…because they couldn't use…or even hold onto it… anymore."

Wilfadge looked at Teelila. "You were the one who was supposed to be scouting the P'Lalfan…what about their city?"

Teelila shook her head. "The place was ransacked a *long* time ago. When they had to bump-waddle their way to the ocean like one of those aquatic otariidae animals…yes there was a great deal of things that they couldn't take with them because they don't have the hands to utilize it anymore." She shook her head. "All of the locals got in there after the P'Lalfan departed…and…no one on my Team could find anything…that was left behind…that is in any way usable."

"Maybe that's why they have such a nasty attitude," said Antrong. "They had been able to utilize all that stuff…and now they couldn't even pick it up."

Dwalooa cleared her throat. "The…uh…latest thing…on the Twakon…it didn't make it into this report…for some reason."

Wilfadge looked up. "Something…we need to know?"

"They're starting to expand...their borders. They're doing it forcefully." Dwalooa sighed and looked around. "You remember...that those Sodle...they were bulletproof. It seems that the Twakon have an exoskeleton...same thing. They've decided that because they can't be harmed by normal bullets... they must be superior...and they're going to go conquering."

Hoynama scoffed. "So they're doing their conquering on Ficara?"

Dwalooa looked up sadly. "And the islands in the Ficara Separation group."

Wilfadge sighed. "Should we worry?"

Dwalooa nodded in affirmation.

Hadathoo grunted. "The Sodle...you couldn't tell where they were looking...because of those...eyes. Do these people have the same kind of eyes?"

Dwalooa shook her head. "They have a metallic gray exoskeleton...but their eyes are...normal." She shook her head and scoffed. "Ever since the firestorm...what's normal?"

Wilfadge hung his head. "Now...we have to watch... the Algothon, the Teltermak, the Yagalom-Ayin...the Gabeesh-Or, the P'Lalfan...and now put a closer watch on...the Twakon." He put his right hand over his eyes. "This is becoming painfully repetitive."

Hadathoo sighed. "The things that we have to do for survival."

Dwalooa looked around the table. "Now we have to assign a new Team...to go watch the Twakon full time. Who should we put in charge of this Team?"

Wilfadge shook his hand at her, motioning for her to hold on to that thought for a while. "Before we make any…larger spy Team…I think that we should send only one Team…and let them do some reconnaissance. Do some mind reading…do some watching…and find out just how…arrogant and forceful they are. They might…just get tired of conquering and…stay home for a while. I don't want an all-out war with them…unless I have to."

Ahandi shrugged. "I've got an Officer Leader in my section. She said that she's willing to do some recon…if needed… for the greater good of Owlam."

Wilfadge raised his eyebrows. "Who?"

"Officer Leader, Am-Sisa of Team 50. She and her Team are ready to do the job. All we have to do is tell them…where."

Wilfadge nodded slightly. "Call them. Bring them here. We'll brief them."

Ahandi closed her eyes and concentrated for a few moments. When she opened her eyes she smiled at Wilfadge. "She's on her way."

They all looked at the door. Several moments later, Akantini was ushering in three members of Team 50 – two women and one man.

Wilfadge raised his eyebrows. "Is your Team incomplete?"

"No, Sir," said Am-Sisa. "One of my Team was just getting out of the bathtub…when we were summoned." Her face turned a little red.

Wilfadge nodded. "Fine, fine. So, whom do we have here?"

"I am Officer Leader, Am-Sisa. The two…that are here… are Officer Grade 5, Orng." She pointed to the man. "And Officer Grade 7, Xikinta." She pointed at the woman.

Wilfadge smiled. "Who is missing?"

Again Am-Sisa blushed. "That would be Officer Grade 6, Impilasha."

"You can brief her when you see her," said Wilfadge. "Now, you said that you'd like to do a little reconnaissance for us. Okay, we have a target for you to recon."

Orng gave Am-Sisa a nasty look. Xikinta rolled her eyes in disgust and huffed.

Am-Sisa gave both of them a scolding glare. She turned back to Wilfadge. "Yes, Sir, we're glad to oblige," she said cheerfully.

A woman was ushered in by Akantini. This woman looked very disgusted and her hair was dripping wet.

Am-Sisa looked at her joyfully. "This is Officer Grade 6, Impilasha."

Impilasha looked at the Staff and gave a half-hearted smile.

Wilfadge looked at them with a little concern. He could see that the only one who wanted to volunteer was Am-Sisa. He hoped that it would not turn into a disaster. He looked at Ahandi. "Do you want to brief them?"

Ahandi smiled and flushed. "It is Dwalooa...who was doing some initial recon. Maybe she should give the briefing."

Dwalooa smiled. "I agree." She turned to Am-Sisa. "The Twakon are currently located on the southwestern coast of Ficara. They seem to want to do some expansion of their holdings... to more of the continent and some of the islands in the Ficara Separation area. We need you to follow them, for a while...a little more closely than what I was initially doing. Find out if they're doing any conquering...and if they have any special abilities... especially if they have anything like the Cacktash or the Perfor. Any questions?"

Am-Sisa smiled. "Is there any...time limit on when you want the information?"

"No," said Wilfadge. "Keep on following them... especially if you notice anything strange about their capabilities. If you need extra help...don't hesitate to ask. If we have to put ten Teams at your disposal...we'll do it."

Am-Sisa smiled. "We're glad to be of service, Sir." She looked back at her Team and received a trio of scowls. She looked back at Wilfadge and cleared her throat. "The job will be done in a professional manner."

Wilfadge smiled. "I hope so." He scanned the other faces of Team 50. "If there are no more questions...dismissed."

All four members of Team 50 vanished.

Wilfadge cleared his throat. He looked at Ahandi scowling. "I saw only one volunteer. I saw three rather upset…followers."

Ahandi sighed. "I don't know what's wrong. I've talked to them…several times and…I don't understand what I just saw. All four of them have…always displayed a totally professional attitude. There must have been…something…that I hope doesn't hinder them."

Wilfadge nodded. "Uh-huh! I hope it doesn't hinder anything either."

Two months later, Team 50 came back to a Command Staff meeting.

Wilfadge called the meeting to order and then leaned back in his chair. "Officer Leader, Am-Sisa…what have you to report?"

She shook her head. "They…are for the most part… unstoppable…on land."

Wilfadge leaned forward cocking his head to the side.

She shook her head again. "They…are totally bulletproof… for the small caliber weapons. The larger caliber…may sting them…but all that does is slow them down for a few heartbeats. If the bullet…from a large caliber weapon does penetrate…again… it only slows them down. A…wall…or any other type of barrier… doesn't do much to stop them. We watched them go through a wooden barrier…like it was paper. A concrete barrier was bashed down…with their fists. A metal barrier…took them a little longer to bash through." She took a deep breath. "A little longer…but not much." She looked around at the Staff personnel.

Dwalooa leaned forward. "You're going to have to go into a little more detail than that."

Am-Sisa looked confused. "Sir?"

Dwalooa smiled. "Bulletproof...but not totally... slowed...but only partially. Let's not forget that you said that they're unstoppable...on...*land*."

Am-Sisa looked at Impilasha.

Impilasha sighed and walked up to the table. "Sirs, the small caliber bullets...they do just bounce off. We didn't even see a dent...or impression. The larger caliber bullets, a few of them got the attention of the Twakon that was hit. I did see one... where a bullet penetrated." Her entire body shuddered and she had a look of total repulsion on her face. "I saw one...Twakon... who got hit by a large caliber bullet that did penetrate...the chest. It stopped and...convulsed a couple of times...and then spit the bullet out of its mouth." She looked off to the side. She looked as if she were fighting regurgitation. "It...then...went back into battle...as if nothing had happened...and I saw...no form of... bleeding."

Antrong interjected. "Did any of them have any pulse weapons?"

Am-Sisa shrugged. "We only saw two...that were firing pulse weapons. Those weapons did knock some of the Twakon down..."

"One of them was *beheaded* by the pulse ray," said Orng.

Am-Sisa cleared her throat nervously. "Yes…there were a few…who were killed by the pulse weapons. The Twakon…then focused…primarily on the Heyyah…who had the pulse weapons… and…" She cleared her throat again. "…they mercilessly stomped those Heyyah…into a pile of bloody goo."

Wilfadge nodded. "All right, they can be killed by pulse weapons. Maybe the time has arrived to get our 459's out of storage and…see if we can get them working again."

Hadathoo shook his head. "We didn't find anything wrong with the weapons. We were having trouble with finding good power packs."

Wilfadge glared at Hadathoo. "Then let's take a *hard look* at the power packs!"

Hadathoo nodded. "Yes, Sir."

Wilfadge snarled and turned back to Am-Sisa. "They're unstoppable…*on land*! What did that mean…specifically?"

Am-Sisa turned to Orng.

Orng walked up to the conference table and smiled. "They did attempt an amphibious assault on the two islands that are the southernmost in the Ficara Separation group…Boric and Nachitok. I don't know how…but the people on Boric were ready and waiting for them. As soon as the boat got within range… the Heyyah on Boric launched these…small explosive projectiles. The projectiles…that hit the boat…did some pretty extensive damage…to the boat. I was on the boat…and I had to switch to Observation dimension…because when those things go off…they are…LOUD! I did see…three of the Twakon…who lost…an arm or a leg…if they were too close to the explosion. They tried to turn the boat back…but the attack continued. It was finally too much for the boat and it sank. That's when I saw that…the Twakon have the swimming, and floating, capability…of a rock. I did a little… underwater recon…and…the Twakon…they do drown easily. They're nowhere near…like those little red mudbabies that lived in the lakes…in and around Owlam."

Am-Sisa put a hand on Orng's shoulder and gently pushed him back. "Once the people on Boric found that they could kill Twakon…by drowning…they radioed the people on Nachitok… and the boat that was headed there…was bombarded with those explosive projectiles…and it was blown to pieces. There've been no more attempts…by the Twakon…at going to other islands. They're doing all of their conquering…strictly on land…on Ficara."

Wilfadge sighed. "We definitely need to get the power packs back in working order for the 459's. Why don't we give that puzzle to that Officer, Kiyalee?"

Teelila shook her head puzzled. "She's a mechanic! What is she going to do with a complicated electronic component?"

Wilfadge looked affronted. "There are electronic components in a truck. If she has kept that old truck of hers running…there had to be a few repairs to the electrical system. If she can keep an old truck running…even the electronics…give her a busted power pack and see what she can do with it."

Teelila sat there with her mouth hanging open. She then

looked off to the side and shrugged. "It couldn't hurt."

12

Kiyalee looked at Soolchakan in horror. "Are you... joking?!"

Soolchakan huffed. "No, I am NOT! The Supreme Officer and the Command Staff have made this decision. They want you to look at this...schematology...and..."

Kiyalee got in his face. "SCHEMATIC...not schematology."

He snickered. "See? You're already half way there. You know what they're talking about."

She shook her head and huffed several times. "It...just isn't...the same thing."

Bonarain sat down next to her and put her arm around Kiyalee's shoulder. "You've rebuilt the battery for your big old 161 three times. I know...because I watched you do it. That's an electrical component. It *is* the power pack for your truck. Is it possible...that the power pack for the 459...could possibly be... that different...or overly complicated?"

Kiyalee looked at Bonarain and huffed a few more times, while attempting to come up with an argument.

Soolchakan placed the schematic for the 459 power pack on the table in front of Kiyalee. "Your people are depending on you. You've shown some extraordinary capabilities...and will power...at keeping that 161 in running condition." He smiled. "Why can't you use that same hard-headed attitude...here?"

Kiyalee huffed a few more times. She looked up from the booklet at Soolchakan and stuck her tongue out at him. She grunted in anger and opened up the booklet. She sighed as she looked down the list of parts on the first page.

Bonarain was looking at the list and was totally baffled at what she was seeing. "Can...you read this...stuff?"

Kiyalee nodded. "Yeah. It's just a listing of the parts...the resistors...the diodes...the capacitors...the relays...along with a few other special parts." She pointed at the second column. "That shows how many of each part you need...and what their strength is."

Bonarain leaned back smiling sheepishly and looking even more bewildered. "Strength?"

Kiyalee sighed. "Yeah. There are nineteen different resistors listed. Each one has a different resistance level." She pointed to one of the lines. "Like this one...here is the resistance level and it says that you need sixteen of them in the power pack. This one has a different resistance level...and you need twenty-two of them. This other column...shows what the symbol for that part is...on the schematic."

"Oh...good," said Bonarain helplessly. She turned her face away and cleared her throat in order to try and get some of her composure back. She sniffed and turned back to Kiyalee. "So what you're saying…this information…makes sense to you…and you just need…to take the parts and put them together…like a big puzzle."

Kiyalee grunted. "This is a lot more complicated than some child's puzzle."

Soolchakan tried to add some encouragement. "But you *do* understand it."

Kiyalee sighed. "This is just a listing of the parts." She turned a few pages. "This is the schematic that shows how they're hooked up…together…to make the thing work…properly."

Bonarain's jaw dropped.

Soolchakan tried to make sure that Kiyalee did not see Bonarain's consternation. "Can you read this…and make sense of it?"

Kiyalee shrugged. "All you have to do is follow the lines…and make sure that you hook everything together…the way it shows."

"Oh…good," said Bonarain still looking hopelessly befuddled.

Soolchakan smiled at her. "So…you can at least…try."

Kiyalee sighed. She ran her finger along a line. She rocked her head back and forth as she followed the line. She held her finger on a line and went back to the listing in the front. She found what she wanted and went back to the page she had marked.

She sighed again. "I…guess…I can try." She looked up a little miffed. "They should have those computer repair people looking at this as well."

Soolchakan patted her on the shoulder. "I'll tell the Command Staff. If we can get some more people…who know what they're doing…to work on this…it might go a lot faster… and take some of the pressure off of you."

Kiyalee continued following lines on the schematic. "Thanks."

Soolchakan and Bonarain went into the kitchen to leave Kiyalee alone studying the schematic.

After the door was shut, Bonarain turned to Soolchakan. "Did you see all of that…*h'oolyach* on that page?"

"Yes, I did."

"And she can…understand it."

He smiled. "Good!"

She shook her head. "I hope…I don't have to…teach that stuff…to anybody."

He chuckled. "If you do…you know who your primary assistant is gonna be."

Bonarain nodded. "You're right." She looked at the pantry. "What should we have for lunch?"

"Food," he said with a big grin.

The next day Soolchakan was checking on any new news

that was going on in the world. He was bothered by the fact that he heard several voices coming from downstairs. These were voices that he was not used to. He shut down his computer and went downstairs to check on the din. He saw Kiyalee and sixteen other people, in the dining area, all looking at copies of the schematic on the power packs for the 459's. He walked up to the nearest table. "Hello...uh...do I know you?"

The man at the table stood up. "Officer Grade 3, Sunggosh. I'm the Team Leader for Team 1001. I...and everyone else in here...we work computer repair. Your Team member asked us to come here and...maybe assist in repairing...or rebuilding the power packs."

Soolchakan nodded. "Do you think you can do it?"

Sunggosh snickered. "The schematic is rather regular. I don't see a problem...as long as you know how to read a schematic."

Soolchakan looked at the page Sunggosh had open. All he saw was a bunch of lines and silly looking symbols. He chuckled. "Well...have a good time." He went into the kitchen to get something to eat.

Bonarain and Chyning were in the kitchen. Instead of going out to the dining area they stayed in the kitchen eating at one of the counters.

Bonarain looked up at him as he entered. "Find out anything that you didn't know?"

"Nothing I care to discuss," he said dejectedly. "I didn't

know that electronics had such...weird workings...and the way that they're drawn on paper."

She sighed. "As long as those people understand it...I'll stand off to the side and let them do their job."

After the three of them finished eating, they considered that it was silly just standing in the kitchen waiting for the meeting out there to end. They walked out into the dining area to see what was happening.

A woman was standing near the bar, looking as if she had taken over the meeting. She was momentarily distracted when she followed the gazes of all of the people in front of her and glanced back at the rest of Team 7016 as they came out of the kitchen. She turned back to the group. "As I was saying, so far...all of the power packs that we've opened up...they all seem to be in good working order...they just haven't been recharged in quite some time. My suggestion is...we put each one in a charger...and see if it'll hold a charge. If it will...wonderful. If it won't...what can we do to repair it?"

Another woman scoffed. "Since they haven't been charged up...in who knows how many years...according to the specs... it'll take at least three days to get any of them up to full power."

One of the men chuckled. "Then the sooner we get them in the chargers - the sooner we find out."

The leader of the group sighed. "According to the information that I have...each apartment, here in the gorge, has at least one charger. We're going to have to get everyone's permission to use their chargers for...uh...how many power packs do we have?"

"156," said a woman.

"All right, let's start knocking on doors and get these things charged up. As soon as we find out how many are good... the sooner we'll know how many we need to manufacture."

Another woman stood up. "I already sent a mental communication to Wilfadge. He is all in favor of the charge up... and has allowed us to go into the apartments that aren't occupied. That way...we can do it without upsetting that many people...in their apartments."

The leader nodded. "You got a list?"

The other woman closed her eyes and started sending the information to all of the other members of the computer repair Teams.

People started picking up power packs and vanishing until the only one left was Kiyalee. She looked up at her Team members and smiled. "I have to get these power packs into the chargers...in ten different apartments...here on the twelfth level."

Soolchakan nodded. "And let them charge up for three days."

Kiyalee nodded. She picked up two power packs and vanished.

Chyning looked around confused. "Each apartment...has one...charger?"

"Yes," said Bonarain.

"Where is it?"

Soolchakan snickered. "Ask Kiyalee when she gets back."

Kiyalee had Jumped back in for two more power packs. "Ask me what?"

Chyning was a little startled because she had not noticed Kiyalee coming back so quickly. "Uh…where…the power pack chargers…where are they…in the apartments?"

"They're in the garage. The vehicles were supposed to be in the garages…so they put the chargers in there as well. That way you didn't have to go very far in order to get your packs recharged."

Chyning shrugged. "Oh…okay."

Kiyalee grabbed two more power packs and vanished. After distributing all of the packs that she was responsible for, she came back. "What's ready to eat right now?"

Bonarain looked toward the kitchen. "There's still a few of those fruit plates that Chyning put together."

Kiyalee nodded. "That sounds good." She headed for the kitchen.

Soolchakan followed her in the kitchen. "Who was that bunch that was here?"

"Those people are the four Teams that are computer repair specialists. I figured that if anyone knew anything about electronics…that was the ones that I needed to bring in on the job."

"Just in case any of them come visiting...if you're not here...what Teams are they?"

"1000, 1001, 1002 and 1003."

Soolchakan nodded. "Okay, sounds good. Do you think that you'll be able to do something with the power packs?"

Kiyalee pulled a fruit plate out of the refrigerator. "I hope so. It isn't as hard as I thought it'd be. They're...batteries...that are a little complicated...but...nothing I can't handle...as long as we have sufficient parts."

Soolchakan smiled. "I knew that you could do it. You've kept that 161 going for over 100 years, so I knew you were capable of this."

She scowled at him. "You just don't think that I can shoot worth *h'oolyach.*"

"No...I don't think you can't shoot...I *know for a fact* that you can't shoot."

She snarled at him and made a threat as if she were going to throw the fruit plate at him. He made a hasty retreat out of the kitchen...while snickering.

Three days later, Kiyalee was sitting at a table, with all of the power packs that she was responsible for, with the packs opened. She was doing some tweaking with her precision tools in order to make sure that everything was working as they were supposed to be...when charged up.

The next day all of the Teams were back in the dining room of the gorge apartment of Team 7016. They were wondering how to test all of the power packs. They had multimeters where they could put leads against leads and tell if it was charged up. This did not tell them if it would work in a 459.

The leader, Officer Grade 3, Tula, from the previous meeting was standing against the bar. "The only way to really test these things…is to put them in a 459…and shoot it."

Kiyalee huffed at her. "Where are we going to do that?"

There were several opinions on where they should go. None of them were approved of because they could very possibly have a witness somewhere who would see that the Owlamites still had pulse weapons and that might put them on someone's number one hit list for conquering. They did not want anyone to know… until that enemy was being fired on.

Soolchakan got tired of the bickering. "Hey, everybody… why don't you take it to the Desert dimension? So far…no one has seen or heard…any life…in that dimension. If you happen to flatten a few sand dunes…who is going to care?"

Tula looked at all of the other computer repair personnel. "That sounds like a pretty good idea to me. We can take our instruments to that place…and like he said…if we flatten a few sand dunes…who cares?"

No one in the room had any arguments.

She smiled. "Get the triangles together and let's…hop." She turned to Soolchakan. "Since it was your idea to go there…

the rest of your Team can carry the equipment."

Bonarain and Chyning both gave Soolchakan a very dirty look. He snarled at them and told them to pick up the equipment.

They all made the hop to Desert. The members of Team 7016 all got a good laugh when they saw a pile of the huge steel flood doors that they had stolen from the Algothon flotilla.

Officer Grade 3, Sunggosh walked up to the laughing quartet. "I thought you said that there had been no sightings of life here."

"There hasn't," said Soolchakan through his giggling.

"Then where did all of those...metal walls come from? It took technology to put those things together and..."

Soolchakan interrupted him. "And that technology was Algothon. We stole those from the Algothon armada that was on its way to Owlam to kill all of us. We didn't have any place better to put the things...at that time. We just haven't had an opportunity or need to come back here and get them."

Tula snickered. "I think...that now would be a perfect time to use them...as targets."

"But we might need the things...later on," said Bonarain.

Soolchakan shook his head. "We haven't found a need for them yet. If we destroy one or two of them...again...who cares?"

They started setting up the special devices. It was a series of four triangular sensors that had to be set up in a line – perfectly aligned. Because of the sand, with no solid foundation, it was very difficult…until Soolchakan suggested that they use one of the steel gates, which was laying flat, as a solid foundation. Once they moved the sensors onto a flat surface, the equipment was ready in a very short time.

Tula sighed. She pulled Soolchakan off to the side. "Thank you for some excellent suggestions. I know that…some of the other personnel…are a little miffed because you…won't shut up…but…so far your suggestions have been very good. I don't mind if you keep talking."

He smiled back at her.

Bonarain looked at the setup. "I see four…triangles on stands…and they're lined up…for…what?"

Kiyalee pointed at them. "You take a 459 and aim it through the four triangles. Once you have it aligned, you pull the trigger. The beam goes through the center of all four triangles and as it goes through, the power and speed of the beam is measured and we get it all on the computer here."

Bonarain nodded. "Okay…I…think I got it…I hope." She continued watching still looking a little confused.

Tula looked over at Chyning and smiled. "You're not doing anything constructive. Why don't you hop back to Home… and bring us all a bunch of cool water?"

Soolchakan looked at Bonarain. "Why don't you help her?"

Bonarain and Chyning both gave disgusted looks and then vanished. They came back rather quickly with several cases of cold bottles of water.

Tula sat down at the computer. "I've got the power packs that I charged up next to the cannon." She looked up at Soolchakan. "Since we have to have everything the same...for each power pack...I need the same person firing the cannon on each test. How about you?"

Soolchakan shrugged and sat down, getting ready to fire the cannon. He picked up one of the power packs and installed it. He noticed that the 459 was bolted into place in order to keep any movement of the gun to a minimum. 'That should keep the tests honest,' he thought. 'If the gun doesn't move and the triangles don't move...the only difference is the power packs.' He powered up the cannon. "Ready!"

Tula nodded. "Now, Sunggosh is going to stand behind you. He'll tap you on the shoulder and you pull the trigger. When he taps you on the shoulder again...let off the trigger."

Soolchakan nodded. "Simple enough."

Tula looked around. "Everyone ready?" She signaled to Sunggosh.

Soolchakan felt the tap and pulled the trigger. The familiar red beam shot through the center of the four triangles and created a sand storm out of the first sand dune that was in the way. Moments later he felt the tap again and let off of the trigger.

Tula looked at her computer screen and shook her head. She looked off to her left. "Zozz, what do you have?"

He shook his head. "It's only putting out...at 91%. That

pack should be giving 100%."

Tula nodded. "Nowma…what about you?"

She looked up. "I confirm 91%."

Tula sighed. "Seennka?"

She did not look up. She continued concentrating on the screen. "91%."

Tula hit a key on her computer. "Okay, one more shot with that power pack and then we move on to the next one."

The second shot came up with the same results. Soolchakan pulled the power pack out and Sunggosh marked the power pack at 91.

There were nine more power packs that Tula had taken care of and they all showed output between 88% and 91%. Next were the ten that were the responsibility of Sunggosh. They all showed power output between 86% and 92%. Officer Grade 3, Shanah brought up ten more. They showed the same dismal output. Officer Grade 3, Atsuska brought nine power packs up to the cannon. Her results were between 87% and 90%. Officer Grade 5, Zozz brought his nine power packs. His showed between 85% and 90%. Officer Grade 6, Hiyshee brought her nine up next. Most of hers were between 89% and 92%, with the exception of one that showed 74%. Officer Grade 6, Loskani brought her nine up. 87% to 91%. Next Officer Grade 6, Jeeshee brought her nine up. 85% to 90%.

Sunggosh leaned forward and whispered to Soolchakan. "75 down, 81 to go."

Soolchakan wiped some sweat off and took a drink of water.

Kiyalee was next in line with her nine power packs.

Soolchakan placed the first one in and waited for the gun to power up. He took another drink of water and noticed that the cannon was ready much quicker than with the other power packs. All of the computer technicians were surprised at this revelation.

Tula sighed. "Test number 76. Are we ready?"

Soolchakan felt the tap on his shoulder. He fired. There was a dune that was further away...that had not really been hit... that was now a dust storm. The other tap and he let off of the trigger. He heard nothing from the technicians. He looked back at them and saw all four of the ones at the computers staring wide-eyed at their screens.

Tula leaned back. "Uh...I get...108%...of normal power output." She looked at the other three who confirmed 108%. She looked at Sunggosh. "Second shot."

Soolchakan was tapped on the shoulder and pulled the trigger. Again the beam shot out...seemingly further than any of the other power packs had accomplished. Another tap on the shoulder. He looked back again.

Tula sat there shaking her head. "108%...again." She checked with the other three who again confirmed. She cleared her throat. "Next!"

The second power pack from Kiyalee put out 106%. The third power pack put out 108%. The fourth put out 107%. The fifth put out 110%. The sixth put out 107%. The seventh put out 108%. The eighth put out 107%. The ninth put out 109%.

Tula stood up. "Who did this? These power packs are above standards."

Kiyalee smiled sheepishly and swallowed. "I…did a little…tweaking…inside the packs. I saw, what I thought, was an imperfection…and…I adjusted…all nine of them."

Tula stood there motionless and expressionless for several moments. She turned to Sunggosh. "Where's that 74% piece of junk?"

Sunggosh looked at the ones that had already been tested. "Here it is…I found it…why?"

Tula motioned toward Kiyalee. "Give it to Officer Kiyalee…and have her…tweak that silly thing. See if it makes a difference."

Kiyalee took the pack. She looked up defensively. "I… have to go back to the gorge…all my tools are there…and…"

Tula huffed. "Quit yapping about it and GO! Tweak it or…change its diaper…wet nurse it…or do…whatever you can! Just…do it…and bring it back."

By the time Kiyalee came back, they had finished another 52 power pack tests. No one else had come up with anything past 92%. Kiyalee gave the "tweaked" pack to Tula. They continued with the other twenty packs. Again, the results were all between 85% and 91%.

Tula looked at the freshly repaired pack. "Okay...put this thing back in the gun."

Soolchakan looked at her. "Is this the last test?"

Tula sighed. "Yes, it's the last test for today. I don't think that any of us could take much more."

Soolchakan powered the cannon up. The tap on the shoulder and he fired. The tap on the shoulder and he stopped.

Tula shook her head. "105%!" She looked at the other three who confirmed. She shook her head. She signaled Sunggosh.

Soolchakan got the tap on the shoulder and fired. Another tap and he stopped.

Tula sat there nodding. She stood up. "Okay! Everybody... gather up all of the equipment. Let's all go back to our homes. We'll get something to eat, we'll take a bath...and then...we go back to apartment 12-562...the home of Team 7016...and we all learn how to...*tweak*!" She looked at Kiyalee. "I don't know what you did...but...if it can take the weakest power pack that we had...and turn it into a dynamo...I wanna find out...quickly!"

Team 7016 got back to their apartment with all of the equipment that they were responsible for.

Bonarain went to Kiyalee. "What did you do? I mean... you fiddled with those power packs...and the ones that you... messed with...were superior to all of the others. So...what did you do?"

Kiyalee gave a highly technical explanation of what she

did, talking about the components, minor adjustments and a special attachment. When she was finished Bonarain was standing there, slack-jawed, even more confused than before. Everything that Kiyalee had said went completely over Bonarain's head.

Soolchakan tapped Bonarain on the shoulder. "Aren't you SO glad that you asked her that?"

Bonarain turned to face Soolchakan, still staring dull-eyed and open-mouthed. "Shuddup!" She turned and headed for the stairs.

Chyning giggled. "She probably needs to wash her ears out as well."

Kiyalee looked at Soolchakan. "Did you understand what I said?"

Soolchakan smiled. "Not one single word!"

Chyning was still giggling as she shook her head.

Kiyalee shrugged. She headed for the stairs, unbuttoning her shirt. "Time for a bath."

After everyone had cleaned all of the sweat off and had a full stomach, they all reconvened at apartment 12-562.

Tula sat down with the power packs that she had charged in front of her. "Okay, Officer, Kiyalee...what did you do?"

Kiyalee looked around at all of the faces. "Uh...does everyone...have their precision tools?"

Tula smiled. "Are we going to need them?"

Kiyalee shrugged. "You can't do *h'oolyach* without them."

Everyone in the room, who were not members of Team 7016, vanished. Shortly after that, each one started reappearing in their seats…with precision tools.

Tula looked up. "We're waiting."

Kiyalee looked at Bonarain. "I don't know how to teach."

Bonarain smiled. "Just show them…or tell them…what you did…and how."

She picked up one of the big round power packs. She flushed as she looked out at all of the other personnel. "Okay… uh…you get out the…number 3 four-point screwdriver…and you open up…the part of the power pack…that sticks out…when it is installed in the 459." She looked over at Bonarain.

Bonarain smiled. "Good…so far."

Kiyalee sighed in relief.

Bonarain sent a quick mental message to Kiyalee. She needed to be doing the same thing in order to give a step-by-step instruction on what was being done.

Kiyalee quickly grabbed one of Tula's power packs and started opening it. She got the outer plate off and looked up. All of the students were now staring at her, waiting for the next step. She again looked at Bonarain.

Bonarain sent the mental message of showing them the

next step.

It took quite some time, however, all of the 156 power packs had been adjusted, according to the information supplied by Kiyalee. Tula decided that all of the power packs should be placed in chargers again and left there for two days of full charging. After that, they would gather all of them and go back to Desert for testing. All of the personnel took their power packs and headed out to place them in the chargers.

Bonarain sat there with a tear rolling down her cheek.

Soolchakan noticed her pained look. "What IS the matter with you?"

She looked up and sniffed. "I've never felt so…stupid…in my entire life."

He closed his eyes and pondered for a moment. He opened his eyes. "Stupid…in regards…to…what?"

"Did you hear her explanations?"

"Yes."

"Did you understand any of it?"

"No."

"And…you don't feel…stupid?"

"No. I don't because I never studied electronics. Kiyalee had to learn electronics in order to achieve the task she was given – keep that truck running. So she learned electronics – all of it. Now…what's your problem?"

She scoffed. "She's telling them to…put the pit in the pat and move the pet to the pot and…hook the pitty-pat to the potty-put…and…I don't know what all…and…they understood…every word she said…and all of the instructions…and I still don't know what they did."

Soolchakan sighed. "She was speaking their language. They understood it. That is what was important today. I know that you may not believe it…but you did help, immensely, today."

Bonarain looked at him confused. "HOW?"

He leaned closer and smiled. "You *taught* Kiyalee…how to *teach*. It was your encouragement and coaching that helped her get the message across to them. If you hadn't taught her to teach…they'd still be in the dark."

Bonarain's lower lip started quivering. Tears ran down both cheeks. She sniffed several times and then hugged Soolchakan. "Thank you," she said through the sobs.

"You're welcome," he said softly as he comforted her. "Now…let's go get a good hot mug of kwatha. I think we both need some…in order to have a really good ending to the events of today."

Bonarain let go of him and headed to the kitchen. "Good idea." She sniffed several times as she wiped the tears off her cheeks. "Sometimes…not many but sometimes…you are capable of being very sweet."

She did not see the scowl on his face as he followed her into the kitchen.

Two days later, they tested all of the power packs again. All of them ended up with ratings over 100%. The lowest one got Officer Grade 6, Brong a little chiding as one of his power packs only hit 103%. All of the rest were 108% or better.

A report was sent back to the Command Staff that there were sufficient power packs and 459 cannons. They could take care of any assault by the Twakon. They all hoped that they would not have to utilize the cannons against the Twakon.

Ahandi had to turn in a new report. The Gabeesh-Or were on the move. They had heard of this upstart Elf people on the southwestern coast of Ficara…those silly Twakon. They were causing problems trying to conquer the continent. What arrogance! The only ones who should be in charge of the Ficara continent… and then the world…was the superior race – the Gabeesh-Or.

Wilfadge hung his head. "What is wrong with…some of these people? Why can't they…just let others alone? Why do they…after all this time…decide to go conquering…when no one else has ever been able to do any complete world domination?"

Hadathoo was equally disgusted. "Do they have pulse weapons? Are their weapons capable of doing any fatal damage to the Twakon? If not…they're in for one nasty surprise."

"Maybe we should just stay out of this one," said Teelila. "Just sit back and watch…and see if one of the antagonists knock off the other one…without us having to do anything."

Wilfadge looked up. "That is a wonderful idea."

Dwalooa scoffed. "We'll definitely find out which one is stronger."

"Once we find that out...they'll realize the same thing," said Shyshee. "Then...they just might...try to start some worldwide domination."

Wilfadge sighed. "If that occurs...then we will absolutely get involved...of course we'll do it secretly." He looked at Ahandi sadly. "Keep your spy Team watching. We'll see what happens... and figure our next move from there."

Hadathoo huffed. "I still haven't heard an answer to my question!"

Everyone looked at him confused.

"Do they have pulse weapons?"

Ahandi shook her head. "Oh...I'm sorry...I forgot. Yes, they do. From what I understand, they are not as powerful as ours, but they do have them."

Hadathoo nodded. "Then they might have a fighting chance against the Twakon."

"Maybe they'll both kill each other off and then we won't have to worry about a thing," muttered Till.

Antrong looked at Till in shock. "It speaks!" He looked around the conference table. "That's the first thing I remember hearing him say...since he was promoted to Senior Officer."

Till gave him a nasty look. "It's difficult getting a word in edgewise with all of you people talking all of the time."

Wilfadge snarled. "Be that as it is...let's make sure that we keep getting updates on this...argument between the Gabeesh-Or and the Twakon."

Team 58 was assigned the task of watching the Gabeesh-Or as they advanced south towards the Twakon. Team 232 was assigned to watch the Twakon as they headed north. Neither Team was very happy about having to watch the two groups as they moved towards each other. Both adversarial sides were committing atrocities against anybody that was unfortunate enough to be in the path of either antagonist.

Officer Leader, Nasnana of Team 58 sent mental communications back about how the Gabeesh-Or were taking any livestock that they found, any crops that they found and any possessions of tribes of Heyyah that they found. They were utilizing all of it for themselves, leaving the victims with nothing. According to the Gabeesh-Or this was all tribute that belonged to the conquerors anyway.

Officer Grade 4, Ishikaniki of Team 232 was reporting the same kind of devastation in regards to the Twakon.

The reports from both Team Leaders also included numbers. The Gabeesh-Or had over 200,000 in their military force.

The Twakon had around 40,000. One problem with the Twakon was that no one could distinguish gender...or age. There were no outward markings of any type and this race did not seem to have any use for clothing. Their ranks (if someone could call it that) were markings that were painted on the top of the right shoulder. There seemed to be some of the Twakon, who were shorter than the regular seven and a half taja, however, the short ones were just as destructive as the larger ones.

At one time, Officer Grade 7, Nokoona of Team 232, observed one of the Twakon apparently giving birth...during a march. The Twakon that was identified as the newborn was able to walk, without any problems, by the time it was ten days old. Nokoona had not been able to see if there was any nursing of the infant either. It was ready to eat solid food, just like the adults, on the second day of life.

Both sides advanced relentlessly and destructively towards each other. Before leaving their respective homes they had only heard of each other and started their advances. If either were getting any updates on the location of the other side, it was a complete mystery to the Owlamites who were simply watching.

Wilfadge gave the order, again, to make any attempt possible at reading their minds. According to the reports, they were both advancing directly towards each other and he wanted to find out exactly how they knew which way to go.

A report came back from Team 232 of another Elf race that the Twakon...did not see. This race was called the Untarba. It was another race that had a jet black exoskeleton, however, they did not seem to want to conquer. When the Twakon got near any of them, they would simply roll themselves into a ball and give the appearance of a black boulder just sitting there. They could stay rolled up for quite a long time as well. After the Twakon departed their area, they unrolled and went to repairing the damage left behind. They seemed to be living in harmony with the surrounding Heyyah tribes in the area. The Untarba were somewhat like the Twakon in that there were no outward signs of gender. There seemed to be no body hair. The Untarba stood only six and a half taja in height...and showed no belligerency towards anyone else.

The Command Staff was relieved that these Untarba did not want to join the Twakon and they were a lot nicer than the conquering types.

Nasnana reported back to the Command Staff that the Gabeesh-Or were receiving some kind of radio messages from... somebody. Whoever it was they were not identifying themselves or where they were. They were able to give some very accurate information on the exact locations of the Twakon, in regards to where they were going and what they were doing. So far, any effort to find out who was on the other end of the radio transmissions ended in total frustration.

Ishikaniki was finally able to report back that they had been able to delve into the minute brains of the Twakon. They had rather low intelligence and they used mainly single syllable words. They were getting radio communications as well and these messages were giving them some very accurate information on the location and activities of the Gabeesh-Or. She had not been able to determine exactly who was on the other end of the communications.

Wilfadge looked at the reports. "Someone is orchestrating this *h'oolyach*! Someone out there...wants to see these two races…meet and…destroy…one or the other…or both…or…I don't know what I'm saying. The speculation could drive you completely *chogo!*"

Ahandi threw her copy of the report down. "Four people… spying on the Gabeesh-Or…just isn't enough. Someone has to be watching them…and giving their location to the Twakon… and vice versa. We need…a lot more people…scouring the area around the two forces…in order to figure out who the perpetrator actually is."

"Irritating!" Wilfadge hung his head. "I didn't…want to involve a lot of people…because I didn't…want any major involvement by us."

Hadathoo sighed. "It is irritating…but we've got to get someone out there…and see if we can find out something. The Algothons could be behind it…because they just might want to see how powerful and/or tenacious these two peoples are."

"That's true," said Dwalooa. "If these two had wanted to conquer…why did they wait over 100 years to start? Someone is supplying them with tactical information. We need to find out who…and why."

Wilfadge looked up with a look of disgust. "Send…fifty Teams…each…to the main ones that are out there. Get them scouring…on both sides…and ahead of the two adversaries. Let's see if we can determine who the real nasty is in this mess."

Three days after the deployment of the extra Teams, the information came in from both sides of the advancements.

Wilfadge growled as he read the report. "Oh... *H'OOLYACH!*"

Antrong shook his head as he read it. "How...and why... are the Teltermak doing this? What do they hope to get out of...a war between these two factions?"

Shyshee shrugged. "Maybe...they're going to try to make friends with the winner. They'll come out and say...look how we helped you. Why don't you join up with us...and we'll do some real damage...to...all of the others?"

"That doesn't sound realistic," said Hadathoo. "All of the reports that came in...in the past and the ones that we're getting today...still say how...both sides think that they are a gift from... their god...to be the one who controls all of the races of the planet. They don't want to share in any power or glory. I don't see either one of them making any alliance...with anybody."

"So maybe the Teltermak just want to see both sides so badly weakened by an all-out battle...that there is nothing left of either race...to cause any future trouble," said Teelila. She shook her head. "Make your enemies destroy each other...then you just dance in and take over. Speaking of the Teltermak...when did they show up on Ficara? All of our intelligence information had them on Lusaratia and a couple of island chains."

Antrong scoffed. "They've had time to spread themselves all over the place. They seem to have gone mainly to the other hemisphere...and escaped from us here...in this hemisphere."

Wilfadge looked at Teelila sadly. "They spread themselves out and...like you said...they weaken their most powerful enemies by making them destroy each other."

Hoynama grunted. "But…what about all of the others that they're devastating on the way to this…ultimate battle? What are the observations here…by the Teltermak?"

Wilfadge shook his head. "It tells…something about them. These…Untarba. They didn't have one single fight. They hid. That tells…that they are *not*…a foe that needs to be reckoned with."

"I don't know about that," said Shyshee. "They hid… and allowed the Twakon to pass by. The Untarba…were not… cornered. If they had been cornered…maybe their reaction would have been drastically different."

"Again, the speculations can drive you crazy," said Wilfadge.

Hadathoo snickered. "Why don't we do a little messing with the Teltermak? They have some kind of…forward posts… where they're doing a lot of watching and spying on the two sides. Why don't we…upset a few of their forward posts?"

"That would only postpone the inevitable battle," said Till. "The unfortunate peoples that are in the path of the devastation… will still suffer the same catastrophic problems…afterwards. What good will it do to befoul the Teltermak posts?"

"It'll divert the attention of the Teltermak," said Hadathoo. "It'll give them something to wonder about…as to just who is messing with them."

"Give the order," chuckled Wilfadge. "Let's give them a

taste of their own medicine. You want to mess with others? Well, someone is going to mess right back."

Antrong snickered. "Hopefully…we can mess with them and they won't be able to figure out who did it. Then…they'll have a real conundrum to worry about."

Nasnana had the perfect opportunity to befoul a Teltermak team. There were three of them sitting under a tree on the top of a bluff. Two of Nasnana's Team, Yod and Leebatha got up into the tree and caused a rather large branch to fall down and…do some major damage to the heads of the three Teltermak.

Once the three Teltermak were sufficiently brain-damaged, Nasnana was able to determine exactly how the Teltermak had been able to orchestrate this entire situation. They had a small device on their radios. The device altered your voice when you spoke through that specific microphone. They could sound exactly like one of the high ranking Gabeesh-Or, giving orders and directions as if they were from a forward reconnaissance position or team. Nasnana gave the Gabeesh-Or some very confusing instructions and this halted their advance for several days. Once she relayed this information to Ishikaniki, the advance of the Twakon was slowed with confusing instructions as well. They now had all of the information that they needed to foul up the communications from the Teltermak to either side.

Now it was the Teltermak who were getting a little frustrated over the fact that their perfect plan was being scuttled and it sounded as if their own personnel were the ones doing the damage.

Wilfadge was discouraged over the fact that Senior Officer, Till had been absolutely correct. All that the actions of the Owlamites did was slow the advance of both parties. The battle was going to happen. Postponing it was accomplishing nothing. If either side stopped moving forward, all they did was abuse the locals even more. Neither the Gabeesh-Or or the Twakon were suffering any great loss at being slowed. Just allow them to find each other and start destroying each other and find out exactly who was stronger between the two factions and then get an idea about the further plans of the Teltermak in the aftermath.

Ahandi clicked her tongue. "All right, Sir. What do we tell our primary spies, in regards to the advance?"

Wilfadge sighed. "Let those two groups of arrogant *bimyocks* meet…and let them…destroy each other. We'll find out which one is the bigger problem…and maybe we can follow these pesky Teltermaks and find out where their main command post is…on the Ficara continent. The Teltermak seem to be popping up everywhere and they're getting their noses involved in the business of everyone else. I don't like where it appears that they're going or what they're doing."

Teelila held up the latest report. "They're still almost three hundred kilotaja apart. We can't seem to be able to speed up their advance. We can slow them, but we can't speed them up. Once we get them…involved in their destruction of each other…then we'll get some more people following those Teltermak and…find their main hideout."

Wilfadge nodded. "I don't really want to get involved… with fighting anyone right now…but if the Teltermak continue to interfere…with everyone else…the same way that the Cacktash and the Perfor were doing…we may have to get involved."

Hoynama looked confused. "I don't understand…what you mean about the Teltermak. They're messing with others…but they're not…messing with us right now."

"This could be a prelude," said Wilfadge. "Instead of trying to enslave others…when they're at their strongest…the Teltermak get them to kill off each other. *Then* they take over. The enslaved are now battle weary, and are grabbed before they know what's going on. You jump them while they're trying to reorganize after a battle, before they can figure out their losses or if they even won the battle."

Hadathoo looked disgusted. "Jump in, take over, control them…and don't allow them any time to figure out what happened. I wonder if they have some of those electric collars that the Cacktash and the Perfor were using. If they do, that's probably how they plan on doing most of the controlling."

"I wonder if those things would work on the Twakon," said Shyshee. "Someone observed one Sodle holding another Sodle by the neck…and the victim was not choking or gagging. That exoskeleton just might protect them from more than we think it does."

"Let's worry about that…if the Twakon win…and the Teltermak try to enslave them…utilizing those nasty collars," said Hoynama.

"Good idea," said Wilfadge. "We'll have another meeting…after the confrontation."

13

As the two factions continued their march of destruction towards each other, the Command Staff continued cringing each time they heard of another town or village being devastated by the two Elf races.

There were several walled cities that each one passed by. The citizens of those cities had been warned in advance (by the Owlamites) and were well hidden from the two destructive hordes.

The Owlamites did make a few friends by giving the warnings. They met several new races of Elf. The Akraneth-Ozen. They had pale skin, they stood just over six and a half taja and they had long pointed ears that pointed straight back.

The Parenk. They stood right at six and a half taja. They had gray skin and green hair. They did not like any of the wars that were going on and according to what they were told by the Owlamites, they would not fight, they would just hide – friends, but they would not form an alliance with anybody.

The Ibka-Sar. Another race that stood right at six and a half taja. Their skin was light tan and they had long gray quills growing out of their head, instead of hair.

The Tunkatil. They were a pale-skinned race that stood just under six taja. The Owlamites that first met them were glad that these were a very amicable people. They had long, sharp horns that stuck out the sides of their heads and they were very capable of using the horns as lethal weapons.

Wilfadge and the rest of the Command Staff were glad to make friends, however, they wondered just how many of these new friends they could depend on in a battle situation.

The fateful day of the two forces meeting drew near. The Owlamites, along with the pesky Teltermaks, were all wondering what would take place when they met.

Then Natsa arrived at the Command Staff conference room. She walked in while the Staff was waiting for a further update on the situation on Ficara. "Sirs…I have some…bad news to report."

Wilfadge groaned. "Just what we need right now." He shook his head. "Okay, don't spare us any feelings. Get it out, so we can all get over the suffering as quickly as possible."

She sighed. "Sirs…we've broken the code that the Yagalom-Ayin were using. They *have* isolated all seven of the ingredients of *Tuzine*. They are now…trying to determine…the exact parts of the plants…and the cooking instructions."

Ahandi snarled. "Have they given this information to the Teltermak?"

Natsa smiled and looked off to the side shaking her head.

"Surprisingly...no! They're keeping it as their own secret."

Dwalooa looked confused. "How...did you finally... break the code?"

Natsa flushed. "We...finally decided...to do some... intense mind reading...and mind controlling."

Wilfadge shook his head. "All this time...and NOW...you finally decided to utilize some mind reading skills?"

Natsa flushed again, shrugged and snickered a little. "We...found that we had originally...done it wrong. Once we...broke through...and understood...a few of their language idiosyncrasies...it became easy."

Wilfadge nodded. "How many...of them...are sure of the ingredients?"

"They all are, Sir. They all...confirmed the seven ingredients...and are now...performing different attempts...at the cooking procedures."

Hadathoo hung his head. "We may have to perform... mass murder...in order to defend our *Tuzine*."

"This is horrible," said Teelila.

Wilfadge sighed loudly. "Do we have any idea...how many of the Yagalom-Ayin exist...in the world today?"

Natsa nodded. "They number about 17,000."

Ahandi's jaw dropped. "But...all this time...and...their numbers are less...than ours?"

Natsa shrugged. "Don't forget...they just went through a nasty battle...alongside the Teltermak. They did suffer...some pretty huge casualties. Their main weapon is the venom in their fangs. They have to get up close and personal in order to utilize this weapon." Natsa shook her head. "They paid a heavy price for that specific form of battle against their enemy."

Shyshee slammed a fist on the table. "Is there...any way... to scramble their information...on the *Tuzine* and...slow them down...or stop them from figuring it out?"

Natsa shook her head sadly. "They have all committed the ingredients to memory. They wanted to make sure that they all knew the ingredients...and once they figure out the cooking formula...they're determined to commit that to memory as well."

Wilfadge flopped back in his chair. "This is a horrible time to have to make a decision like this. We're waiting for the report on...the battle...or battles...between the Gabeesh-Or and the Twakon and now...we have to deal with the Yagalom-Ayin... without tipping our hand...or knowledge...to those *chokwad* Teltermaks."

Hadathoo looked around the table. "Maybe we should... all of us...go home for a day or two and think about what our final decision on this should be."

Dwalooa cleared her throat. "What about Algothon? Those people are trying to isolate the ingredients as well. Have we heard anything from our people there?"

Wilfadge groaned. He sent a mental message to Officer Leader, Ota. Moments later she was ushered in to the conference room.

Ota looked around at the Staff. "What was it that you needed, Sirs?"

Wilfadge gave her a friendly smile. "We've found out that the Yagalom-Ayin have isolated all seven of the ingredients for *Tuzine*. Now, they're working on the proper mixing and cooking procedures. Have the Algothons…come any closer to finding out anything about our *Tuzine*?"

"Oh!" Ota looked shocked. "That…that's terrible! Uh… no…Sirs, the Algothons…they haven't come any closer…yet. They keep on trying to compare any of their findings to kwatha. They're still hung up…on that. What…are we going to do…about the Yagalom-Ayin?"

Wilfadge hung his head.

Hadathoo looked up and sighed. "We may have to…do some rather nasty destruction…to the Yagalom-Ayin…in order to defend…our property."

Ota grimaced and shook her head. "Yes, Sir," she said meekly.

Wilfadge sighed. "Does anyone have any better ideas?" He stared at the table waiting for an answer. When he received no answer from anyone he stood up. "Meeting adjourned…until we hear any more news…from either Satroco Isle or Ficara."

The word came in from Ficara. Officer Leader, Nasnana

and Officer Grade 4, Ishikaniki were standing together on a bluff overlooking the two antagonists. They were both standing their ground, looking over the other while making tremendous noises of bellowing and banging all kinds of objects together.

Nasnana shook her head. "I don't understand this...first part of the...hostilities. All they're doing is trying to see who can make the most noise."

"They're trying to make themselves mentally ready to go...fight...and make all attempts at crushing their enemy," said Ishikaniki.

"A sea of pearl coloring on one side and a sea of gray on the other." She huffed. "They won't have a hard time determining who their enemy is."

"I just wish I could determine...gender...on those Twakon. They...don't seem to have...any outward difference... whatsoever...even in the way that they pee."

Nasnana huffed in horror. "You...you've watched them... PEE?"

Ishikaniki shrugged. "They don't hide it. They...just stop...stand there and...let fly. They have no modesty about it... at all."

Nasnana grunted. "That's disgusting."

"Yes, they are."

Nasnana saw some movement. "There they go," she said calmly. She sighed. "The carnage is about to begin."

The Twakon all raised their fists and started charging at the Gabeesh-Or at a full run. The Gabeesh-Or did not move for several moments. Then they started their charge. Some of the Twakon had rifles and started firing with deadly results. Several of the Gabeesh-Or stumbled or staggered…or just fell dead in the middle of their run. The Gabeesh-Or started firing back. Their rifles did nothing to the charging Twakon. None of the Twakon appeared injured until the two factions were in range of the weak pulse weapons that the Gabeesh-Or had. Then some of the Twakon started falling as well.

Ishikaniki scoffed. "Do we really have to stand here…and watch this?"

"Unfortunately…yes. Wilfadge wants a complete report… on just how badly the Twakon are hurt by…either bullets or pulse beams."

Ishikaniki sighed. "Bullets…no…beams…yes."

"What about bullets at close range?"

"From all of our observations…of them ravaging other places as they advanced…I don't remember seeing any Twakon being killed by any bullets…anywhere…no matter how big the caliber. The bigger caliber made them stop and…grunt in pain… but they weren't *stopped*."

Nasnana sighed. She sent a mental call to the rest of her Team who were out scouting for the Teltermak. She knew that the Teltermak were probably very interested in the outcome of this battle…or battles…if it went that far.

Officer Grade 7, Leebatha answered the call. She had found the Teltermak and reported that they were sitting…watching…and giggling.

Nasnana sent the message for her Team to stop them from giggling…or sending any more transmissions to their home base.

Five more Teltermaks were introduced to Jahong's Death… along with some of their equipment.

Nasnana shook her head. "Your Team…do they know where the Teltermak are…that were following the Twakon here?"

Ishikaniki nodded. "We've been keeping an eye on them."

"Are they…enjoying the spectacle…in front of them?"

Ishikaniki frowned. She sent a mental message to her Team members. A few moments later she sniffed. "The…Teltermak… are now…enjoying an acid bath…in Shogoot's Search."

Nasnana nodded. "That may bring a few more Teltermak out here."

"I don't know. According to my Team…the Teltermak that they were watching never did give an accurate location…of where the Twakon were."

"So…if the Teltermak team…that we were watching… were just as negligent…the Teltermak higher ups…will have to send out a search party…or several…in order to find the battleground."

Ishikaniki scoffed. "Tough!"

Two days later, the battle was still raging. Many of the combatants just fell where they were from exhaustion. They would...somehow...get some sleep. When they awoke, they would go back to fighting.

Nasnana scoffed. "Surely...some of them...are getting a little hungry by now. I...haven't seen any...field kitchen...or anyone going back...for food...or any form of medical treatment. What's the matter with these people?"

Officer Grade 4, Yod of Nasnana's Team 58, pointed up to the sky. "They're here. They've got some of their kites circling overhead...watching the fun." He snarled at them. "I wonder if they're...just enjoying it...or if they're also trying to find their missing personnel."

Nasnana looked up and nodded. "Wasn't there...a report... from someone...about Jumping up on those kites...while they're flying...and detaching the canvas...from the frame?"

Ishikaniki nodded. "I remember reading something about that."

Nasnana looked at Yod and smiled. "Why don't you try it? See if you can just loosen it a little...so that they don't fall. They just...descend...rapidly. Maybe they can survive hitting the ground...right in the middle of the battle...and become part of it."

Yod let out an evil chuckle. He looked up at the kites and vanished. Moments later one kite started a rather rapid, spiraling descent as some of the material had become loosened from the frame. Another kite started spiraling down…then a third…and a fourth. All of the rest of the intact kites swerved off to the west towards a high bluff. Two more kites ended up falling before the Teltermaks were able to safely land…right next to two Owlamite Teams (who were in Spy dimension).

Owlam and Teltermak were all watching from the high bluff now. The six kites that had been sabotaged all landed in the middle of the battlefield. The Teltermaks tried to use their pulse weapons to defend themselves, however, you cannot fire 360 degrees at all times and they were quickly overwhelmed…and killed…by either being shot or bludgeoned. The more powerful pulse weapons that the Teltermak had were not utilized by the combatants on the field…with several Gabeesh-Or and Twakon being cut in half by the deadly beams.

Officer Grade 6, Doyndon, of Ishikaniki's Team snickered when he looked at the Teltermaks. He nudged Ishikaniki in the ribs. "Those *bimyocks*…are standing dangerously close to the edge…don't you think?"

Ishikaniki nodded slightly. "Yes…they are," she said flatly. "That is so irresponsible of them."

Doyndon walked up behind one of the Teltermaks doing a little flexing. He did a practice kick. He smiled and kicked the Teltermak, as hard as he could, right in the middle of the butt cheeks. The Teltermak went flying over the edge, screaming as he fell.

One of the Teltermaks shouted in anger. "Get back! Everyone get back from the edge! What's going on here? Have we…suddenly gone…*mombik?*" He looked around and huffed. "Be careful!" He snarled. "Before we all go…anywhere else… or do anything else…everyone go back and check the lacings on your wings. I don't want to see any…more…deaths from some… *vogoth* mistake."

All of the Teltermak complied and started doing thorough inspections of their kites.

Nasnana cocked her head to the side. "That guy doing all of the yelling…is he in charge? Does anyone here…remember the Teltermak ranking system?"

Officer Grade 7, Kayfina nodded. "I'm pretty sure that his rank is called Silver Standard. That makes him equal to…an Officer Grade 5."

Nasnana nodded while frowning. "Thank you. Does anyone see…another one of them…that has a higher rank?"

Kayfina shrugged. "I think…he's the only officer. All the others…are enlisted ranks."

Nasnana nodded again. "Okay. He's the big one…here."

Doyndon stood there with a big smile. "Should I send any of the others over the edge?"

Nasnana smiled back. "Not while they're over fifteen taja away from the edge. That'd look too suspicious."

Officer Grade 7, Nokoona walked up to the two Team leaders. "I count eighteen of the kites up here."

"Oh…thank you," said Nasnana. "That leaves…thirty-five Teltermaks up here and…thirteen dead ones…down there."

Ishikaniki frowned. "Are you trying to figure out a way… to make more of these *bimyocks*…dead?"

"If there were more dead Teltermaks…it wouldn't hurt my feelings…but…I don't want them to be able to…go back and say that there was any death…that they can't explain."

"That sounds reasonable."

"Not unless we can kill all of them."

Ishikaniki gritted her teeth. "Yeah…thirty-five of them… and eight of us. We'd need a little help."

"I'm thinking about that." She shook her head. "Nah! We'll let this bunch go back…with a report of some stupid and tragic accidents." She sighed. "However…if any of them do… get a little too close to the edge again…I guess that…they could… fall off as well."

The battle continued on into the night. They could hear sounds of battle still going on, however, they could not see any of the carnage that was taking place below. They did see a few of the beams from some pulse weapons go off, however, they could not tell who or what was being hit by the beams. As the sun started showing the first signs of morning light in the east, the sounds started dissipating.

Leebatha looked down at them rather confused. "Why… are they covered with mud? It hasn't rained…during this whole affair."

Yod groaned. "That...*mud*...is not dirt mixed with water... it is dirt...mixed with blood."

Leebatha moaned in disgust and put her hand over her mouth as she turned away, looking as if she were about to lose her breakfast.

Nasnana huffed. "So...what's left down there?"

Doyndon shook his head. "The only ones that I can see... that are still moving are the Twakon. They're walking around... stomping on the heads of all of the Gabeesh-Or...making sure that they're dead."

"How many...Twakon...are left?"

He shrugged. "It's hard to tell. They're spread out...and moving. It's difficult to count them. From what I can see...I'd estimate...that there are...less than fifty of the Twakon left."

She scoffed. "Fifty! Several days ago...both races... numbered in the tens of thousands. Now...one case of extinction... and one...reduced to...less than one hundred." She shook her head and walked to the edge. "HEY YOU *BIMYOCKS*...WAS IT WORTH IT?"

He cleared his throat. "Uh...you are in...Spy...they can't hear you."

She sighed. "I know. I was just...venting."

One of the Teltermak women carefully walked over to look out on the battlefield. She stayed a safe distance from the edge.

The Teltermak officer was eating something (that the

Owlamites did not want to guess about). "What do you see, Chooshoosh?"

She turned back to the officer. "The only thing that I see moving…Twakon. They're making sure…that all of the Gabeesh-Or are dead, Sir."

"Are they spread out?"

"Widely, Sir."

He nodded. "Okay, we'll wait until they're all gathered in a clump. It might take a while…so…everyone get well rested."

It was nearly midday when the remaining Twakon were finally satisfied that they had dispatched all of the Gabeesh-Or. The surviving group all joined together near the center of the battlefield. After a quick count, it was determined that there were forty-two Twakons that were still alive.

Nasnana noticed that the Teltermaks were all holding their noses. Apparently there was a rather foul stench coming up from bodies that had been killed on the first day of battle.

The Teltermak officer looked at his people. "All right! You know what is supposed to happen now. Everyone to your wings…and let's get this job done."

All of the Teltermaks headed for their kites. They prepared themselves and waited for a signal from the officer. He gave the signal and they all started running towards the edge of the high bluff. Once they were airborne, they started firing down at the surviving Twakon with their pulse weapons. A few of the Twakon had pulse weapons and they were able to return fire. Before all of the Twakon were killed, they managed to bring five of the kites down, with fatal results for the ones in the fallen kites. The kites circled overhead for quite some time, looking for any movement… by anyone. When they were satisfied that no one down there was alive, they turned north and flew off.

Nasnana shook her head. "Now…the Twakon…are extinct as well."

Ishikaniki hung her head. "Time to send a report to the Command Staff."

Wilfadge looked up from the report. "Two more races… extinct. I wonder if the Algothons…or the Teltermak…are happy."

Ahandi blew her breath out slowly. "Do you think that they'll go after the P'Lalfan next?"

Wilfadge shook his head. "Why? What harm…can the P'Lalfan do to anybody…if they're not on a beach somewhere… on the Aerisau continent? The only people that they can… aggravate…are fishing villages. They certainly can't conquer anyone…even if they wanted to. All you have to do is stay away from the beach area."

Dwalooa tapped her fingernails on the table. "Is there a possibility…of another race…somewhere…that might want to… start some conquering?"

Hadathoo scoffed. "How are we supposed to know that?"

She shook her head. "We can send some of our people

to other places…find out about other races and then go in there
and…read a few minds. Find out if they have any plans of…
expansion…of their territory…and how it might affect us…and
see if those *chokwad* Teltermak are…anywhere near there…
stirring up trouble."

Wilfadge rubbed his temples. "Unfortunately, that
sounds like a pretty good idea. Start having our people…
search the continents…a little better…now that we're more
familiar with a lot of the planet's geography. Find…any
and all…people…with nasty attitudes…or desire…to…
add to their holdings…by military means. Once we've
established who the conquerors are…we keep an eye on them."

"That could take a while," said Shyshee.

"Then let it," said Wilfadge. "I'm very tired of…surprises."
He looked up. "Maybe if we can get a head start on some of these
world dominators…we can cut the number of casualties…before
another blood bath even starts?"

Four years later, Wilfadge got his report.

On the continent of Cifpasica, there was a race called the
Af-Kawder. They stood just over five taja in height. They had
pale skin and a black nose. Among their own they were sticklers
for the law. They treated others with complete contempt. After
all the time since the firestorm attack, they numbered well over
900,000, however they did not seem to be the conquering type.

Another race on Cifpasica was a race called the Bising.
They were seven and a half taja in height, had what was described

as "emerald" colored skin and they had enormous heads. Anyone who came within twenty kilotaja of their city was killed instantly... without any form of a trial. These people were very greedy and it was advised that they be watched carefully.

The Bloynid were a race on Aerisau. They had a somewhat dark complexion, they stood six taja in height, they numbered over 1,500,000...and they had retractable claws like felines. They liked to claw people to death, however, they did like to keep in their own area.

A race called the Bohereth-Rahanan-Or were located in a very southern part of South Chilamte. They stood just over seven taja in height and were another race of people who had green skin. They numbered about 800,000, however they did not seem to have any ambitions of world domination.

The Fastern were a race that Wilfadge was familiar with, from information that came from the Turgon Wall. They stood nearly eight taja in height, had dark brown skin and fangs. These fangs were just nasty looking – no venom. They lived on the far eastern, northern peninsula on North Chilamte. They were nasty and cocky, but not the type to conquer. They did not have enough organization for that particular plot.

The Feeror were a race of pale skinned people who lived in central Aerisau. They stood five taja in height and had a flat brown nose. Another group that was a stickler for laws among their own and a different set of rules for any outsiders. Because of their short stature, they did not seem to pose a world dominating threat.

The Filkont were in the northwestern part of Ficara. They

were about five and a half taja in height. They had pale brown skin and large, flat, ribbed ears. They numbered over 1,000,000. So far, they showed no signs of trying to conquer anyone.

The Grod were located in northern Aerisau. They stood nearly seven taja in height. Dark tan skin and very nasty looking pointed teeth. They did not like anyone, however, they did not seem to pose a threat…at this time.

The Ikogo were somewhat like the P'Lalfan. These people had arms. They had flippers instead of legs…and they had gills. They had become very adept at controlling certain beach areas along the far southern portions of North Chilamte. Because of the fact that they had no legs, it was not likely that they could conquer very much of any land area. Another thing that made it hard to accept them as conquerors was the fact that they numbered less than 100,000.

The Kafal-Shan lived in a southwestern part of North Chilamte. They were six taja in height and instead of fangs, they had tusks that grew out of the side of their jaws, going directly through the cheeks. They had brown skin. They would trade with others, however, if you trade with them…count your money carefully afterwards.

On the far eastern part of the Lusaratia continent they found the Kalawb-Rahanan-Or people. They had greenish-white skin and stood six taja in height. They had a rotten attitude towards everybody, however with numbers less than 90,000, they did not seem to be any kind of a threat.

In the southwestern part of Neopaure, the Merkab-Kara

were found. They were under five taja in height, they had black skin that would shine when exposed to sunlight. They also had enormous hands and feet. The sleeves of their shirts and cuffs of their trousers had to be very large in order to fit over those gargantuan features.

In central Lusaratia, they found the Noga-Or. These people did have some delusions of grandeur and were doing a lot of talking about world domination. Seeing as how they numbered around 150,000, they were not able to figure out how to carry out their domination plans. Another problem for their plans was that they also were a race whose skin glowed in the dark, so sneaking up on anybody was impossible. They were about six and a half taja in height.

The Opoteeve were located in south central Ficara. Just over seven taja in height and another race with bright green skin. They numbered over 700,000, however, they did not have any plans of world domination. As a race, they collectively had a very nasty attitude towards others, however, they did regularly send their prisoners to the Turgon Wall and they did trade with Owlam for *Tuzine*.

The Orek-Karaw were located in the far southern region of Aerisau. They had light tan skin, they stood over seven and a half taja in height and over 60% of their height was their extremely long legs. You might not be able to outrun an Orek-Karaw, however, they were not the domination type.

The Parash-Zanab were a pale-skinned race that lived in northern Aerisau. They were slightly less than six and a half taja in height and had a whip like tail that they could use as a nasty weapon. It was advised to keep an eye on these people because they did appear to have some rather high ambitions of controlling…as many people as they could.

The Perek were a race of dark tanned people who stood six taja in height and had feline like claws on both their hands and feet. They numbered almost 2,000,000, however they did not have any ambitions of dominating anyone else. They did do some very nasty things to anyone who entered their territory…without permission.

Wilfadge was getting a little bored at reading some of this information and was a little startled when the next race listed was the P'Lalfan. Yes, they had nasty attitudes towards others, however, the only people that they could cause any grief to were coastline fishing villages. They could not conquer anyone.

The next race listed was the Pryato who lived in the southwestern part of North Chilamte. They stood just under five and a half taja, had ebony skin…with blue and purple striped hair. No one seemed to see them as a threat because they numbered less than 60,000.

The next race was listed as a high probability of being dangerous. They lived in the southern part of North Chilamte. The Rakab-Rosh had dark, shiny green skin, they stood about seven and a half taja…and while standing up straight, their knuckles dragged the ground…unless they held their arms up. If they spread their arms out, they had an arm-span of almost ten taja.

Another race in northern Aerisau was the Shan-Ad. They

stood about seven and a half taja in height, had brown skin...and had a very difficult time eating because they had both fangs and tusks. While they numbered almost 2,000,000, they were not looked upon as much of a threat, because they seemed to have a diet of certain vegetables that only grew in that area of Aerisau.

The Tekaylath-Sar lived in central South Chilamte. They stood under five taja in height. They had ebony skin with all black hair, teeth, eyes and eyeballs. They hid very well at night and were the main suspects in many nighttime thefts in that area. During the day, they stayed inside the walls of their city and communicated with very few people at all. They were not looked upon as a threat.

The Teeve were located in northeastern Aerisau. Another race with milky green skin and green eyeballs. They stood just under six and a half taja in height. They were not looked upon as a threat because they numbered less than 100,000.

The Teltermak were listed next and their locations were numerous.

The Tendixive were located on the eastern coast of North Chilamte. They stood just under five taja, had ebony skin and they spit venom from somewhere in the back of their mouth. While some thought they may be dangerous because they numbered around 1,500,000, they did reluctantly trade with others and they did send all of their prisoners to the Turgon Wall.

The Tsaylaw-Ozen were located in south central North Chilamte. They stood just over five taja in height. They had pale brown skin and pointed ears. The ears were topped with sharp poisonous spikes. They were not looked upon as a threat because

Dara J. Carr

their poison attack had to be too close for comfort in any fight.

The Weesak people were located on the southern coast of Lusaratia. They stood seven and a half taja in height, had tan skin and ten fingers on each hand. While they numbered around 1,000,000, they did not appear to be very ambitious.

The Yagalom-Ayin were listed next. Wilfadge scoffed at this because they already knew what these people were doing. They had isolated all of the ingredients of *Tuzine*, however, after over 30,000 attempts at figuring out the recipe, they had not figured it out yet.

The last group in the listing was the Zaberd. They stood six and a half taja in height and had aqua skin. They lived on the southern coast of Cifpasica and numbered less than 60,000.

Wilfadge looked up from the report. "Does anybody have any special comments on this report?"

Dwalooa grunted. "I still don't understand why the Yagalom-Ayin haven't revealed to the Teltermak...that they've isolated all seven ingredients."

Antrong snickered. "That's all they've got! If they let the Teltermak know the ingredients...they could end up in a stew pot themselves. I wouldn't put anything past those Teltermaks...as something that they're *not* evil enough to do."

Teelila turned the report over. "I see that we have a whole list of possible enemies. Are there any reports of any new friends?"

"Yes," said Hoynama. "There's a group on South Chilamte...called the Yazeemay. They're kind of tall...they have dark yellowish skin…and purple eyeballs. They're friendly enough. They're pranksters…but…nothing that is mean or deadly."

"There's another race in western Aerisau," said Shyshee. They call themselves the Plyskenlil. They're rather short, they have light brown skin…and a long straight horn that sticks right out of the center of their forehead. They're a very friendly people who do everything they can to please as many people as they possibly can. I don't know if they'd be worth a hang in a fight, but, they…probably wouldn't fight against us…unless we attack them."

Wilfadge nodded. "So we got a couple of races that we really don't have to worry about at all. Do we have some people… watching the really dangerous ones on this list?"

"Absolutely," said Hadathoo. "We have Teams that take turns watching their leadership. There are a few that are making plans…but they always seem to get bogged down when trying to answer the question: How do we do it? If any of them ever do answer that question…our spies will let us know very quickly."

Wilfadge chuckled. "So now…we're doing what we were trained to do initially. We're watching. We're not doing it the way that we did originally but…watching others…that is one thing we know how to do…watch."

Antrong looked around at the faces of the others at the table. "And while we're watching…are we keeping a good, close watch…on the ones that do seem to have some ambitions? There are twenty-nine races listed here…six that are extremely dangerous to us...according to the report...two of which we were already aware of...but...are we going to end up spreading ourselves too thin...watching all twenty-nine races?"

Wilfadge was staring at the table sadly. "We can rotate a few Teams on each one. I don't think that any of them...will try to start anything...that is really...overly ambitious...without first talking to the top leaders. No one would keep a secret like that from their leaders...unless they have some kind of an internal rebellion. Then...we'd see a big mess within...before they could start on any crusade to take over the world."

"It'd be great if we could watch those infernal Teltermak a little closer," said Dwalooa. "Where did we find their main leadership?"

"We haven't," said Hadathoo.

Dwalooa shook her head. "But...what about the *Tuzine* laboratory? Isn't there someone who has to report to the higher ups...about any results from there?"

Hadathoo sighed. "All done by radio transmission. We haven't figured out where the receiving end is...yet." He grunted. "We haven't gotten our multi-fat-headed thin-lick communicator on line yet, so we don't know where the receiver is...only the sender."

Shyshee let out a nervous chuckle. "Remember that the Teltermak and the Axswain made a pact...along with Zee-Altha? Is it possible...that the main leaders of the Teltermak...are somewhere on the same island with the few remaining Axswain?"

Wilfadge cocked his head to one side in thought. "This is one possibility. I don't know if anyone has looked at that. We'll check that and see. I really would like to know exactly where they are hiding. It's infuriating not knowing...and they seem to be the only race that...we don't know where their main headquarters is...anymore."

"I think I know of a way to pull them out of hiding," said Till.

Wilfadge looked up. "I'm listening."

Till cleared his throat. "Let the Teltermak know...that the Yagalom-Ayin...have all of the ingredients...and are currently working on the cooking instructions."

"That's risky," said Ahandi. "It might only bring out a group of experts in torture...who'll try to extort the information from the Yagalom-Ayin. I don't think that it'll bring the leadership to Satroco Isle just to extract information from...an alleged ally."

Wilfadge sighed. "Let's all go home...and contemplate some thoughts on...a way to smoke the Teltermak leadership out. We really need to find them...and keep an eye on them."

The meeting was adjourned.

14

For twelve years everything seemed to be going well. There were a few skirmishes between some factions here and there, however, it was nothing major so it did not concern the Owlam Command Staff. Most of the time there was peace.

A call came in from Officer Grade 4, Indayazz. She was the Team leader for Team 399. This was the Team that was currently watching the Parash-Zanab in northern Aerisau.

Wilfadge got the telepathic message from Indayazz and called the Command Staff to the conference room.

Hadathoo walked in looking rather glum. "Why can't some people just leave well enough alone? Why...after all this time...does someone have to get stupid...again?"

Wilfadge shrugged and shook his head with a rather sad look on his face. "I don't understand it either. We were all like that...a little...before the firestorm. Now...we have some people who..." He shook his head again. "...I don't know."

After all of the Staff was there, Akantini ushered Officer Grade 4, Indayazz into the conference room. She asked if any of them needed anything before she went back to her office. No one said a thing. They just stared at the guest. Akantini departed silently.

Wilfadge sighed in a rather loud manner. "Okay, Officer, Indayazz, what is going on with these Parash-Zanab?"

Indayazz smiled helplessly. "As I reported...they're on the move...and they're being very destructive." She took in a deep breath and let it out slowly as she looked at all of the faces. "They're heading south from their city...and they have taken everything with them. Each village that they come to...they quickly take all of the citizens that they can...and herd them ahead of their entourage...as a buffer between them and the next enemy. They hold the families of the villagers hostage and tell the men that they'll be the leading edge of the next attack. If they try to fall back...they'll be killed by the Parash-Zanab. They are to attack... relentlessly. If they fail...and survive...they will get to watch their own family...get executed...in a slow and cruel manner."

Teelila scoffed. "So these *chokwads* can't even do their own fighting?"

"No, Sir, they make their prisoners do the fighting. They seem to be heading towards another city called Dardsrom. They seem to be, but we can't really prove it...yet. The Elf race there... they're just over seven taja in height, they have a medium brown skin...that is covered...all over with thin wisps of pure white hair. The Dardsrom are a rather amicable bunch that number about 3,500,000. Since the Parash-Zanab only number about 500,000, they're...pressing other people into the fray to do their fighting for them."

Dwalooa frowned. "Have you been doing any mind reading...to determine if this is their goal...and why?"

"Yes, Sir. While their accent is...rather strange...it seems that ever since the firestorm...all they've been doing is building up their armory. They found out that the Dardsrom have been building their city...and are now doing some commerce trading of their own...with the surrounding areas. The Parash-Zanab...want all of that...without having to build themselves up to it. They want to control."

Till snarled. "Is it possible that this is just the beginning... of a much longer campaign?"

Indayazz nodded sadly. "Absolutely."

Hadathoo was looking at some data. "So the Parash... whatever...are just under six and a half taja...and they number about 500,000. They want the Dardsrom...who stand just over seven taja...and have seven times the population of the Parash-Zanab." He scoffed. "And they don't have the guts to take them on by themselves. They have to press other...unwilling Heyyah into their service."

"Yes, Sir," said Indayazz. "This also includes another Elf race called the Rasixer. "Those people are about five and a half taja in height, they have gray skin and they have these gargantuan eyes...that somehow allow them to see in the darkest night, just as easily as we can see during the day."

Ahandi grunted. "How many of the Rasixer are there...I mean...does this add a large portion to the unwilling entourage?"

"No, Sir. As far as we can determine…the Rasixer number a total of around 120,000. They've shown themselves to be a rather fun loving…albeit sneaky people…they don't really want to harm anyone…they just like playing pranks…at night."

Wilfadge sat there shaking his head. "You say they…put all of their prisoners in the front…and use them as a buffer. What about their rear flank? Do they have much protection there?"

Indayazz smiled weakly. "I…don't know. I…could get Chachay to go take a quick look, if you like…Sir."

Wilfadge cleared his throat. "Uh…Chachay? Who…is Chachay?"

Indayazz bit her lip. "Officer Grade 4, Chachay. She is the Team leader for Team 1902. She has been…working with my Team…399…for a few days…on the mission."

Wilfadge smiled. "Well?"

Indayazz smiled. "Yes, Sir!" She closed her eyes and tilted her head back. She sent a telepathic message to Chachay. Without opening her eyes, she was verbally relaying what was now going on in northern Aerisau. "Team…1902…is deploying behind…the mass. They…are spreading out…to look over…as much of…the group…as possible."

"Good so far," said Ahandi dryly.

Wilfadge admonished Ahandi with a glaring look.

Indayazz continued. "There…don't appear…to be any… hostages…in the rear area. All of the hostages…are kept…near the front...in the middle. There appear to be at least...twelve... command type vehicles...with a lot of...strange colors...and... fancy colored flags on top...of each vehicle."

Ahandi frowned. "Is there any kind of...rear guard?"

Indayazz moved her head around as she was getting messages from the rest of Team 1902. "There...are guards... along the left and right flanks...but...nothing...in the rear."

Dwalooa chuckled. "Team 7016 still has a working 161. Send them to that rear area...and have them use a 459 cannon... and take out some of their command vehicles."

Wilfadge nodded. "That sounds like a good idea."

"Hold on," said Teelila. "Are we going to send...just one Team?"

Wilfadge shrugged. "Who else has a working vehicle... that can mount a 459 or any other pulse cannon?"

Teelila opened her mouth to say something. She stopped herself and contemplated the question. "I...guess...no one does... any...more."

"No one ever thought of setting up anything for the cannons on any of the new acquisitions," said Hadathoo. "Until someone comes up with a mount, for other vehicles, that 161 of Team 7016 is the only one that has that capability."

Antrong chuckled. "What's the problem? They can shoot from Spy dimension. Aren't they the ones who discovered that particular trick?"

Teelila shrugged in resignation. "Team 7016 it is."

Soolchakan received the message from the Command Staff. He got out of the tub and did not bother drying off. He wrapped a towel around himself and walked downstairs to where the three women were planning where to start on harvesting the *Shoonshook* plants that were ready. All three women looked up at their dripping wet Team leader.

He scowled at Kiyalee. "I hate you," he said in a dull manner.

Kiyalee instantly got defensive. "What…did I do now?"

"You kept that 161 in working order. Now…since it is the only vehicle…in all of the city of Owlam…that can mount a 459…we have to go into battle."

Three female jaws dropped at the announcement.

Bonarain got hold of her senses first and stood up. "What battle?"

He sighed. "The Parash-Zanab, in northern Aerisau, are on the march. They've taken several Heyyah villages and are using those unfortunates as shields and soldiers. The Command Staff has discovered that those *bimyocks* are not protecting their rear. We have to go to Aerisau and pulse cannon their rear…to show them that someone knows about their nonsense and is ready to cause them some grief as well."

Bonarain and Chyning both looked at Kiyalee as if they

had something sour in their mouths.

Kiyalee shrugged and smiled back. "I'll go get the truck ready."

"All three of you will go get the truck ready. I want the 459 mounted before we go."

There was a knock on the door.

Soolchakan sighed. "Come in!"

The door did not open. An Owlam man came through the door in Ghost dimension and then hopped back to Home dimension. He looked at Soolchakan. He shrugged looking a little perplexed. "I'm Officer Grade 6, Tozo of Team 1902." He looked Soolchakan up and down again. "I'm here...to Jump you to Aerisau...when you're ready."

Soolchakan sniffed. "Right! You can make yourself useful...while I'm getting dried and dressed. Help them mount the 459 on the turret."

Tozo smiled. "Yes, Sir...no problem." He looked at the women and smiled.

Kiyalee smiled back. "The truck is in the garage. Let's go."

The three women led the visitor to the garage while Soolchakan headed back upstairs grumbling to himself.

After drying himself as quickly as possible and getting dressed, he headed down to the garage to get ready to go. He wondered if the mounting still worked at all. It had been quite some time since they had attempted to set it up. He shrugged. With Kiyalee taking care of that truck, he was positive that she could repair any damage prior to Jumping to Aerisau. He was right. Kiyalee was applying some fresh grease in the turret area, in order to make sure that the cannon could be moved easily. Bonarain was doing the swiveling while Kiyalee greased it.

Chyning was standing off to the side chatting with Tozo about where they were going.

Soolchakan walked over to Tozo. "If you're finished gossiping, we're ready to go?"

Tozo smiled. "As soon as your people are sure that everything is fully functional."

Soolchakan grunted. He looked up at Kiyalee. "Well?"

Kiyalee put the grease gun in a tool box along with a greasy pair of gauntlets. She smiled at him. "Ready."

"Turn the cannon to the rear, lock it down and let's go."

All five were in the truck and Tozo Jumped them to Aerisau in Spy dimension. While Team 7016 looked over the twelve "possible" command vehicles, Tozo telepathically contacted the rest of his Team 1902. The three women of Team 1902 walked in front of the 161 and waved at the people inside the truck.

Team 7016 was introduced to Team 1902: Officer Grade 4, Chachay, Officer Grade 6, Vinvee and Officer Grade 7, Nisataka.

Soolchakan was standing up in the turret looking over the twelve target trucks in shock. "Who painted those things?

They look like…they were painted by…someone who is totally colorblind. They also look like each one came from a different manufacturer. Look at the differences in body style!"

Chachay snickered. "They do like things to be… ostentatiously garish…and a little…unique."

"That's an understatement," said Bonarain.

Soolchakan shook his head in disgust. "Let's get the cannon unlocked and ready."

Kiyalee grunted. "Which one are you gonna shoot first?"

Chyning snickered. "The ugliest one."

Kiyalee looked at Chyning bewildered. She shook her head. "Which one is that?"

Chachay laughed out loud. "That's a good question."

Bonarain looked at the trucks in horror. "Let's go with that…purple…and green…and orange…thing. That thing has got…at least…ten flags on top…and no two are the same color."

Soolchakan shrugged. "That's as good as any." He scoffed as he powered up the cannon. "Ridding the world of that grotesque thing…will be a *monumental* pleasure." He aimed the cannon and waited for it to beep.

Chachay waved at him. "Shouldn't we be a little closer?"

He looked down from his vantage point. "Were you at the Axswain wall when Nagasoom had us attack?"

"Of course I was…why?"

"What kind of vehicle were you in?"

"We had a type 74…Small Sprint Vehicle…why?"

"I was in the seventh row…and I hit the wall from there with one of these 459 monsters. You probably had the old 456 and it just doesn't have the same range as this destructive machine."

Chachay looked a little surprised. "O…kay….let's see it…destroy something."

Bonarain hollered out. "Uh…people…before we make something blow up…why don't we all go to Observation dimension…so we don't have to listen to any explosions?"

"Good idea," said Chachay.

All eight of them made the hop…with the 161 in tow.

Soolchakan looked at the target vehicle. "Again, getting rid of that…atrocity…will be a pleasure." He aimed the cannon and hopped the business end of the barrel into Home. He opened fire, hoping that he was hitting the fuel tank…or somewhere close to it.

The explosion was almost immediate. It was so violent that it made all of the Owlamites flinch. Even though all of the twelve Parash-Zanab trucks were spaced about fifteen taja apart, when the target truck blew up, the trucks on either side of the explosion were knocked onto their sides from the concussion. There were several more explosions as things that had been inside the truck started blowing up as well.

Bonarain chuckled sheepishly. "I think…it might be a…

munitions truck."

Kiyalee looked at the mess. "Past tense - was!"

There were numerous Parash-Zanab in the area who had been blown over – and probably killed. The ones who were still standing (or kneeling) were shaking their heads and rubbing their ears...with shocked looks on their faces. Several others were heading towards the burning wreckage, attempting to rescue anyone that they could.

Nisataka snickered. "Should we give them a chance to recover...or should we go ahead and blow up another truck?"

Chachay looked up at Soolchakan and pointed. "I really don't like that ugly thing over there."

Soolchakan scoffed. "Which one? They're all ugly!"

"The one that's striped...four shades of green, three shades of blue and two shades of orange...not to mention their poor taste in colored flags."

He shrugged and pointed the cannon to the right. He aimed at the unsightly truck and fired. There was another equally violent explosion as that truck went up in flames and toppled two more of the enemy trucks. Once again there were several residual explosions that were almost as bad as the initial blast.

Tozo shook his head. "What are they putting inside those things!?"

"I don't know," said Soolchakan. "We may have a problem though. I think that some of them saw the origin of the second shot. I'm hopping the whole gun back into Observation. As soon as the…residual blasts are over…let's go to…Spy and see if we can listen in to what they're saying."

"Bonarain is already trying to read some of their minds," said Chyning.

"So is Vinvee," said Nisataka.

Soolchakan looked at Chachay. "That's good enough…for the moment."

Chachay nodded in agreement.

Bonarain opened her eyes. "There were a whole bunch who saw the second shot. We need to move."

Vinvee nodded in agreement.

Soolchakan nodded. "Everyone…mount up! We'll move…to a different location…before the next shot."

Several of the Parash-Zanab walked to the area where the 161 had been parked originally. They looked around in any and every direction trying to figure out where that deadly beam had come from.

While the Parash-Zanab were doing their search, Kiyalee drove the truck directly through a crowd of the enemy as they were attempting to do some first aid to the injured.

Chachay looked around. "Where do you want to take your next shot from?"

Soolchakan shrugged. "Anywhere is fine with me. We

know they can see the beam…but not any of us. I can destroy their vehicles at will…without having to worry about anything."

Chyning scoffed. "At least these people aren't anything like the Cacktash or the Perfor…reading our minds or sniffing us out."

"Amen," said Tozo.

Nisataka groaned. "Please take that…ugly truck over there out next."

Soolchakan shook his head. "Which one…again…they're all ugly."

She pointed. "The one that is…striped and…at least forty different shades of green."

He chuckled. "My pleasure." He aimed the 459, hopped the business end into Home and fired.

Once again the result was almost immediate. This truck exploded and one part of the roof flew way up in the air. No one paid much attention to the flying piece until it came back down… killing two Parash-Zanab in the hard landing. There were the numerous residual explosions that took place, just like the other two trucks.

Chachay shook her head. "I don't know what they're storing in those trucks…but it is…totally volatile."

Kiyalee pointed to another truck. "Take out that six-wheeled atrocity next."

Soolchakan aimed and fired. The results were just like the

other three explosions.

The difference this time, however, many of the Parash-Zanab saw the originating point of the beam. They all started firing their weapons in that direction. Soolchakan noticed this and hopped the entire gun back into Observation.

Chachay sat there with her mouth agape. "Those... *bimyocks*...are...shooting each other! They saw the beam...and are firing...hoping to hit the invisible object...but they're killing each other instead."

Soolchakan grunted. "What a bunch of *melafathan dobops*!"

Finally, a Parash-Zanab Officer made enough of a din of his own and stopped everyone from firing. It was too late for at least forty of them. There were several of them that were obviously dead and there were several others that would die...soon.

The entire population was halted as the Parash-Zanab attempted to get chaos back to order and try to figure out just exactly what had happened.

Nisataka was looking up in shock. She pointed up. "Is that what...I think it is?"

Everyone else looked up as well.

Chachay let out an angry grunt. "That...is a bunch of... Teltermak kites. You don't think...that they have something to do with this...march of destruction...do you?"

Soolchakan shook his head. "Right now...I wouldn't put

anything past those parasites."

"I'll go check," said Vinvee. With that she vanished.

Chyning looked around. "Did she...go up there...to the kites?"

"Not the first time," said Tozo. "She goes up there and listens to their conversations."

Soolchakan smirked. "Does it help any?"

Chachay nodded. "Yes! She's come back from riding with them with some pretty good intelligence data."

Soolchakan nodded. "Okay...good."

Bonarain looked back around at the mess that had been made on the ground. "Should we wait for her return...or should we...damage...a few more vehicles?"

"We've stopped the forward progress of the march. We've created a big puzzle...not to mention a medical headache for them," said Chachay. "Let's wait...and see what she reports when she comes back down."

After a rather long wait, Vinvee came calmly strolling up to the front of the 161. "I think we need to give the Command Staff a little briefing on those *chogo* Teltermak. I heard some interesting reports...by them...to their headquarters."

Soolchakan chuckled. "Should we bust up a few more trucks before we go...or should we just go?"

Vinvee pointed towards the southwest. "I saw another

group of trucks over that way…when I was up there. If we…"
She cleared her throat. "…*bust up*…another truck…it should be
in a different location. That'll cause them Teltermaks to be even
more confused."

Chachay frowned. "Aren't we…supposed to be causing
the Parash-Zanab a lot of confusion? Why do we want to cause
the Teltermak…some confusion?"

Vinvee smiled. "Before…I give you a report…I'd like to
make sure of something. If you blow up another truck…or two…
over there…I'll listen in on their transmissions and get a little bit
of confirmation." She vanished.

Soolchakan looked at Chachay. "Okay…what now?"

Chachay shrugged. "Let's go over there…and blow up
a couple of trucks. She's probably gone back up there and is
listening for their transmissions to their headquarters."

He shrugged. "So who's going to Jump the truck…over…
wherever?"

Bonarain got up on top of the truck in order to get a better
look. She climbed back down in the truck. "Is everybody ready?"
After seeing a group of nods, she Jumped the 161 to a part of the
Parash-Zanab mob where there were ten large trucks, currently
parked, because of the mess that had happened at the rear of their
group.

Soolchakan snickered. "Don't tell me to blow up the
ugliest one. They're all so…garish and ugly…I can't tell which
one is the ugliest."

Tozo pointed. "Take out that big one with the bad taste of…at least eleven different colors"

Soolchakan nodded. "How close are we to it?"

Chachay shrugged. "About sixty taja."

He checked the power pack. It showed that it was still at 91% power. He aimed at the big truck and pulled the trigger. The spot where he aimed started glowing red. Less than one heartbeat later, the 161 was surrounded by flames. Everyone in the truck looked around in shock as this truck had gone up with a massive explosion that covered a lot more area than what they figured. There were a few very large residual explosions that occurred as well. When the flames (for the most part) subsided and the cloud of dirt and smoke started going down, they were finally able to see that the explosion from the first truck had made five other trucks blow up as well.

Tozo chuckled nervously. "I'll bet she's getting a truckload of transmissions from those *chokwads*."

"Well don't interrupt her," said Chachay. "We still need… any information that we can get…from any of their transmissions… as to what they're doing here…or anywhere."

They sat there for quite a while, watching how the Parash-Zanab were reacting to the disaster that had just hit them…again.

Vinvee finally showed up. "I think that we need to get to headquarters…while all of this stuff is still in my head."

Chachay nodded. She closed her eyes and sent a telepathic message to headquarters. She opened her eyes. "According to

Akantini, we go to headquarters and Team 7016 can go back to their home."

"Oh...no, no, no," said Soolchakan. "I wanna hear what she has to say. You don't make an announcement like that...and then leave me hanging in the dark."

Chachay chuckled. "Okay, head to your parking spot in the big lot near headquarters."

Bonarain Jumped the group to the parking lot. The entire group then proceeded to the Command Staff conference room. Akantini was a little surprised to see eight personnel instead of four. When it was explained that Team 7016 did not want to wait for the information, especially since they had been involved, Akantini gave up arguing and ushered them into the waiting room.

Akantini smiled. "There's someone else in there right now...giving a report on the stuff that's going on at Satroco Isle." She pointed at a table. "There's some refreshments there that you can partake of...while you're waiting."

They were all more interested in the report on the *Tuzine* situation.

A woman was giving the report. "So far, Sirs, the Teltermak are still unaware of the seven plants used in the ingredients. The Yagalom-Ayin still haven't told them. So far...using the seven ingredients, the Yagees have attempted over 300,000 different recipes. None have worked."

Wilfadge sounded surprised. "What? 300,000 and... nothing close to getting it down?"

The woman chuckled. "No, Sir. The main reason…*we* are aware of the fact that with the *Shoonshook*, you use only the deep roots. So…every time they put the roots, any part of the root… (chuckle) …we added a little cyanide to the mixture. Now…they don't add any root at all…and so…they're getting nowhere."

The entire staff got a big laugh out of the sabotage.

"As long as you're keeping them…frustrated," said Wilfadge. "…keep them guessing…and bewildered."

"Yes," said the woman. "Thank the Great Maker for Spy dimension."

There was a chorus of "Amen".

Wilfadge spoke up. "Are there any other questions for her?"

Silence.

"Thank you for the report. You are dismissed."

Akantini went to the door. "Sir, there's a group here, with a report from the Parash-Zanab situation."

"Okay," said Wilfadge. "Bring them in."

Soolchakan held his Team. "We can wait out here and hear it."

Chachay nodded and led her Team into the conference room. "Sirs, I am the Team Leader for Team 1902. We were just in the middle of their mass movement…and with the aid of Team 7016, created a chaotic situation where their advance has been slowed…if not stopped completely. While watching their reaction to the situation…it was observed that the Teltermak were flying on their kites…very high…over the mass.

"There's not much we can do about that," said Ahandi. "They have just as much right to observe as we do."

"No, Sir," said Vinvee. "It's not observation. The Teltermak are steering them."

"You have my attention," snarled Wilfadge.

"Thank you, Sir," said Vinvee. "After we blew up a couple of the Parash-Zanab trucks, we noticed that there were five Teltermak kites flying overhead. I Jumped up there and listened to see if I could glean any information. They said that the Parash-Zanab were being attacked by…the same 'Ghost Assassins' that attacked the city of Teltermak and ran *them* out of their home."

Hadathoo laughed. "They still don't know that it was us who attacked them."

"No, Sir, they don't." said Vinvee. "Our people were in Observation dimension and we blasted that hole in the wall from there. Apparently they ran because they found no way to fight an enemy that they can't see…so they ran. They've been trying to find out who attacked them and until we hit the Parash-Zanab… from Observation…with a 459, they haven't seen any sign of what they call…Ghost Assassins."

"I wonder if…what was left of the Axswain…ran for the same reason," said Teelila.

"That's as good a guess as any," said Antrong.

"Anyway," continued Vinvee, "they're now sending several more of their kites out there...over the Parash-Zanab, to see if they can find any more evidence of who the Ghost Assassins are...and also try to get them back on track...for whatever the Teltermak have planned for them...either their trail of destruction or...death."

Dwalooa leaned forward. "Was there any indication of... where the headquarters of the Teltermak...is located?"

Vinvee shook her head sadly. "All they said...was...Home Base. They...gave no indication of where it is...or...anything about it. The response from...Home Base...was for them to make every attempt at getting the Parash-Zanab...back on the move."

Wilfadge growled. "Those pests...are becoming...an even bigger headache than any of us originally thought. They're getting...involved...in controlling...anybody and everybody. It might be...just like the Gabeesh-Or and the Twakon...make them destroy each other and the Teltermak come in and...clean up the residue."

Till scoffed. "Great! The problem here...who on that continent is strong enough or mean enough...to take on that mass and actually hurt them...and still have enough left over?"

"Maybe the move is enough," said Shyshee. "Get them out of their city...into the open...and have them weaken themselves considerably...along with others. Once they've weakened the entire continent...the Teltermaks could take over...without much of a fight."

"We've got to find out what the overall mission is in

steering the Parash-Zanab to…wherever," said Wilfadge. "Who, what, when, where, how and why? Some of them we have… partial answers to. We've got to get more clarification and find out just exactly…anything!"

Chachay scratched her head. "Should we go back there… and do a few more Ghost Assassin stunts?"

"Absolutely," said Wilfadge. "We need to get as many of those Teltermaks out there…talking to each other…and maybe someone'll…spill…something!" He stroked his chin. "Let's get a few more of our people out there with some 459's and do some shooting."

"We can't," said Teelila. "There's only one vehicle… currently in existence…that can properly mount a 459. All the rest of them…rotted away…a long time ago."

Wilfadge slammed his fist against the table. "Then let's get started making a few more. We bought all of those trucks from…whatever that city is. Get a few mounts in them. Make sure that the mounts are temporary and can be taken out of the trucks. That way…the truck won't appear to be something of… war…alone."

Hadathoo nodded. "Until that's done, we need Team 7016 to do several Jumps, in and around that mass movement…and create as much chaos as possible…to keep that mass movement… completely not moving."

Wilfadge smiled at Chachay. "Can you contact Team 7016 and get them back out there?"

Chachay turned to the door. "Officer, Soolchakan?"

He walked to the doorway. "Yes, Officer, Chachay?"

"Did you hear what he said?"

"I certainly did."

"Are we going to need any extra power packs out there?"

"It sounds like a good idea to me."

Wilfadge grunted. "Have you been sitting out there…all this time?"

Soolchakan smiled. "Yes, Sir, we have. May I make a further suggestion?"

"Oh, by all means."

"Get about one hundred more Teams out there…to the Parash-Zanab area. If the Teltermak are as nosey and manipulative as what we think…they may be sending…who knows how many more kites out there for observation. We need a bunch more people out there for our own observations…of the Teltermak."

Wilfadge looked at the Staff. "Make that two hundred Teams. Start calling people out there…right now!"

All of the Staff closed their eyes and began sending out telepathic communications to get more Teams into the action.

Soolchakan walked into the room. "One more thing… make sure they go into Observation…if they're on the ground. The last truck that…I blew up…the blast was…to say the least… tremendous. If we'd been in Spy dimension…we'd all be deaf.

Tell them to wait until they're on a Teltermak kite before they switch to Spy."

"Done," said Wilfadge. "Anything else?"

"I'll make other suggestions if I think of any."

Wilfadge nodded. "Good. Get your truck out to the... mess and...make it a...bigger mess." He held his hand up as if to signal Soolchakan to stop. "Another thing – since your truck is the only one left that can mount a 459...I'll have some Teams standing by with additional 459's...just in case anything goes wrong with yours."

Soolchakan smiled. "Thank you, Sir." He turned back to his Team.

Kiyalee was standing there looking a little disgusted. "We have our 459 and the spare in the bracket on the inside of the truck. We have twelve power packs. What else do we need from anyone else?"

"More backups won't hurt," he said calmly.

"Are you questioning my capability to keep that stuff working?"

He gave her a warm smile. "Not at all. The thing is...in any military confrontation...you need to hope for the best...but prepare for the worst."

Bonarain scoffed. "That works in any endeavor of life."

"Let's get back out there," said Soolchakan.

Chyning looked surprised. "Shouldn't we wait...to show some other Teams how to Jump to that specific spot?"

"Chachay and Team 1902 can do that," said Soolchakan. "Let's move out."

They Jumped to the truck and then Jumped back to the battlefield.

Soolchakan did a quick scan of the sky. "Uh...Bonarain... call Wilfadge...and tell him...there's well over forty Teltermak kites....here...already."

Bonarain looked up through the turret. "Oh, my! Forty... at the very least!" She sat back down and closed her eyes.

Soolchakan sighed. "Okay...Kiyalee...which of their trucks...do you hate the most?"

Kiyalee let out a little "humpf". "That gaudy brown and green one...way over to the left."

Chyning shook her head. "I've flushed, prettier looking stuff, down the toilet."

Soolchakan aimed the cannon. "Consider it history." He fired.

Again there was a tremendous blast.

Chyning let out a squawk. "Are they ALL munitions carriers?"

Soolchakan looked up. The Teltermak had seen the beam coming from his cannon. There were several of them that were

circling directly above the truck. He snickered. "Let's Jump…
oh…say…two kilotaja from here…and I'll take another shot."

Kiyalee smacked his leg. "Which way to you want?"

He pursed his lips. "Pick one."

Kiyalee laughed. She looked off to the right, shrugged and
Jumped the truck.

All four of the Team saw a truck that was about eighty taja
directly in front of them.

"You've got to be joking," said Bonarain.

Chyning shook her head. "Oh…please kill it…now!"

Kiyalee looked as if she had a bad taste in her mouth.
"Who…designs these eyesores?"

Soolchakan shook his head, aimed the cannon and fired.

All three women said "thank you" at the same time.

The blast from the last target sent a very large tire directly
at Team 7016. The huge tire landed directly on the front of their
161.

"I'm so glad that we're in Observation," said Kiyalee. "If
that thing had actually landed on my truck…ooh…I'd be so mad."

"I'll bet you would," said Bonarain.

Chachay was suddenly standing next to the truck. "Have
you looked up lately?"

Soolchakan glanced up and his jaw dropped. The sky

was now full of kites. "There's got to be...over two hundred... where'd they all come from?"

Chachay shook her head. "From...almost every direction. Don't shoot any more of the enemy trucks...and maybe some of them'll go back home. We'll be able to follow them...and find some of the satellite stations...and then glean more from that as the day goes on. Go ahead and take your truck back...and we'll call you if we need you."

Soolchakan did not look down. He continued staring at the multitude that was flying overhead. "I want a report...on what you find...please!"

"I'll keep you informed," said Chachay.

Team 7016 Jumped back to their home.

15

Twelve days later, Soolchakan was sitting in the dining area eating a stew that Chyning had cooked up. She was wanting a critique of the stew, seeing as how it was a brand new recipe she had come up with. He was not paying much attention to the stew, he was paying more attention to the report from Officer Grade 4, Indayazz on the Parash-Zanab.

When the trucks started blowing up and the Parash-Zanab saw all of the kites flying overhead, the Parash-Zanab assumed that the sabotage was coming from those people up above…and started firing on the Teltermak with everything that they had…and they did have pulse weapons.

211 kites were shot down and 134 escaped. There was an Owlamite on each kite that escaped and they were able to find several little hideouts that the Teltermaks had established on Aerisau. Hideouts where they planned to stay because they had their families with them.

As a result of the Teltermak being seen and shot at by the Parash-Zanab, the Teltermaks had to do their reconnaissance from a much further distance. The distance had to be from the side because the Parash-Zanab pulse weapons were able to shoot them out of the sky, even from great height. This was when the Owlamites found out that the Teltermaks were steering the Parash-Zanab, the same way that they had steered the Gabeesh-Or and the Twakon. The problem here was that Owlam could not figure out the exact destination of the mass movement. The original target was thought to be the city of Dardsrom. Now they were not sure at all. Even if they could, they were not sure how to protect the involuntary soldiers that were kept as a buffer between the Parash-Zanab and…whom it may concern.

Chachay got a report from one of the people spying on a Teltermak site. She looked at her map of Aerisau. "According to what she said…the Teltermak want…this mass to go to the city of Barratokefin. Who are those people?"

Officer Grade 5, Mikmika of Team 339 checked her information. "They're a black-skinned people. They're seven taja in height and…they have black teeth as well. They're sticklers for the law. They obey all laws…to the last degree of the law…and they expect any visitors…to do the same."

Chachay nodded. "Anything about their numbers?"

"Last report we got…shows…about 400,000."

"So they got their hostage fighters to give them a better advantage than what they had before."

Indayazz walked up. "Wilfadge wants another attack by our Ghost Assassin Team. He heard that the Parash-Zanab were starting to move again and he wants them slowed…as much as possible."

Chachay cocked her head to the side. "Does he want the city of Barratokefin warned...as well?"

Indayazz shrugged. "He didn't say...but...it couldn't hurt. Has anyone been there...yet?"

"I have," said Officer Grade 6, Jojomon of Team 399. "I scouted the place about six days ago." He looked a little worried. "They're not the type that...is going to eat me are they?"

Indayazz chuckled. "No...they won't eat you, but they will jail you if you break any law of theirs."

"Wonderful," he said sarcastically. He sighed. "I'll...be back...as soon as I can...if I can." He vanished.

Indayazz looked at the map. "I think we should check on some of these other places as well. Warn...everyone...no matter what."

Chachay nodded. "I find it hard to argue with that."

Soolchakan looked around him at all of the Parash-Zanab vehicles. "Are they all painted...with bad taste in mind?"

"I think so," said Bonarain. "I haven't seen one color combination...that I could consider...even slightly good looking."

He looked up. "Everyone get their binoculars. Look for any sign of Teltermak."

Chyning crawled up through the turret to the top of the truck. "What do we do if we see one?"

He snickered. "We get closer so that both sides can see each other...and maybe we get a few more Teltermak killed in the process."

Kiyalee held up a pad. "Did you see this report from Indayazz?"

Soolchakan did not look down. "No...why?"

"According to what she's been able to find out...your blasting has killed over 6,000 of the Parash-Zanab."

He looked at her pad in shock. "Those explosions...were more damaging than I thought. Over 6,000 dead and...2,100 wounded. I wonder why...there are more dead than wounded. That usually doesn't happen."

Kiyalee scoffed. "Because these *bimyocks* kill anyone who can't continue. If you're wounded and you can still function... you live. If you need a stretcher...you're dead."

Chyning shuddered. "How...benevolent!"

Jojomon returned to where Indayazz and Chachay were waiting.

Chachay frowned at him. "What took you so long?"

He sighed. "Those Barratokefin were adamant that I give a similar warning to another city. They don't get along with that other city, so they suggested that I do the talking."

Chachay nodded. "What city?"

"Zerowa-Mashak. Those people are…nice. They're another black-skinned bunch…about seven and a half taja and they have long sharp quills…all over their bodies. They don't wear much clothing…because the quills…tear through just about anything."

Indayazz smiled. "So…did you warn them?"

He looked affronted. "Of course! I did it in the name of harmony…with some of the peoples of the planet. There's enough enemies out there."

"Thank you," said Indayazz.

Wilfadge was in the tub washing is neck when he received a mental communication from Akantini. It had something to do with the advance of the Parash-Zanab. He sent back that he was in the tub and would be at the conference room as soon as possible. He also told Akantini to call the rest of the Command Staff. He finished his neck and got out of the tub.

Hadathoo arrived (what he thought would be last because of something he had to take care of). When he walked in, the only one who was still absent was Wilfadge. He smiled at the rest of the Staff. "Does anyone know what this is about?"

Everyone shook their head and went back to any refreshments they had with them.

A short time later, Wilfadge walked in, with damp hair. "I was in the tub when I got the call," he muttered.

Considering the mucus that was coming out of the scales on the backs of their necks, no one questioned him further.

Wilfadge sat down at the head of the table. "Officer Akantini! What are we here for?"

Akantini came in, ushering an Owlam Team in behind her. "This is Officer Grade 4, Joyntee. She's the Team Leader for Team 538 and she has something to report."

Joyntee smiled at the Staff. "This is my Team, Officer Grade 6, Intsima, Officer Grade 6, Zhardok and Officer Grade 7, Fanasina. We've been following the Noga-Or for several weeks and…they're headed from Lusaratia to Aerisau. They got on some huge ships…with all of their belongings…five weeks ago and they should land on Aerisau within three days."

Ahandi stood up angrily. "FIVE WEEKS AGO…and we're just finding out…NOW!"

"Sit down," said Wilfadge calmly. "We'll find out… why…" He frowned at Joyntee. "…I hope."

Joyntee chuckled nervously. "Yes…Sir!" She swallowed. "I would have reported it earlier…except…we had no idea where they were going…at first."

Everyone on the Staff gave her a questioning look.

She continued. "The location…where they left Lusaratia… it should have only taken sixteen days to get to Aerisau. They… zig-zagged…and even turned around…all over the place and…we weren't sure…whether they were going to Aerisau, Cifapasica or Ficara…or even back to Lusaratia. Then…five days ago…there were some…Teltermak kites…that appeared high overhead…and they all got *directly* on track…straight to a harbor on the southern tip of Aerisau. They haven't turned from this heading…since the Teltermak showed up."

Wilfadge closed his eyes and hung his head. "The Teltermaks," he whispered with a snarl. He looked back up. "So… the Teltermaks are steering this bunch…to Aerisau. Is there any indication…that it has anything to do with the southern advance of the Parash-Zanab?"

"Yes, Sir. When they got…on track for Aerisau…some of their Commanders pulled out some paperwork that specifically gives them all kinds of information about the Parash-Zanab."

"Wait a moment," said Shyshee. "According to this… information here…there's only about 200,000 Noga-Or. Why… are they going after a much larger enemy…out in the open?"

Joyntee bit her lip. "Those figures are…wrong. They had…over half of their population hidden…in some mammoth caves near their city. The correct number is much closer to 450,000."

Dwalooa was looking through the information on her pad. "What do these people look like?"

"They're about the same height as us…just over six and a half taja and they have fluorescent skin."

Dwalooa looked more confused. "Another bunch with fluorescent skin? What color of…fluorescent skin?"

Joyntee smiled helplessly and shrugged. "It all depends

on the angle…that you're looking at them from. Sometimes…
white…sometimes blue…sometimes purple and sometimes…
gold."

Antrong scoffed. "Do they do the color change…on
purpose?"

"No, Sir, it is just…something about each individual…and
the angle that you're looking at them."

Wilfadge sat there drumming his fingernails on the table.
"So…once again, the Teltermak are interfering with the lives
of many others. They…got the Gabeesh-Or and the Twakon
massacred. Now…they're trying to do the same to…the Noga-Or
and the Parash-Zanab. They got away with it once…now…they
want to do it again. Why?"

Till shrugged. "Get rid of any possible enemies…that have
any ambitions of world conquest…and then…you can dance in and
take over. You just have to make it look like those antagonists…
were the primary perpetrator in the war…and meanwhile…you sit
by looking totally innocent."

Teelila shook her head. "And we can't expose them…to
the rest of the world without…exposing ourselves…as far as what
we've been doing…so far."

Hoynama sighed. "We would be exposing ourselves to the
Teltermak as well."

Wilfadge snarled. "Okay! So it looks like we may not be
able to stop this war. Is there a way that we can get those hostages
out of the way?"

Hadathoo smiled. "Are the Parash-Zanab protecting their rear yet?"

"I haven't heard anything yet," said Wilfadge. "Why?"

"We've been mounting tripods in the back of some of those newly acquired trucks," said Hadathoo. "Those tripods can mount a 459 and you can fire from it. I just would not want to be moving and firing at the same time. If we take all of the trucks that are prepared to fire a 459 and do a mass attack on their rear…it might make them move the hostages…to the rear."

Antrong shook his head. "Or it might only make them thin out…the front and the flanks."

Hadathoo chuckled. "Yes, but that would still be fewer people in the front or on the flanks that have to be rescued."

"That still doesn't answer the question of how we rescue… any of them," said Ahandi.

Till snickered. "Disguise ourselves as some heavenly host that has come down to pull the innocent out of the way of being harmed."

"I don't think that the Great Maker would approve of that," said Wilfadge. "No, we do everything covertly. We go into the area where the families of the battling hostages are kept. We free them and then…do some mind manipulations…to steer them to safety. Once they're free, we manipulate the battling hostages to get out."

Till smiled. "If we're going to mind-manipulate the families out of there…the safest direction would be to the battling hostages. That way, the battling hostages know that their families are free…and then there won't be any need to mind-screw them."

"I like that," said Dwalooa.

"So do I," said Wilfadge. "It may take three thousand Teams to get it done…but that doesn't matter - it'll be worth it. We get the hostages out of there…and…"

Hadathoo growled. "The flying Teltermaks are sure to see a mass exodus of hostages. How do we prevent that?"

Till snickered. "Before the battle starts, the Teltermaks – who are in the area – start having some mass malfunctions with their kites…and then they have no way to observe the exodus or the battle. By the time they're able to get any more kites in the area, most of the battle will be over and the hostages will be gone…without the Teltermaks having any clue as to how they got away."

"This is going to take some careful timing," said Teelila.

Hadathoo shook his head. "Wait a moment! We haven't even found out how the Parash-Zanab are going to react to a mass rear attack. We have to find out what they do with the hostages… before we execute the second phase and start the rescue. If they move ALL of the hostages to the rear…phase two is not necessary."

Wilfadge nodded. "Absolutely correct! How many of those trucks…including Team 7016 are ready to do a mass… Ghost Assassin attack against the rear?"

The four Master Officers closed their eyes and sent out telepathic communications to all of the people under their individual command. After all four had finished the communications they looked at Wilfadge.

Wilfadge turned to Ahandi. "Sector One?"

"We have six, Sir," said Ahandi.

"Sector Two?"

"We have eight, Sir," said Teelila

"Sector Three?"

"We have seven, Sir," said Dwalooa

"Sector Four?"

"We have seven tripods and Team 7016," said Hadathoo.

"That makes twenty-nine 459's that can go into action now," said Wilfadge. "That should make a considerable amount of wreckage among the Parash-Zanab. Get them out there and let's get this treacherous ball rolling. One word of warning…tell them to check and see if there are any hostages who're already in the rear echelon. If there are…we may have to change the attack."

The four Master Officers sent out the new communication. As soon as they were finished, they opened their eyes and nodded to Wilfadge, giving him the ready signal from all of them.

Wilfadge looked apprehensive. "Any reports of hostages in the rear?"

All four shook their heads.

Hadathoo cleared his throat. "How long should we

maintain the attack?"

Wilfadge looked off to the side. "Tell each Team to...check their power pack. As soon as it gets down to...oh...say...20%...get out of there...and then we'll wait for a report from our watchers."

The four Master Officers relayed the order and once again looked at Wilfadge.

The Supreme Officer hung his head and sighed. "Open fire," he said sadly.

Soolchakan did not really try to aim the 459. He just pulled the trigger and swept back and forth in several crowds of the Parash-Zanab. He was sickened as he saw severed body parts flying randomly around. He noticed, with peripheral vision that some of his colleagues were blowing up trucks. The damage was incredible. The loss of life was mounting up in numbers that would sicken anyone.

He stopped every few moments and checked his power pack. By himself he had probably massacred over a thousand of the enemy and his power pack was still over 85%. He snarled and kept on firing.

The Parash-Zanab were firing back with any weapon that they could get their hands on. They, like the Owlamites, noticed that there were some kites flying overhead. Some of the Parash-Zanab switched their aim to the kites above. Bullets had a hard time reaching the kites, however, the pulse weapons did not have the same handicap and several kites came crashing to the ground with fatal results for the Teltermak that were on those specific ones.

The kites flew off or up, attempting to get out of range…
with Owlamite passengers on board.

To his left, Soolchakan heard a loud explosion. That did not
make sense. All of the Owlamites were in Observation dimension
and they should not be able to hear any of the explosions unless it
was…something Owlamite that was blowing up.

Indayazz sent out a frantic mental communication…just as
a second explosion sounded off to the left again. She was telling
all of the personnel to stop firing and get their entire 459 cannon
back into Observation.

He stopped firing, powered the cannon down and looked to
his left trying to figure out what had happened. From his vantage
point on top of the 161 he could see some smoke coming up from
two of the Owlam trucks. Both trucks vanished. He figured that
they probably Jumped back to Owlam to visit the Medical Teams.
He was still very curious as to exactly what had happened…and
how many may have been hurt.

The Supreme Commander gave a telepathic order for all
of the cannons to be brought back to Owlam until they could
investigate the explosions and find out what did happen.

The Owlamites who were able to hitch rides with the
surviving Teltermaks were able to find a few more hideouts that
their old nemesis had on Aerisau. It was now appearing that those
cannibals had been spreading their people all over the place and it
would take quite a while to get all of them located and cataloged.

Five days later the report on the explosions in Observation came out. Somehow the pulse weapons of the Parash-Zanab had hit the very tip of the 459 cannons of two Teams. When the enemy beam hit, the 459 beam reacted with some kind of a backwash to the power pack, resulting in the explosion.

On Team 6643, two women had been standing in the back of the truck when the explosion occurred. Officer Grade 5, Avasoona and Officer Grade 7, Ee-Manasima were both killed instantly.

On Team 6682, the same thing had occurred only there was only one woman in the back of the truck operating the 459. Officer Grade 7, Denyisa was killed instantly in the explosion.

To complete these two Teams again, the incomplete Team 5709 was disbanded. Officer Grade 5, Oymani and Officer Grade 7, Tway were transferred to Team 6643. Officer Grade 7, Neenahasa was transferred from 5709 to Team 6682.

Further reports were coming in from the Owlamite spies who had ridden with the Teltermaks to their lairs. More communications to the Home Base, however, still no clues as to the exact location of the base. The radios they were using were the type that could communicate with any other radio (of that sort) any place in the world. The Owlamites were getting no closer to finding the location.

Indayazz reported that even though the attack was of a short duration, the results had been devastating. The Parash-Zanab had lost thirty-two trucks and over 28,000 troops. They were now moving over half of their contingency of hostage fighters to the rear echelon, seeing as how that was the only direction that they had been attacked from...so far

Wilfadge dropped the report. "How do we avoid...any more fatal accidents like this...backwash explosion?"

Antrong looked up. "Don't sit in one place...very long. Open fire...with two or three bursts...hop the cannon back into Observation and...Jump...somewhere else. Fire two or three more...keep Jumping."

"Sounds good," said Wilfadge quietly. "Get that order out to all Teams right now." He shook his head. "According to the ratio...they lost 9,333 for each one that we lost. I still don't like any losses...never have."

Till looked up from the report. "I think that we haven't answered...or even asked the biggest question...yet. How are the Teltermaks...obtaining control...over these people? How can they...control and manipulate...an entire population...to follow so blindly? They get them to leave the safety of their city...with...EVERYONE! Every man, woman and child...every occupation...every...*thing*...as well! How? I can understand the radio communications...where they steer them...but...why do all of these people...follow...so blindly?"

Dwalooa gasped. "Drugs! I...remember...several years ago...the Algothons drugged their entire city...looking for spies. Is it possible...that the Teltermaks have manufactured...some... drug...that they can use to get and keep control of...an entire population?"

"That makes more sense than anything that I can think of,"

said Wilfadge. "The only other possibility is mass hypnosis." He growled and shook his fists. "Now...we have to find...not only their home base...but...a chemical plant...where they make all kinds of...mind controlling pharmaceuticals!"

"These people are really becoming a massive pain... everywhere," said Hadathoo. He scoffed. "Even if we...kill a few...satellite stations..." He shook his head. "...it doesn't get us any closer to...either...home base...or a chemical plant."

Teelila looked around. "What about Satroco Isle?"

"No," said Wilfadge. "Everything on Satroco is devoted to analyzing *Tuzine*." He sighed. "I already checked on that."

Shyshee shrugged. "What about that island...where the Axswain are living? Is it possible that they could be using the Axswain...the same way that they're using the Yagalom-Ayin?"

"No," said Wilfadge. "I've had a few Teams go there and check. Right now, all that the Axswain are trying to do...with their tiny population...is survive."

"I wonder who is next," said Hoynama. "If they kill off these two antagonists...they're bound to have another target...or targets...in mind." She shook her head. "No telling who that could be."

The Noga-Or had landed and were marching north. Joyntee gave the exact location to the Command Staff. Indayazz gave the exact location of the Parash-Zanab and it was estimated that it would be approximately eight days before they were in shooting range of each other.

Wilfadge was sitting there quietly pondering. "Has anyone considered the exact way that we're going to rescue hostages and keep them from becoming…extinct casualties?"

"Yes," said Hoynama. "Start rescuing them now." There was a chorus of "What" as she sat there gloating. "If the Teltermak can manipulate them…with drugs…or hypnosis…why can't we try a little of the same thing? We get in there and make them…or at least the night guard, get a little lazy. They all…are blinded…or distracted…or…knocked out. While they're…doing the 'other', we then unshackle the families and get them out of there with the rest of their families. We can probably keep the Parash-Zanab distracted for…two days. That should give the hostages enough time to get away and make the Teltermak forget about trying to get them back together." She smiled triumphantly.

"That'll require a little coordination…as far as keeping the Teltermak kites busy," said Teelila.

"I don't think we'll have a problem there," said Hadathoo. "According to those flying cameras…there's a big storm front moving in on the Parash-Zanab location." He smiled. "The kites can't fly in any storm." He shrugged. "I don't think that the hostages will mind…departing the area…even if it is raining…as long as they can get out of there…alive."

Wilfadge sat there staring at nothing in particular. "Call… *everybody*! The only ones who will not be involved in the rescue… are the ones who are spying on the Teltermak and the Algothons… or the people at the *Tuzine* trading stations. When the storm hits…

and night falls…all hostages are going to be rescued." He looked around the table. "When I say that all personnel are going to be involved in the rescue…I mean US…as well."

Over 20,000 Owlamites were at the Parash-Zanab location (in Observation dimension). It took all day to determine the locations of the families and the fighter hostages. Once that had been covered, the Owlamites looked to the west and watched the storm front move in. They started a mass thought wave process. They made the Parash-Zanab feel cold and afraid as they watched the dark clouds roll in. When the light rain started, all of the Parash-Zanab headed for cover…anywhere.

Now the Owlamites had to act fast. They had to free over 200,000 families from shackles and get them to move towards the hostage fighters. None of them had been kept in any of the trucks. They were in long lines, chained together so that they could be controlled easily. Many of them sat there looking in disbelief as the manacles just fell away. They looked in fear for their captors. It was a little difficult giving them the courage to move, however, it was finally accomplished with some strong mental manipulation. They made them even more afraid of being caught *without* the manacles on their wrists. This made them move.

Getting the hostage fighters in the forward positions was rather difficult as well. Once again the Owlamites had to put mental images of fear of being caught by their captors without any chains. They herded every one of them to the rear area. By the time they got all of the hostages to the rear area the rain was coming down hard. The entire area was nothing but one huge muddy quagmire.

There were several of the Parash-Zanab that noticed the hostages moving. They, at first, got up to attempt to stop the mass movement. A quick hop of their faces into the Stink dimension and they were on their hands and knees…with something else on their mind as they knelt there heaving up everything that they had eaten in the last day. Several others found out, the hard way, about Jahong's Death dimension.

The storm did not let up when the sun came up. It was hard to tell if it was day time at all because of the clouds. The storm lasted all day and on into the night. By the time it let up… all hostages had been on the run for over a day and a half and they were scattering in many different directions making it impossible to recapture any large contingency of them.

The Parash-Zanab were now going to have to do their own fighting…and the Teltermak were absolutely baffled as to how 200,000 family members and some 65,000 hostage fighters had disappeared from the area so completely. The Teltermak made numerous transmissions about the conundrum to Home Base, however, there was still no clue as to the location of Home Base.

The march of the Parash-Zanab continued south. The march of the Noga-Or continued north. The Owlamites could not seem to find any way possible to stop the meeting between the two. The Teltermak had done their job very well in making the two ambitious races go head to head…to the death.

The two groups finally got in screaming range. They both stood their ground making all kinds of noises trying to outshout the other side. The noise making took up most of the morning.

The Owlamites who were there were very glad for the existence of Observation dimension. They sat there quietly waiting to see what would happen.

Suddenly the sky was full of smoke trails as both sides started attacking with artillery. The shells were landing in each enemy camp with deadly results.

Indayazz started laughing and pointed up at a Teltermak kite that had been hit directly by one of the flying artillery shells. The kite and the two occupants fell to the ground in flames.

"I'll bet the other kite flyers are trying to get a little higher," said Joyntee.

"You can't go too high," said Chachay. "The higher you go, the colder it gets and the thinner the air. At a certain point... you can't breathe."

"That'd be interesting to see," said Officer Grade 4, Ambad of Team 967. He chuckled. "It'd serve them right."

Vinvee stood up. "Oh...*h'oolyach*...here they come!"

Everyone looked up. The Noga-Or and the Parash-Zanab were now running at each other at full speed and firing their weapons as they charged. Hundreds in the leading edge of both sides were being cut to pieces by pulse weapons or blown apart by conventional projectile weapons.

Mikmika scoffed. "Is this for real? Look at that! There's a Noga-Or woman...and she's...attacking...with a baby on her back! How stupid is that?"

Indayazz started looking around at both sides. "There… is a bunch of women…from both sides…pregnant…or with children…and…THIS IS RIDICULOUS!"

Chachay shook her head as she saw a pregnant woman get beheaded by a pulse beam. "What possesses them?"

"Teltermak drugs," said Ambad bitterly.

Vinvee looked at her Team Leader and spoke angrily through her teeth. "Can I go up there and bring those *chokwads* down?"

Chachay scoffed. "Be my guest. You can do it with my blessing."

Vinvee vanished.

Indayazz squinted as she looked up. "How many are up there?"

Joyntee looked around the sky. "Nine…I think."

"Make that eight," said Chachay as one of the kites came falling down like a rock.

"Seven," chuckled Indayazz. "She doesn't take very long to destroy one of those things."

They counted as each one of the kites started falling.

Moments after the last one was falling, Vinvee reappeared among her colleagues. "Shall we get out of here? Both sides are converging here and it…is getting a little crowded."

Indayazz looked around. "There's a hill over there. That's

a good spot. When we get there we can switch to Spy dimension…
unless it gets too loud."

They all Jumped to the spot that she was pointing at. When
they arrived, they heard someone making a rather frantic one-
sided conversation on a radio. A Teltermak woman was reporting
the falling of all of the kites over the battlefield. She insisted that
they get some more Wings overhead in order to be able to keep
track of the outcome. She was thrown into Jahong's Death before
she could get any kind of response from the other end.

Joyntee smiled. "Zhardok, why don't you listen in on that
radio…and see if she does get a response?"

Officer Grade 6, Zhardok snickered. He went to the radio
and sat down, giving the equipment the once over.

One of the Parash-Zanab trucks went up with a deafening
explosion. All of the Owlamites flinched and started rubbing
their ears. Indayazz mentally gave the order for them all to go to
Observation dimension.

Zhardok decided that it was going to be impossible to hear
anything on the radio with the ringing in his ears so he hopped the
entire radio setup into Shogoot's Search so that it could dissolve in
the acid…and the Teltermak would not be able to use it again.

One of the artillery shells from the Parash-Zanab hit an
ammunitions truck. There were several Noga-Or who were killed
in the initial blast and many others who ran for their lives as the
ammunition started going up.

Joyntee turned away. "I can't watch this anymore." She

looked up trying to think of anything else other than the mass slaughter that was happening behind her. She saw two Teltermak kites coming in. "We've got company!" She turned back to the other Owlamites and saw that none of them had heard her. They were all still rubbing their ears. "**We've got company**."

This time, all of them turned and looked where she was pointing.

Indayazz stamped her foot in frustration. "**We're going to have to go to Spy dimension in order to hear them**."

Most of the others groaned at the thought, however, they did make the hop and got closer to the spot the radio had been sitting in. All of them assumed that they were going to be looking in that spot for their missing radio operator.

The two kites landed with four Teltermaks on them. There was one officer and three enlisted.

Indayazz frowned. "**What's that officer's rank**?"

"**I think he's called an Icon...or Icon Second**," sent Jojomon.

Indayazz nodded. "**What about those enlisted**?"

All of the Owlamites shook their heads. The enlisted had not been that important.

The officer glanced around angrily and started shouting. "WHERE IS SHE?"

"This is the place, Icon Vevbron, I helped her set up," said one enlisted.

The officer glared back. "Then she should be here, shouldn't she. Why isn't she here? It's probably because you came to the wrong place!"

"But...Sir...you saw the marker on top of that boulder! This is the place...I swear it...Sir!"

Vevbron looked up at the boulder. He glanced around angrily again. "Yes, I saw the marker. So...this should be the place. She's not here...and hasn't transmitted for quite some time. Look around! Find her!"

One of the other enlisted picked up a satchel. "Here...Icon Vevbron...here's some of her equipment."

Vevbron snarled. "That *mombik* abandoned her post!"

The third enlisted looked at the officer confused. "Sir... how could she...abandon her post...with all of that heavy radio equipment?"

Vevbron opened his mouth to say something and froze. He stood there like a statue pondering the question. His shoulders sagged and he looked around confused. "Find her...and then we'll get some answers." He grabbed the satchel and opened it. He started looking through the contents. He let out a squawk of surprise as the satchel disappeared out of his hands.

"**Kill all four of them**," sent Indayazz as she grabbed the satchel.

In a very short time, four more Teltermak, along with their kites, were dissolving in the acid in Shogoot's Search, while Indayazz started rummaging through the satchel.

"**There might be something in this thing that we can use**," sent Indayazz. "**I might have to turn it over to someone who's a little better at recognizing intelligence data**."

Joyntee watched as Indayazz continued looking in the satchel. "**What happens when they send more of their people, not just to search for that woman...but to search for the other four as well**?"

Indayazz chuckled. "**If they do...they'll have an even bigger mystery on their hands. What happened to all of the kites that were originally here, flying overhead? What happened to the radio operator and all of her equipment? Now, what happened to the search party that came out here after her**?"

Ambad shook his head. "**Sneaky**."

Indayazz smiled back at him. "**If they send another search party...the same happens to those *bimyocks***."

Ambad shrugged and started scanning the sky for any more kites.

They eradicated three more search parties before the sun went down.

This battle was different than the Gabeesh-Or/Twakon battle. This time, when the sun went down, the hostilities ended and both sides went back to their camps to lick their wounds and count the dead.

Joyntee looked at the carnage below them. "What time do

you think those *doovofts* will start tomorrow?"

Indayazz scoffed. "It doesn't matter. It'll be too early…no matter what time they start."

The Command Staff were sitting in the conference room, all feeling rather gloomy. They were getting reports from the battlefield and it was all bad. Even children were going into battle, some armed some unarmed. Between the two races the war had started with almost one million total. The first day, the fatalities were at least 25%. The second day cut both populations down considerably again. Both sides went back to their areas to take care of wounds for the second evening.

A mental call came in to Teelila. She looked up startled when she received it. She had not been expecting any private communication unless it was from one of her Team members.

Wilfadge looked at Teelila inquisitively. "Is something wrong?"

She smiled nervously. "A…mental…communication… uh…just a moment, Sir." She closed her eyes to concentrate and respond to the caller…whoever it is. She groaned and laid her head on the table. "Everyone open up…for a communication, please."

Wilfadge shrugged. **"This is the Supreme Commander. Who are you and what do you need**?"

The response came back. **"This is Officer Grade 4, Nydizya. Team Leader of Team 470. I'm currently**

watching the Bising...and they've just gone on the move...just like the Gabeesh-Or and the Twakon. They're abandoning everything in their city, except food, clothing and ammunition. They're going on the march to battle."

All of the Staff let out different moans, groans and snarls.

Wilfadge sighed. "**Where are they headed**?"

"**Sir...they're headed to...the city of Owlam.**"

"**Hold on**," sent Hadathoo. "**Those *bimyocks* are on Cifpasica! What are they planning on doing to get here...to North Chilamte**?"

"**Sirs, it seems that they have somehow arranged for transport...for all of their people on ships that are waiting in a harbor...in the northeastern part of Cifpasica. Even though there's about 350,000 of them, there are enough ships to carry them all...along with all of their stuff.**"

Wilfadge looked around the table. "Ships! I seem to remember that we've been there before. We sank the entire flotilla that the Algothon came up with. I think that we'll have to do the same thing here."

Hoynama grunted in disgust. "Before we drown an entire race...I think that we should try to stop them from getting here by some other means."

Wilfadge snickered. "How?"

She shrugged. "We mess with the navigators on the ships. We keep them running in circles, until we determine just how much they really want this and if the Teltermak are behind this mess as well."

Wilfadge sat there pondering. **"Officer, Nydizya, how long will it be before they get to the harbor and start uploading?"**

"It's a good eight days march. Then it'll probably take about two days for all of the loading. Then... depending on weather...it'll take about fifteen days to get to North Chilamte."

Shyshee interjected. "Then...depending on where they disembark here...we'll then know how long a march it will be to arrive here...at our city."

"They're not going to get to North Chilamte," growled Wilfadge. "If we can redirect them...and make them forget about us...we'll do that. If they're determined to get...here...and... fight us..." He hung his head. "...then we'll drown them. I still want a full investigation...as to whether or not the Teltermak are controlling them...or if this is their own motivation." He leaned his head back. **"Officer, Nydizya, keep your eyes open for any of the Teltermak. If you see any...try to find out how involved they're...and get back with us."**

"Yes, Sir."

Ahandi cleared her throat. "Do you want me to call out those Teams that sunk the Algothon ships?"

"Might as well," said Wilfadge. "They may have to do it again."

"Team 7016 was involved in that as well," said Shyshee.

"I'll call them out there," said Hadathoo. "Maybe with Team 470, those Teams that studied the ships and Team 7016, we can find out a lot about any Teltermak involvement in this mess."

Wilfadge stood up. "We *really* need to find this…Teltermak Home Base."

No one disagreed.

Wilfadge looked around the room. "Anything else… today? No? Meeting adjourned."

16

Wilfadge ordered some of the 459's to be taken out to the battlefield on Aerisau again. If the Teltermak were going to do their same eradication that they had pulled with the Gabeesh-Or and the Twakon, he decided that the Ghost Assassins would strike again…against the Teltermak.

The Battle between the Noga-Or and Parash-Zanab raged on for three more days. The last day, between the two combatants, there were less than five thousand total. The last day there were no children out on the battlefield…except for the dead ones that had not been cleared from the field earlier.

The Owlamites stayed in Observation dimension so that they did not have to put up with the smell. Several hundred thousand dead bodies, some of them were now five days old, were getting to be too much for them to stomach.

The remaining antagonists attacked. As they attacked, the Owlamites noticed that there were numerous Teltermak kites coming in from several different directions.

By now, there were eighty of the trucks with tripods ready to fire 459 cannons at any enemy. Indayazz gave a mental order that some of the kites were to be allowed to return to home base so they could report that the Ghost Assassins were antagonizing the Teltermak again.

Indayazz looked up at the kites and noticed that there was one that had a gold colored stripe in the sail. She ordered Vinvee to go up and investigate and see if this was some kind of high ranking Teltermak. Vinvee was back very quickly.

"That man who's doing the observing," said Vinvee. "His rank...if I remember correctly...is Army Leader."

Indayazz looked at her pad for some reference. She smiled. "An Army Leader is...equivalent to a Master Officer. That means that...there's only one rank higher than that *doovoft*." She looked up at the kite again. **"All personnel who have a 459 cannon ready...aim at that Teltermak kite that has the gold stripe on the sail. He's the same as a Master Officer. We're going to take him out. All of you who have your 459 warmed up and ready...fire...NOW!"** She flinched as she saw that almost all of the cannons had been ready and in less than one heartbeat, the Teltermak officer and his kite were turned into several thousand giblets that came falling down. There was not one single piece that was large enough to hurt anybody, on the ground, if it hit them.

All of the Teltermak fliers saw the beams and many of them panicked. Several made sharp turns doing their best to escape... in any direction. Several of them attempted to gain some altitude. A few others, in their panic, slammed into each other and totally destroyed their aerodynamic capability. There were eighteen kites that came plummeting to the ground with screaming Teltermaks attached in the harnesses.

Since the Owlamites were in Observation they could not hear the screaming, however, the combatants on the field did. Many of the ground fighters looked up and had to scramble out of the way as the kites came crashing down.

Indayazz smiled as she looked at how the Teltermaks had changed their flying pattern. There were no more formations of circling kites…at least not over the battlefield.

Once the ground combatants saw that all of the falling debris had landed, they went back to their hostilities. By the time the sun was high at midday time, the war was over. The only thing that the Owlamites or Teltermaks could see moving were three Noga-Or men. Nothing else was moving.

Indayazz stood there with her teeth clenched as she saw the three men moving around, firing their pulse weapons at any and all of the dead bodies of Parash-Zanab. She could not understand why they kept on firing, when the dead could not feel the pain ever again. Before she could react, several Teltermak kites came swooping down and finished off the last three Noga-Or with pulse weapons. She ordered all of the 459's to open fire on the Teltermak.

Nineteen more Teltermak kites became casualties before eleven others all veered away and fled in great haste. The eleven, however, did have an unknown passenger on each of them.

Wilfadge looked up. "How many more days before the

Bising get to the harbor?"

Teelila shrugged. "According to what we were told, they should be there tomorrow."

Wilfadge sighed as he looked up some data. "The Bising are…just over seven and a half taja…they have…extremely large heads…and they have…" He frowned at the screen. "…emerald green skin?"

"That's what it says," said Hoynama. "I wonder why someone had to get specific on the shade of green."

Wilfadge looked up. "We've got all four of the Teams that sank the Algothon ships in place. What's the report on Teltermak involvement?"

Dwalooa scoffed. "According to Nydizya…total involvement. Those *bimyocks* are so brazen…they're travelling with the Bising. No disguises, nothing covert. The Teltermaks are giving them all kinds of guidance as to where the harbor for embarkation is, the time to travel to North Chilamte, the harbor where they get off the ships…and the most direct route to the city of Owlam."

Hoynama picked up her pad. "The Teltermak are travelling with their radio equipment as well. They make regular reports to Home Base on the progress. The Bising are following…with no objections of any kind…as to who is in charge."

Wilfadge leaned back in his chair and folded his arms across his chest. He stared at the ceiling. "As soon as the ships are…four days out of port…start sinking them. First of all…if the Teltermak are on the ships as well…grab their radios. Get all of the radios…on all of the ships…here. No communication of any type with anybody for the Teltermak. Sink the ships and don't let them call anyone. Make sure that all lifeboats are useless as well. No one, who is on any of the ships, survives this folly." He sniffed. "No one but us…will ever know what happened to that armada." He looked back down at the table frowning. "How many ships are there?"

"Thirty-one," said Ahandi. "That would make around 11,300 Bising per ship."

Hadathoo cleared his throat. "In order to get all of that destruction accomplished, we're going to need more than five Teams over there…taking care of this unhappy business."

Wilfadge cocked his head to the side. "So send fifty more Teams…get them briefed and get to work."

While picking some Teams, Shyshee looked up. "Who's going to give the briefings?"

Wilfadge snickered. "Isn't Team 7016 involved in this? They were involved in the last sinking of a large naval group. Who knows better than that Officer, Bonarain…how to teach people what to do?"

"Yes, Sir," said Shyshee as she went back to her pad.

While the Bising were arriving in the harbor area to start uploading, Bonarain was giving briefings on how to sabotage the ships and the lifeboats.

After she finished, Soolchakan stepped up. "We   were told that we had to silence all of the Teltermak radios. We'll need to assign one person specifically to each Teltermak that gets on any of these ships. As soon as the command is given to start the...eradication of the group...the first thing to go will be the Teltermak radios. Next will be the ship's radios. Then we start sinking ships."

One of the Owlamites who was listening, raised his hand. "When do we sabotage the lifeboats?"

Soolchakan smiled. "Anyone who is not assigned to the forty-one Teltermaks that we've identified in this multitude will start that sabotage now."

Another one raised her hand. "How...exactly...do we do it...so that they don't notice...here in port?"

Soolchakan smiled. "Remove...certain vital parts of their engines. Take all of the fuel cans, take half of the fuel to Owlam and replace it with water from the ocean."

Another woman raised her hand. "Why don't we just take all of the fuel?"

"Because we still want the smell of fuel in the can. They check how full the cans are and take a sniff. The fuel floats on top of the water, so all of the water will be at the bottom. Once they're out there and...someone tries to fuel up a lifeboat engine with contaminated fuel...even if the engine starts...it won't run... very long." He cleared his throat. "Once we're out at sea, hop any and all oars into...whatever dimension your devious little heart desires. In the bottom of the lifeboats...hop several of the main slats into Ghost dimension. They'll see the slats and won't be able to figure out how the water is gushing through…when everything appears to be intact."

Nydizya came up. "All of the ones who've been specifically assigned to shadow a Teltermak…go now. All of the rest of us… to the lifeboats."

Chyning was one of the personnel who was assigned to keep close tabs on one certain Teltermak. He was going to be on one of the last ships to depart from this harbor, wherever it was on Cifpasica. She followed him to a private room that he was going to occupy on the ship. She was disgusted with the fact that none of the Bising got any private rooms, but all of the Teltermak did. She started daydreaming about ways that she was going to destroy this monster, while she watched him set up his radio.

Soolchakan, Bonarain and Kiyalee were on the same ship that Chyning was on. They were now going from lifeboat to lifeboat doing all kinds of nasty things to sabotage them. That business took all day.

When they finished killing all one hundred and fifty lifeboats, Kiyalee sat down with her pad and did some figuring. "This doesn't make any sense."

Bonarain stretched some sore muscles in her back. "What doesn't?"

"Okay, there's…one hundred fifty lifeboats."

"Right."

"Each one can hold about thirty people…fifty…if

absolutely necessary."

"Right."

"That comes out to seven thousand five hundred that can squeeze in the lifeboats."

"Okay…so what's the problem?"

"Don't you remember? They said that there were going to be over eleven thousand Bising on each ship. Then you have to add any Teltermaks on board…not to mention the crew."

Soolchakan had been listening with some disinterest. Now, his curiosity button had been punched. He looked around the main deck of the ship. "I wonder if they have any…inflatables…that're stored away."

Kiyalee scoffed. "They'd have to have enough inflatables to hold almost four thousand more."

Soolchakan nodded. "That could be…the plan. They're probably hoping that they won't have to use any of the lifeboats. But…if they do have a problem…they'd have to have sufficient lifeboats for all…or else…if this thing goes down somebody's already dead…before any decisions are made as to who gets on which lifeboat." He licked his lips. "No responsible ship leader would set out to sea…without sufficient lifeboats or life rafts…be they solid or inflatable." He closed his eyes and mentally called Nydizya. **"Soolchakan calling Nydizya…can you hear me**?"

She came back sounding a little impatient. **"Yes, I can… what's so important now…that you have to interrupt me**

now?""

"One of my Team members came up with a math problem on the lifeboats. There aren't enough boats... in case the ship sinks."

Nydizya mentally scoffed. **"Is this...a problem?"**

"The problem is...they might have some inflatables that are stored away. This would mean there are sufficient boats and rafts on board. We may have to do some more damaging, sabotaging and sinking... once the big boats start going down."

She pondered the problem for several moments. **"I see your point. Okay, I'll let everyone know to keep a lookout...once we start sending these things to the bottom...to look for...anything other than the lifeboats that we can see.**"

"Thank you, Sir." He turned to Kiyalee and smiled. "Now, she's aware of the situation. Now, we all have to keep a lookout for any lifeboats...other than the ones that are stored on deck."

Bonarain snickered. "I don't think that we're gonna have much of a problem sinking these things. Look at those first two ships that they loaded. Look how low they're sitting in the water. Then look at the ones that haven't been loaded yet. There is a huge difference."

Kiyalee shook her head. "I think that they've...just thrown the safety rules out completely."

"Remember," said Soolchakan. "It's the Teltermak who are in charge of this move. They don't care how many Bising die out on the sea. They just want them to kill most of us...or all of us...so they can get rid of both of us."

Kiyalee grunted. "I'm really...*really*...getting to hate those Teltermaks."

Bonarain sighed. "I can't think of one Owlamite who isn't tired of those nasty people. How many times did they try to kill us...with or without the help of the Axswain...or the Zee-Althans? They just get on your nerves and stay there. I have a funny feeling that one day...we're going to have it out with them...and it is gonna be messy."

Kiyalee smiled. "Maybe we should allow the Algothons to make another firestorm weapon and hit those rotten Teltermaks."

"That wouldn't do much good," said Soolchakan. "They're too scattered...all over the place."

They sat there for two days waiting for all of the loading to be completed. The ships that had loaded first had their main decks lined with Bising that were leaning over the rails losing their breakfast, lunch and dinner. Still none of the ships were scheduled to depart until all of them were completely loaded.

Soolchakan sat down on the deck in frustration. "If they do have any inflatables...they're well hidden...or just packed away real good in some unmarked containers."

Bonarain scoffed. "Or maybe they're not here at all. Did

you think of that?"

Kiyalee yawned. "How's Chyning doing with her pet Teltermak?"

Bonarain snickered. "He's not the main *bimyock*, so she's just as bored as he is. He's only sent out one message and that was a radio test."

Soolchakan sniffed. "Since we've finished screwing up all of the lifeboats, let's go visit her. See if there's anything that we can do to give her some more excitement."

"I'll stop by the gorge on the way," said Kiyalee. "I'm going to pick up some fresh hot kwatha."

Bonarain raised her eyebrows. "Do you know which room she's in?"

"We've been there at least six times since we finished the lifeboats," said Kiyalee smugly. "I know the way."

Bonarain shrugged and followed Soolchakan to the room.

Chyning was sitting on a chair next to the bed. She looked totally bored.

Soolchakan chuckled. "Is it really that bad?"

Chyning stuck out her tongue and made a choking noise. "I think that his mommy didn't give him enough toys when he was growing up. He can't keep his hands off of...that...*thing*." She looked off to the side and sighed. "Whoever I made this mad... I'm gonna go to them and apologize, every day, for the next ten years."

Soolchakan sat on the desk. "You know that it went by rank as to who got assigned to be a garbage watcher."

"Well...he still hasn't turned that radio off and...he still hasn't made any transmissions since the first test...to make sure that it works." Chyning closed her eyes. "Other than that...he likes to...*play* with himself."

Bonarain looked around. "Uh...where is he?"

Chyning looked a little sick. "In the bathroom...and no you don't wanna know what he's doing."

Kiyalee Jumped into the room with a platter full of mugs.

Chyning sniffed and smiled. "At least something can go right...even in this rotten place."

Each one of them took a mug of kwatha and started spooning through them looking for the biggest lumps.

The Teltermak came out of the bathroom completely naked. He walked over to a full length mirror and started flexing (what few) muscles he had, trying to show off for...who knows what. "Oh...when I get back home...sweet Kofsheeza...what I'm gonna do to you!"

"Probably make her as sick as you're making me," said Chyning caustically. She turned her back on him so that she did not have to watch his megalomaniacal show.

Kiyalee reached into a utility pouch that was on her belt. "I can't stand this." She pulled a small precision tool out and walked over to the Teltermak. Before Soolchakan could stop her, she stabbed the Teltermak in the posterior with the tool.

He jumped in shock and turned around looking throughout the small room while rubbing the pained spot and uttering several curses. The Teltermak went to the radio. He changed the frequency on it and keyed the microphone. "This is Silver Standard, Hoochooshik…in room Borag 121. Something in this room…just bit me. I need to talk to you about it…NOW!" He put the microphone down.

A response came a few moments later. *"I'm sorry, Sir, but I can't come down right now. We're getting ready to shove off."*

Hoochooshik picked up his microphone. "I don't care what you're doing, get down here…before I *shove* you!" He pulled his hand away from the pained area that he had been rubbing and saw that he had blood all over his hand. He backed up to the mirror and tried to see anything that could give him a clue as to what happened. He took a hand towel, wiped a large amount of blood off of his rear and threw the towel on the bed.

Kiyalee took her tool, wiped blood from the towel onto it, wiped some of the fresh blood on the sheet and threw the towel on the floor.

They waited for the knock on the door. It took longer than they thought it would.

Hoochooshik went to the door and opened it. "It's about time!"

Kiyalee looked at the man just outside the door. "What is that?"

"A Tendixive," said Bonarain. "They're the ones who can spit venom."

"They'd have to have something going for them," said Chyning. "He's less than five taja tall."

Soolchakan looked at the newcomer. "He could easily hide at night…with skin that dark."

The Tendixive looked up. "All right, Silver Standard, Hoochooshik…what is so flaming important?"

Hoochooshik turned his backside to the Tendixive. "Look, Ship Leader, Wafk! Something bit me! It bit and took a chunk out of me!"

Kiyalee was trying to use some mind manipulation on the Tendixive. She was attempting to steer him towards the bloody mess on the bed…it worked.

Wafk walked directly over to the bed. He shook his head and looked up at Hoochooshik. "You called me down here…to report that you're a clumsy *thwomok*? You sit down on a…" He squinted to take a closer look at the bloody tool. "…a precision tool…and you try to say that something bit you! Excuse me, but you're not dealing with some silly *ishdible*! Waste any more of my time with…" He held the tool up in Hoochooshik's face. "… hurting yourself because of your clumsiness and you'll spend the rest of the trip in the lockup and then probably get a nice reservation at the TURGON WALL!" He threw the tool down on the bed and stormed out, slamming the door behind him.

Hoochooshik picked up the small screwdriver. "What…

but…where…how…I've never…" He let out a few more unintelligible syllables in confusion and frustration. He walked over by the desk and threw the tool in the trash. He picked the towel up and went back to reexamine his still bleeding rump. He looked at himself in the mirror. "If that useless little *protch* ever talks to me like that again, I'm gonna jettison the little *fonk*… somewhere between here and Chilamte!"

Soolchakan chuckled. "Oh there's gonna be some jettisoning going on all right."

Bonarain sighed. "Let's see…Bising passengers that want to go to Owlam and kill us. Tendixive people driving *this* ship… maybe others in the flotilla. Teltermaks controlling the whole mess. What next?" She gave Kiyalee an inquisitive stare. "Did you do some mental manipulations on that Tendixive?"

Kiyalee gave her a great big grin. "Why do you think he found the screwdriver so quickly?" She turned her gaze to the trashcan. "Speaking of which…" She walked over and retrieved her tool. She wiped the blood off and put it back in her pouch.

Hoochooshik finally got the bleeding under control and bandaged his injured hip.

Chyning sipped a little of her kwatha. "I wish he'd put some clothing on."

Soolchakan looked at the bottom of his mug. "We have to get back out there and start sampling some Bising thoughts. Remember they want us to find out just how devoted to this crusade these Bising are."

"But they're all drugged," said Kiyalee. "How can they possibly be responsible for what they're doing?"

"Not up to me," said Soolchakan sadly. "We collect what we can and pass it on to the Command Staff."

Wilfadge was in the tub cleaning his neck when he got the call.

"This is Officer Grade 4, Nydizya calling Wilfadge. Can you hear me?"

Wilfadge rinsed his washcloth out. **"Yes, I hear you. What did you need**?"

"Sir...the Bising are not coming to the city of Owlam to kill us. They've been given orders, by the Teltermak, to go to the city and capture as many of us... alive...as they can."

He stopped rinsing the washcloth and just sat there in surprise. **"We're supposed...to be spared...for...what... or...why**?"

"Sir, since we can't read the minds of the Teltermak, we haven't been able to figure that one out. All we know is...the Bising are being told that there'll be a special reward for every one of us that is captured... alive."

He sat there contemplating the possibilities and was getting absolutely nowhere. **"Thank you, Officer, Nydizya.**

As soon as you can get any more information on this puzzle...please...don't hesitate to call."

"Yes, Sir."

After several moments of sitting there baffled he sent out a call to all of the Command Staff. There was going to be a meeting at midday, to discuss this conundrum.

Wilfadge informed the Staff of the orders to the Bising. All of the Staff were sitting there with stupid or stunned looks on their faces as they all attempted to figure out why they were to be spared. After the Teltermak had gone to great lengths to exterminate several races, they were going to utilize the Bising as...herders. The Bising would be herding Owlam livestock. Why?

Teelila was the first to speak. "I think we should distract the Teltermak with a problem of their own."

Wilfadge raised his eyebrows. "Such as?"

"Our people on Satroco Isle have decrypted the writings of the Yagalom-Ayin."

"I know."

"So...give the Teltermak all of the decrypted data...and let them know...the Yagees have betrayed them. The Yagees have isolated all seven of the prime ingredients of *Tuzine*, but they haven't been able to come up with the proper recipe. By now, the Yagees have tried over 400,000 recipes and none of them have worked...because our people keep contaminating the pot...if they use *Shoonshook* ROOT. The Teltas won't get the recipe right...

either…without *Shoonshook* ROOT."

"But it should give them a very nasty distraction, in regards to the betrayal by the Yagees." Wilfadge groaned. "Still…do we dare let the ingredients out?"

"It should be a huge shock…to all of the Teltermak," said Hadathoo. "It might distract them…with a battle…with the Yagalom-Ayin."

Wilfadge looked around the table. "Any other ideas?"

There were none.

"So…who is in charge out there?"

Hoynama looked at her pad. "Officer Leader, Boneech is in charge of watching the Teltermak and Officer Leader, Natsa is in charge of the Yagalom-Ayin."

Wilfadge shook his head. "Inform…both of them…and tell them to stand back…and watch what happens."

Teelila mentally informed Boneech, while Dwalooa mentally informed Natsa. Moments later, both Boneech and Natsa were being ushered in by Akantini.

Boneech walked up and leaned on the conference table. "Excuse me, Sirs, but…have you lost your mind? You want us to give up the…ingredients to…the Teltermak?"

Wilfadge glared back at her. "We have to come up with something…to distract the Teltermak…even if it is something that is temporary. Anything that'll rattle their cage and let them know that their faithful friends, the Yagalom-Ayin…aren't really so faithful after all. Then…they'll be suspicious of anybody that they try to befriend. That should…hopefully…set them back…a little."

Natsa tapped Boneech on the shoulder. "Don't worry, we've completely turned them away from using the *Shoonshook* deep root…or any root. Every time they try to put any part of the *Shoonshook* root in the mixture we poison it. They'll never get the correct recipe."

Boneech hung her head. "Okay! If we're going to blow their shorts off…we might as well get back there…and watch the fun." She looked up. "I'm…sorry for the explosion…Sir."

Wilfadge bowed his head slightly.

Both women vanished.

Till smiled. "How long should it take?"

"Hopefully…not very long," said Wilfadge. "Let's…sit here and wait…for a little while."

Boneech and Natsa both contacted Wilfadge and informed him of an uproar by the Teltermak and a sudden battle, to the death, between the two former allies. The battle did not last very long. Even though the Yagalom-Ayin were badly outnumbered, they did have their poisonous fangs as well as a few pulse weapons of their own.

Immediately after the battle was over, the Yagalom-Ayin went to the stewpots, minus their teeth and poison glands, and the surviving Teltermak started pouring over all of the data that had been amassed by the Yagalom-Ayin, even before some of them had received any medical aid in their wounds.

Wilfadge stared at the ceiling. "It was...*only*...a short distraction. It was a distraction to the people in that island chain. It didn't affect the Bising move at all." He hung his head. "Make sure they know the Bising armada is to be sunk. No survivors... of any race."

Nydizya gave the order. The radios of the Teltermak were Jumped to the gorge. The ship radios were close behind. Many of the Owlamites grabbed and Jumped a great deal of the Bising weaponry to the gorge as well. The sinking of five ships was almost immediately after that. The alarms went off and it was mayhem as the Bising panicked and headed for the lifeboats.

The ships crews were able to get things under control rather quickly as they forced the Bising to line up near the lifeboats. As the first boats were lowered into the water, full of Bisings, they sank immediately, leaving all of the Bising floundering in the water.

A second lifeboat was lowered, empty, in order to rescue all of the ones in the water. When it sank just as quickly, now, it was complete pandemonium.

Meanwhile, five more ships started sinking and the catastrophic outcome was the same on each one of those ships.

Now it was revealed that there were numerous inflatable lifeboats that had been stored under the solid lifeboats. The Owlamites had to go back to the first five sinking ships and sabotage the inflatables as well. A few sharp knives, ripping through the underside of the life rafts made the panic grow in intensity. People were grabbing anything that they could find that would float, jumping into the water with their spur-of-the-moment life raft and then having to fight off everyone else for ownership of the item.

The water was now full of sinking ships, drowning Bising, blood and scavenging and predator fish.

Now that they knew where the inflatable rafts were, there was a decision made to get into the storage areas and Jump the rafts to Owlam, before sinking the ships. This way, the fight for inflatables was avoided and the panic went to the worst degree very rapidly.

Before the day was ended, the Bising became the fourteenth race to become extinct. They were not very good swimmers because their enormous craniums threw them off balance and the only way that they could float was to lay back in the water. They were easy prey for the large sharp-toothed carrion eating fish that were now in the area in tremendous numbers and were in a feeding frenzy.

Several of the carrion eaters died as well after eating any of the Tendixive people…and being poisoned by the fresh venom in their glands.

The forty-one Teltermaks all died in shock, wondering how the plan could have gone so badly wrong and horrified that they could not report this mess to their superiors.

It took the Teltermak High Command almost fifteen days

to realize that their plan, to capture the Owlamites alive, was a complete failure…and no one had a clue as to how, where or why the Bising armada had disappeared.

The Bising armada was sunk and there seemed to be no more enemies…at the moment…that were threatening Owlam. The only thing that was going on now, with any Owlamite Teams were the ones spying on Algothon, the ones that were spying on the Teltermak on Satroco Isle, the *Tuzine* trade just outside the walls of Owlam and a few other Teams that had some odd jobs.

Soolchakan was a little tired of what he had been tasked to do over the last few months and felt the he needed to burn off a little steam…or maybe a lot of steam. He went to the garage and got in his red truck. He Jumped it to a spot just outside of the wall of the city of Owlam. He made sure that he was nowhere near the *Tuzine* trading tables. He looked around to make sure that no one was near him and hopped the truck back into Home dimension. He turned the truck towards the east and slammed down on the throttle. The truck spun its tires in the grass and took off.

He remembered that shortly after the firestorm had hit, this entire area had been nothing but brown dead vegetation. Soon thereafter it was just brown dirt. Now, one hundred twenty-four years after the firestorm (and after borrowing a lot of vegetation from the Forest dimension, it was green again.

He kept the throttle at full. He remembered also that this entire area was, for the most part, a very flat plains area. There were a few bounces here and there, however, he did not care about that. All he wanted to do was run as fast as possible and as far as possible, just to get some of the anxiety out of his system.

Fourteen races that had been created by the firestorm weapon were now totally extinct and the Axswain could be number fifteen, seeing as how there was around two hundred of them currently existing. He wondered how many of the lives that he had personally taken. He felt that he should be sickened by the numbers, however, for some reason it did not bother him. That thought was what bothered him. Why did he not care?

Time went slowly. The kilotajas that he was putting on the truck passed quickly. He kept on heading east...just to help burn off the confusion that was bothering him at this time.

On and on he sped, pushing the engine to the limit. It did not really bother him if he blew the engine because he knew that Kiyalee could fix it and he also knew that he could easily Jump the truck back to...wherever Kiyalee needed it, in order to fix it.

He snickered as he saw a familiar site ahead of him off in the distance. He was approaching the wall to the destroyed city of Teltermak. He snickered for a very short time. All of a sudden he felt a cold chill go down his spine. He let off of the throttle and hopped the truck to Spy dimension. He wondered if his eyes were deceiving him. He looked up over the city of Teltermak and he saw several of those repulsive Teltermak kites flying over the city.

He let off of the throttle and let the truck coast to a stop. He took the truck out of gear and got out. He walked around in front of it, while still staring up at the kites. He leaned back against the front of the truck and felt some rather intense heat coming off of the engine of the truck. He decided to leave the truck here to cool down while he did a little investigating on foot...with the use of a few Jumps.

He then remembered that there had been a rather large hole in the wall...on this side of the city. It had been repaired. That was no small task.

He Jumped up to the top of the wall and stared out over the repaired city of Teltermak. It was once again a large metropolis. Maybe not as large as it had been before the Algothons had attacked, however, it was still looking very well for a city that had been demolished by the firestorm weapon.

He Jumped down to the ground level inside the wall and looked around. He spent nearly three days looking over the city. He found several buildings that looked rather important and checked them out completely.

With his jaws clenched tight, he Jumped back to his truck. He got in the truck and Jumped back to the garage. He sat in the truck fuming for quite a while and then realized that he had not really had much to eat in the last three days. He got out of the truck, went to the kitchen and had a rather hearty meal.

The three women walked in the kitchen talking. They noticed that he had several plates scattered on the counter.

Bonarain smiled. "I guess...you were a little hungry...for some reason."

He looked at her sadly. "Over the last three days, I was...a little too busy to eat. When I got back here, I remembered and...I ate something."

"Several somethings," said Chyning.

He smiled at Kiyalee. "My truck...might need a little attention."

Kiyalee simply nodded as she pulled a jug of fruit juice out of the refrigerator.

Bonarain crossed her arms and looked at him sternly. "Okay, what's wrong?"

He sighed. "Get ready for another battle."

All three women froze and looked at him in shock.

He cleared his throat. "I have to go talk to the Command Staff...and let them make the decision as to...whether or not...we go back into battle."

"Oh, no," said Kiyalee. "You don't stop there. What is going on?"

He hung his head. "I don't want to have to repeat myself. You can go with me to the Headquarters Conference Room. You'll find out then."

Bonarain let out a grunt of exasperation. "When do we leave?"

He sniffed. He looked at the three women and smiled. "Did you want to get something to eat first?"

All three of them stood there akimbo with nasty looks on their faces.

He shrugged. "Let's go."

Team 7016 Jumped to Headquarters. The Command Staff personnel were all leisurely walking into the conference room. Some of them noticed the appearance of Team 7016 but gave them little notice as they continued into the room.

"I have some important information for the Command Staff," said Soolchakan.

Hadathoo looked back at him. "Unless it is *extremely* important, we don't have time for any fooling around."

Soolchakan snarled and then shouted. "I FOUND THE TELTERMAK BASE HEADQUARTERS...just in case any of you are interested!"

All nine members of the Staff froze in place. Several of their Team members did the same. Many of them turned and looked at Soolchakan with shock in their eyes. The three women of Team 7016 were equally shocked.

Wilfadge smiled at Soolchakan. He raised his right hand and beckoned, with his index finger, for Soolchakan to follow. He walked into the conference room.

The entire Staff, plus Aides, rushed into the conference room and took their places. Team 7016 followed. Soolchakan walked up to the end of the table while his Team members stood behind him with anticipation written all over their faces.

Wilfadge gave him another smile. "You have our attention." He looked around at the others. "Our UNDIVIDED attention."

Soolchakan took a deep breath. "I was…burning off some steam from the latest confrontation that I went through. I ended up…driving my truck…to the wall that surrounds the city of Teltermak. I saw the breach in the wall has been repaired. After doing a Jump up to the top of the wall, I spent three days walking around inside the…*rebuilt*…city of Teltermak. I looked for any building that looked…official. I found five. One of them…IS…the Home Base of Operations for all of the people of Teltermak. I was in the primary radio room…when three different calls came in. They responded with that same…succinct answer: Home Base acknowledges." He cleared his throat as he looked at all of the faces. "They have rebuilt…most of the city. They have a…somewhat large population there…and I saw…quite a few high ranking Teltermaks. They are back…to…being a power in that city again."

No one in the room spoke for several moments as they were sitting there stunned, attempting to devour the information.

Teelila closed her eyes. "Is there any estimate on population count?"

"No, Sir, I don't have that…estimate…other than quite a lot."

Wilfadge rubbed his forehead. "Those sneaky *chokwads*!" He smacked his fist on the table. "All this time we've been looking…at island chains and other continents and…all the time they were right next door."

Hadathoo grunted. "We need to get someone in there and get us an estimate."

Wilfadge smiled at Soolchakan. "Thank you for that information. We'll take it from here. You may go."

Soolchakan nodded courteously and turned around to go. Bonarain, Kiyalee and Chyning were still staring at him in shock. He suddenly stopped and froze with a stunned look of his own. He turned back to the Staff. "Uh…Sirs…I just thought…"

Hadathoo snarled back. "You've been dismissed! You may go!"

Wilfadge interjected. "Wait a heartbeat there, Hadathoo. This man found the Teltermak Home Base. If he has something else to add…I *will* listen!"

Hadathoo turned to Wilfadge and smiled. "As you wish, Sir."

Wilfadge looked at Soolchakan. "What is it?"

Soolchakan looked as if he were going to pass out. "Teltermak! Those people have been rebuilding…who knows how long? We never checked the city of Teltermak. We never patrolled it." He looked up at the ceiling then back down and drew in a deep breath. "When was the last time that any of us… checked…the city of Axswain…or the city of Galsino…or…Zee-Altha?"

Once again, all of the Staff members were staring at Soolchakan in shock.

Wilfadge stood up looking rather angry. His teeth were clenched and he was doing some very controlled breathing. He looked around the table. "Sector 1 Commander and Vice

Commander…you and your Teams will go to Axswain…and check things there. You will not send any subordinates! YOU will go and do the reconnaissance yourselves."

Ahandi and Antrong both stood up. Together they said: "Yes, Sir!"

Wilfadge continued. "Sector 2 Commander and Vice Commander…you and your Teams…no subordinates…will go to the city of Galsino…and perform the reconnaissance there."

Teelila and Till stood up. "Yes, Sir."

"Sector 3 Commander and Vice Commander…you and your Teams…again no subordinates…will go to the city of Zee-Altha and perform the reconnaissance."

Dwalooa and Hoynama stood up. "Yes, Sir."

Hadathoo smiled weakly. "Is there anything for…me to do?"

"Sector 4 Commander and Vice Commander…go to the city of Teltermak and…start counting…and get me an estimate as quickly as possible."

Hadathoo and Shyshee were both standing. "Yes, Sir."

"If the cities of…Axswain, Galsino and Zee-Altha…have any population of Teltermak…I want to know immediately. Once you've informed me of…any presence…of Teltermak…then you can start counting as well."

Wilfadge looked at Soolchakan and smiled. "Are there… any other suggestions…as to what we…might look for?"

"Yes, Sir," said Soolchakan flatly. "Since they've done it in the past...I suggest that we get those...Teams of tunnel killers involved as well. We all know how the Teltermak love their tunnels. Why should they stop now?"

Wilfadge closed his eyes and grunted in disgust. "Yes... someone notify that Officer...what's his name...Eeleeg! Get him...and the rest of his...tunnel killer...accomplices...and start looking for tunnels."

Teelila nodded. "Yes, Sir...immediately!" She turned to her Aide. "Officer, Amafee...notify Officer, Eeleeg immediately... of this entire meeting and get him working on Teltermak...now. Tell him that if we find any Teltermak in the other cities, he'll have to inform his other colleagues to get to those cities and start looking for tunnels as well."

Amafee nodded. She closed her eyes and started sending the mental communication to Eeleeg.

Wilfadge flopped down in his chair. "Officer, Soolchakan... do you have any more...helpful suggestions?"

Soolchakan smiled. "Sir...if I think of any...you will be the first to know."

Wilfadge smiled weakly. "Thank you." He looked around the table. "Let's move it people...NOW!"

Suddenly, the only people in the room were Wilfadge, Akantini and Team 7016. Then Team 7016 vanished.

Wilfadge looked at Akantini. "I wonder how long they've been rebuilding."

Eleven days later, the Command Staff was back in session. Wilfadge had invited Team 7016 as special guests for this meeting.

Wilfadge leaned forward. "What do we have to report from the city of Axswain?"

Ahandi looked at him and smiled. "The city of Axswain… is a training center for the Teltermak. There are always…at least…a thousand kites flying over the city…day and night. There's enough light from the city that…they can see where they're flying or landing. My…Team members…Nashisi, Kiykay and Koolong… they're with Antrong's Team and…they're all reconfirming…our estimate of…about 250,000 Teltermak in residence…in Axswain."

Wilfadge looked at Soolchakan. "It seems that your counsel…was indeed very good. So far…you were correct."

Soolchakan smiled back. "Thank you, Sir."

Wilfadge cleared his throat. "What do we have to report from Galsino?"

Teelila just sat there with a blank face. "According to what we found there…they are now attempting to find the recipe…for *Tuzine*. They have another drug that they're working on and they have quite a large amount. There was an instruction booklet that we found…in regards to that drug. Don't ask me to name the drug… none of us could even guess how to pronounce it. It IS the mind controlling drug. You just introduce it into the city…or village… water system…and in about five days…you start controlling all of the inhabitants." She swallowed. "We estimate that there are close to 300,000 Teltermak in that city…at this time."

Wilfadge nodded. "Kites in one city…drugs in another." He looked at Dwalooa. "Sector 3…what is your report?"

Dwalooa shook her head. "The city of Zee-Altha… has been turned into a major military training base. It is also a place where they are manufacturing all kinds of ammunition… conventional ammunition. I didn't see any pulse weapons of any sort. All of them are training with conventional weapons." She took in a deep breath and let it out. "We estimate around 300,000 Teltermaks in that city."

Wilfadge bit his lip. "Officer, Soolchakan, I'm very glad that you took your little trip to Teltermak." He looked at Hadathoo. "What else did you find out about that city?"

Hadathoo looked sad. "It is definitely their Home Base of Operations. They get reports…from…I have no idea how many… places…all over the planet. They always give that same short reply. The Teltermak are…everywhere. Right now, they're very confused…at the Home Base, as to how the Bising venture…just vanished. They're troubled and they're sending out some scouts to try to find out anything that they can to uncover the disappearance of the convoy." He shook his head. "We estimate…that there are around…400,000 Teltermaks…in the city…and over half of them are under the age of fifteen."

Wilfadge frowned. "What? Where did you come up with that figure?"

Hadathoo leaned back. "From what we saw…it appears that…as soon as a Teltermak woman is…able to start bearing children...she does! I saw many females...who looked very young...and each one of them had...several children. They're doing everything that they can to procreate themselves into a... great multitude."

"I saw the same thing at Axswain," said Ahandi. "They had a lot of...what looked like family homes...and all of them were occupied by a woman...with several small children."

"Same thing in Galsino," said Teelila.

Dwalooa nodded. "Even in a place where they're manufacturing all kinds of dangerous explosives...numerous dwellings...one female and several children."

Wilfadge scratched his chin. "So those *chokwad*s have us surrounded." He looked up and frowned. "Where's that tunnel killer?"

Teelila closed her eyes and made a mental call to Eeleeg. Moments later, Akantini was ushering him into the conference room.

Wilfadge smiled at him. "Officer, Eeleeg...have you found anything?"

Eeleeg sighed. "Yes, Sir, we have. There are two large tunnels coming from Teltermak and two from Zee-Altha. There is nothing from Axswain or Galsino."

Wilfadge frowned. "Why...nothing from those two...I wonder?"

Eeleeg shrugged. "Axswain is where they're training on

kite flying. Those things wouldn't work very well in a tunnel. Galsino…drugs. They don't want to introduce the drug… anywhere…except the water system. Since our water system is completely independent…of any public river or stream…they have a problem trying to figure out how to deploy it…on us. The other two cities…they can sneak up on us from Teltermak with troops. They can plant…who knows how many explosives…from Zee-Altha."

"Are the tunnels under Owlam…yet?"

"Oh, no, Sir. They're all over twenty kilotaja away from getting under our wall."

Wilfadge nodded. "A few well-placed explosives will prevent them from getting much closer."

Eeleeg smiled. "Yes, Sir."

Wilfadge let his breath out. "So…where do we begin with…?"

At that moment there was a bit of an argument out in the hallway. Akantini was telling someone that they had to wait. A woman argued that it could not wait.

The other woman barged her way into the conference room. "I'm sorry, Supreme Officer, but…this is extremely important!"

Wilfadge was a little upset over the interruption. "It had *better* be important for you to interrupt *this* meeting." He cleared his throat. "Now, who are you and what is to so important?"

"Sir, I am Officer Grade 3, Nahansika. Team Leader for

Team 1594. I've come here to tell you that the Rakab-Rosh are on the march. A march just...like the Bising...except the Rakab-Rosh were already on this continent. They're located in the central part of the southeastern peninsula. Sir, they have thousands of vehicles and...their convoys will be here...at the city of Owlam... within six days. Sir...they're coming here...to conquer us...with orders to take as many of us alive as they can. I can tell you that the Teltermak *are* behind it, Sir. Those *chokwad* Teltermaks are with the convoys...leading them...our way."

Wilfadge sat there with his teeth clenched. "I'm learning many new ways to hate those...cannibalistic monsters."